The Curious Cases of Sherlock Holmes Volumes 1 and 2

By

Stephen Herczeg

First edition published in 2021

Hardcover ISBN 978-1-78705-764-7

Published by MX Publishing
335 Princess Park Manor, Royal Drive,
London, N11 3GX
www.mxpublishing.co.uk

Cover design by Brian Belanger

To Carol

for always being my muse

To

Derrick and David

Without whom none of this

would ever have happened

Contents

Copyright Notices

First published in Beyond the Adventures of Sherlock Holmes - Volume II by Belanger Books (Nov 2020)

The Adventure at Dead Man's Hole ©2019
First published in The MX Book of New Sherlock Holmes Stories - Part XX: 2020 Annual (1891-1897) by MX Publishing (Jul 2020)

The Case of Vanderbilt and the Yeggman ©2020
First published in The MX Book of New Sherlock Holmes Stories Some More Untold Cases Part XXIV: 1895-1903 by MX Publishing (Nov 2020)

The Adventure of the Second Body ©2020
First published in The East Wind Blows by Belanger Books (2021)

The Tranby Croft Affair ©2020

The Adventure at Castle Metzengerstein ©2020

The Case of the Borneo Tribesman ©2021
First published in The MX Book of New Sherlock Holmes Stories - Part XXVII: 2021 Annual by MX Publishing (Jul 2021)

Foreword

by David Marcum

Sometimes over the last few years – and especially during the tumultuous events of 2020 (and now 2021) – I've thought about connections that we all have now that simply didn't previously exist. For many of us, not that long ago, our world was very small – family and co-workers and the people we saw in our towns. But with the connections of social media – for good or bad – we now have links to people all over the world that we would have never known otherwise. If the COVID pandemic had hit just a few years ago, I personally wouldn't have had any specific concerns about people outside of my own local sphere – it would have been horrible, but nameless and faceless. Now, by way of connections through mutual admiration of Sherlock Holmes, I "know" many people from around the world – even if we've never met in person (yet) – and my concern over their well-being and safety, and my joy at their triumphs and good news, exists in a way that wouldn't have been possible before.

One such person that I'm very glad to now "know" in this modern sense is Stephen Herczeg, Author.

I first became acquainted with Steve while editing a book of sequels to the original Sherlock Holmes stories. He had previously written a Holmes tale that was included in the Belanger Books collection Sherlock Holmes: Adventures in the Realms of H.G. Wells (2017), and now he wanted to write a sequel to "The Engineer's Thumb". As a diligent editor, I'm always happy to receive new stories, and I'm always hoping that the author will be good – which means to me that the stories are written in the mold of the original Canon in the voice of Dr. John H. Watson – and also that the author will become a reliable repeat contributor. Steve is both of these.

His enthusiasm is notable and always welcome. He always wants to join the party. When he doesn't know something about The Canon, he's always very happy to learn, and he's great to work with.

Whenever I've been involved in editing a new Sherlock Holmes anthology – for either Belanger Books or MX Publishing – Steve always steps up, with stories that are Watsonian and uniquely interesting. When I also began editing new Solar Pons anthologies, he wanted to be part of those as well.

Like many of us Sherlock Holmes pasticheurs, Steve isn't in it to get rich. (In the case of the MX anthologies, he – along with the rest of us – donates his royalties to the Stepping Stones School for special needs children at Undershaw, one of Sir Arthur Conan Doyle's former homes. So far, the nearly two-hundred contributors from around the world have raised over $75,000 for the school, and no end in sight!) We write because we enjoy it – as painful as the process is sometimes – and also to add to the Great Holmes Tapestry. Another benefit of writing for these various Holmes anthologies is that they give us opportunities to produce more stories that we otherwise might not attempt, and after a while, we step back and see that we've written a good many of them.

And that's what has happened for Steve: After being in so many Holmes anthologies, he now has a plethora of adventures with his name on them, ready to be collected into his own book. I'm personally thrilled that this volume now exists, and that people who possibly didn't have a chance to read these stories when they originally appeared in various anthologies can now enjoy them collected in one place. I very much hope that this book will be followed by Volumes II and III and so on . . . .

I'm very glad, in this time of worldwide worry, to know Steve, and to have enjoyed his stories. Sit back and dive in – and let the present fade away for a while as Watson tells us another excellent adventure of his friend, Sherlock Holmes . . . .

David Marcum
February 2021

Foreword

by Derrick Belanger

It was on July 12, 2017 when I was first introduced to the talented Sherlockian author Stephen Herczeg via email. Mr. Herczeg wrote to me, starting off as he always does with a friendly "Gidday!" and asked if I'd consider including his story "The Curious Case of the Sleeper" in my anthology Sherlock Holmes: Adventures in the Realms of H.G. Wells. I read his story, and replied with a strong YES! "The Curious Case of the Sleeper" does a remarkable job of blending the writing of H.G. Wells with that of Dr. Watson's adventures. Add in a touch of Dickens with the ending, and you have a wonderfully imaginative mystery.

That was the first of many stories by Mr. Herczeg which I'm proud to have published. What amazes me with Herczeg's work is how he is able to create an excellent Sherlock Holmes pastiche no matter if he is working in the boundaries of Doyle's traditional Victorian England or if he is pushing those boundaries and incorporating elements of science fiction, horror, or steampunk. Take for example his excellent, "The Body at the Ritz". In this story, Holmes is called in to solve the mystery of a body found in an alley outside the Ritz hotel. The plot follows a traditional Holmesian narrative where Holmes and Watson are their 19th century selves; however, it also has them living in a steam powered world of horseless carriage lined streets and dirigibles covering the skies.

While this anthology focuses specifically on Herczeg's works around Sherlock Holmes, I would be remiss if I didn't also give a shout out to his wonderful writings of the other Sherlock Holmes, the one that resides in Praed Street, Mr. Solar Pons. Herczeg's Pontine works featured in The New Adventures of Solar Pons have Sherlock Holmes's successor with his partner, Dr. Parker, solving crimes in the early twentieth century, just as August Derleth intended. As Herczeg does with his Sherlock Holmes writing, sometimes he bends the rules a bit with his Pons stories. In "The Rondure of Cthulhu," his piece in The Necronomicon of Solar Pons, the Praed street sleuth is pitted against the monsters from the world of H.P. Lovecraft. The story is an excellent piece of detective and weird fiction. I highly recommend seeking out Herczeg's Pontine work which is just as good as his Holmes writings.

One last point I'd like to make about Mr. Herczeg is how willing he is to push himself to keep writing new pastiches. Whenever I send out a call for new Sherlock Holmes fiction, Mr. Herczeg is always the first to respond, eagerly taking on the challenge of adding more stories to his personal Holmes canon. I'm sure this anthology will be the first of many.

Keep visiting 221 B Baker Street, Mr. Herczeg. We look forward to more thrilling adventures!

Derrick Belanger
February, 2021

The Curious Case of the Sleeper

I am fairly certain that if I had not been along at that precise moment then neither myself nor Sherlock Holmes would have ever heard of Thomas Graham or as he became known to the two of us, the Sleeper.

It was a bright day in July. A mid-summer heatwave was pummeling London with an unbearable ferocity. Even in my light frock coat, I could feel the pools of perspiration under my arms and the intermittent stream as rivulets ran down my side. I would have much preferred to have been home with my beloved, but Sherlock had called upon me to come with great haste.

As I walked briskly down Baker Street, I noticed a group milling around the entrance to 221b, my destination.

Mrs. Hudson was on the doorstep, attempting to convince the group to move away. I increased my pace to help out my dear colleague's housekeeper.

"I say, what seems to be the problem, Mrs. Hudson," I said.

She looked at me; hope crossing her face, then indicated the rabble before her.

"It's this lot Doctor Watson," she said.

I finally took in the members of the group. There were four young street urchins and an older man of about forty years. He was marginally taller than the children and likewise dressed in dirty rags and bare feet. I addressed him directly.

"What is the meaning of this Sir?"

He did not seem to hear. One of the urchins turned to face me. I recognised him. Tommy Bones he was called. He was one of the Baker Street Irregulars, Sherlock Holmes' personal network of spies and aides.

"Sir, this man, sir. 'e was down at the river bank. 'e don't make no sense. We thought that Mr. 'olmes might be interested in 'im".

I looked down my nose at Tommy.

"Is that all?"

Tommy's eyes roved around before sheepishly returning to gaze into mine.

"We thought there might be a couple o' coppers in it for us".

"That's more likely," I said.

I looked the man up and down. His eyes were slightly glazed and he stared off into the distance, vaguely taking anything in. He was certainly a mess. His clothes were rags that threatened to disintegrate if the slightest breeze were to touch them.

"He'd be better off at the hospital if you ask me," said Mrs. Hudson.

"I tend to agree with you there," I said.

I reached into my pocket and pulled out tuppence. I handed it to Tommy Bones.

"Run along now Tommy. We'll take this gentleman off your hands".

Tommy looked into his hand, his eyes lit up. He showed the other children then ran away yelling back over his shoulder "Thank you, Mr. Watson".

"It's Doctor Watson," I almost yelled, then thought better of it. I turned back to the dishevelled specimen before me.

"What should we do with you then?" I pondered out loud.

"Send him on his way I reckon," said Mrs. Hudson.

"I don't think he's quite right in the head. I'd like to examine him first and then he may need to go to the Hospital. I'll just take him inside," I said.

Mrs. Hudson looked terrified.

"Mind my floors then, I've just washed them. You can take him upstairs into the parlour. His nibs won't mind. He doesn't care how dirty the floors are," she said.

I helped the poor fellow up the stairs and brought him into Sherlock's parlour. It was empty. I assumed the great detective was out, which annoyed me more as he was the one who had sent for me.

I helped the distressed fellow sit down on the settee and began to give him the once over. His gaze continued to focus on distant objects, his eyes steady and unmoving. His clothing was very odd. A collarless, cuffed shirt. A pair of knee-length knickerbockers and no shoes. His feet were caked with mud. His right hand was covered in something black like soot, his left with dirt and blood from various scratches. He was unshaven and his hair was unfashionably long and matted with dirt.

I checked his pulse. Strong. Constant. His temperature. Fine. His breathing. Steady. I pulled out my stethoscope and listened to his heart. I gave him a cursory check for wounds, bumps and abrasions, but he was whole and unmarked. Within a couple of minutes, I had come to the conclusion that this man was perfectly healthy.

Mrs. Hudson came into the parlour. She carried a small glass half-filled with amber liquid. She looked at me and smiled.

"I thought a small brandy might help your friend here," she said.

She bustled over to the man and held the glass beneath his nose. His hand rose, grabbed the glass and downed it in one swallow. He continued to stare into space, but his head shivered slightly as the alcohol hit his stomach.

"Well I thought it would do more than that," said Mrs. Hudson. She shrugged, took the glass and wandered off.

I watched her go then turned back to my patient. It seemed to me that this man had lost his mind. He was beyond my help and would need another sort of professional. My train of thought was broken by a voice behind me.

"What the devil do you have here Watson?"

I turned. Sherlock stood in the doorway, dressed in a smoking jacket and eyeing us both with a slight expression of bemusement.

"One of your boys, Tommy Bones, brought this man to your doorstep. Mrs. Hudson wanted to turn him away. I wouldn't have it. The man seemed to be outside of his own mind. I wanted to examine him to make sure he was not injured or suffering some ailment that I could fix, but he is fine. What bothers him is beyond me, Holmes".

At the mention of my friend's name, the dishevelled gentleman's face snapped towards my voice. His eyes focused on us and uttered the first words he had spoken.

"Holmes?" he asked.

I stepped back in surprise. The man turned his head towards Sherlock. His eyes locked on my compatriot's face and examined him for a moment.

"Siger Holmes?"

The man stood slowly to rigid attention. His hand came up in a salute.

"Captain Siger Holmes?"

Sherlock's eyebrows rose. He returned the man's salute.

"At ease," said Holmes.

The other man dropped his hand and sat down once more. His eyes drifted off again.

"What in God's name was that all about?" I asked.

"Watson, I'm shocked to say that have no idea," said Holmes.

"Who is Siger Holmes?" I asked.

"That's a name I have not heard in a long time. Captain Siger Holmes was my great grandfather. He commanded a small naval vessel and died during the fourth Anglo-Dutch war in the late 18th century".

"How would this man know that?"

Sherlock studied the man carefully. After a moment a small grin crossed his face.

"Very clever. Very clever".

"What do you mean, Holmes?"

"Well Watson, we have here an unidentified man. He wears a shirt with no collar and long sleeves with the remnants of a ruff on the cuffs. This type of shirt would be worn with a cravat or similar, under a frock coat with a vest. His hair is long and untidy. If clean it would be worn swept back and tied. I would think it could lend itself to being powdered. He has a scraggly beard, uneven as though left to grow naturally rather than being trained into any particular style. He wears knickerbockers without any socks or shoes. What do those fashion choices indicate to you?"

"Very out of date?"

"Yes. Well done Watson. Then couple that with his knowledge of my great grandfather who died over a hundred years ago".

"Okay. But what does it mean?"

Sherlock shook his head.

“Watson, Watson, you do disappoint me sometimes,” he said.

Sherlock moved in front of the man and came to attention.

“What is your name sailor?” he said in a commanding voice.

The man stood bolt upright and saluted.

“Lieutenant Thomas Graham, sir,” he said.

“Who is King?” Sherlock asked.

“King George the third, sir,” Graham said.

“What?” I blurted out.

Sherlock held up a finger to silence me.

“What year is it?”

An expression crossed the man’s face, indicating in his mind that it was indeed Sherlock Holmes that was the mad man.

“Well it is 1790, sir,” he said.

“Indeed,” said Holmes “at ease again Sailor”.

The man dropped his hand and sat. He seemed a little more aware of himself now and looked around the room instead of straight ahead.

I sidled up to Holmes and said, "What in the blazes is going on? Is he mad? Should we get him to a sanatorium?"

Holmes smiled.

“Watson. What we have here is one of two things. Either it is a man who has prepared himself to carry on in the persona of someone from the late eighteenth century”.

“Or?”

“Or he is indeed a man from the late eighteenth century”.

“That’s impossible,” I blurted out once more.

“Well that is for us to discover, isn’t it?”

That smile still played on his lips.

“This could be a most satisfying mystery. I thank you for bringing it into my home,” he said.

I started to say something but Holmes turned his attention back to the man.

“My dear fellow. What is the last thing you remember before my young compatriots found you and escorted you here?”

The man started to rise. Holmes held out a hand to stay his ascent. The man looked up at Holmes instead.

“I remember waking up. In a dark room. I was on a small cot. I found a door and staggered out into a long tunnel. It was so musty and dark. I don’t know why I was there. I managed to find some light and headed towards it. I came out at the river. It was very strange. There were boats and buildings that I’ve never seen the like of before in my life. I tripped and fell into the mud. I must have passed out because when I awoke, that young rapscallion was kneeling next to me. I thought he was going for my purse. I barked at him to get away and tried to stand, but I fell to my knees again. Tommy talked to me and convinced me to come to you,” he said.

“Good advice, I think. What’s the last thing you remember before waking up?”

“I,” he started, then stopped, closed his eyes urging his mind to remember.

“I had been sick. A fever. It had been days since I had slept. I took a sleeping draft and went to my bed,” he continued.

He looked up at Holmes and said “and then I woke up in that accursed room”.

Holmes’ face remained stoic. He has never been one for emotion has our Sherlock Holmes.

“You said that you went to your bed. Where? What address do you live at?”

The man said, "I live above my shop, at number 5 Moorgate. Just south of the last remnants of the London Wall”.

I’d had enough “what the Devil is he talking about? London Wall? That was demolished well over …”

Holmes put a finger to my lips. Turned to face me. “Shhh. Let the man continue. Do you not see a pattern forming?”

Confused, I resigned myself to stay silent and grumpy. Once again Holmes was keeping me in the dark.

Holmes prompted him again “describe your home to us; it might help us locate it”.

“I was a simple blacksmith before I served in the Navy. When I returned I used woodworking skills I'd picked up to expand the business and become a wainwright. One of London’s best. We repair the coaches and wagons that frequented London. Business is very good and we are about to expand our premises. I had meetings with a financier today as I recall. I must return to my abode”.

He started to rise. Holmes went to him and gently pushed him down again.

“I think Mr. Graham that you should take some time to recover. You must be famished and thirsty”.

Graham nodded.

“Come to think of it yes. I am,” he said.

Holmes said, "Watson can you get Mrs. Hudson to organise some food and drink for our friend here”.

I moved away but Holmes called out again.

“Oh and a suitable change of clothes as well”.

I nodded and moved away.

When I returned, Holmes was standing before Mr. Graham dressed and ready to leave. I was a little taken aback as I’d only been gone a few minutes.

“Well I’m glad you can move when you want to,” I remarked.

“I’m intrigued Watson. I want to believe that Mr. Graham here is actually from the eighteenth century. I know that is highly improbable, but there is a chance and that excites me”.

***

We arrived at the bank of the River Thames within the hour. The sun was still high and biting. Again, I was a streaming bath of sweat. Holmes, as usual, showed no impediment from the heat. His concentration was solely on the job ahead.

On our way, we made two stops. One to purchase two paraffin lanterns, the other to find Tommy Bones. It was he who now led the way.

“We found him down here,” Tommy said as he led us down the stone steps.

Even from above, I could make out a small indentation in the drying mud of the riverbed. Holmes moved up to the depression and stooped down to investigate. He searched all around, examining every minutia. Finally, his eye fell on that which he sought.

He stood up and moved towards a small concealed opening in the wall beneath the street above.

“Give Tommy a couple of coppers will you Watson,” he said as he moved off.

Grumbling, I reached into my pocket and once again paid the young street urchin.

He doffed a make-believe hat and said "thank you, Mr. Watson,” and scurried away.

“Doctor,” I shouted then turned to follow Holmes.

He stood at the entrance of a small passage; his lantern lit and held out to light the way. He turned and looked towards the depression then slowly scanned the ground back to the entrance.

"What is it, Holmes?" I asked.

“Do you not see Watson?” he asked me back.

I looked closer. Lit my own lantern and stooped down to examine the floor of the passage. Immediately I could see a set of footprints in the soft dirt covering the floor.

“Well that should make things easier,” I said.

“Indeed Watson,” said Holmes and bolted into the passage. I followed along behind through the cramped confines.

Several times I brushed the walls and my coat caught on the rough surface. I grumbled my annoyance prompting a reproach from Holmes.

“Yes, the coarseness of the brickwork explains the scratches on Mr. Graham’s hands doesn’t it,” he remarked.

I’m sure he could see the expression on my face as realisation hit. I kept quiet not wanting to give him any further ammunition against me. It was a lot cooler in the corridor than outside. I gave silent thanks.

Holmes kept up a tremendous pace, but finally, he stopped before a wooden door set into the side of the passage. The door was shut. Holmes held up his lantern to examine the structure. He leant up against it and listened.

I started to speak but he held up a finger for silence. After a moment he pulled away from the door and grasped the handle, squeezed it and pushed the door open.

“What the devil was that about?” I asked.

“Well Watson, our Mr. Graham left this room in a bit of a daze, so you should ask yourself, why would the door be shut? It would seem improbable that he would have closed it, doesn’t it?” he said.

I thought for a moment. Was about to say something but realised Holmes had already entered the room and kept it to myself. I followed him in.

The room was very Spartan with a dry, dusty, dirt floor. A small cot lay in one corner. The sheets were askew and filthy. There were footprints in the dirt near the bed, they overlaid each other in a messy pattern, but a single set led away towards the doorway. A cloying smell emanated from a small bowl on a stand near the head of the bed.

I moved towards it to have a closer look.

Holmes spoke from across the room “I wouldn’t go too close to that if I were you Watson. Unless of course, you'd like to take the place of our Mr. Graham”.

“What do you mean Holmes?” I asked.

"Those herbs are what was keeping our sleeper in a state of perpetual slumber,” he said, "a distant cousin to the European valerian, procured from South America I would say. I smelt it as soon as we entered”.

I backed away from the herbs, it was then I noticed the cold. I couldn’t believe it. I looked around and noticed several boxes that held large blocks of ice. I breathed out. A cloud formed before my face.

“Makes you wonder why a sleeping man would need it to be so cold doesn’t it Watson?” asked Holmes “possibly to keep his vital signs low and to avoid any stimulation”.

I looked towards his voice and found Holmes stooped down on the other side of the room. He held the lantern before him. I could make out a faint set of shoe prints.

Mr. Graham had indeed had a visitor.

I looked back at the doorway. There was a trail of shoe prints leading out of the room, but not into it. I looked back towards Holmes and found him staring at me.

“Well done Watson,” he said, "notice anything else?"

He started to examine the wall next to him. I looked back at the shoe prints and finally found what he was talking about. A heavier set of prints had been made near the wall, but with the heel closest to the wall, as if someone had stepped out of the wall and into the dirt-floored room. A trail of shoe prints led across the floor to the doorway where they exited the room.

The wall itself was fairly barren. It was plain stone brick with a single candle holder to one side. Some of the bricks were cracked and chipped, and a lot of mortar had fallen out over time. I guessed that this room was a few hundred years old, probably made when the original foundations of this part of London were laid.

"Ah-ha," said Holmes, pushing his finger into a gap in the mortar.

A loud click rang out in the silence and a section of brickwork, as tall as a man, pushed out from the wall. Holmes moved up to this new feature and prized the brickwork away from the wall. It formed a door and swung easily away from the wall. He looked back at me with a wry smile on his face.

"And that's how a man can walk out of a wall," he said.

Before I could answer Holmes had disappeared into the hidden corridor. I followed along in his wake. A short entrance led to a stairway that rose for about twenty feet and alighted at a corridor that was tight and very dark, our lanterns emitted a feeble glow that illuminated very little.

Suddenly, Holmes stopped. I pulled up short almost crashing into him and setting him on fire with my lantern. He turned when he felt the heat on his back.

"Look out Watson. I think I have enough light of my own thank you very much," he said.

He turned away and I heard a soft click. Then the corridor was flooded with light. I brought my hand up to shield my eyes. As they adjusted, I realised Holmes had found another hidden door. He pushed it open and stepped through.

I entered and found him standing before another door at the end of a wood-panelled corridor. He listened intently. I moved up to him and started to say something. His finger came up to silence me.

He turned his attention back to the sounds from the other side of the door, then without warning twisted the doorknob, pushed it open and walked through.

I heard a gasp from the room beyond and Holmes say, "Ah, Mr. Miller, I presume".

Another voice said, "who the Devil are you?"

I bustled into the room to find a portly man standing behind a desk staring at Holmes with a look of total surprise on his face. His jacket was draped over a nearby chair, his vest was open and sweat stains marred the pure white of his dress shirt.

Holmes had assumed a posture of complete arrogance near the centre of the room. He faced Miller, but his eyes roamed the room taking in every minute detail.

Miller moved out from behind the desk affronted at the arrival of two strangers in his study.

“I ask again Sir, who are you? What are you doing in my study?” he said.

I realised it was time to step in.

“I apologise, Sir, for this inconvenience. On behalf of my friend here, let me introduce ourselves. I am Dr. John Watson. This is Mr. Sherlock Holmes,” I said.

Miller’s face showed shock at the mention of Holmes’ name. He stuttered before responding.

“Sh...Sherlock Holmes,” he said, "why would you be coming from that corridor. Please explain yourself, Sir." His voice didn’t seem to have the conviction of his words.

Holmes smiled.

“I think you know exactly why we’ve come through that doorway Mr. Miller,” he said.

“I ... I don’t know what you mean,” he blustered.

“Your shoes seem to say something else,” said Holmes.

I looked down at the large man's shoes. The soles had a small patina of brown dirt on them. Miller didn't even bother to look down, just tried to gather his thoughts.

“My shoes are dirty. It’s not a crime,” he said.

“No that’s true. It is not a crime,” said Holmes “but I think the authorities would look dimly at someone that confines a person against their will, uses their identity to forge corporate documents and takes over their company”.

“What? Lies nothing but lies,” he said.

Holmes walked to the desk and reached across to a pile of papers. It was then I noticed the nameplate with "Charles Miller" engraved on it. Holmes pulled a paper from the pile, studied it for a moment then held it up. It was on letterhead for a company called Graham Coach Builders. At the bottom was a series of black smudges that I recognised as fingerprints.

"I think you'll find these fingerprints belong to a man that once resided in the small room at the end of the passageway beyond the corridor from which we entered. A man who has rested in slumber in that room for quite a number of years. A man who is the original owner of the company that you represent Mr. Miller,” Holmes said.

Miller blustered “what man? There is no man downstairs. I”.

He thought for a moment. Smiled.

“Yes. I use that room for somewhere quiet to rest and escape the trials of the day. I find it very serene,” he said, "in fact, I have just returned from a mid-afternoon nap”.

Holmes smiled.

“I think not Mr. Miller,” he said “the sweat stains beneath your armpits belie that fact. It would seem strange that anyone, even someone of your girth, could raise a sweat in that cold room”.

Holmes shifted and moved closer to the desk.

"I put it to you, Mr. Miller. You were in that room earlier, but you found it empty. In your panic, you went into the adjoining passage and came out at the river. From there you searched high and low before returning to this office. That explains your sweaty underarms and the dirt on your shoes".

“Rubbish,” said Miller “absolute rubbish”.

Holmes continued “I will also put it to you that the man who normally resides in that room is none other than Mr. Thomas Graham. The founder of this company. That man”.

Holmes pointed to his left. Miller's head, and mine, swivelled in that direction. On the wall above the fireplace was a large portrait of a man that had a strong resemblance to our dishevelled guest.

I gasped. Miller shuffled slightly forward. His hand went to the desk for support. He laughed.

“That man has been dead for a hundred years,” he said, "you must be insane my dear Sir”.

“I don’t think so. In fact, I know so. Mr. Graham is at this moment sitting in my parlour. Very confused, but very alive,” he said "I think he would be very interested to know that the great-grandson of his business partner has been keeping him alive and running the business in his stead”.

Miller’s face turned red with rage.

“This is an insane accusation. How dare you?” he said.

"Admit it, Charles. Your family has been running these Coachworks for a hundred years, haven't they? In the name of Mr. Thomas Graham’s family, but his family does not exist does it?” he said.

“What do you mean Holmes?” I asked.

“Thomas Graham brought in a partner in 1785 by the name of George Miller. They built the company up but Miller remained as a silent partner, not a co-owner. George Miller gave Graham a concoction that caused him to slip into a deep sleep. One that has lasted for a hundred years. During that time, they have sown the tale of a reclusive Thomas Graham and family,” he reached for the paper again and held it up “and used his fingerprints in lieu of a signature for all official and legal documents”.

He placed the document down and turned to Miller.

“Is that not correct Mr. Miller?” he asked.

Miller’s face had turned purple. He snatched up a letter opener and launched himself at Holmes.

Holmes, well versed in various styles of fighting, simply stepped to the side, threw a hand out and flipped poor Mr. Miller onto his back. The letter opener went clattering across the floor.

At that precise moment, the doorbell rang.

“Ah, a most opportune moment, I believe,” said Holmes.

Within a few moments, Inspector Lestrade led a newly attired Thomas Graham into the office. Lestrade looked at Miller then at Holmes.

"What have you been up to Holmes?" he asked.

Holmes held out his hand towards Miller.

"This is Mr. Charles Miller. I'm sure he will have an interesting tale to tell you about our Mr. Thomas Graham, who is the true owner of Graham Coach Builders," he said.

Graham looked around the room. His eyes spied his portrait. He moved closer.

"I remember when this was painted. It was three years ago," he said.

"I think you'll find it was a hundred and three years ago," Holmes said.

Graham turned and looked at Holmes as if he was mad.

"What do you mean?" he asked.

I walked over to Graham and led him to a settee.

"I think you might want to sit down for this," I said. We both sat.

"Mr. Graham, this man is Charles Miller. I think you knew his great grandfather George," Holmes said.

"Yes. George. My good friend," he looked around "where is he?"

"I'm afraid he's been dead for about eighty years," said Holmes "but I don't think he was really your friend. Do you remember his giving you a draught to help you sleep?"

Graham smiled "yes, yes, he was worried I was a little tired and worn out. He prepared me a draught to help me sleep".

"Well you did sleep," said Holmes, pausing for effect "for a hundred years".

"What?" Graham gasped.

"Beneath this building. You slept. Kept cold and safe but in a perpetual slumber thanks to some South American herbs. While George and his heirs managed the company and built it up to quite a large enterprise, but they never had full control because you had never signed any part of the company over to George. They lived well off of your company. Used your fingerprints instead of your signature to keep control. There is a legend they spread that you had retired to the country and your family remain there," he said.

Lestrade spoke up "I've heard of Thomas Graham and his family".

"Very good Inspector," said Holmes, his condescending voice lit large for all to hear "and now you've met him".

Lestrade's face dropped. Confusion reigned.

"What?" he asked.

Holmes turned and held a hand out towards Graham.

"This is Thomas Graham. Alive and in the flesh. Confused and a century out of place, but he is here," Holmes said.

Lestrade stepped forward. Looked at Graham. Turned and looked up at the painting. Looked back at Graham. Shook his head.

"Can't be," he said, "that's impossible".

"It does sound highly incredible," I added.

"And I would say the same thing if the evidence was not mounting up before me," Holmes said, "but let's ask those involved".

He stepped over to Mr. Miller.

"Would you mind getting up Mr. Miller? It's a little bothersome having to look down at you like this," he said.

Miller slowly rose to his feet. Lestrade sidled up next to him. Stopping any chance of his escape.

"Now Mr. Miller. Can you verify what I've said so far?"

Miller still steamed. He looked at Holmes with a stare that could wither an oak tree. Holmes noticed and simply smiled.

"What was that?" asked Holmes.

Miller's eyes narrowed, but a certain swagger grew within him.

"I said nothing, but everything you've said Mr. Holmes is to be expected from someone that many think insane. Your crazy story has no basis in fact. You present some unknown man. Claiming him to be the long-lost owner of this company and concoct a tale about kidnapping, drugging and fraud," he said.

He turned to Lestrade.

"My dear Policeman, I think you should remove these gentlemen from my premises before I ask you to lay charges against them. I have a mind to seek legal representation as I feel you have besmirched my good name," he said, his chest puffed out in faux irritation.

"Really," said Holmes. His hand moved to his pocket. He stepped towards Miller and pulled his hand out. It was now full of something.

"I picked up a handful of the herbs that we found in the room downstairs," he said as he raised his hand "if you deny my accusations then you have no problems taking a deep sniff of them". He stepped towards Miller and shoved his hand in the portly man's face.

"No, keep that away from me," Miller said as he recoiled in abject horror and stepped backwards, tripped over a small ottoman and fell heavily on his immense rump.

Holmes stood over the man, looked down and smiled.

"I assume that you are now happy to corroborate my story then?" he said.

Miller dropped his head.

"Yes. Yes. My great grandfather started this whole mess," he said. He turned and pointed at Graham. "It was his fault," he continued "he denied my ancestor his share. He wouldn't bring him into the business as an equal partner".

Graham looked surprised.

"What are you talking about Sir? I always treated George with the utmost respect. We have always been equal in everything," he said.

"But you wouldn't make him a partner," Miller retorted.

"We have been in negotiations for many weeks. George has been ...," he stopped for a moment, looked over at the portrait then back to Miller "had been seeking financial aid to buy half of the business off of me. I had been patient and wanted to bring him along with me".

He stood up and walked to the portrait.

"I can only think that George had come to his wits' end and couldn't raise the capital," he said. He turned back towards Miller.

"If he had only come to me. I would have worked with him. I'm not an unreasonable man. Never have been. George knew I'd raised all the capital myself and brought him in when the business was growing quite well. He worked hard but didn't have any money behind him. I paid him half of all the profits in the hope he could buy-in," he continued.

He walked forward shaking his head.

"But poor old George. He couldn't save a penny. Spent everything he earnt I'm afraid. I assume your Great Grandmother played a large part in it," he said.

"Here, watch what you say, Sir," said Miller.

Graham held up a hand to stop his protest.

"I apologise, she was a remarkable woman. Gloriously handsome and very strong-willed. A fine woman, but very ambitious I'm afraid. This whole thing was probably her idea, not George's," he said.

"What would you have us do with Mr. Miller here?" asked Holmes.

Graham turned to face Holmes.

"That is an interesting question, Mr. Holmes. I have spent the best part of this day confused and a little lost. You and Dr. Watson here have convinced me that I was asleep for a hundred years, an incredible slumber, but in my mind, I have only awakened from a single night's sleep. In all normality I would have been in this office," he looked around once more then continued "well in an office a bit less salubrious than this one, going about my work".

He walked back towards Miller.

"Instead, I find myself with a company that appears to have grown to a level of grandeur that I could only have dreamed of".

He pointed at Miller.

"Because of this man's ancestors. My good friend and his progeny, in my absence. I can no less take that away from them and claim it as my own as I could let them continue without me," he said.

"Does that mean you wish to form a partnership with Mr. Miller here?" asked Holmes.

"I think it does, dear Sir," said Graham. He turned back to Miller and placed a hand on the man's shoulder. "What do you think Charles? Want to take on an apprentice and teach him the ways of this newfangled company you've grown?"

Miller was taken aback for a moment. Then he asked "As a partner? A full partner? No more sneaking around with fingerprints?"

Graham nodded.

"I think your great Grandfather would be proud if you did," he said. Graham held out his hand. Miller looked at it for a moment then took it in his own.

Lestrade piped up "hold on, does that mean there has been no crime? A man was drugged and held captive against his will for a hundred years and now nobody is to be charged".

Holmes nodded his head.

"As strange as it seems Inspector, that seems to be correct," said Holmes "in fact, I think we three can leave these two gentlemen to their future partnership".

Lestrade looked dumbfounded. He stood in a huff, grabbed up his hat and thrust it on his head.

"Take heart Inspector, your journey was not a total loss. You brought Mr. Graham here as I asked and were on hand in case things went against my initial expectations and Mr. Miller here became a source of concern. As it is all has worked out well and peace has been accorded," Holmes said.

Lestrade didn't look convinced.

"Fine," he said then doffed his hat to Graham and Miller "I bid you gentlemen goodbye, but I will make a note of this for future reference".

Graham walked over and held out his hand to Lestrade. "Thank you, Inspector. I'm sorry you didn't find the crime that you wanted, but you have been instrumental in helping me none the less," he said. Lestrade shook his hand, eyed Miller one more time then turned and left.

Holmes walked over to Graham, took his hand and shook it.

"I'm glad we could help in your restoration, Mr. Graham. When originally presented with a case as curious as yours, I was a little perplexed, but once all the evidence was collected and the illogical removed, it was fairly obvious what had occurred. One would be remiss with not acknowledging the bizarre nature of your story but I would hope that your future will be less so," he said.

"Thank you, Mr. Holmes," said Graham. He leant towards me and grabbed my hand "and thank you Dr. Watson. Without your charity I would have wandered these strange streets and fallen afoul of its denizens".

"My pleasure Sir," I said.

Holmes piped up "we should be going Watson. Mrs. Hudson will wonder what has become of us".

He turned and moved off. I doffed my hat to Miller and Graham once more and followed.

Back in the bright sunshine, Holmes began to fill his pipe with the contents of his pocket.

I was dumbstruck but managed to say, "isn't that from the basement room?"

Holmes smiled. "Don't be foolish Watson. This is pipe tobacco, always was. I must admit that I have taken Mr. Miller's herb in the past. Left me unconscious for three days. I wasn't going to touch it again and obviously neither was Mr. Miller".

We walked along for a while, basking in the sunshine until I broke the silence.

"What do you think will happen with Messrs. Miller and Graham?" I asked.

"Well, Watson. Mr. Graham left a small local wainwright one day, returned to one of London's largest carriage makers the next. With developments in such things as the internal combustion engine and two astute businessmen joining forces, I can only imagine good things to come for them," Holmes said.

"I can see the name Graham and Miller coachbuilders, or maybe Miller and Graham?" I said.

"A bit of a mouthful, perhaps they'll just use the first letters?" Holmes said.

"Mmmm, MG does have a certain ring to it," I said.

The Adventure in Nancy

. . . wherein Victor Hatherley of "The Engineer's Thumb"

finds himself in new danger . . .

Though it had been many months since I witnessed the most unfortunate series of events that led to the demise of my true friend, Sherlock Holmes, my grief had started to dissipate and I could finally begin to expound on and document several adventures that occurred in the months preceding his plunge into the Reichenbach Falls whilst wrestling with that dastardly villain, Professor Moriarty.

As with many of the more intriguing of Holmes's cases, it all started with the simplest of requests but continued with the two of us sent off to the wilds of France and Germany, dragged into a world of espionage and conflict of an almost global nature.

Our adventure started one bright spring morning. I was seeing patients whilst Mary was away in the country visiting with the children and family for whom she was once governess. Although I missed her dearly, I was kept busy with the somewhat trivial nature of my patients' maladies.

Upon hearing an urgent pounding at my door, I almost bowled over the person who was next in line for my services in my hurry to answer. Standing diligently on my doorstep, I found a young postman holding a message for me. I took the envelope and thanked the man, sending him away in my haste to have at the contents.

As I turned and opened the message, I noticed several sets of eyes staring back at me. After I read the message, all thoughts of doctoring vanished.

I apologised profusely to the people in my waiting room and bade them goodbye. I told them that a family emergency had arisen and that I had been called away from London. I would post a note on the door when I returned to active duty. There were many grumbles, but quite a few sympathetic murmurs as my patients left. A small part of me retained a deep level of regret and worry, but I read the message again to re-energise myself.

The message was, of course, from my good friend Sherlock Holmes. He wished me to meet him in the Stranger's Room at the Diogenes Club at two o'clock that very afternoon. The club was an interesting place and one that Holmes frequented occasionally, but usually in the company of his brother, Mycroft.

***

The hansom dropped me off at the entrance to the club. To the uninitiated, it could have been any manner of establishment. The small leather-clad double doors that served as the entrance were manned by Wilson, the club's affable footman.

I nodded to him as I climbed the short staircase and received a familiar nod in return. I don't think in all these years that I have ever heard Wilson speak. I've often thought that he holds to the traditions of the club with a vice-like grip, or he is in fact mute, and as such has found the perfect occupation.

Wilson opened the doors for me and I stepped into the dark womb of the club. Taking off my coat and hat, I left my accoutrements with Smythe at the cloakroom and continued down the silent hallway toward the Stranger's Room. I saw many an older gent sitting alone in the various rooms leading off from the hallway. Silence was their creed, every one of them. The club frowned on any form of verbal communication and instituted a policy whereby any member or visitor caught speaking would be given a notice of offence. Upon three offences, they would be brought before the committee and could find themselves banned.

The one place where this rule was relaxed was the Stranger's Room.

I came upon the entrance and stepped inside. As expected, I found Holmes. He sat in a chair facing towards the door and spoke in a sullen, quiet voice with a man, opposite him, who was hidden from view.

I moved up next to Holmes's chair and turned to face the hidden man. A smile came to my face as I recognised him.

"Hello, Doctor," Mycroft said as he looked up at me. "Please sit, won't you," he continued holding a hand out to indicate the vacant chair beside him. "I've already taken the initiative to order coffee and brandy," he finished.

"Thank you," I said as I took my seat.

It had been a while since I last laid eyes on Holmes's older brother. He had barely changed. He was what I could imagine Sherlock Holmes would look like with a couple of years of sedentary lifestyle and a hearty appetite to boot. Mycroft retained the Holmes's tall physique but encased in a soft, thick wrapping. Where Sherlock was wont to wander the streets in search of interesting subjects and puzzles to vex his mind, Mycroft simply sat, sipping coffee and brandy, and partaking of whatever fare was on the offering.

But they both had the sharpest minds that I would ever know in my lifetime. Mycroft's was a degree sharper and more encompassing than Sherlock's due to these simple lifestyle choices. Where Sherlock would expend intellectual and physical energy in the pursuit of answers, Mycroft would sit back and cogitate in comfort until the answer appeared in his mind.

I studied each of the Holmes brothers, in turn, mulling over in my mind what this meeting was all about. I was about to speak when a butler entered wheeling a trolley towards us. Mycroft immediately held up a finger to shush my question as it formed on my lips. I closed my mouth and watched as the butler served our coffee, brandy, and an assortment of cakes and scones.

Mycroft took a scone, slathered on jam and cream, and sat back to enjoy the delicacy. I had brandy, while Holmes simply poured himself a cup of coffee, adding two sugars and stirring it slowly until the butler turned about and left. He tapped his spoon against the side of the cup and gently placed it in the saucer. The tinkling of the chinaware in the quiet space was almost deafening.

After taking a sip and returning his cup to the saucer, Holmes leant forward and said, "Now that we are both here and have been served, would you like to tell us the reason for this meeting, dear brother?"

Mycroft finished his scone, wiped his mouth on a cloth napkin, and then sat back in his chair, steepling his fingers and looking across them at the both of us.

"I believe," he started, "That you are both familiar with a young Mr. Victor Hatherley."

My mind flashed and I blurted out, "The engineer. Lost a thumb, down Reading way. Was almost killed by a mad German."

"Yes, that would be him," Mycroft said.

Holmes simply smiled and considered Mycroft for a moment before he spoke.

"You've taken him into your service, haven't you?"

Mycroft looked slightly indignant.

"Well, not me personally – far too low level for me to be involved – but members of the government approached Mr. Hatherley to assist in certain matters," he said.

Holmes's smile increased as he noticed a note of discomfort in Mycroft's appearance and voice.

"What matters?" he asked, "Would they have anything to do with the remnants of the machine we found in Colonel Stark's house?"

Mycroft blanched at Holmes's quick appreciation of the situation.

"Why, yes they would. Again, I would remind you this has nothing to do with me. I only made the knowledge of the situation available to other members of my Department."

"And what Department would that be?" Holmes pressed a hint of a smile on his lips.

"Never mind about that," Mycroft retorted.

I was beginning to get lost in the conversation, so tried to bring it back to the obvious.

"What exactly is wrong with Mr. Hatherley?" I asked.

Mycroft turned his attention to me and away from the prying eyes of his brother. He regained his composure and smiled his little ingratiating smile towards me.

“Well, that is one of the main questions. My superiors are unsure what has happened to Mr. Hatherley. They haven’t heard from him for a while, so it would seem he has disappeared.”

“Where was he?” Holmes asked.

“Nancy, in the eastern Alsace province of France,” Mycroft said.

“France?” I asked, “What the devil was Hatherley doing there?”

Sherlock Holmes smiled broadly and chuckled.

"I think you've nailed it, Watson," he said, "It was the Devil's work, wasn't it dear brother?"

Mycroft’s face turned bright red with indignation as he said, “He wasn’t working for me.”

***

As is often the case with Sherlock Holmes, a whirlwind of action blows up around him and I find myself quite swept up in the torrential eddies that swirl in his wake.

Mycroft furnished Holmes with the details of a “safe house”, as he called it, in a mostly rural part of the town of Nancy. He revealed that Nancy itself had been under siege from a torrent of refugees escaping the Prussian invasion of Alsace-Lorraine, beginning in 1870. What was once a tiny rural town had doubled in size over the past two decades.

I was unsure if it was the probable increase in the criminal population, as well as a proportional increase in good folk, that was the problem. Holmes was playing a quiet game within his own mind and would only divulge tiny details at any time.

I must admit I was becoming quite frustrated and almost contemplated staying in England and leaving Holmes to his quest, but I had grown to like Mr. Victor Hatherley during our brief encounter of some time before. If he had been placed in danger by Mycroft’s compatriots, then I felt it was my duty to help in any way possible. Plus, if there had been foul play, a medical doctor’s help might be at the top of the agenda.

Besides, Mycroft had mentioned that his superiors did not want to send any more agents to avoid any diplomatic embarrassment, which meant Hatherley was on his own.

After the Diogenes Club, Holmes and I parted ways to return to our respective homes and prepare for our journey to eastern France. I prepared a message for Mary and had a servant take it to the telegraph office to send it to her, letting her know that I expected to be gone at least a fortnight, if not longer.

I bade my servants goodbye and took a hansom to Baker Street to meet up with Holmes. He had taken Mrs. Hudson into his confidence and she was busy helping him pack – though her aid consisted mostly of suggesting items for Holmes to take and him shaking his head and removing them from consideration. Finally, she threw up her hands and went off to make some tea.

Holmes quickly threw some basic items into his carryall and closed it, cursing "Damnable woman," under his breath. He dropped the bag near the doorway and turned to me.

"All set, Watson?" he asked.

I nodded, "I would be more so if you would actually tell me what is going on."

Holmes chuckled, "All in good time, my dear Watson, all in good time."

I shrugged and slumped down on his settee, just as Mrs. Hudson returned with afternoon tea. She began pouring cups for each of us and then moved in closer to me.

"Do you know what's going on, Dr. Watson?" she asked.

I shook my head, "I know scant details of what is behind it all. But, I do know we are to head for the eastern part of France to investigate the disappearance of an old acquaintance."

"Oh," she said, "Well, please look after him. You know how bad he is amongst the English. The good Lord knows how the French will take to him." I chuckled at her comment. She turned to watch Holmes pottering about amongst his chemicals, tools, and books, shook her head sagely, and then left the room.

I continued to watch Holmes whilst sipping my tea. He filled a small bag with a few bottles of dry chemicals and a small cache of tools. I didn't catch what any of the items were but was mindful to check at a later date in case my old friend had snuck in any of his store of illicit chemicals.

Holmes moved to his carryall and slipped the bag into it. Then he retrieved his frock coat and deerstalker hat from a nearby rack. I took this as a signal for us to leave and placed my cup down.

Holmes was already gone before I gained my feet, so I hurried after him and onwards to whatever fate awaited us.

***

With a quick goodbye to Mrs. Hudson, who stood on the doorstep, we boarded a hansom cab and made our way to Victoria Station. Our progress through the busy station was eased by my tall friend's ability to scythe through the crowds of London, and we were quickly aboard our next mode of transport, the train to Crowley.

Although I love train journeys and would be most appreciative of reading a full narrative of the trip, I have decided to limit my account to just the relevant destinations. From Crowley, we changed trains for Dover and the English Channel. There, we boarded a steamer bound for Calais. It was whilst sharing a cabin that I became acquainted once more with my erstwhile companion's annoying habit of snoring. By morning he was well refreshed from a deep slumber, while my head was pounding with the continuous internal replay of Holmes's wood-sawing noise.

After a hearty breakfast in the steamer's buffet, we alighted on French soil and quickly made our way to the railway station. There our journey took us north to Lille to meet up with the Brussels-to-Paris line. Finally, we arrived at the Gare du Nord and found ourselves in the splendour that is Paris in the spring.

My elation was brief as Holmes bustled me off to a nearby hotel and reminded me that we were not here on holiday, but on important business. I was mindful to book two rooms, which amused Holmes, who quipped, "What would Mary say about the extra expense?"

I retorted, "I have the receipt and will send the final bill to Mycroft for complete recompense. In the meantime, I need my sleep."

Holmes merely smiled as we made our way to our allotted rooms.

Even though the room was small, the bed was wonderfully soft. I fell into a deep sleep and awoke to the bright sunshine streaming in through the parted curtains. A noise from the corner of the room grabbed my attention. I started in shock when I saw Holmes sitting in the chair in the corner.

"Oh, do pull yourself together Watson," he said.

I asked, "What in blazes are you doing in my room, Holmes?"

"Time was getting away from us while you slumbered. Now, come on. Time is wasting and we have far to go."

He turned on his heel and left.

***

I met up with Holmes a short while later in the café next to the hotel. We dined on croissants and *café au lait* before making our way back to the station to continue our journey east.

I must admit that I was a little disconsolate at being in the city of romance without my dearest Mary and any time to enjoy the place. However, I was thrilled to see the city's newest landmark as our train pulled out of the station and ran along the edge of the Seine towards the outskirts of the city.

I pointed out the *le Tour Eiffel* to Holmes. Surprisingly, it piqued his curiosity slightly. He studied it while it remained in sight. Once the scenery returned to the simple suburban landscape of any great city, Holmes sat back in his seat and resumed his private thoughts.

I withdrew a notepad from my bag to begin sorting through the notes from our many adventures when Holmes piped up.

"It is a pity that such a marvellous accomplishment will have such a short life," he said.

"How do you mean?" I asked.

"Monsieur Eiffel was only granted a permit for the tower to stand on that location for twenty years. They will be compelled to demolish it in 1909. A shame really," he said.

"I'm surprised that you would be so sentimental over such a thing," I replied.

"As we have seen on so many occasions, the ingenuity of the human mind is wasted on frivolous pursuits that make no genuine contribution to the pool of knowledge as a whole."

He waved a hand towards the disappearing tower and continued, "Monsieur Gustav Eiffel was commissioned to build a simple entrance to the World's Fair, but he chose to go beyond his brief and built a possible contender for one of the wonders of the modern world. And his marvel will be consigned to the scrap heap because of some simple-minded bureaucrat's insistence on the rules. I find such things a little depressing, Watson."

With that, he pulled his hat low over his eyes and resumed his recumbent posture. I took this as my dismissal and turned my attention to my notes, but Holmes's words played on my mind for much of the remainder of our trip.

Around noon, we arrived at Reims and were made to change trains to continue on to our destination. We took luncheon on the next train and stayed for coffee and a smoke, mostly to pass the time before resuming our seats.

The sun was starting to dip below the western horizon by the time we reached Nancy. We departed and were lucky to find a hotel near the station which could provide us with a pleasant, if not simple, meal along with our twin rooms. I still wasn't going to lose any more sleep to Holmes's snoring – not while I was secure in the knowledge that Mycroft would repatriate any expenses. I hoped.

***

The morning broke brilliant and glorious with a serene silence that one could rarely find amongst the hustle and bustle of London. Holmes and I made our way downstairs for our morning repast and found a small nearby café. We settled at a small table outside in the sunshine and broke our fast on croissants and coffee, a little habit I'm sure we would continue to develop before leaving France.

Holmes sat back and seemed to me to be enjoying the scenery and soaking up the ambience, but that was shattered when he spoke.

"Watson, we have much to do today. Our first port-of-call post-breakfast will be the address gifted to me by Mycroft. I am hoping that a local hansom can take us directly there, as it is a little way out of town."

He stood up so abruptly and looked down his aquiline nose at me a stern expression on his face.

"Well, don't dilly-dally. Time is wasting."

I quickly downed my coffee and proceeded to cough on the last dregs. Holmes wandered off to look for a hansom, I assumed, so I walked inside the café to pay for our breakfast.

At the counter was a large bearded man who looked at me with suspicious eyes. I asked for the bill in my best broken French. He continued to stare at me as if I had just insulted the President before replying, "English?"

I nodded.

"*Trois francs et quarante*," he said.

I handed over a five-franc piece. The bearded man kept his eyes on mine the whole time as he took my coin and slid a selection of coins back to me. I was mesmerised by his gaze and not a little perturbed. I picked up the coins without looking, pocketed them, and turned to leave. I walked to the doorway and quickly looked back. The man was gone. I stepped out into the sunshine and felt the coins jingle in my pocket. It was only then that I noticed the weight of them.

My knowledge of French currency was not up to date, but I was intrigued by the size of one of the coins. I withdrew it to have a look. It wasn't French, but a German 1 Mark coin. I thought about walking back into the café, but Holmes chose that moment to join me, looking down at my new acquisition.

"What have you there, Watson?"

I held it up for him to view. Its unblemished surface glistened in the sunlight.

"Ah," he said, "I think you have stumbled onto quite a find."

He turned on his heel and headed for a small open carriage drawn by a single chestnut horse. He seated himself in the rear and looked back at me. I pocketed my coin and hurried after him. He spoke fluent French to the driver, well beyond my capacity to understand, and the horse was whipped into action.

We cantered through a few winding village streets before the houses gave way to wide open fields. The blue sky above provided a wonderful counterpoint to the greenery below. I drank in the blissful sight again.

Within a few moments, however, we turned into a long tree-lined drive and emerged from the shadows before a small but picturesque farmhouse. The carriage pulled up and Holmes leapt out and hurried away, calling over his shoulder, "Pay the man, there's a good chap."

I stepped down, reached into my pocket and pulled out my coins. The driver perused the offering before him and reached for the Mark. He picked it up, turned it over in his hand before huffing and dropping it back in my hand. He proceeded to pick out a few francs then doffed his cap to me.

I said, "*Merci, Monsieur,*" but received only a slight grunt before he flicked the reins and moved off.

"How rude," I thought to myself before hurrying over to where Holmes was studying the front door. I watched the driver disappear down the shadowed laneway before I spoke again.

"I get the idea that we aren't exactly welcome in this area," I said.

"Has any Englishman ever been welcome in France? Besides, the locals around here are probably a little more wary of the English since the denizens of this house moved in and then disappeared."

The lock suddenly clicked. I turned to see Holmes withdraw his lock picks and push the door open. He pocketed the tools and strode into the house.

***

The interior was dark but lacked the mustiness associated with long-abandoned houses. The only smell that greeted us was the strong tang of machine oil.

Holmes's shoes made a rather loud clopping noise as he strode down the main hall and into a reception room at the end. I followed closely behind and peered into the rooms that led off the corridor. Each was fairly Spartan, containing an unkempt bed made from a single mattress lying on the floor. There were three of these bedrooms. I stopped by the doorway of the last room and studied it for a moment.

At first, I believed that the bedding had been swept back by the man who had reposed within, but upon closer examination, I realised the bed had been searched. The blankets and sheets stripped back to show the mattress. In fact, the mattress in this room had been slashed open. The straw padding spilled out on to the floor as the intruder searched for something within.

I turned and hurried after Holmes to show him my find. I stepped out of the corridor and into the reception room itself. I had expected to find a cluttered room that would explain the goings-on, but it was devoid of all furniture and fittings, except for a fireplace with spent ashes along one wall, and an overturned wicker chair across the room from it.

Holmes was kneeling and examining some small rents in the wooden floor. I peered down near where I stood and saw similar marks. They consisted of holes with splintered edges and a large number of scratches radiating off and around them, looking as if someone had ripped a fixture out of the floor by twisting, pulling, and finally levering it out.

"Holmes," I began, only to be cut off when the target of my question looked up and put a finger to his lips. He stepped across to the middle of the room and gestured for me to accompany him. He kneeled again and withdrew a small glass bottle from his pocket. I could see some metal shavings on the floor before him but nothing else.

He poured some white powder from the bottle and blew it across the floor. As a result, the powder highlighted a series of faint white rings that I hadn't seen before.

"Watson, could you please pass me the 1 Mark coin that you were given today?" he said.

I quickly dug out the coin and put it in his outstretched hand. He bent down, placed it on the wooden floor, and slid it into one of the round grooves. It fit perfectly. He tried a few others nearby and showed them to be of the same size each time.

"What does that mean?" I asked.

"Come on. Surely you've picked up on the reason for us being here, or at least the reason for our Mr. Hatherley having been here, haven't you?"

"Refresh my memory again, if you will."

Holmes stood and handed the coin back to me. He walked to the far end of the room and pointed to the most splintered hole.

"Do you know what these holes with the splintered wood around them were for?" he asked me.

"I assume that something was secured to the floor and then removed in a rather rough way," I said.

Holmes smiled, "Well done. And the indentations?"

"Perhaps there was something heavy resting on some hidden coins," I answered.

"Would it not be more logical if the indentations were made by a machine as it was worked, rather than somebody trying to hide a few German Marks?" he said.

"Hatherley and that infernal machine that he was employed to investigate," I said. "The German was using it to press counterfeit English coins."

"Yes. But that machine was destroyed by the fire in the house at Eyford," he said. He scanned the room again and walked over to a pair of double French doors. Several deep scratches led to the door and appeared to extend beneath them. Holmes grabbed both handles and thrust the doors open. The scratches finished at the doorstop, but deep gouges were cut into the grass outside.

"This was a similar machine, wasn't it? But it stamped out German 1 Mark coins," I said.

"Exactly, my dear Watson, exactly. A much smaller version, but basically a hydraulic press for coining."

I pondered long and hard. There were many thoughts running through my head, but I think I managed to put it all together. I studied the floor, the grooves and the scratches, and then joined Holmes at the doorway and looked out across the grassed area beyond.

"Hatherley, an engineer, familiar with hydraulics – the only Englishman to have seen Stark's machine."

Holmes smiled his little sardonic smile and nodded slightly.

"You told Mycroft about Hatherley's adventure. Mycroft employed Hatherley to create a coin press identical to Stark's."

"Well, not Mycroft himself, but one of the other areas within the government."

"But why bring it here? Why the German Marks?"

"Ah, that was the bit that had embarrassed Mycroft, and why he wants to avoid any further involvement. Around two years ago, Germany installed a new Chancellor, Wilhelm II. As a commemoration of that event, a new currency was minted to replace the previous version."

I reached into my pocket and pulled out the extremely shiny and new 1 Mark coin. I flipped it over and studied both sides. It was the first time I had noticed that the minted date was from two years earlier.

"Yes. That's right Watson. Very shiny for its age, is it not?"

"I still don't understand, Holmes. Why would our government be minting fake German coins in France?"

"But Watson, we are only about five miles from the German border. The nearest large town would be Colmar, and further north is Strasbourg. With the change of Chancellor, the German economy is in a state of flux. The perfect time for a discreet form of sabotage to occur using fake currency. The counterfeit coins would be used in exchange for real currency, which would then be taken out of circulation. At some stage in the future, either the fraudulent currency would be found out, or a story would be leaked to the appropriate authorities. A scandal would ensue, and the populace would lose faith in the country's currency, thereby undermining the economy."

"How devilishly clever," I said. "But if this has happened, where is the machine? And the men?"

"That is the question that Mycroft has sent us to answer. There are only two solutions that I can see at this stage. One, the men felt the need to remove the machine and themselves to a safer location, or, two, they were removed by force. There is not enough evidence in here to conclude anything, so we must investigate further or wait for further clews to be presented."

With that, he strode out through the double doors and across the grass. I followed and noticed a small storage shed, possibly for wood, at the rear of the property, and a large unkempt area of long grass and overgrown foliage nearby.

I wandered over to the small shed as Holmes looked around the overgrown area. It was as I approached that I noticed the blackened chimney stack poking out of the roof, and to one side a large pile of coal. Intrigued, I tried the latch on the door, and to my delight, it opened, bathing the interior in light.

My questions were answered quickly, as inside the small shed was a blacksmith's forge with a large metal pot, spattered with solidified silver metal. A rolling press stood nearby. A tray lay before the pot, which would take the liquid metal and set it in strips ready for rolling or pressing into the appropriate thickness. From my rudimentary knowledge of metalworking, I assumed this was used to mix the alloy required for the coin press.

Excited at my discovery, I hurried out to find Holmes.

He was staring at something in the deep underbrush at the very rear of the property. I started towards him and began to speak as I approached.

"Holmes, I have found something rather marvellous," I said.

He held up a finger and stopped me in mid-sentence.

"What?" I asked.

"Listen," he said.

I did and could hear the sound of a horse trotting along at quite a pace. The clatter of a cart being pulled accompanied the horse.

"Quickly! They come, as I assumed they would," Holmes said. He then ducked into a long thicket of grass and lay prostrate in such a way as to keep an eye on the rear and one side of the house.

"How in blazes did you know?" I asked, joining him.

He brought out his pistol and checked that it was loaded and ready.

"Shh! If you must know, the two gentlemen behind us told me all I needed to know. I assume our friend who comes was signalled by either our driver or your friend in the café," he said.

"Gentlemen?" I asked then turned around to peer into the tangled growth behind us.

"My God!" I uttered as my eyes fell on the corpses of two poor, unfortunate men that lay hidden behind us. Both lay on their backs. They had suffered at the hand of a knifeman as their lifeblood had drained from the deep slashes across their neck. I studied them for a moment longer before the sound of the cart driving up before the house snapped my attention back.

"Neither one is Hatherley," said Holmes, "I assume they were the hired help or muscle, sent to assist him with the operation. They would not have known of the machine's workings, and therefore they were considered dispensable by our government's foe."

"Do you think Hatherley is still alive?" I asked, dreading the answer.

"I cannot be sure," he said, "As long as his skill is still required, then he should be alive, maybe even safe."

I looked once more at the two unfortunates behind me. Holmes noticed and, knowing my propensity for empathy, spoke again.

"We can mourn those two later, but at the moment we must concentrate on the possibility of finding Mr. Hatherley, and above all maintaining life ourselves."

The possibility of my own death hit home very quickly and realigned all my senses to the task at hand. I pulled my revolver out and ensured that it was fully loaded.

Through the still air of the countryside, we heard the cart driver open the front door and enter the house. Holmes got to his feet. I joined him, and we began a quick trek through the underbrush via the side of the house, circling round to the front.

"That's a stroke of luck," he whispered as we came around the front.

The cart stood all alone. The man hadn't brought any company. It had two seats up front for the driver and a passenger and a large flat-bed behind for transporting cargo. The entire rear was covered by a large canvas sheet. This was probably the same cart used to move Hatherley's machine.

Holmes moved along the side of the house, being careful to keep away from the gravel path and to only step on the grass and dirt area running along the building. I followed and arrived at the rear of the cart just a moment behind him.

He pulled up the canvas and climbed beneath. Again I followed and resumed a most uncomfortable position next to him.

"Now we wait," he said.

For what seemed like an eternity we lay in that stiflingly small area beneath the canvas sheet, listening intently, but only hearing our own breath and hearts beating.

Finally, the front door slammed shut and a key turned in the lock. The crunching of gravel indicated that the man was making his way to the cart. It lurched as he hopped back into his seat.

He mumbled under his breath, "*Niemand hier. Stark wird wütend sein. Dumme englische Männer.*" – Roughly, "No one is here. Stark will be unhappy. Stupid Englishmen."

On hearing the name Stark, my eyes opened wider. I stared toward Holmes in the darkness, and could barely tell that his face was impassive. Again he put his finger to his lips.

The man said, "Hah!" and whipped the reins. With a whinny from the horse and steps upon the gravel, the cart pulled away from the house.

Holmes lay back and closed his eyes. I tried to do the same but my hands closed tighter around my pistol as my mind imagined what would come next.

***

We bumped along for well over an hour. The growling in my stomach was almost as loud as the clattering of the cart as it trundled along the roadway. I looked across at Holmes, still laying back in a supine pose. He snapped awake when the cart slowed and veered to the right. The sound of the wheels rolling across gravel followed.

Holmes pulled out his revolver and held it at the ready. I hadn't let mine go but had to admit my hand was feeling very numb and sore. We travelled along for another five minutes before the cart finally stopped.

We heard the driver drop-down from his seat and move away across the gravel. Holmes held up a finger until the noise died down and we appeared to be alone. When all was quiet, we slid across to the edge of the cart and peered out.

The world beyond the cart was an empty space devoid of any movement. I took this as a good sign and quickly escaped the cramped confines. Looking around, I now had a better view of our environs. We had found ourselves in the side courtyard of a large stone mansion, enclosed by a thick stone wall shielding the building from view.

Holmes joined me and motioned towards a small door nearby. We both hurried across the gravel expanse as quietly as possible. Luckily the door was unlocked and we scampered inside.

We found ourselves in the tradesmen's boot room. There were a number of well-worn and dirty pairs of boots and galoshes strewn about the place. Several slickers and coats hung up on a rack along one wall. Two doors led away, one near the entrance and one at the rear. I tried the near door and peered through.

"Kitchen," I whispered to Holmes. He nodded and indicated the rear door. I made my way there and found it led down into the cellar.

"Let us make our way downstairs for the moment until we formulate a plan," he murmured.

The journey downstairs was quite a desperate affair, as there was no light to guide us. Holmes pulled out a small box of matches and struck one. The feeble light allowed passage but little more, and soon we stood on the firm but damp cellar floor. Holmes looked around and found a candle on the near wall. Lighting it chased a bit of the darkness away and gave us more confidence.

"Where the devil are we, Holmes?" I asked.

"I don't know for certain, but from my calculations, I believe us to be in a country mansion in the Bezirk Lothringen Department in Alsace-Lorraine," he said.

"Germany?"

"Yes. Hence the driver's speech to himself."

"All right, I'm curious. How did you come by that judgement?"

"To begin with, the farmhouse in which we started was situated about five miles northeast of Nancy, not very far from the German border. Our driver cantered along at approximately ten to fifteen miles an hour. We travelled for just over an hour, so are now up to twenty miles from Nancy."

"And the direction?"

"Ah, you possibly observed me during our journey, did you not?"

"Yes. I thought you were reposing in contemplation, as you are want to do."

"Close, Watson, close. As we got undercover, I found a small tear in the canvas and situated myself below it. I made the tear a little larger and concentrated on the beam of light emitted by the hole. It shone onto my crossed hands and I watched the direction that the beam moved as the cart journeyed on. At this time of the year, the sun travels across the sky at about a sixty-degree angle, higher in summer, lower in winter. The spot from the sun was closer to my face than to my boots, which meant we were lying north to south and the cart was moving east, or slightly northeast. From my knowledge of the area, we would have passed into western Germany after about fifteen minutes, and are now well into the country."

"Extraordinary," I remarked.

Holmes smiled his laconic smile that usually accompanied one of his brilliant deductions.

"Thank you, Watson. Simple elucidation based on the evidence. Nothing more."

"Indeed," I said.

I found another candle, lit it, and walked around the cellar. It held bric-a-brac and other items useless to our endeavour and had just the one entrance.

"I would think this is an old disused root cellar. We will need to enter the kitchen or exit the building if we are to proceed," he said. I nodded my agreement.

Back in the boot room we sidled up to the kitchen door and listened for a moment. Silence. I unlatched the door and stepped into the deserted room. My stomach grumbled as I spied the makings of a decent lunch. Bread, cold meats, and pots of butter and jam sat upon the bench in the middle of the room.

"No time for that, Watson," said Holmes as he moved past and sidled up to the exit doorway. He listened intently and withdrew his revolver. I pulled mine out quickly and a small part of my mind became nervous with anticipation.

Suddenly, he waved at me to move to the other side of the doorway. I flattened myself as much as possible against the cupboards there. Holmes did the same on his side, hiding slightly behind the door.

A young scullery maid entered the room, singing a soft tune to herself and completely unaware of our presence. She placed the tray she carried down on the bench and began to put the luncheon makings onto it.

Holmes quietly closed the door and slid home the latch. I moved towards the young lass in expectation of her startled reaction.

"*Fräulein*?" said Holmes, not too loudly, but enough to be heard.

The young girl turned, spied Holmes and his gun, and opened her mouth to scream. I ducked towards her and put my hand across her mouth to stifle any noise. Holmes put his finger to his lips.

"*Sh, sei ruhig. Wir werden dich nicht verletzen. Ja*?" he said.

My rudimentary German translated this as, "Be quiet. We won't hurt you. Yes?" I'm not sure it worked that well, as the young girl's eyes were ready to pop out of her head in fear. I tried talking calmly to her.

"It's all right. We mean you no harm. We are looking for a friend of ours," I said in my most caring doctor's voice.

Either my words or expression seemed to work. She calmed down and tried to speak. I pulled my hand away, ready to slap it back in place if she cried for help.

"*Englisch*?" she asked.

We both nodded. My German at least extended that far.

Our confirmation seemed to fill her with either hope or confidence. She stood tall and continued to direct questions to Holmes, whom she figured was the best person with whom to speak.

"*Bist du hier für den Engländer? Meine herrin, sie kann helfen,*" she said. ("Are you here for the Englishman? My friend, she can help.")

"*Ist der Engländer am Leben? Warum sollte deine herrin helfen wollen*?" Holmes asked. ("Is the Englishman alive? Why would your mistress want to help?")

I was lost but assumed they were talking about Hatherley and another person. I tried to wrack my brain for details of Hatherley's original adventure with us. I remembered a woman and a portly man being involved.

"*Sie hat sich in ihn verliebt. Sie möchte mit ihm fliehen,*" she said. ("She fell in love with him. She wants to escape with him.")

Holmes chuckled at this last confession.

"What is it, Holmes?" I asked.

“It seems our Mr. Hatherley has won a young girl’s heart during his imprisonment. That should prove useful to us, I think,” he said.

“*Wie heißt deine herrin*?” he asked. (“What is your mistress’ name?”)

“Elise,” she replied.

Immediately, I knew what was going on.

“Elise. The young girl that tried to convince Hatherley to escape Stark’s clutches last time,” I said.

“Yes, Watson. Funny how matters of the heart play out, isn’t it?”

The girl sidled up next to the door. She quietly opened it and looked through. We stayed back but listened intently for any sound from beyond. She finally turned and motioned for us to follow her through. Holmes and I both made sure our revolvers were primed, just in case, and trailed after her.

The maid scurried down the hallway beyond the kitchen and stopped at the end. She waited while we caught up, then looked through before moving across the open foyer beyond. Holmes followed her to the foot of a staircase leading to the upper floors. I lagged behind slightly, searching for any evidence of others in the house. It was then that I heard the noise.

From deep within the bowels of the ground floor there came a whooshing noise, followed by the creak and groan of metal and finally a clanking noise. The whoosh became higher pitched and a tinkling of metal followed.

I started to move towards the noise when the scullery maid spoke.

“*Mein Herr! Nein*!” she said.

I turned to find the maid’s face aghast with fear. Holmes stood beside her with a look of grave concern on his own. He nodded up the staircase and proceeded to climb. The maid turned and scuttled upwards herself. I shrugged and took one last look in the direction of the noise as it became louder once more. With no one to back me up, I decided discretion was the better part of valour and joined the other two in ascending the staircase.

***

In short time we came to a doorway at the far end of another corridor. The maid knocked once then let herself in. Holmes and I bundled our way in without waiting, rather be caught in an open room than an enclosed corridor.

A beautiful woman sat at a small dressing table in the middle of brushing her hair. At the sight of the three of us, her face dropped.

"*Mein Gott, Gertrude, was bedeutet das*?" she said. ("My God, Gertrude, what does that mean?")

"*Diese Engländer sind hier für herr Victor, meine dame*," Gertrude replied. ("These Englishmen are here for Mr. Victor, my lady.")

Elise placed her hairbrush down and stood up to face us.

"English?" she asked with very little accent, "You are here to rescue Victor?"

Holmes stepped forward.

"Yes. I am Sherlock Holmes and this is my associate Dr. John Watson. We have been sent to locate Mr. Hatherley and bring him back to England. Do you know if he is safe, Madam?"

Elise sat down. Her eyes dropped to the floor. There was an obvious air of loss in her pose. I could take no more and stepped forward.

"He's dead, isn't he?" I asked.

Elise's face shot up. Her sad eyes locked onto mine. Tears welled in those eyes and threatened to pour down her cheeks. She shook her head from side to side.

"No. No, he is not dead. Death would be better than this. That monster has him caged downstairs. He makes him work that infernal machine from dawn till dusk. That noise is all I hear, apart from the occasional scream from my dear Victor."

She dropped her head into her hands and sobbed.

"And it's entirely my fault."

Gertrude moved across and put her hands on Elise's shoulders and cooed to her in a soothing voice.

"*Mach dir keine Vorwürfe, meine Lady. Du wusstest nicht, dass das passieren würde*," she said.

Holmes provided a vague translation, possibly for my benefit. "'Do not blame yourself, my lady. You did not know that would happen.'"

"Now, now, my dear, do not blame yourself. Tell us what happened so that we may help solve this conundrum," he said.

She dried her eyes with a small kerchief hidden in her sleeve then looked up at us and told her story.

***

"A few weeks ago, Gertrude, myself, and Karl, our driver, went to Nancy. I was tired of being cooped up and wanted to peruse the local dress shops. Karl went off, so Gertrude and I wandered the high street. I looked around and spotted him. Victor Hatherley. The engineer I had saved in England. I could not believe it.

"I hurriedly wrote a note and tasked Gertrude with delivering it. Victor hurried over to me but said he needed to return to his dwellings and could we meet up again the next week.

"I agreed and we bid each other goodbye. My heart fluttered at our meeting. There had been something there since our first encounter, and it still remained.

"I didn't realise it at the time, but Karl had been sitting at a nearby café and saw the entire reunion. It was when he noticed Victor's disfigured hand that he remembered one of the Colonel's tales. He made enquiries and found out the location of Victor's home.

"As soon as Karl told the Colonel, he went mad and ranted about how the engineer had destroyed all his plans in England. I could hear him from my room and knew that no good would come from this.

"I cried myself to sleep, but when I awoke, the Colonel and his men were gone. I confided all to Gertrude, but neither of us knew what to do. I paced the house all day until late that night when they arrived back with a second cart containing something large under a canvas covering. I watched from my window and saw a fourth man, with a bag on his head, taken from the cart and into one of the large rooms at the rear of the house. The Colonel and his men worked into the early hours to move the covered item inside. I tried to watch and listen but finally fell asleep, waking with the sun streaming into my room.

"I crept my way downstairs and was greeted with the hiss and whir of some great engine. I approached the origins of the noise but found my way blocked by Karl. Innocently, I asked what all the commotion was about. He told me some fable about a new printing press that the Colonel was using to publish his memoirs. He pressed me with the urgency of the work and that the Colonel was not to be disturbed.

"I left knowing full well what those noises were. They mimicked the infernal machine that the Colonel had been using to press coins in England. I did not know the connection between the machine and Victor at that stage, but I was committed to finding out.

"Later that night, when all was quiet and I was sure the Colonel and his men had retired for the evening, I used the servants' passages to steal my way into the downstairs rooms where the machine had been positioned. There I found Victor, bound, gagged and chained to a wall. I was horrified and tried to unbind him, but the chains were beyond my strength. Victor was unconscious and had suffered from multiple blows to his back and chest.

"I stole away when I heard the main door open and returned to my room. I haven't been back since and fear the worse for Victor."

***

She began to sob again before saying, "I blame myself. If only I hadn't sent Gertrude after him on that day in Nancy."

Gertrude tutted and rubbed Nancy's shoulders again.

I looked across at Holmes. He stood quite rigid, cogitating on all we had heard. He peered at me. A small smile came to his lips and he winked.

"I do believe, Watson, that it is now that we shall find out our true mettle. I think our first course of action is to disarm and disable our enemies. Then we release the hostage and escape."

"Sounds simple when you say it like that, Holmes," I said. "Should we destroy the machine while we're at it?" I added sardonically.

"Of course we should." He turned his attention back to Elise.

"Now, Madam, can you show us to these internal passages so that we may confront this Colonel Stark."

***

Holmes, myself, Elise, and Gertrude made our way through the tight passages that wound through the house and kept the servants from the view of the gentry. We stopped outside of a small doorway. Holmes stayed, and the rest of us went on towards the lower levels where the machine and our unfortunate engineer were to be found.

From the account that Holmes told me later, I pieced together his encounter with the Colonel.

He opened the doorway with nary a sound and quietly stepped into the Colonel's study. Stark sat at his desk with his back to the small entrance.

Holmes stood stock still, withdrew his revolver, and pointed it at the Colonel. He started to speak but the Colonel beat him to it.

"So, Englander, you have come to rescue the disabled engineer?" he said in very good English.

Holmes was shocked and taken aback. He retained enough presence of mind to thumb back the hammer on his revolver.

"Yes, I have actually. If you would be so good to release him to me, we'll be on our way," he said, hoping that his bravado would destabilise the German.

"I can't let you take him. I need him to operate the machine," he continued without looking around.

"I'm sure the Kaiser would be interested in your continuing to mint counterfeit coins."

"True, just as much as he would dwell on the knowledge that another government was doing the same. *Your* government in fact. He may wish to talk to you about that."

"I am but a private citizen, and have only a loose connection to the forces of government."

Holmes sidled around the edge of the room to get a better look at Stark's face. He much preferred to debate face-to-face so he could study the untold language of his foe.

Stark looked up from his work and studied Holmes for a moment. A smile played on his face. A smile that disturbed Holmes more than he would have liked.

"What do you find so amusing?" Holmes asked.

"Oh, you are exactly as he described."

"Who described?"

"An old colleague of mine with whom I became reacquainted with during my stay in England. He warned me that our paths may cross if I pursued my goals. Interesting how it all came down to us meeting in the middle of Germany, rather than England. My friend will be most annoyed when I tell him how you were dispatched."

Holmes became confused.

Stark then yelled, "Karl!"

The driver burst into the room brandishing a large cleaver and headed straight for Holmes. He brought the gun around but it was knocked from his hand, with one sweep of the cleaver, and skittered away. Holmes ducked back and felt the wall behind him.

Karl brought the cleaver up and down in one sweep. Holmes ducked sideways and dropped to the floor. The cleaver struck the wall, splitting the wood and becoming wedged. Holmes lashed out with one foot and caught Karl in the knee. A loud crack drove him to the ground, where he howled in pain. Holmes gained his feet and stepped back towards the driver, smashing his fist into the side of the man's face. Karl's head slammed into the floor and his body dropped into an untidy heap and stopped moving.

Holmes retrieved his revolver and pointed it at Stark. The man looked more annoyed than frightened.

"*Hans, Ich brauche hilfe hier*!" he yelled. ("Hans, I need help here!")

The door opened again revealing a larger man than Karl. Hans held a small pistol in his meaty hand and pointed it at Holmes.

"*Erschieß ihn*!" Stark yelled. ("Shoot him!")

Hans smiled. Holmes ducked to one side as the sound of the gun retort echoed through the room. Hans' smile slowly faded from his face and a small dribble of blood ran from his mouth. He toppled and fell to the floor, revealing to Holmes my shocked self, standing behind him, holding a smoking gun.

"Watson, what fabulous timing."

Holmes quickly rose to his feet and turned to face Stark. The Colonel looked extremely annoyed. He stood up and opened a small desk drawer.

"Fine. I'll do it myself," he said and dragged a revolver from the drawer.

Holmes pre-empted Stark's actions and leapt forward, driving his right fist into the German's jaw and knocking him backwards. The Colonel crashed to the ground and lay still.

"My word!" I said as I walked up next to the desk.

Holmes looked down at what had preoccupied Stark's attention when he entered the room. A broad smile came to his face.

"Interesting."

***

Holmes and I sat across from Mycroft in the Stranger's Room once more. The fire burnt low, even though a bright summer's day reigned outside.

"Hatherley?"

"Safe and healthy."

"And this Stark – a habitual coiner, but not working for the Kaiser?" asked Mycroft.

"Correct. It was only luck that drew him to Hatherley's machine. With it, he planned to recoup his losses from his English experiment and set about undermining the new Kaiser himself – thereby doing your work for you."

"It wasn't my work, as I've said. But why did you stop him then?"

"There were innocents involved, and I have no care for the matters of government at large."

"And where are these innocents now?" I asked.

"Elise and Victor have been furnished with a country estate and an allowance," said Mycroft. "They will not pose a problem."

"And this Stark fellow?"

Sherlock Holmes smiled, "We left him and his driver secured by the chains near the machine. On our way to Nancy, we notified the local *Polizei* that they may be interested in the goings-on at a nearby mansion. I'm sure Stark is a problem to nobody by now."

"Good," said Mycroft, "This has been a very embarrassing affair, all told."

"Quite so. But I think that it still has the potential to become more than just embarrassing. If not investigated further from both of our perspectives, it threatens to endanger not just ourselves but the general populace as well."

"What makes you think that?"

Holmes reached into his jacket pocket and withdrew a letter he had taken from Stark's desk. He slid it across the table. Mycroft picked it up and opened it.

"It's not the contents you should worry about, just the seal at the bottom."

The red wax seal was indented with a stylishly curved capital "*M*".

Mycroft's expression changed to show slight worry and confusion.

"This is not my seal," he said.

"Correct. Think harder and you will understand the gravity of the situation."

Mycroft stared at the seal until the penny dropped. He looked back at Holmes, fear writ large on his face.

"*Moriarty*!" he said.

The Case of the Gila Monster

During my friendship with Sherlock Holmes, I have, on numerous occasions, found myself over-awed by the breadth of knowledge that resides behind those aquiline features, and also been humbled by his immense understanding of all things medical. At times I have been left mouth agape in surprise as some esoteric piece of information springs forth from that immense intelligence.

These incidents have been quite frequent and ego-shattering, but none so much as the time Holmes solved the mystery surrounding a death from the bite of a Gila Monster.

It was a wonderful spring day and I was enjoying a late afternoon cup of tea in the back garden behind my Kensington practice. I had seen numerous patients all day and rewarded myself with some peace and quiet. The serenity was sadly broken by the appearance of my beautiful wife, Mary, at the rear door.

"Sorry to bother you, John, but we've received a late patient. I suggested that she return in the morning, but her manner was ever so compelling that I thought it best if you see her now," she said.

I stood up and replied, "Quite alright, dear. It will probably be nothing, but I would rather quieten her fears now than allow any to develop further overnight."

I moved to the door, but Mary placed a hand upon my chest stopping me short. She glanced over her shoulder then leaned in close to me, whispering, "She's a formidable lady. If I was to have an opinion, I would think that her problems are all in her mind. But of course, you are the doctor."

I smiled and patted her on the shoulder. "I'm sure they are, but I've never met a patient that could pull the wool over my eyes."

Mary allowed me to pass and I stepped through into my consulting room. My patient spied me and immediately stood up to greet me.

My wife was right. The lady before me was an astounding specimen. She stood just short of six-foot-high and was quite rotund as well. She wore an extremely tight-fitting black tulip skirt and a matching black blouse wrenched over her enormous bosom and brought in tight at the waist. Her hair was pulled back into a high bun, giving her face a fierce expression, even at rest.

She had the look and presence of a private school governess. My only thought was pity for her students.

Her face split into a fierce smile and she said, "Dr. Watson, thank you so much for seeing me at such short notice. I have to apologise, but I didn't know where else to go."

I bade her to sit and took my seat behind my desk.

"What is it I can help you with Mrs, ah . . . ?"

"Bell," she answered, "Mr. Moira Bell. I live not far from here on the edge of Regents Park with my son."

It was then that this remarkable woman lost all composure and showed that underneath her gruff exterior was someone full of emotion and love. As soon as she mentioned her son, a torrent of tears poured forth from her eyes and she sobbed uncontrollably into her sleeve.

I jumped up, raced around the desk, pulled a clean kerchief from my breast pocket, and offered it to the distraught woman. She took it, wiped her eyes, and then blew her nose into it. As it was an inexpensive silk kerchief, I decided to let her keep it.

I quickly found Mary and asked her to brew some tea while I attended to Mrs. Bell.

The troubled woman finally calmed down once the offer of a cup of hot tea was made. She began to tell me her tale whilst sipping the brew.

She was a local resident who lived in a line of properties that edged onto a lovely part of Regents Park, not far from the London University College. Her family had possessed one of the three-storey Georgian houses for well over a hundred years, and she had inherited the lease on the passing of her father almost thirty years previously.

She lived alone with her grown son, Julius, as her husband had died in the Afghan war. I told her my own war tale and was able to provide a larger level of empathy towards her because of it.

She went on to explain that her son was a Professor of Zoology working at the University College. He possessed a rather large and exotic collection of snakes and reptiles, which he kept in a room on the second floor.

"A herpetologist?" I asked.

"If you insist," she answered, indicating to me that she had no real interest in her son's profession. "It was those damnable lizards that caused all this trouble."

I pushed her for more information and was finally told that her son had been arrested for manslaughter. A man named Hyram Shrubb had forced his way into their home and had died as a result of being bitten by one of her son's lizards, a Gila Monster from America.

I frowned internally at this revelation. Gila Monsters are venomous, but to my knowledge are rarely deadly. Most victims are usually left with horrid wounds caused by the strength of the jaws rather than from the venom.

At the remembrance of her son's current whereabouts, she began to sob all over again without revealing any other pertinent details. I quickly went to her aid to calm her once more and prescribed a relaxant to help her sleep that evening. I also suggested that a friend of mine might be able to shed more light on the facts of the case and help to unearth the true nature of this horrid affair. She then admitted that it was my friendship with Holmes that had led her across town to see me.

Once she was calm again, I helped her out of my rooms after securing her address and said that I would bring Holmes to her home at precisely eleven o'clock the next day.

Through a veil of drying tears, she agreed, thanked me for my service, and marched off home.

As I watched her go a small thrill went through me. I know that my good friend Holmes requires constant stimulation of his mind to keep the *ennui* at bay, but during these quiet times, I find myself in such a need as well.

This case also promised the need for a high level of medical knowledge, and there was hope that the depth of my experience would be of use to Holmes.

Sadly, that was not to be.

***

I arrived at the front doorstep of Mrs. Bell's home on Cumberland Terrace at a few minutes of eleven. The day was quite warm and I found that I had underestimated the walk and was awash with perspiration.

I had removed my hat and was mopping my brow with a fresh kerchief when I noticed Holmes walking towards me. He was elegantly dressed as always and tapped along with his cane. He had left his hat at home and showed no sign of being overheated.

"Good morning, Watson, and what a wonderful morning it is!" he said, admiring the building before us. "Poisoning by venomous lizard. Not a regular occurrence in London, one would think."

"Indeed."

We both studied the house before us. It was part of a long series of terraces flanking this side of the park.

"I took the liberty of walking around the back of the houses. There's an alleyway running along the buildings used by the night soil men and a gate through which one can access the park. Very convenient for a quiet evening stroll or for accessing the rear doorway unseen," he said.

I nodded in agreement, unsure of what he meant.

We turned to mount the steps to the front door but were disturbed by a commotion next door. Two men were struggling to manhandle a settee down the steps and into a large cart parked by the roadway.

I turned and watched their antics just as the lead man slipped off a step and tumbled to the pavement below, bellowing in pain. By the time I reached him, he was sitting up and holding his right ankle.

"I'm a doctor. I can help if you like," I said.

"Ow! It's my ankle! I nearly broke it!" he cried.

I gently pulled his hands away from his foot and straightened his leg out. The ankle was certainly swollen. I moved the foot about, which elicited more howls of pain. To stop his moaning, I lowered his foot and spoke to him.

"I don't think it's broken," I said as I reached into my pocket for a card, "but you certainly won't be doing any more furniture moving today. I suggest you make your way home, rest, and put some ice on it to take away the swelling,"

He took the card and I continued. "Come and see me tomorrow – or better yet, the next day. I'll be able to tell how badly damaged it is by then. Meanwhile, stay off it."

"I'll 'elp 'im get 'ome," his friend offered.

Another man emerged from the doorway with an angry expression on his face.

"Here, what's all this laying about then?" he asked.

I stood up and addressed him.

"I'm afraid your man has had a rather nasty tumble. He's sprained his ankle or worse. I'm a doctor, and I've told him to rest up for a couple of days before coming to see me about it."

The man was indignant.

"I can't wait up for him to get better. I need this place emptied today," he said.

He pointed to the man on the ground, "Get up, Harry, or you're fired!"

Harry's eyes lit up in fear. He tried to pull himself up but screamed in pain as he put weight on his leg and collapsed again.

"I think that answers that question, then," said Holmes.

The angry man turned to face the detective.

"And what do you care?" he asked.

"Nothing, really. I'm just a casual observer, but anyone can see that if this man is not fit to work, then the work will not get done."

The angry man turned back to Harry, ready to blast him again.

"And why are you in such a hurry?" asked Holmes.

The angry man turned once more, "What's it to you?" he said.

"Just a casual observer," repeated Holmes evenly.

"Well, if you have to know, this whole place," he indicated the line of terraced houses, "Is going to be pulled down and replaced by nice, new, modern houses."

I was horrified.

"Why destroy these wonderful buildings? Who would do such a thing?" I asked.

"I think the answer to that, Watson, is pretty much under your nose," said Holmes.

I looked at him and saw that he was staring at the wagon behind me. I turned and read the sideboard of the cart. *Shrubb Brothers*.

"I've never heard of them," I said.

Holmes smiled at me, that smile I had seen far too often for my own liking. I'd missed something again.

"I think you'll find, Watson, that one of those brothers is exactly why we are here."

I once again urged the injured man to rest, much to the annoyance of his employer, and then joined Holmes on the neighbouring doorstep. Holmes smiled at me and indicated the door.

"Well, it's your case so far, Doctor," he said.

I stepped up and lifted the heavy knocker. I rapped only once before the door was unlocked and opened. It revealed a sallow-faced young maid. She looked at us wide-eyed through the crack in the door.

"Can I 'elp you, sirs?" she asked.

"Yes. Dr. Watson and Mr. Sherlock Holmes, to see Mrs. Bell. We are expected," I said.

"Oh, yes, sirs. Please come in," she said as she backed away and opened the door for us to enter.

We stepped into a small entry hall that proved a little too tight for both Holmes and I together. The maid squeezed past us, locked the door, and withdrew the heavy iron key. She moved to a nearby wall stand and hung the key on a hook next to its twin. A third hook remained empty, so I placed my hat upon it. The maid once again moved past and motioned for us to follow her into a room off to the right.

"Does that key unlock the rear door as well?" Holmes asked.

The maid was surprised by the question and shrank back slightly. "Yes. Yes, it does," she said.

Holmes simply nodded.

We entered the small reception room and found Mrs. Bell sitting by the window, reading the day's newspapers. She looked up and brightened when she saw me, and then eyed Holmes with a curious lift of her eyebrow.

"Mrs. Bell, I'd like to introduce my good friend, Mr. Sherlock Holmes. I've described the scant details of your son's case to him, and he is very interested in hearing more to see if he can indeed provide help."

Mrs. Bell began to rise from her seat. Holmes gallantly tried to stop her with a gesture but was too slow. He was taken aback when she rose to full height and met him almost eye-to-eye, something that happens rarely for Holmes, especially with women.

Mrs. Bell held out her hand and said, "Mr. Holmes, I am very pleased to meet you. I am Moira, but I do prefer Mrs. Bell in deference to my late husband."

A small grin came to Holmes's mouth as he shook hands with the dominating presence that was Mrs. Moira Bell.

"Please tell me all about your son's troubles, Mrs. Bell," he said, indicating her chair. Holmes and I took seats on the small settee nearby. My friend sat back and steepled his hands before his face, his standard pose when absorbing facts provided to him.

Mrs. Bell began her tale.

"My son has been charged with the manslaughter of a very nasty man, Mr. Hyram Shrubb. My son, Julius, lives here with me and is a Professor of Zoology at the University College, just down the road. He specialises in the study of lizards and snakes."

"Herpetology," Holmes said, "Yes, Dr. Watson informed me. To be honest, that was probably what piqued my interest the most. I have heard a lot about your son and would dearly love to meet him. I can assure you that I will do all I can to clear this little matter up for him."

Mrs. Bell continued, "Oh, thank you. Well, this Mr. Shrubb turned up on our doorstep one day and barged past my poor Milly uninvited."

"Your maid, I presume?" asked Holmes.

"Why, yes. I'm sorry. He stormed into this room and blurted out his introductions, and then laid out an offer to buy the lease on my house. I was far too perplexed at his gruff manner to even consider such a request unannounced. I sent him away without another word, but he didn't leave it there. He turned up several days in a row, but Milly, God bless her, held her ground and wouldn't let him in. After the seventh time, he arrived when Julius was home, so I agreed to meet him again and hear him out."

She took a deep breath before returning to her story.

"We met in here with tea and biscuits to present an amicable setting. Mr. Shrubb called himself a 'property developer'. He is purchasing all the houses along this street with the idea of demolishing them and building a new set of larger terraces to serve the officers of the nearby Regents Park barracks. Julius became very nervous at this talk. Our house has been in my family for over a hundred years. Julius was born here. He's never known another home. He's a good boy and would never hurt a fly. He needs this house, as it's near to the University which is his life, and he needs the space to store his collection."

Holmes sat forward, a slight glint in his eye, "I take that to be his collection of reptiles," he said.

"Yes," she continued, "My Julius has a large collection of reptiles upstairs, with some very rare breeds that even the London Zoo doesn't possess." She made a slightly disgusted face. "I never go in there myself. Dreadful things," she finished.

"And that's where the Gila Monster is housed," asked Holmes, sitting back and resuming his contemplative pose.

"Oh, yes. That's also where everything went wrong."

"Go on."

"Well, I told Mr. Shrubb that there was no way that I would even contemplate selling. Julius was much relieved. Mr. Shrubb tried to offer more money to persuade us, but my mind was made up. I don't need any money, as my poor unfortunate father, God bless him, was well invested. I shan't be in need for the rest of my life and neither will Julius. Mr. Shrubb left in quite an angry mood and I hoped that would be the last we saw of him."

"But it wasn't," I said.

"No. Not at all. That meeting was a fortnight ago. Earlier this week, I was at my bridge club, Milly was out at the grocer, and Julius came home early to feed his collection. He stepped in through the front door and heard screams coming from the second floor. He ran upstairs and found Mr. Shrubb lying on the floor with Julius' favourite – his Gila Monster – clinging to his arm. Julius went to his aid and managed to pry the lizard away from Mr. Shrubb's arm. He then put the reptile away, latched up the case, and then attended to Mr. Shrubb. My dear boy managed to bring the man down to this room just as Milly returned. They both helped to tend his wound and call him a hansom. He kept blubbing that he found the door unlocked and was looking for me. He stumbled into the reptile room and was attacked by the lizard. The last they saw was his slumped form in the seat of a hansom, taking him to Dr. Brown's surgery around the corner in Robert Street. Frankly, no one thought any more of it until the police came two days ago and took my poor boy away. Manslaughter, they said, caused by the lizard bite. They blamed Julius for leaving the cage open."

"Hmm," said Holmes, "I think I'd like to see this reptile room and then, Watson, I think we should pay a visit to Dr. Brown."

***

The reptile room was more crowded than I had presumed. It was located in what was a rather large second-floor bedroom, but it seemed to shrink when filled with a dozen or so large wooden framed enclosures with glass sides. Each had a glass lid and held a single specimen.

Holmes moved around the room, a look of delight on his face as he stared into each of the reptile tanks. He stopped by one and studied it.

"Ah," he said, "*Vipera berus*. The common adder. The kingdom's only venomous snake, but really quite shy and harmless."

He moved on to another that contained a brown snake lying on a flat rock.

"*Naja haje*, the Egyptian Cobra, also known as the Asp. It was this snake that was thought to have been used by Cleopatra to commit suicide. Very good, very good."

He moved on and stopped by another enclosure.

"Ah, and here is our little mischief-maker himself."

Inside the glass cage was a fat, squat lizard with a pink and brown mottled body and black face.

"*Heloderma suspectum*, the Gila Monster. Native to the southwestern United States and northern Mexico. I'm not sure if I'm more impressed in seeing it, or the fact that Professor Bell managed to find one and keep it alive."

He studied the cage and unlatched two slide bolts near the top which caused the front to fold down. The lizard hardly moved with the door open and simply looked at Holmes for a moment before falling back to sleep.

"Hardly the vicious killer of legend, hey, Watson?"

"Is it still alive?" I asked.

Holmes chuckled and relatched the door.

Just then the room's door opened and Milly walked in with a tray of food scraps. She saw the two of us and a slightly shocked look came to her face.

"Oh, I'm sorry gentlemen. I can come back and feed these beasts later."

"Never mind that, Milly. Please ignore us, will you. Go about your chore," said Holmes.

Milly moved to the nearest cage and opened the top. She dropped some scraps inside and the resident lizard wandered over to eat. She replaced the lid and repeated the exercise with the next few tanks.

Holmes watched with interest.

"Milly," he asked.

The young maid almost dropped the tray in shock. She turned sheepishly to face the detective.

"Yes, sir?"

"I assume that Professor Bell usually feeds the reptiles."

She nodded.

"Since he's indisposed you've taken up the challenge."

Again she nodded.

"I noticed that you only feed them through the top of the enclosure. Do you ever need to open the front?"

"Oh, no, sir. Julius, er, the *professor* always uses the top. 'E would only open the front if 'e was moving the animal to another enclosure, and then 'e would use those."

She pointed at a pair of thick leather gloves hanging from a peg on the wall.

Holmes studied the gloves, looked back at the Gila Monster sitting on its rock, and then turned to me.

"Watson, it's time to visit Dr. Brown."

***

We were shown into Dr. Brown's room just as his last patient before lunch left.

Behind the desk sat a man of about sixty years of age with a ramrod-straight posture. He was quite bald but possessing of a luxuriant grey moustache and a monocle held in with his right eyebrow.

A quick look around his room showed the standard paraphernalia of a modern doctor. A full-sized human skeleton hung from a frame in one corner. A gurney sat against one wall with a curtained area for undressing next to it. On the wall behind the desk was a small but marvellous collection of artefacts from the east.

A Ghurkha knife stood on a stand in the middle of a mantlepiece that framed the grate of a small fireplace. On the wall to either side were framed copies of the doctor's professional certificates and a letter with the seal of Her Majesty. I strained to read the letter, but only made out a comment about service to the Crown. It looked very similar to the one that I had received.

"Let me introduce ourselves, Dr. Brown. I am Dr. John Watson, and this is Mr. Sherlock Holmes," I said. I pointed to the Ghurka knife and asked, "You served in India?"

He looked around for a moment and turned back with a smile of fond remembrance, "Yes," he said, "I was an officer in the Indian Army for more than twenty years." He studied me for a moment, "And yourself? You have the air of a military man as well."

I nodded with a slight bow. "In Afghanistan, until I was injured."

He looked at Holmes, taking in my tall companion's presence for a moment before directing his enquiry at the detective.

“Sherlock Holmes. I have heard of you, sir, but never believed I would find myself in any need of your services, so forgive me if I am surprised to find the reverse.”

A small smile crossed Holmes’s face. “Let us not take up too much of your time,” he said, “A couple of days ago, you received an emergency patient by the name of Hyram Shrubb.”

The doctor nodded, “Yes. Lizard bite. Very strange and nasty.”

“I know it may constitute a breach of privacy, but could I enquire as to how you treated the bite?”

“Well, I don’t wish to let out my secrets, as it wasn’t something well known among British doctors.”

“Could it have been with the administration of a weak mix of strychnine?”

The doctor looked aghast. “How in the blazes would you have known that?” he asked.

I was just as shocked. “Yes, Holmes. How?”

Holmes’s face possessed that smile generally reserved for me when I’ve been surprised by one of his deductions. He took a deep breath and enlightened us.

“Dr. Brown, before you even spoke, your Ghurka knife told me that you lived in India. I presumed that you would have served as a doctor for most of that time.”

“Yes,” said Brown.

“Mr. Shrubb presented to you with a bite from a Gila Monster. He may not have known the actual species, but you would have seen fang marks and much damage caused by the bite. I expect that you would have treated him as if he had been bitten by a venomous animal.”

“Well, yes. Once I treated any infection, I naturally took the precaution to treat for poison.”

“And coming from India, where the standard procedure for cobra bite is to use strychnine, a treatment developed in Australia in the 1850s to care for bites from their local snake population, as it contains species far deadlier than the cobra of India.”

“Yes. Correct again. Amazing. You got all that from a Ghurka knife?”

"You would be amazed what information Holmes can gather from the smallest of sources," I said.

"Thank you, Watson," Holmes said. "By the way, Dr. Brown. Do you know that your patient, Mr. Shrubb, died the very next day?"

Brown's face dropped in complete shock.

"What? That's impossible. Once I administered the strychnine and settled him down here for a little while, he was right as rain. I loaded him into a hansom and sent him home. I'm flabbergasted."

"Quite so, but I would have experienced the same reaction if I were in your place. I do give you my promise that we will return and explain what happened when I have solved it myself, which will be quite soon," said Holmes, "I thank you for your time, Doctor."

He spun on his heel and spoke to me.

"Watson, if you will, I think we should take a visit to Scotland Yard. We need to see the unfortunate Mr. Shrubb."

***

Martin, the young mortician, looked up as Holmes and I entered. He was just finishing his lunch and had probably expected a little peace and quiet. He stood up quickly and addressed us.

"Dr. Watson, Mr. 'Olmes. I wasn't expecting anybody today. What can I do for – "

He was cut off by the arrival of Inspector Lestrade, who seemed a bit flustered. He carried the small note from Holmes that had been passed to him by the desk Sergeant on the floor above.

"Ah, Inspector," said Holmes, "I believe you will find the following of interest."

"Why did you drag me away from my luncheon to come down to this God-awful place?" Lestrade asked.

Holmes ignored the question and instead addressed Martin.

"If you would be so kind to please direct us to the corpse of the unfortunate Mr. Hyram Shrubb, Martin."

Martin put his sandwich down and pulled the napkin from his collar before skirting a few gurneys and stopping before one covering a large bloated body.

"'E's a big 'un," he said, before pulling back the sheet to reveal the corpse below.

"Thank you," said Holmes. He bent forward and looked at the man's face, studying the mouth and nose while making small humming noises to himself – something to which I have long become accustomed when Holmes investigates. He pulled out his glass and had a closer look at the man's nose. I did find this particularly odd, as I could see the bite mark on the man's left forearm quite clearly.

Finally, Holmes moved away from the man's face and studied the bite. From where I stood, I could see that the flesh on the arm had been ravaged by multiple teeth marks. The lizard had latched on with considerable force and thrashed about before being pulled off. There were two larger holes on opposite sides of the bite which were deeper and more pronounced. I took these to be the venom-bearing teeth.

Holmes's examination of the bite was remarkably short as he moved away from the area and fixated on the man's upper forearm. I could see more puncture marks, which I presumed were from the injections administered by Dr. Brown.

Holmes rose and stood staring at Shrubb's corpse for a moment before turning back to Martin.

"The Coroner hasn't performed an autopsy," he said.

It was more a statement than a question.

Martin replied, "No. No, 'e 'asn't. 'E said that we know 'ow the man died, so no need to mess 'im up any more."

Holmes's face screwed up. I knew that he viewed such actions and sloppy, as they restricted the amount of information that could be gleaned.

"Why do you think that would be important?" Lestrade asked, "We know it was the lizard, and we know that this professor was the lizard's owner. Case closed."

A short flash of fury leapt to Holmes's face before he replaced it with calm. I believe that Lestrade barely missed a thorough lecture.

"Because, Inspector, this man is extremely obese. I dare say a good shock of any sort could have caused him to keel over. Also, do you not think it would be a good idea to ascertain the amount of venom in his system? I've seen the lizard in question. Unless it had friends working with it, then it wouldn't have been able to generate enough venom to kill a man of this size."

With that, he placed his lens back in his pocket and abruptly departed, speaking over his shoulder as he did.

"Thank you, Martin. Your help has been admirable. Inspector, I think you should meet Watson and me at the house of Mr. Hyram Shrubb and his brother in two hours. I will announce my findings there forthwith. Please bring Professor Bell, for he has nothing at all to do with this unfortunate event and you can release him afterwards."

I gave thanks and said my goodbyes before following after Holmes.

***

We took luncheon in The Rag nearby in Pall Mall. My status as an ex-serviceman held me good stead amongst the military folk that inhabited the place, and Holmes was always welcome once his identity was known, even though he'd never served Her Majesty in the armed services.

Throughout the meal, I kept prodding him about the solution to the case. His only answer was to smile, nod, and say, "All will become clear." A most infuriating affair it was. He seemed more intent on studying the diners at several other tables, most of whom wore very high-ranking insignia on their jackets.

"My word, this is a very prominent gathering for this time of day," I remarked.

"Yes," said Holmes, "One would almost imagine that we are centralising some of our garrisons in preparation for another campaign."

"I'm sure it's nothing to do with war, Holmes. Just a gathering of officers."

Holmes simply smiled.

***

At a little after two, we were the first to arrive. Holmes went straight to the door and knocked. It was opened by a pasty-faced doorman, who eyed us with slight suspicion.

"I am Sherlock Holmes and this is Dr. John Watson. We should be expected."

The doorman nodded and replied, “Yes, sirs. Mr. Shrubb was informed of your imminent arrival. He has seen fit to meet with you in the parlour.”

He stepped back and allowed us to enter. The foyer was quite luxuriant with deep-grained woods and leather. The doorman led us down a short corridor and into a spectacular room lined along every wall with bookcases, each crammed with leather-bound volumes in nearly perfect condition, and a small number of display cases holding an assortment of bric-a-brac.

Both Holmes and I were quite taken aback by this room. Neither of us has any expectations of such a place in a house occupied by a pair of bachelor property developers.

It was then I noticed a man sitting in a high backed chair towards the far end of the room. He was the spitting image of his brother, but lacking most of the weight. For a split second, I imagined the Holmes brothers, with Mycroft lying in the Scotland Yard morgue and Sherlock sitting before me.

“Gentlemen,” he began, “Welcome to my home.”

He rose and stood a good two inches higher than Holmes. He made his way towards us and held out his hand to me first.

“I am Aubrey Shrubb,” he said and took my hand.

“John Watson,” I replied.

He turned to Holmes and repeated the action, remarking, “And you would be the famous Sherlock Holmes.”

“I’m sorry about what happened to your brother,” said Holmes, shaking and finally releasing Shrubb’s hand.

“Yes, damnable strange way to die, that. Who would have thought such an intelligent man would allow his creatures to run free and attack any innocent person who happened upon them? Very negligent, it would seem.”

“That is partly why we are here. Mrs. Bell has asked me to investigate a little further and determine just how your brother came into contact with the lizard, and what happened afterwards.”

“I think the police have worked all that out, haven’t they? He was bitten by a venomous lizard and it killed him. Case closed.”

“Forgive my cynicism, but the police are likely to take the most obvious answer when investigating a strange case such as this. I much prefer to look at all the facts and evidence before jumping to conclusions.”

The sound of the door knocker filtered in as the second group of guests arrived at the Shrubb residence.

“Ah, speaking of the police,” said Holmes.

Moments later, the doorman showed a slightly aggrieved Lestrade and a very perplexed and dour-looking man, who I assumed was Professor Bell, into the parlour.

Shrubb took one look at Bell and asked, “What is *he* doing here?”

“I thought it best to have the professor here to provide any expert information concerning the Gila Monster, and to be on hand to defend himself if required,” said Holmes.

“Hmm. I only agreed to this because your note said that you had new information that would shed light on Hyram’s death. I was hoping that you would find something to convict this man with murder rather than manslaughter,” Aubrey said, his contempt for Bell on show as he spat out the word man.

“Well, it could go either way,” said Holmes, “To move things along, would it be possible to see your brother’s rooms? My understanding is that he had a suite of apartments on the second floor and that he was found in his own drawing-room."

“Yes. The rooms are as he left them. I haven’t had the heart to let the help tidy up yet.”

***

The second floor was a large and sumptuous collection of rooms styled in a more minimalistic way than the parlour below. I assumed that they reflected the less austere tastes of the younger and larger of the Shrubb brothers.

The climb up the stairs also left me a little breathless and I wondered how a man of Hyram Shrubb’s girth would have found the journey. It was later that I discovered there was a lift, which explained quite a lot.

Aubrey Shrubb led us down a short corridor and into a large but modestly decorated drawing-room. There was a sizeable wooden desk at one end, with a small collection of leather-bound volumes on a set of shelves behind it. I pulled a book down and looked closer. They were mostly books relating to the history of London's property transactions. It seemed this room doubled as Hyram Shrubb's office, or else his work was also his hobby.

I turned back from the shelf and found Aubrey directing Holmes to a large chair in the far corner. The elder Shrubb brother pointed to a stain on the carpet and spoke.

"My poor unfortunate brother was found face down here. His last act was to expel his luncheon – hence the stain. I did allow the maid to clean the results after the police allowed it."

Holmes turned to Lestrade and said, "Did your men take samples for examination?"

"Why?" Lestrade asked.

Holmes closed his eyes for a second, pursed his lips, and said, "Because it would have been a trivial exercise to determine the contents of his stomach, revealing how much venom was in his system, and also what else may have been ingested."

"Right," said Lestrade.

Holmes turned back to the scene and moved to a small table next to the sitting chair. Opening the drawer, he pulled out a bottle of white powder and a half-full syringe containing a clear liquid. Holmes picked up the bottle, uncorked it, and dabbed a small amount of the powder on his finger. He tasted it, nodded, and smiled. I questioned him as he put the bottle down.

"What is that?"

"My old friend – though a lot more concentrated than my favoured seven-per-cent solution," he said.

"Cocaine?" I remarked.

Aubrey piped up with a hint of offence. "What my brother did in his own house is none of your business!"

"Indeed," said Holmes. "But it must be taken into consideration with all the other evidence."

He turned and scanned the room, seeking out *minutiae*. His eyes fell on me, and then the desk. He strode over and stood behind it, opening the top drawers and rifling through them.

"Hello, what the blazes do you think you are doing?" yelled Aubrey, "That's Hyram's private business!"

He started to move towards Holmes but Lestrade placed a hand lightly on his shoulder.

"I'd let Mr. Holmes finish, sir. If there's something that we've missed, then he is most likely to find it. I'm sure he's not interested in any private affairs of your brother's."

With that, Holmes finished looking through one of the bottom drawers and stood up withholding his prize – a large iron key.

Professor Julius Bell yelled out in surprise, "That's our missing key! We thought that Milly had lost it. She got a right dressing down from Mother. No wonder she cried so much. I had to console her for hours."

Lestrade turned to look at the professor, who suddenly realised he'd said too much. A sheepish look came across his face.

"Well, she was very upset," he added.

All eyes slowly returned to Holmes, who placed the key in the middle of the vacant leather desk pad. He looked around all of the faces full of anticipation and smiled. "This, gentlemen, is the vital clew for which I have been searching."

"But what does it mean?" I asked.

He ignored me and turned towards Shrubb.

"Mr. Shrubb. You and your brother are highly successful property developers, a new occupation that takes the city's old and derelict districts and renews them for the next generation and in turn attracts a tidy profit. Is that not right?"

Shrubb nodded, "Yes, why?"

"Your brother wasn't used to failure, I think. He studied the city and chose the best locations for these developments – hence his detailed volumes of property transactions and locations in London. A well-versed man in that field, I would presume."

"Yes. He was the educated one. He found the properties and I organised the workmen and ran the operation."

"So, his latest venture was to revitalise parts of Regents Park, with the view of establishing residencies for the officers of the nearby

Regents Park Barracks and the new garrisons that will be moving there soon."

"We had already convinced most of the residents to depart, and were almost ready to demolish."

"But one held out."

"Yes. Mrs. Bell wouldn't sell. Even when we made a higher offer than to any other resident."

Holmes held up the iron key.

"And that's what drove your brother to purloin this key and gain access to the Bell residence when he believed all to be away."

"How dare you besmirch my brother's good name!" said Aubrey as he stepped towards Holmes.

Lestrade intercepted him and posed a question of Holmes. "How can you be sure that Shrubb took that key from the Bell residence?" he asked.

"When we arrived, we noticed that there were only two keys on the rack near the front door. Professor Bell has told us that there was a third which seems to have gone missing. Mr. Shrubb was found inside the house when all occupants had left. I would say that his claim that the door was unlocked was a fantasy. With this key, he could have entered from the front or back, as both doors use the same lock."

"Why did he break-in?" asked Lestrade.

"Ah, well, that's where I must presume a little, until of course more evidence is unearthed that proves me incorrect. The sticking point of the sale of the house was Professor Bell's residency at the University College. His mother would not have them move. The facts as they standpoint to Mr. Shrubb entering the house with the express purpose of removing one of the venomous reptiles and probably placing it in Mrs. Bell's bedroom."

"Preposterous!" said Aubrey.

"Possibly, but if Mr. Shrubb could cause a ruction between mother and son because of the reptile collection, then he may have thought he could convince Mrs. Bell to sell up."

"Yes, Mother is proud of my work, but she doesn't like my collection," said Julius.

"But that lizard bit him. It's obviously vicious and," Aubrey pointed at Julius, "*he* is responsible!"

The professor looked shocked at the accusation. "I would never – " he started before Holmes cut him off.

"You have no need to apologise, Professor Bell, I have seen the lizard in question and it is a somewhat sedentary beast. Can you explain to us how and why the Gila Monster in question would act the way it did?"

Julius Bell's posture changed completely as his professional stature was called upon.

"The Gila Monster, especially the male that I possess, is rather slow and sluggish. They generally don't attack unless provoked."

"If someone were to pick one up, would that be enough to elicit an attack?"

"Possibly, especially if it was handled roughly. A Gila Monster will bite and latch on for dear life then thrash around until they subdue their prey," Julius said, "That was how I found Mr. Shrubb. My lizard had bitten him on the wrist and clamped its mouth shut with some force. I had to remove it with a stick."

"But it wouldn't attack unless picked up or moved?"

"Yes, that's right."

I felt I had to step in and clarify things. "So, what you're saying is that Mr. Shrubb stole a key from the Bell's household, and then came back when they were away and tried to pick up a venomous lizard to put it in Mrs. Bell's bedroom, but was himself bitten."

"Precisely. We already heard from the maid that the cases are rarely opened fully, so the lizard had to be extricated from its confinement, which probably aggravated it enough to attack," said Holmes.

"That doesn't excuse this man!" said Aubrey Shrubb, pointing at the professor. "He kept dangerous reptiles in his house, waiting to leap on unsuspecting victims and kill them."

"Yes," said Lestrade, "Regardless of whether Mr. Shrubb entered illegally, he was still killed by the professor's lizard, which is manslaughter under the eyes of the law."

"Ah, but did the lizard kill him? What say you, Professor?"

“As I explained to the police, it’s simply not possible for my Gila Monster to inject enough poison into a man of Mr. Shrubb’s size to kill him. Even if he had ingested the entire poison sack, he would simply have been rendered prostrate for a matter of hours and lethargic for a good week.”

“Quite so. That was also my estimation. If the neurotoxic poison of the lizard didn’t kill him, we should then look at the treatment,” Holmes turned and addressed me directly. “Watson, of the doctor’s use of strychnine in treating the lizard’s venom?”

Searching my memories, I stated, “Strychnine is itself a poison, but like many poisons when administered in small doses acts as a stimulant. I’ve never come across its use in this way, but I would assume it is used to stimulate the nervous system to counteract the retardation effect of the neurotoxin.”

“Exactly. And what of cocaine?”

“Again, another stimulant. The two together would engender an extremely vigorous reaction from the heart and respiratory system.” I clicked my fingers as the penny dropped. “By God, Holmes! I see where you are going.”

Lestrade looked as lost, as always. “What are you suggesting?”

I continued, “The dual actions of the strychnine and cocaine on a man of Mr. Shrubb’s size would have put such a strain on his heart that it would have seized, if not burst.”

“And as I found out in the morgue, Mr. Hyram Shrubb was a very habitual cocaine user, with many injection marks in his left forearm.”

Holmes pointed at the syringe.

“I’m sure that if we test the contents of that syringe, it will be a very highly concentrated dose of cocaine. I would presume that Mr. Shrubb was in intense pain from the lizard bite and mixed himself what he thought a heavy dose of pain relief, but to his poor luck, turned out to contain the seeds of his own demise.”

Aubrey Shrubb stepped forward and said, “Are you saying that my brother accidentally did it all to himself?”

“Yes. Through his actions, your brother paid the ultimate price.”

Holmes turned to Lestrade. "I would think that the death should be put down to misadventure. I'm sure that the Bells would be most happy to remain out of any further enquiries."

Lestrade nodded and gave Aubrey Shrubb a look of contempt which made the taller brother shrink back. "I'll do that, but I'll be making some notes about the practices of Shrubb Brothers for future reference."

He turned and stormed out.

Aubrey Shrubb looked apologetically at Professor Bell and tentatively held out his hand. The professor took it in his own and gave it a perfunctory shake.

"No hard feelings, I hope," said Shrubb, "I can only apologise for my brother's actions, but can assure you I knew nothing about them."

Julius eyed him with suspicion before begrudgingly nodding his acceptance and turning to leave.

"Professor," Holmes said.

Bell turned and saw Holmes holding the iron key.

"Yours, I believe," he said.

The professor walked over and took the key, saying, "Thank you, Mr. Holmes. I can't tell you how much that I'm in your debt. I'm sure my mother has made some recompense offer, but I would be prepared to increase whatever it was."

Holmes smiled, "No need for that. This has been a most interesting day and has broken the monotony with much verve. There is only one reward I would be most interested in seeking."

"Name it, sir, please."

"I would love to return to your reptile room and discuss all things herpetological with you, at your leisure."

The professor's face lit up with glee.

"Oh, any time, sir, any time! I would also be delighted for you to attend my lectures at the University College whenever you have the time. From what I've seen and heard today, I believe that there are things I can indeed learn from you."

"I'm sure we can both benefit," said Holmes, "I will check my calendar and take you up on your offer."

Still beaming, the professor pocketed the key, turned on his heel, gave one last desultory look at Shrubb, and exited.

Shrubb's face was aghast with all that had happened. He looked around his brother's room as if every artefact held a level of danger and betrayal in his mind. He finally stepped towards Holmes.

"I am in awe of your deductive skills, sir, and owe you an apology as well. I truly believed that young man meant ill to Hyram. I was possibly blinded by a brother's love, but now see what Hyram was up to. Sadly, his actions have left me with several terraced houses that serve no purpose in my business – business that I will need to re-examine in case there are other occurrences of this kind."

He turned, shoulders slumped and trudged out of the room. I watched his tall figure reduced by bereavement and betrayal and almost felt a touch of sympathy towards him. I told Holmes as much as we stood alone in the dead man's parlour.

"I wouldn't be too sad for him, Watson. His pride has been damaged more than anything else. I don't think the loss of his brother will affect him too much. It's more the damage to his reputation that worries him. With all that's happening in this city at the moment, I'm sure a person like Mr. Shrubb will recover and build an empire with a renewed vigour. I just hope he refrains from utilising the devious methods of his kin."

> *I leaned back and took down the great index volume to which he referred. Holmes balanced it on his knee, and his eyes moved slowly and lovingly over the record of old cases, mixed with the accumulated information of a lifetime. ". . . Venomous lizard or gila. Remarkable case, that!"*
>
> Dr. John H. Watson – "The Adventure of the Sussex Vampire"

The Adventure of the modern Guy Fawkes

Most of the adventures that involve my companion Sherlock Holmes are of a rather mundane nature, involving a cross-section of the folk who live the bulk of their simple lives within the great metropolis of London.

Sometimes, however, Holmes is called upon to decipher mysteries that involve the upper echelon of modern society, and on rare occasions, his investigations are tangled up with even the highest levels of Government. Such was the case when I opened the front door to the frantic tapping of a distraught young man dressed in a heavy woollen suit and bowler hat, the distinct attire of the civil service.

He handed me his card, which announced him to be "*Godfrey Jones, Under-secretary of the Committee of Imperial Defence*". I held my hand out to shake his hand and introduce myself but was greeted with his coat and hat. Though slightly taken aback, I took it in good humour, as his distress seemed to overwhelm him.

"Thank you, my good man, I'm here on orders from the secretariat to seek out the services of Mr. Sherlock Holmes. Is he at home?" he asked.

I pointed to the stairs and said, "If you follow me, I'll take you to him." I backed away and allowed him entry.

We found Holmes reclining in his favourite chair, smoking a pipe and reading the daily paper. "This would be the man you are after," I said to Jones as I placed his coat and hat on a nearby chair. I extended my hand again and finally introduced myself.

"I am Doctor John Watson, Mr. Holmes's associate," I said and indicated Holmes, "This is Mr. Sherlock Holmes."

His face dropped a little and his cheeks flushed red with embarrassment. He held out his hand and took mine. "Oh, I am sorry, sir, I didn't realise."

I smiled and let go of his hand. "Never mind," I said and indicated a free chair. I handed Holmes the card and turned to leave to ask Mrs. Hudson for tea, but was greeted at the door by our landlady with a laden tray containing tea, three cups, and biscuits.

I smiled and remarked quietly, "You are a wonder, Mrs. Hudson."

She placed the tray on the side table and turned back towards me, a slight smile on her lips. "Yes, I am," she agreed as she moved past me.

While the tea steeped, I took a seat a little way from Jones and watched the proceedings.

Holmes carefully folded his paper and placed it to the side. I noticed that he had left a specific article on the top to continue reading later. I took note of the strange headline, "*Robbery at Woolwich Artillery Base*". He read the business card and then looked up and studied Jones for a moment, I presumed that he was gathering data and forming an opinion about the man. I smiled to myself as I also observed Jones's agitation at Holmes's silence.

Finally, Holmes looked up into the young man's eyes and spoke. "Well, Mr. Godfrey Jones of Her Majesty's Civil Service, it is a pleasure to make your acquaintance." He rose and shook the young man's hand. "If I'm not wrong, you are a clerk, having been in the service for some six years after leaving Rugby Public School at the requisite age of seventeen. You once played rugby as well, but since moving to London have relinquished your sport. You are also married with a small child."

Jones's mouth dropped open. "How? How?"

A smile developed on my face, I'd seen this time and time again but was a little perplexed at how Holmes had gleaned such details in such a short time. "Yes," I said. "How did you work all that out?"

"Quite simply, Watson." He indicated our guest. "Mr. Jones here is about twenty-two or twenty-three years of age. He sports a dark blue tie, with light blue-and-green diagonal stripes – the traditional colours of Rugby college. Plus I cheated. You are wearing your school's pin on your lapel."

Jones looked down at his lapel. Holmes smiled at the last remark, and I winced internally for missing that obvious detail.

“Mr. Jones here is also wearing a suit that is of a slightly out-of-date style, possibly purchased on his promotion from clerk two or three years ago. It is now heading towards retirement itself. He is quite well built, which suggests a history of sporting endeavours, but is sporting a slightly pronounced belly which indicates those days are over. He has a simple gold band on his left ring finger, and there is a small crusted stain on the right shoulder of his coat, which indicates spittle from an infant nestled there. Am I correct?”

Jones was still staggered in amazement.

“Yes. Yes, sir, you are correct on every detail. No wonder they wanted me to come and fetch you.”

He sat down heavily, his brain whirring at a frantic rate, trying to take all of Holmes’s abilities on board. I passed around cups of tea to break the tension.

Holmes sat back and sipped, his steely gaze still locked onto young Jones. “Who told you to come fetch me?” he asked.

Jones sipped his tea to steady his nerves and answered, “The Secretary, through his assistant, asked me to bring you immediately.” He looked at the cup of tea in shock and placed it down a little unsteadily.

“He said immediately. I . . . I . . . must bring you back,” he said standing up and taking us both a little by surprise.

Holmes smiled, “I’m sure it’s not so urgent that we can’t finish our tea.”

Jones looked at the both of us and realised we weren’t going to move. After a moment, he sat down again and picked up his cup.

“I – I have a hansom waiting outside,” he said.

“Good, good. That will save time, and you can tell us all about why you are here,” said Holmes.

Jones looked surprised again. “I’m sorry to say that I have been sworn to secrecy and was told to simply fetch you and bring you to the Houses of Parliament. Once there, all will become clear,” he said.

Holmes’s face showed a wide grin.

“Oh, really, how very intriguing. Someone was relying on your innocence to stir my curiosity. Very good,” he said as he drained his cup and placed it on the side table. He stood. “Well Watson, shall we prepare ourselves and go with young Mr. Jones *here to see if there is* some game to be had in this little adventure?" He smiled to himself and added, "I feel that my brother is mixed up in this somewhere."

***

The hansom pulled up on Great George Street, about fifty yards from Westminster Bridge and across the road from the clock tower. Luckily for us, Big Ben was silent, as it was a good twenty minutes to the hour. The sound of that great bell is fixed in the minds of Londoners, but at that close distance, it tends to have a dire effect on one's hearing.

We followed Godfrey across the street towards the magnificent site that is the Houses of Parliament. I looked up and down Great George Street and was surprised by the number of uniformed constables milling about. Usually one would see the odd bobby walking near the houses, but on that day, I spied a good half-dozen.

I thought to myself, "Something must be afoot."

Jones led us around the lush grass of the Speaker's Green, below a small arch in the side of the building, and up to a wooden door set back from the pathway.

He rapped twice on the door and announced himself. A heavy lock was turned and a bolt drawn before the door swung back into the building. A large cloud of smoke blew out of the open doorway, causing all three of us to cough. It slowly dissipated, revealing a heavy-set man with a ruddy complexion who eyed all three of us suspiciously whilst chomping on his cigar.

"Ah, Mr. Parsons," said Jones, evidently aware of the man's identity, "This is Mr. Sherlock Holmes and his associate, Dr. John Watson. The Secretary asked me to fetch them to investigate the, ah, the little problem."

The ruddy-faced man looked Holmes and me up and down then drew on his cigar again before *harrumph*-ing and stepping back from the doorway to allow us passage. He peered out through the entrance once more before slamming the door behind us and bolting it shut.

"This is highly unusual, but I've orders from upstairs, so follow me, please," he said, letting the last word hang in the air before walking off along the long dark corridor leading away from the door.

I could detect a small grin on Holmes's face as he turned and followed Parsons, looking around from time to time to discern any details that might prove useful.

Jones walked next to me and spoke. "Please excuse Christopher. He was formerly in the Army and takes a lot of pride in maintaining the security here," he said.

"I was in the Army myself," I replied, "and I can quite understand. I can also see that he wouldn't like the idea of civilians simply waltzing in."

"Quite so," said Jones.

The corridor was a long, painted brick affair with no decorations of any kind. Every twenty yards or so, a small gaslight provided the only illumination. The barren nature told me that it was a service tunnel, used mostly by the cleaning staff or tradesmen who needed to access the underbelly of the Parliament buildings. Every so often we crossed another corridor and passed by dull, grey doors that were firmly shut. The only sounds were our footsteps on the ancient tiled floor.

Parsons stopped and opened one of the doors, revealing a set of stone stairs leading further down into the bowels under the building. A single gaslight shone on the ancient stone steps and allowed us to safely descend. The exit door led to another dimly lit passageway that headed off at a right angle to the one above.

We traversed this next narrow passage for about fifty yards before Parsons stopped, bent down, and picked up a small paraffin lamp. He lit it from his cigar and indicated an open archway leading into another passage perpendicular to the one in which we stood.

"I don't generally let civilians into this area," Parsons said. "Not within protocol, but . . . ."

Holmes finished his sentence for him, "You have your orders," and stepped through the arch.

We all followed and found a wide room with a doorway at the far end, along with a multitude of pipes running across the ceiling.

Parsons stepped up to a nearby gaslight and brought more illumination into the room by lighting it with his cigar. I noticed the pipes were a mix of dull brass and ceramic. I assumed they carried both water and sewage, and hoped they were watertight, as the thought of any leaks down here filled me with dread.

It was then I looked down and saw several small barrels, sitting in a neat pile, nestled against one wall.

Holmes spoke up, “I take it that this is either a storeroom or the source of your little problem."

“These appeared last night. One of the guards was doing a routine check, before I started, and found them. He reported to the duty clerk, then suddenly some shiny-bottom starts yelling ‘Guy Fawkes!’ and all hell breaks loose,” said Parsons.

Holmes stepped up to the barrels and brought his lamp closer. Suddenly, he stepped back again and handed the lamp to me. “Keep this at a distance, will you Watson? I need to examine these barrels, but don’t want the flame to get too close,” he said. He turned to Parsons and said, “Do your protocols mention anything about smoking near explosives?”

Parsons looked sheepish and stepped back a couple of yards.

I approached Holmes and held the lamp at a suitable distance. Even from there, I could see traces of a black substance on the lid of one of the barrels. My rudimentary knowledge of explosives came to the fore.

“Is that - ?” I asked.

“I think so,” Holmes answered.

He looked toward a brightly lit room through the door at the far end. He picked up a barrel and marched off towards the doorway. I started after him, but he held up a hand to stop me.

“No need for us both to be in danger, Watson,” he said.

I stood, mouth agape, as he strode away.

“In danger?” I said to myself.

I watched from afar as Holmes placed the barrel on the ground just inside the room and pulled off the lid. He stared at the contents for a moment before dipping a hand into the barrel and bringing it out, full of black powder. He let it spill through his fingers and then rubbed two together with the remnants of the powder on their tips. I could see a smile play on his face and realised something was up. I hoped to be privy to it soon.

Holmes dipped his hand again, replaced the lid on the barrel and poured a small pile of the powder onto the lid. He picked up the barrel and turned back towards us.

Something just inside the other room grabbed his attention. He examined it for a moment before returning to us.

"Good news?" I asked.

"Interesting news, I think," he replied.

He placed the barrel on the floor, away from the others. I spied the small pile of black powder on top.

"Gunpowder, I presume," I said.

Holmes smiled and said, "That's what our perpetrator would lead us to believe."

He turned, plucked Parsons's cigar from his mouth, and rammed it into the little pile of powder.

We all reared back in terror.

The cigar simply sizzled slightly and let out a small stream of smoke. The powder remained inert.

"What in blazes?" said Parsons.

"It's sand. Fine, black sand, and ground-up charcoal with a small amount of black powder," Holmes said.

"Good Lord," said Jones.

"Why?" I asked.

"I'm not sure at this point," said Holmes. "But something of this nature would be to sew discontent and terror, or to distract attention from another act." He turned towards Parsons, who was fishing out another cigar. "As you have said, the public isn't allowed into this area, so who would have access?" he asked.

"Guards," he said. "Cleaners. Maintenance crew. Why?"

Holmes pointed to the next room and said, "There is a cleaners' trolley sitting in the adjoining room. There are traces of the same black powder, so I am assuming it was used to transport these barrels. You would also have noticed that there is no fuse leading away from the barrels."

All three of us looked at the base of the pile. I felt ashamed that I had missed such an obvious clew.

"The only way to ignite this lot would be to set fire to a barrel itself, which would leave no time for the perpetrator to escape," said Holmes. He looked to the ceiling and posed another question. "And the room above?"

"That would be the House of Commons," said Jones, who had been silent for quite some time. "It's the main reason this was elevated beyond internal security and kept on the quiet."

"So the whole Guy Fawkes analogy is quite within reason," I said.

Holmes grinned then stepped towards the wall at the end of the room. He looked to the ceiling and through the doorway, then paced out the distance between the wall and the barrels.

"Twenty paces," he said pointing at the wall behind the barrels, "And this wall would be in the centre of the room to provide support for the chamber floor above."

He pointed to the ceiling and continued, "I propose that whoever sits on the Government benches above this point is the subject of this plot."

***

We re-assembled in the chamber of the House of Commons, several feet above the barrels of weakened black powder we had examined minutes previously.

The House was luckily empty as Parliament wasn't sitting that week. Holmes stated that this fact indicated that the barrels were merely a distraction from the true nature of this conundrum.

Parsons stood near the entrance with his arms folded and a scowl on his face. "I don't know why you need to be in 'ere," he said. "It's very out of the ordinary for Johnny public to be allowed access to the chamber. But – "

I finished his sentence, more in desperation at the man's insistence on protocol than anything. "You have your orders."

He nodded, grim-faced. At least he had disposed of his foul-smelling cigar. I assumed even he wouldn't deign to smoke in the chamber – much to my relief.

Holmes was indifferent to Parsons's complaints. He was busy taking in the grandeur that is the chamber of the House of Commons.

He paced the floor of the room between the two rows of benches, stepping up to the beautiful wood-panelled walls at either end and examining them in detail. He knocked a couple of times, eliciting a shocked response from Parsons. "'Ere, what you doing?"

Holmes looked over at him and replied, "Ensuring that I'm correct in my assumption that the solid stone wall below us is in fact the same wall that this wood panelling hides from view."

Content in his deduction, he proceeded to pace out his measurements from below. He repeated the process a couple of times then turned to face the Government benches.

"Whoever sits in this area would have been the most affected by the blast from below," he said pointing at the green leather-upholstered bench, "*if* it were true gunpowder."

Godfrey Jones strode over and checked the location. He pointed to Holmes's right. "The Prime Minister sits there. To his left is the Chancellor," he said, pointing out each imprint in the leather as he turned. "Then the Foreign Secretary, the Home Secretary, and the Secretary for Defence,"

"Any of those last three," said Holmes, "could have been sitting directly above the bomb."

"But you said it wouldn't work," commented Parsons, "so it doesn't matter who it was,"

"As I said," added Holmes, "I think it is a distraction, aimed at sending a message, rather than inflicting any wholesale damage."

"Speaking of messages," interrupted Jones, "I think that brings us to the next piece of information that you should see."

Holmes and I both turned to look at him with slight surprise on our faces.

***

Jones brought us to the outer office of Sir Nigel Attleby, the Home Secretary. We entered and found a rather attractive woman sitting behind a desk looking extremely frazzled. She looked up as we entered, and her face dropped even further. "What is it now?" she asked.

Jones answered her with a calming voice, "I'm so sorry to disturb you, Miss Plumb, but these are the men that are helping us with the little problem downstairs. Sir Nigel also requested that they be brought to him when appropriate."

Her demeanour changed as she realised why we were there. "Ah, yes, I understand," she said, rising from her seat and stepping up to the padded leather door. "I'll see if he's free then," She knocked and waited until a muffled reply came from within. Opening the door, she entered and shut it before we could see inside.

Jones turned to us. "Please forgive Miss Plumb's mood. In addition to the barrels downstairs, we have a visit from King Alfonso of Spain next month, plus the Queen will be spending the summer at Balmoral. The Prime Minister has asked for an increase in security on both fronts due to this incident. Sir Nigel has been tasked with coordinating it all, which means it falls to Miss Plumb, his secretary."

I raised an eyebrow. It was quite unusual for a woman to hold such a position. Miss Plumb's reappearance broke me from my thoughts. She opened the door and stepped into her office, allowing us to file into the Secretary's room.

Holmes was at the end of the queue and stopped briefly next to the young lady. "Does your husband work in the Home Office as well?"

The woman's face dropped in shock. I turned in time to see it and assumed that my good friend had once again performed one of his miraculous observations.

"But, how – how could you know?" she stammered. "I've never seen you before in my life, sir."

Holmes simply smiled and nodded towards her hand. "You disguise it well, but your wedding bands have left a light mark on your ring finger. Perhaps you should leave them off for an extended time to allow the skin to darken in line with the rest of your hand," he said.

"I couldn't do that," she answered. "My husband would become enraged if he caught me without them. I only leave them off here to keep the peace amongst the other girls."

"I understand," he answered and tapped the side of his nose. "Your secret is safe with me."

"Thank you, sir. Sir Nigel signed a waiver for me when I married. David wanted me to resign, but then he left the Army and the money dried up, so I asked Sir Nigel if I could stay until David found employment. Really, I didn't think I'd be here this long. Poor David. He hasn't been himself since . . . ." Tears quickly formed in her eyes. She excused herself and fled from her office.

I walked over to a surprised Holmes and asked, "Something you said?"

"I think, perhaps, Watson, that there may be some deeper emotional strife within young Miss Plumb's marital circumstances," he said.

***

Inside Sir Nigel's office, the Home Secretary was a far different man than I had imagined. One tends to form an image of members of the upper levels of the civil service as stocky men tending to fat from their desk-bound lifestyle and with the ruddy complexion of those who indulge in the demon drink a little too much.

The man who stood up and moved out from behind his desk was nothing like my cerebral musings. Sir Nigel Attleby was an athletic man in his early fifties. He was tall – even taller than Holmes – with chiselled features that would have had many a young lady swooning from his attentive gaze. He raised his hand and thrust it towards Holmes. "Mr. Holmes, I presume. A pleasure to meet you. Your brother has spoken well of you on many occasions," he said. "He and members of his department have worked closely with my own people at numerous times over the years." He turned in my direction. "And you would be Doctor John Watson, yes?" he asked.

I took his hand and shook, letting go before replying, "Yes. That I am, Sir Nigel."

"I've heard that you're the chronicler of Mr. Holmes's cases," he said, smiling again. "I don't think you'll find much to write about from this little nuisance."

"Interestingly enough," I said, "it is usually the seemingly mundane adventures that prove to be the most fascinating."

"Well, let's hope this remains as mundane as it seems." He leaned back against his desk and held out a hand to the three chairs before him and then looked up Parsons. "You'll be fine standing, won't you?"

Parsons scowled at the suggestion but nodded his head. Holmes, Godfrey Jones, and I took the proffered seats.

Sir Nigel studied each of us in turn. "Now, I know that Parsons has shown you the little display downstairs."

We nodded, and I noted, "You seem to be very calm, given that there's a large pile of gunpowder-filled barrels sitting below the House of Commons as we speak."

His expression remained calm. "Yes, but no one will be in there for another two weeks. So whoever put it there either didn't realise or didn't care. There was no way the barrels would go unnoticed for that period of time, and if ignited, they wouldn't have hurt anyone and would have just been a nuisance. They're safe enough now until we determine what's going on. So, yes, I am calm."

I peered at Holmes, who was studying Sir Nigel. "And you are correct," said Holmes, "The bomb, as it has been called, is merely a diversion. The powder in the barrels is not explosive, and there was no method to detonate it anyway. I'm still trying to discern what the person's motivation was in planting the barrels."

"I may have a clew as to the motivation," Sir Nigel said. He reached behind him and picked up a small handwritten parchment from a pile of paperwork. He turned and handed it to Holmes, who quickly read it. I noticed his eyebrows raise and a wry smile cross his lips. He then handed the page to me. It read:

We, the members of the Sudanese Mahdist Revolutionary Army, demand the immediate full-scale withdrawal of all Anglo forces from our country. If our demands are not met, we will unleash terror and hell upon the Parliament of Great Britain the likes of which have never been seen."

It was signed "*Mahdi Muhammad Ahmed Bin Abd Allah*".

I turned towards Jones and offered the page to him. He waved it away which told me that he'd already seen it. I gave it back to Sir Nigel. "Is this real?" I asked.

Sir Nigel peered at the page whilst answering, “Her Majesty’s troops are currently engaged with Egyptian, Italian, and Ethiopian forces in the Sudan, fighting against this Mahdi Muhammad Ahmed’s army of militiamen.”

“Would they have the resources to undertake an operation of this kind on British soil?” asked Holmes.

Sir Nigel thought for a moment then stared into Holmes’s eyes, his expression had turned serious. “No, no, I don’t think they would, but that’s not to say that some other nation, or group of people, has provided them with the resources. I’m still not overly worried as I prefer to think that this – ” He waved the page about. “ – is another diversion, as you call it. But I don’t know what the true objective is.”

At that moment, Sir Nigel’s now-composed secretary popped her head in through the connecting door and spoke. “Sorry to disturb you, sir, but the Prime Minister would like an update on the incident downstairs.”

“Very good. I’ll be with him shortly.”

The woman withdrew and shut the door quietly. I noticed Sir Nigel’s gaze lingered on the doorframe for a few moments before he turned back to us. I put it down to the stress of the situation, but I found out later that Holmes had other ideas which proved to be correct.

“I would think,” Holmes said, “that you can assure the Prime Minister that the barrels are relatively inert and may be removed without incident. As to what is behind all of this, I will return to my rooms and cogitate upon it further. I believe that it will be a one or two pipe problem.”

Sir Nigel looked a little perplexed by the last comment. “He simply means,” I explained, “that he will need to sit back and smoke one or two pipes and think.”

Sir Nigel’s eyebrows raised. “Oh, an interesting way of approaching a problem.”

“Quite so,” I said.

“Well, gentlemen,” he said as he ushered us out of his office and into the outer office, “I do hope to hear your solution quickly, but as you are aware, my presence has been requested, so I shall have to leave you."

He turned to his secretary. "Please give Mr. Holmes my home address, in case they have any information and need to contact me after hours. I'll be with the Prime Minister for a good while, but we will need to discuss the Balmoral arrangements when I return." The woman nodded and took down a small note to that effect. Sir Nigel then bid us *adieu* and left quickly.

I noticed the woman watch him leave, her gaze staying on the doorway in much the same as Sir Nigel's had earlier. I also observed that Holmes had seen the same thing.

We said thank you and goodbye and left her office. Parsons escorted us to a side door that led out onto Great George Street. As he started to leave, Holmes stopped him. "Mr. Parsons, if I might offer a suggestion." Parsons stopped and looked back a poorly hidden look of contempt on his face. "It might be worth your while to undertake an investigation of the residential premises of the Home and Foreign Secretaries, and anyone else that may have been in the supposed blast radius of the gunpowder bomb," he said.

Parson's expression relaxed slightly. "You think these idiots would try to get them at home?" he asked.

"If they have received local help, enough to get them into the Houses of Parliament, then they might be able to set up a similar bomb, or worse, a *real* bomb, at the home of one of our politicians,"

Parson's eyes grew wide. Holmes's suggestion had hit at the heart of his world. He disappeared quickly, leaving us alone with Godfrey Jones.

"Thank you, Mr. Holmes," he said. "I must admit that I am astounded at your ability to look at the simplest situation and determine so much detail. I can only hope to learn the art of deduction and follow in your footsteps. It would be much more interesting than a life in the civil service."

I smiled a little at this confession, and a wry grin crossed Holmes's face. He answered, "If I were you, I would agitate to be moved to my brother Mycroft's department. Although he doesn't undertake the level of deductive reasoning that I do, he is much more adept at the art than I, and would be a worthy case study for someone in a position such as yourself."

Holmes held out his hand and shook Jones's before continuing, "If I might ask one favour of you: Could you have one of the barrels of black powder delivered to my abode this afternoon. I'd like to examine the barrel further. I believe it will assist in my deductions."

"Of course," Jones said, beaming widely, "Anything to help." He turned, shook my hand, and quickly disappeared back inside.

"A young lad full of admirable qualities, I think," I said.

"Yes, Watson, indeed," Holmes agreed. "I do hope he finds his mark before that place strips him of all ambition."

***

True to his word, young Godfrey Jones arranged for one of the barrels to be delivered to Baker Street later that same day. Holmes was elated and carried it to his chemical corner and then set about his work. I relied on the initial fact that the black powder had been heavily mixed with sand to allay any fears that Holmes's investigations would lead to an explosive result. With that in mind, I decided to leave him to his experimentation and occupy myself elsewhere. He wasn't home when I returned later that evening.

It was late the next morning, whilst I was enjoying some morning tea, that Holmes emerged from his bedroom, looking refreshed and exhilarated.

"Good news?" I asked.

He stretched his arms, smiled and said, "Why, yes, thoroughly good news." He sat down and helped himself to coffee and biscuits.

"Well?" I asked with a touch of impatience.

He smiled, took a sip of coffee and began to explain. "I have found out many interesting facts," he began. "The black powder, as I surmised is a mix of gun powder, sand, and ground charcoal. It will burn, but it isn't explosive in any way. Its purpose was to give the illusion of being an explosive, rather than having any destructive power." He took another sip of coffee, then continued. "The powder itself is interesting. It's the type that was used by the British military up until a couple of years ago, when they changed all formulations to cordite, which isn't as explosive but diffuses much more gas-per-weight, thereby creating a greater propellant effect. The original gunpowder burnt too hot and caused damage to the barrels and firing chambers of many of our guns."

He placed his cup down, rose, and walked over to our sitting chairs. He rooted around the discarded newspapers for a moment and brought out the object of his attention. "A-ha, here it is," he said, brandishing the article that I had spied on the day young Godfrey Jones had come to our door. Holmes read aloud: "'*Two weeks ago, there was a break-in at the Royal Artillery Barracks in Woolwich. The stores were raided, but all that was stolen were twenty barrels of gunpowder destined for destruction. The Army has advised the local constabulary in case any local criminal gangs were involved.*'"

He looked up at me and smiled.

"Sounds as if we may have found the source of the black powder," he said, placing the paper down and re-joining me at the dining table, "although the quantity stolen doesn't equate with the amounts that would be in the barrels found under Parliament. I would estimate that only about two barrels-worth of powder was mixed across those we discovered." "Now, the next question I needed to answer was about the barrels themselves."

"They aren't the same barrels?" I asked.

"No, surprisingly not. The stolen powder kegs themselves would have been much smaller, around nine inches tall and seven inches across, plus the strapping bands would have been made of reed or rope to avoid sparks."

I turned and spied the barrel sitting on Holmes's workbench. It was a hefty size, around two feet tall and one foot across, with distinctly metal banding.

"Yes, exactly, Watson. Those barrels are not the originals. In fact, they were built by a cooper down at the Port of London. I wired him last night and confirmed an order by an unknown buyer two weeks ago. Sadly, he only dealt with the delivery driver, whom he described as a balding man of about forty. He said that he'd never seen the man before, and believed that he would never see him again. I suppose that's the problem with cash payments. A businessman is only concerned with the money, not the details of the transaction."

“Where does that leave us?” I asked.

He took a final sip of coffee, placed his cup down, and looked at me over steepled fingers .“Well, we still have eighteen unused barrels of black powder. We are led to believe that a Sudanese organisation is behind all of this, but the powder was stolen on British soil and the perpetrators procured items from a London-based business and used a local to undertake the exchange. I dropped in on Lestrade to see if there had been any known activity amongst the local Sudanese population, but according to Scotland Yard, the only known Sudanese in London are a single-family that lives in Canning Town. They’ve been monitored since before the war in the Sudan started and, according to Lestrade, are simple dockworkers who escaped from Northern Africa in the early 1880s."

“It’s all a front then?” I said.

“Yes,” said Holmes, “And – ”

We were suddenly disturbed by an insistent thumping on the front door downstairs. Soon, we heard Mrs. Hudson unlatching the door before letting out a surprised cry. Loud footfalls proceeded up the stairwell, causing us both to stand in readiness.

The door to our apartments was flung open and there stood a very flustered Godfrey Jones. He took one look at the both of us and, through a series of strained inhalations, gasped, “Please come quickly. There’s been a horrible accident.”

***

Jones remained tight-lipped throughout our trip in the hansom. I could see he was fidgety and extremely anxious. I tried on numerous occasions to talk to him, but he fobbed me off with mumblings about secrecy.

It was as we pulled out of Pall Mall and into Carlton Gardens that I realised we were heading towards the secretarial residences. The Crown owned several properties in the area which were made available to members of the Cabinet whilst they were in London. The Home Secretary’s address was amongst them.

My concerns grew grave as we passed through a small police cordon that blocked off the end of the street. Inspector Lestrade stood by a young constable and peered into the hansom. “Mr. Holmes?

What the devil is going on? I have orders to let you and only you through," he said.

"All will become clear, Inspector," Holmes answered. "I will inform you as soon as I have finished my investigations."

"Blast!" Lestrade said as the hansom pulled away.

I was still wondering which Secretary was involved when we pulled up outside of Number Three. As I looked out of the cab I became shocked. Holmes even made a small murmur when he viewed the devastation. We quickly exited the hansom to survey the scene.

Carlton Gardens are generally a wonderfully kept set of Georgian Terraced apartments. Each is four stories high, and my understanding is that they contain several bedrooms for residents and staff, with a full-sized catering kitchen, a large dining room for state affairs, and everything that Cabinet ministers might require. They back onto St. James Gardens so that even families with young children had ample room for play and exercise.

On this day, however, the outside of Number Three was a sight of utter desolation. The entrance-way appeared to have been blown apart from below. The front door was missing and the short staircase leading up to the door was simply a smouldering hole with broken masonry and brickwork strewn in a wide arc around the front of the building.

"Good Lord," I said.

"Indeed," said Holmes. "I think we have found the rest of our missing gunpowder – or what remains of it anyway,"

Once the hansom had driven off, Godfrey Jones joined us and simply stared at the hole in the ground at the front of the residence.

"They told me what happened," he said, "but I didn't think it would be this bad."

I turned to him and asked, "Can you tell us which Cabinet minister's residence this is?"

"Yes, it's Sir Nigel's house. The explosion occurred only an hour ago. I was at work at Parliament when I was commanded to fetch you and bring you here," he said.

"The Secretary? Is he . . . ?" I hesitated to finish the question.

Jones shook his head. "No, he's fine," he said.

“I’m afraid that can’t be said for some other poor unfortunate,” said Holmes from a few feet away.

I looked around. He was looking at some dark stains on the cobbles. I knew straight away what those stains meant.

“Oh, my,” I said and turned back to Jones. “Who was it?”

His face bore a look of shock. He stared for a moment then dropped his head. “It was Parsons.”

“Parsons? Why in blazes was he here?” Then I realised. He came on our insistence to check up on the members of the cabinet.

Holmes had wandered over to the very front of the house and was peering down into the void left by the explosion. I joined him to gain a better view. The house had a lower basement level, where I presumed the help lived. A small courtyard was visible below the street, probably available to the staff for their use. Previously it would have been a cosy place to sit and possibly smoke or take tea. Now all the furniture was destroyed, and the plants burnt to cinders.

Holmes stood at the edge of the courtyard wall and was peering with great intent at the blackened vegetation below. “Hmm,” he said, “I need to gain access to the courtyard.” He turned to Jones. “Is there a way that we can enter the house?”

A voice answered from within the house itself. "Yes, Mr. Holmes. Yes, there is," it said.

We turned to find Sir Nigel standing in the ruins of his entranceway wearing a smoking jacket over a pair of silk pyjamas. A stern look crossed his face. “I will give you all the help you need to find this culprit,” he said.

***

Sir Nigel met us at the rear door of the property. His sombre mood persisted, and he quietly led us through to the front of the house where a small staircase led down to the servants’ quarters. He remained behind with Godfrey Jones as Holmes and I made our way down the stairs and out into the small courtyard.

It looked more of a mess up close than before. Holmes immediately set about viewing the entire scene and taking in as many minute details as he could. I watched as he surveyed the wreckage, dropped to his knee from time to time, and pulled out his glass to examine the clews, such as they were.

I scanned the area myself. The two longer walls consisted of the front of the house, with two windows that looked into the servants' sitting room and the solid retaining wall that lined the street side. At one end, a small under-croft appeared to lie beneath the front staircase. It must have been in there that the barrels of powder had been placed. The explosion brought down the staircase and virtually buried the evidence from view. At the other end, two trees had been planted amidst a once-lovely garden bed. A line of planter boxes bordered the bed which had a small sitting area in the centre, the furniture now blasted into pieces. The far wall had a gate that led into the neighbouring courtyard. The gate had been blown off its hinges and could be seen lying beyond.

As I walked over to the garden bed to lessen my view of the devastation, I noticed something completely out of place. More dark stains were spread out across the grass that had been protected from the brunt of the blast by the planter boxes. The bloodstains radiated away from the blast and towards the small gate.

"Holmes, I think I've found something," I said over my shoulder. As I turned, I found him standing right behind me, holding a small item of interest in his hand. It was the stub end of a cigar. Burnt – but still relatively whole.

"Parson?" I asked.

He nodded then said, "What have you found then, Watson?"

I pointed to the bloodstains and suggested we follow them into the next yard. He agreed, and I led the way.

I was astonished at what we found, but I believe Holmes had already deduced this eventuality. Lying just inside the courtyard and hidden from view was a body. He was covered in blood and had received horrendous burns from the explosion. I checked his pulse and found that he was well and truly dead. I managed to turn him over and we discovered that he was a balding man about forty years of age. The evidence suggested that he was the delivery man that had bought the barrels from the cooper.

"Our culprit?" I asked.

“I would think so,” said Holmes, “The evidence is adding up.” He returned to the adjoining courtyard and studied the scene once more.

I joined him and asked, “Do you know what happened yet?”

“I can surmise from the existence of the dead man and this cigar, that our poor Mr. Parsons, by pure accident, thwarted the plan to kill Sir Nigel, and inadvertently took his place.” He pointed to the staircase. “I presume that Mr. Parsons came to the house early this morning, smoking a cigar as was his habit. He stopped on the entrance stairs to finish it off and casually tossed the remnants into the courtyard rather than the street.”

He stepped over to where he found the cigar and pointed out the undercroft and then the line of planter boxes. "Mr. Parsons just happened along at the same moment that our assailant had managed to set up his explosives and was waiting for an opportune time to ignite them. He may have known that Sir Nigel likes to retrieve the daily papers himself of a morning.”

I interjected at that point, “How do you know that?” Then I promptly answered my own question in my head just as Holmes confirmed it.

“I had Sir Nigel watched,” he said. “Now, Parsons tossed his cigar into the courtyard and was most unfortunate to have it land on the line of gunpowder that our assailant had laid down to act as a fuse.”

He pointed to a smudged line of dark black powder which I had taken to be ash or charred detritus from the blast. “The fuse lit and quickly raced towards the black powder. The result is evident.” He pointed to the planter boxes. “Our bomber was hiding behind those planters, which are good and heavy and would have provided adequate protection. When he heard the fuse ignite, however, he stood in surprise, thereby becoming the second victim in this little fiasco.”

“The fool,” I said.

“Quite so,” agreed Holmes.

“Who was he then?” I asked.

“For that, I think it is time to head inside. There is a little more to this story, yet.”

***

We found Godfrey and Sir Nigel seated around a small table in the parlour. Coffee had been served for all four of us, and the two of them had poured for themselves while they awaited our return. Sir Nigel was the first to see us and placed his cup down in preparation for our arrival.

"Gentlemen, I ordered some refreshments – although I'll admit, at the moment, I don't quite have the stomach for food. Devilish time," he said.

"Thank you, Sir Nigel," said Holmes in a rather stern voice, "but I think it best if we move forward as quickly as possible,"

I was taken aback by Holmes's mood. He seemed annoyed at the events that had occurred, and I was a little afraid that he would overstep the mark and damage the relationship we'd built with the Home Secretary.

I assumed he was about to rebuke Sir Nigel for something, but he spoke to Godfrey Jones instead.

"We have found the body of a poor unfortunate in the neighbouring courtyard. The police must have missed it on their first investigation. Sloppy if you ask me, but it does me no good to dwell on it. Would you be so kind as to go out and inform the constables outside, so they can deal with it? Tell them I have investigated and will update Inspector Lestrade in due time," he said.

Jones put down his own cup and rose. "Of course, Mr. Holmes. Do you think it was the man we are after or just an innocent victim?"

"I'm still trying to determine that, but with Sir Nigel's help, I believe I will have a solution before you return," he said.

"Very good," Jones said and rushed off.

Once he was gone and out of earshot, Holmes turned to Sir Nigel. "That was mostly for your benefit," he said. "I think it would be prudent to bring Mrs. Button out so that we can put this despicable affair to bed, so to speak."

Sir Nigel's face dropped in shock for a moment but relaxed into a slight grin. "How the devil did you know?"

"Well, to be honest," he replied, "there was no deduction necessary. I had an inkling as to what has been going on and asked a few discrete questions. My informant apprised me of the affair. Don't worry," he added, "Your secret is safe with me for as long as you require it to be. That was the main reason I sent young Jones away."

Sir Nigel rose and said, "Very good. I thank you for your discretion."

After Sir Nigel left, I turned to Holmes as I just had to ask: "Who is Mrs. Button?"

"Ah, yes. I used some of that time away from Baker Street last night to initiate further investigations. Plus, I called on the services of my irregulars to conduct low-level surveillance, not only of Sir Nigel but his personal assistant, one Mrs. Angela Button," he said. "You know her as Miss Plumb."

"Why would you need to have his secretary observed? What does she have to do with all of this?" I asked.

Holmes smiled. "Oh, I think we'll find that she has everything to do with this," he said in that slightly irritating but knowledgeable way of his.

It was at that point that Sir Nigel returned and stood aside to let the young lady in question into the room. We both nodded in deference to her.

"Mr. Holmes, you wished to see me," she said retaining as much dignity as she could muster, given her presence in Sir Nigel's home.

"Mrs. Button," Holmes began.

She cut him off by saying, "Angela, if you please," a hint of aversion at the use of her married name crossing her face.

"Firstly," Holmes continued, "let me apologise to both yourself and Sir Nigel, but I employed the use of my associates to have you followed last night."

Both began to protest, but Holmes held up his hands. "I also had my people follow the Chancellor, the Defence Secretary, and both of their assistants as well. The main object was to detect if there were any agents of foreign interest doing the same."

Mrs. Button found some inner courage and spoke up, "I know what you see before you must seem like some sordid little affair, but you would be wrong. Sir Nigel and I have a simple platonic friendship, that's all. I've been his assistant for over ten years, well before I was married, and well before he held the position of Home Secretary. I came to him late last night after David, my husband, and I had a row. He was drunk again and accused me of all manner of ills. Frankly, I'd had enough, and stormed out. At that time of night, I had nowhere to turn but here."

Holmes paused for a moment to gather his thoughts before continuing, "Now, Mrs. – ah – Angela, could you describe your husband to us."

A slight look of surprise flitted across her face before she spoke. "A typical Englishman if you like. Just turned forty years old. Keeps his hair very short, in fact, shaves it bald on occasions. Tall. Has started to become a little stocky due to the drink. Why?" she asked.

As the description continued, my face dropped in realisation. I looked across at Holmes who remained stoic. "I was a little afraid of that," he said.

"What do you mean, sir?" asked Sir Nigel, "What does Angela's husband have to do with any of this?"

"Sadly, everything," said Holmes. He indicated the settee and continued, "Madam I think it would be best if you were to take a seat. My explanation may be a little long and, for you, a little disturbing."

Mrs. Button sat down with Sir Nigel standing behind her. Both retained concerned looks on their faces.

Holmes waited until they were settled, and for a little dramatic effect, before he began. "I'm afraid that your husband, ex-Corporal David Button, was the sole perpetrator behind this whole affair. My inquiries have indicated that he served at the Royal Artillery Depot at Woolwich up until six months ago when he was dishonourably discharged for theft."

Tears formed in Angela's eyes and she dropped her head forward. "He wanted to set us up in a little country estate. I was ashamed of his actions, but we'd just married and I've always been told to support your husband no matter what. Foolish man." She looked up, a trail of tears running down each cheek. "I pleaded with Sir Nigel to help out, and he managed to have the charges dropped, but they had to discharge him as a matter of protocol."

Sir Nigel nodded. His face showed sorrow. I wasn't sure if it was for Angela or for himself.

"I managed to get him a job on the cleaning staff not long afterwards, but he showed up intoxicated on several occasions, and even I couldn't protect him," he said.

Mrs. Button nodded, turned, and looked up into Sir Nigel's eyes. He patted her shoulder and she placed a hand on his for a moment before turning back to Holmes.

"David kept blaming me for all his troubles. He said I was having an affair. He said I was making him less of a man because I kept working. Last night was the first time I became scared. He threatened to kill Sir Nigel, and then he threatened me," she said.

"The black powder was from a robbery at the Woolwich depot," explained Holmes. "Several barrels of old stock. The fake bomb under the House of Commons was probably an attempt to scare you, Sir Nigel. It was never going to work, but he must have used what he learned from his cleaning job to get back into the House and plant the bomb. I found a disused cleaner's trolley nearby. Last night, I presume, a combination of drink and his temper caused him to act. He must have arrived very early this morning and brought the powder in via the next-door courtyard."

"Yes," said Sir Nigel, "That's the Foreign Secretary's residence. He lives in Newcastle when Parliament is in recess. A caretaker comes in a couple of times a week."

"Quite so. Now, I am surmising that Mr. Button finished his work. Placed a trail of powder to the barrels in the under-croft to act as a fuse, then waited behind the row of planter boxes for Sir Nigel to retrieve the morning paper. He fell asleep instead and the unfortunate Mr. Parsons arrived early, looked around the front of the house, and lit up a morning cigar. Once finished, he was either about to leave or to knock on the door to ensure all was fine. He flicked the remains of his cigar into the courtyard, where it ignited the trail of powder. Mr. Button awoke to see the powder alight. He stood up just at the same time as the barrels ignited and exploded," Holmes said.

Mrs. Button reacted in surprise. "How do you know he was down in the courtyard?" she asked.

We all realised that she was the only one who didn't know about the body. "Oh, I'm so sorry dear," said Sir Nigel, "I afraid that Mr. Holmes and Dr. Watson found a dead body in the garden next door."

"And it fits the description that you gave of your husband," said Holmes.

A hand shot up to her face as she gasped, her face a mask of horror.

"I am so sorry to break it to you like this," Holmes said. "In your husband's defence, there's no indication that he intended to light the fuse. I believe it may have still been a ruse to scare Sir Nigel away from you."

"No. I loved my husband," Mrs. Button replied, "but of late his delirium over our supposed affair has escalated. The last thing he said as I fled from our house was that he was going to kill Sir Nigel and he had the means to do it. At the time, I took it as another set of his drunken ravings, but it seems . . . ."

She stopped abruptly as tears streamed from her eyes.

I took that moment to begin our excuses. "I don't know if there's much more we can achieve here," I said as I stood.

Sir Nigel nodded as he reached down and comforted the sobbing woman.

We quickly found ourselves out in the street and were approached by Inspector Lestrade, his face a mass of questions. "What is going on, Mr. Holmes?" he asked. "I have a bomb going off in a Government minister's residence. I have two dead bodies, and I've been kept away from the scene of the crime all morning."

Holmes held up a hand to quieten the policeman. "All will be explained, Inspector, I assure you. At this stage, you have the perpetrator, a Mr. David Button, the second corpse found on the scene. What started out as an act against the Houses of Parliament – " Lestrade's face dropped in shock at this revelation. " – has turned out to be a domestic issue with tragic results. For now, please be so kind as to allow Sir Nigel and his houseguest a little privacy for a couple of hours. They have had a major shock. I still need to tidy up one or two loose ends myself, but I assure you I will come by later and explain the full details to you."

Lestrade huffed and stormed off. Waiting was not one of his favourite hobbies.

Holmes took a deep breath and stared up into the clear blue sky.

"Do you think Angela will be alright?" I asked.

Holmes smiled and turned towards me, "I think that after the shock of this tragedy subsides, Mrs. Button may end up acquiring a new wedding ring that she will be more than proud to display, and a new title that will allow her to cease her duties in the civil service for good."

I smiled at his assumptions. "But she said that there was nothing to Button's insinuation of their affair," I said.

"Ah, yes," he said, "but the affairs of the heart aren't always so easy to deduce, even for those directly involved."

He looked down the street towards the devastation in front of the Home Secretary's residence. "I won't be holding my breath waiting for our wedding invitations, but I think it will be a nice surprise when they arrive," he said.

I chuckled to myself and we walked off to fetch a hansom back to Baker Street.

The Body at the Ritz

Life in the late nineteenth century was an active time in the annals of human history, especially in London. Man's intelligence had always set us apart from the greater animal population, but with James Watt's improvements on Thomas Newcomen's original designs for the steam engine having been put in place half a century ago, man's ingenuity had only been slightly outstripped by his imagination.

I sat on the balcony, with my breakfast coffee and looked out across the wide region that is greater London and smiled at the commotion at play as the populace went about their daily lives.

Horseless carriages, belching puffs of steam along with wisps of black coal smoke, trundled along the byways below. Dirigibles, large and small, ferried goods and people through the airways thick with clouds. Great zeppelins ploughed their way through the upper atmosphere connecting countries like never before and opening up new horizons and bringing new peoples into the modern world.

Wars were almost a thing of the past as technological improvements eradicated the ever-present need to gain resources or land from neighbours.

Sadly, though, one element was always present within any society and led to the need for men such as myself and my erstwhile companion, Mr. Sherlock Holmes.

Crime.

Be it theft. Be it murder. Or any of the multitude of variations that the human mind can muster. There will always be a need for a constabulary to investigate and solve the crimes of men, and when the officials are at the end of their tethers, they call upon outside help such as only we can lend.

I finished my coffee and withdrew back inside.

There I found Holmes in an accustomed position. He sat in an easy chair, resplendent in a silk smoking jacket, a pipe in mouth, poring over the daily paper.

He looked up as I entered and smiled.

"A lovely, quiet day, eh Watson?"

I placed my cup on the tea tray nearby as I answered.

"Yes, yes, it is Holmes. A wonderful time to be alive."

He grinned.

"A bit dull though. I've had nothing to perplex my brain for a good week."

I hadn't realised this and became wary. When Holmes was unoccupied his mind slipped into a state of ennui and could have dire consequences as he sought out other means to temper his boredom.

"Don't worry Watson, I'm not going to embark on any drug-fuelled fervour any time soon. I was just remarking that there seems to be a paucity of crime at the moment. Well, crime that requires my attention anyway," he said.

I sighed with relief but made a mental note to monitor my friend's movements in case of any obvious deviations from the norm that would indicate some chemical abuse.

"I was thinking of going to the Diogenes later for luncheon. Mycroft mentioned that he would be there today. It might be good to catch up with him. You never know he may let slip some little snippet of information that leads to an entertaining case," he said.

I agreed and packed up the tea tray and cups to take down to Mrs. Hudson, more for something to do than anything else, though I do like to help our landlady out when the opportunity arises.

As I reached the doorway a *shoomp* noise echoed up the stairway. Holmes looked up and grinned again. I knew the noise to mean the arrival of something in the sealed vacuum tube messaging system.

Moments later, the sound of footsteps on the stairs greeted us and the door opened to reveal Mrs. Hudson holding a rolled-up parchment. She handed the note to me and took away the tea tray.

"Thank you, Doctor, but you needn't have minded, I'm quite able to clear the dishes away," she said with a grin as she bustled off.

I blanched at the slight rebuke, then looked down at the note. It was addressed to Holmes, so I gave it straight to him and waited, curiosity writ large on my face.

Holmes read quietly to himself, then looked up and smiled.

"The game is afoot," he said.

***

On our ascent to the rooftop, Holmes stopped by and handed a note of reply to Mrs. Hudson.

"See this is delivered immediately, and thank you," he said to her.

I was still mystified as to the nature of the original message and intrigued about what faced us.

Once outside, I triggered the cab request lever and immediately a hidden mechanism fired up, filled a small balloon with compressed hydrogen then released it on a long line. The balloon ascended above 221B Baker Street and floated into the sky lanes to be spied by the floating network of viewfinders operated by the Greater London Cab company.

Within a few minutes, we noticed a black dirigible deviate from the throng of others of its kind passing overhead and move in our direction.

I triggered the reverse switch on the mechanism and the balloon retracted to avoid entanglement with the vehicle as it approached.

I finally asked Holmes what the note was about.

He replied, "Lestrade has found a body."

"Nothing unusual in that," I said.

"True, but this one was found in a small alleyway off of Piccadilly."

"Again, nothing unusual."

Holmes smiled.

"Outside of the Ritz," he said.

"Oh," I said, "we've been called on the insistence of Sir Rupert, then?"

Holmes nodded and looked up as the dirigible finished its descent. Its landing claw reached out and grasped the edge of the roof platform letting out a mechanical *clank*.

We bade the pilot a good day and boarded. Whilst Holmes gave him our destination, I sat in one of the front seats so as to distribute the weight evenly. Holmes joined me, and we heard the motors whirr and felt the aircraft begin to rise. With a slight bump, as the claw detached, we were away.

The pilot ascended to join the other airships and craft flying along in the sky lanes and headed south towards St. James's Park. I craned to my right and took much pleasure in viewing the landscape below.

Within moments we were crossing Marylebone and drifting within sight of the lush greenery of Hyde Park. Soon, the architecture changed from the simple Georgian and Victorian terraces of Marylebone to towering neo-Gothic structures clad with shiny bronze scales and plates.

This style of building had only come into play in the last ten years or so and was more a reflection of the tastes of the nouveau riche than for any structural or functional purposes.

The pilot turned the airship and began his approach to the landing platform at the top of the Ritz Hotel.

I viewed the building with a slight amount of awe. The current owner, Sir Rupert Linklatter, had taken the once elegant five-story Georgian hotel and added another five stories all clad in brightly shining brass plating with several glass elevators that traversed the exterior overlooking Piccadilly. At night, the hotel was lit up like a beacon with electric lights playing across the façade, reflecting off the myriad bronze plates and shining back across the roadway below and buildings opposite. It was quite a spectacle, one that I had watched on a few occasions but had never been overly enamoured with.

Sir Rupert had made his fortune from coal mining in the Newcastle region, controlling much of the fuel that drove the new industrial age and reaping the benefits. The Ritz was his domain in London. It provided both a high-cost hotel to the rich and famous and a luxurious inner London sanctum for Sir Rupert and his family.

As could be expected, Sir Rupert's status attracted a high level of protection from those in the upper echelons of the political power base. Holmes had enamoured himself to Sir Rupert a few years back when he helped to discover the true nature of the disappearance of the Countess Bruckheimer from within her suite at the Ritz. Holmes managed to solve the case quietly and quickly without drawing any adverse attention upon the Ritz and Sir Rupert. Henceforth, on orders from those in power, the local constabulary often played second fiddle to Holmes when any crimes were discovered in the general area of the Ritz.

The pilot brought us in to dock at the landing platform built out from the roof of the Ritz. I paid the man and followed Holmes from the craft. A well-dressed couple in their sixties entered the airship and were away before we had even crossed the roof to the Hotel's entrance, such was the pace of modern life.

As we approached the main doors, I saw Holmes nod towards the footman and receive a knowing look in return. I assumed this was one of Holmes's informants and wondered if he would prove useful to us later.

The footman opened the doors for us to reveal a tall, lanky man dressed in a dinner suit, waiting inside. He bowed and introduced himself as Allaister Croan, Sir Rupert's assistant. He shook our hands and led us through the hotel at a cracking pace. I struggled to keep up, but Holmes, being almost as tall, had no trouble.

"Sir Rupert expresses his gratitude, in advance, of you solving this little dilemma," Croan said.

"But the body was found outside, surely that bears no problem for the Hotel," I said.

Croan stopped and turned to face me. His face took on a very serious tone.

"Sir Rupert has a very exclusive clientele. The mere presence of the constabulary fills him with dread, and he would appreciate all avenues being taken to keep the details of this matter private and away from the day-to-day operations of the hotel," he said.

To punctuate his sentence further and to stress the importance to Sir Rupert, he continued with, "And the Prime Minister is evidently aware as well."

He turned and moved on. Holmes dropped back to walk beside me. I could see a familiar grin on his face. Holmes has never been one for power players. To him, a crime is a crime, whether it involves a Prince or a pauper.

As we walked, my eyes strayed to the lush pile of the carpet we traversed. Most hotel carpets consist of a short, hardy pile, but this was long and thick, probably woollen and of an extremely high quality. The swirling black, grey and white pattern that repeated every ten feet or so, was intricate and would have added more to the cost.

Finally, we were shown to a side door that opened out into the alleyway beyond.

Lestrade stood with his arms crossed waiting in impatient anticipation for our arrival. As we stepped into the alley, he unfolded his arms and relaxed slightly. He stepped to his right and unveiled the object of our attention.

Slumped, with his back against the wall was the lonely figure of the victim. His head hung down with his hands folded in his lap and legs jutting straight out from the wall.

He wore a long red velvet frock coat, which was bunched beneath him and soaking up the water from an early morning shower.

Beneath the coat, he sported a beige waistcoat, white collarless shirt and a dark brown cravat. His dark brown tweed pants were tucked into knee-high leather boots. All his clothing was of exquisite taste and smacked of expense. On first observations, this was a well to do man about town. One that would fit into the exclusivity of the Ritz seamlessly.

Holmes approached the scene and circled around to the front of the body, carefully avoiding any clues that may lay in the immediate area.

He scanned the ground, bending down from time to time to observe some ephemera. Satisfied that there was nothing of interest he moved in closer to the body.

"Male, Caucasian, approximately thirty to thirty-five years of age," Holmes said.

He stepped back for a moment, scanning the man's entire body.

"Approximately, five foot ten inches in height, about one hundred and seventy pounds. So not overweight, but not overly athletic," he said.

I piped up with an observation of my own, "There's no hat. The current style for one wearing a frock coat and boots is to accompany it with a top hat, is it not? There are none laying around the immediate area either."

Holmes looked towards me and smiled.

"Very good Watson, very good. What does it tell you?"

"That he either lost it before entering the alleyway or it was taken from him," I replied.

Holmes nodded then reached into his inner coat pocket and extracted his goggles. He placed them over his eyes and turned a small side screw that pushed the lenses away from his face, enabling him to zoom in and magnify some minor details that were invisible to the naked eye. He pulled on a pair of fine kid gloves and for the first time reached in to touch the victim's body.

He gently picked up each of the man's hands, in turn, and examined the palms and especially the fingertips. Murmuring to himself as he did so. He bent down and sniffed the man's palms, which I found a little strange, even for Holmes, but chose to ignore it in the interests of the investigation.

Holmes placed the man's hands back in his lap and turned to Lestrade, addressing the Inspector for the first time since our arrival.

"I assume you have already searched him for identification?"

Lestrade looked affronted.

"I have my orders to leave everything alone and wait for you. I wouldn't want to get Sir Rupert offside now, would I?" Lestrade replied with a heavy dose of sarcasm.

Holmes smiled widely, knowing full well what Lestrade meant.

"Found nothing then?"

Lestrade nodded.

"Nothing at all?" asked Holmes with a hint of surprise.

"Absolutely nothing. Clean as a new bought suit," Lestrade replied.

Holmes murmured to himself.

"Why Holmes?" I asked.

"Because Watson, what we have here is a scene depicting a robbery that has gone a little wrong, resulting in a dead body."

"Yes."

"But if you had just accidentally, or even purposely, killed someone you would take the most obvious things, wallet, watch, maybe keys, and leave quickly. This man has been picked clean, including his hat and possibly glasses or goggles."

He stood and scanned around the area again, then took off his right glove, reached down and felt the collar of the man's frock coat.

"Dry," he said.

"It rained this morning," said Lestrade, "Around seven o'clock."

"Well, that gives us our estimated time of death. Sometime after seven o'clock," I said.

Holmes didn't seem convinced.

"Unless," he said.

He hunkered down and pushed his finger into the man's cheek. There was considerable resistance. He returned his attention to the man's hands and prodded the thenar eminence, the fleshy part beneath the thumb, with his finger. The indentation stayed put for quite a while.

"Rigor mortis is quite pronounced," he said.

"Yes. In this weather I would put the time of death closer to four to six hours ago, not two," I said.

"Precisely," said Holmes as he stood up, "I believe this man was killed elsewhere and dumped here. Why? I have no idea and still need more facts to prove my assumption."

He reached into his coat and extracted a strange tool. It was a long wand-shaped brass cylinder, with a clear crystal at one end and a small crank handle towards the middle.

Holmes turned the handle which caused the device to emit a whirring noise as some unseen engine within began to turn. As the crystal started to glow with an inner luminescence, Holmes moved it towards the dead man's coat.

The crystal cast a faint blue light over the red material, causing several small specs on the coat to glow white with a slight purple tinge.

Holmes stopped and peered closely at a small spec on the man's coat. He again reached into his coat and pulled out a small pouch of tools. Opening it, he extracted a pair of tweezers then picked the spec out from the fabric of the man's coat. He stared at the item more closely, turning it to gain a better look.

"What have you there, Holmes?" I asked.

"A sliver of glass," he said.

Holmes put the sliver aside, then returned to examine the man, murmuring as he moved the wand across the man's coat, hovering over a bright spot on the left lapel. He opened the man's coat and waved the wand across his vest and shirt. No more spots showed up which must have confused Holmes as he let out a surprised little murmur.

He shifted his attention to the man's legs and moved the wand down his trouser legs. He looked at the man's boots and with the tweezers pulled out another clue. He held it up to the light and adjusted his lenses to magnify the object.

"What have you there, Holmes?" I asked.

"A woollen thread. Carpet. Dark grey. Similar to something we saw not long ago," he said.

"The carpet in the hallway of the Ritz," I said.

Holmes nodded and turned the man's legs out to check the backs as best he could. I noticed a scuff mark on the back of one beautifully polished boot. Another nod of the head told me Holmes considered this to be a clue. I decided to let him continue without distraction.

He pulled back and wound the little device's handle again.

Turning to Lestrade, he said, "Inspector, if you would be so kind, can you tilt the body forward so that I can examine his back?"

Lestrade, happy to be useful, leapt at the opportunity and gently tilted the man forward.

Holmes ran his wand across the man's back and let out an exclamation. I moved to a position where I could see his find.

The light now showed several large bright white spots that ran down the man's back from the collar. The spots were ill-defined and appeared to be smudged.

"What the Devil?" I asked.

Holmes said, "Blood, Watson, blood. This little device contains an yttrium crystal, which emits ultraviolet light when stimulated by static electricity. The little crank turns a small leather band inside which charges the crystal. Bloodstains always show up under ultraviolet light, no matter how well you try to clean them. As we have just seen."

He reached in with the pair of tweezers again and pulled out a small spike of glass.

"And more glass," he said placing it to the side.

He brought his hand up to the man's shirt collar and pulled the cravat away. We all immediately saw a small puncture mark at the base of the man's skull just below his hairline.

"Good Lord," said Lestrade, "That wasn't done by some Johnny on the street, that was done by a professional. It almost looks like an ice-pick or needle wound."

"Very true, Inspector," said Holmes, "Very true."

He stood up and Lestrade returned the body to the wall. I piped up as a small memory came to the fore.

"That wound is very reminiscent of the one we found on Professor Bhargava who was visiting Durham University from Paris two years ago," I said.

Holmes nodded; his face becoming stern.

"Yes…Yes it is, Watson. We never found the assailant, but my inquiries led me back to the Vishkanya, a league of assassins for hire operating out of India many years ago."

He stared at the body for a moment then up to the brightly lit upper floors of the Ritz hotel.

"I don't wish to jump to conclusions about the assailant, I don't have enough information for that, but I am sure that this man was killed inside the Ritz and was subsequently moved here. I found a small thread probably from the thick carpet in the hallways. Then there are the specs of glass, and the marks on the back of the man's boots lead me to believe that his demise resulted in a large amount of damage to some furniture."

Holmes looked further down the alleyway, away from the blazing lights of Piccadilly. I followed along, leaving a confused Lestrade with the body.

We quickly came to the corner of the hotel and peered around into another darkened alleyway.

"Aha," said Holmes as he spied something sitting near the wall amongst a pile of similar detritus. He moved over to the pile and grabbed hold of a slender cylinder of wood and pulled the frame of a low wooden table from the pile.

He set the frame upon the three remaining legs. The top was missing but appeared to have been glass as there were shards still attached to the frame mountings on each corner.

"What do you make of it, Holmes?" I asked.

"Not a lot, Watson, but if I was to project a story from what we've seen, I would say that our dead man was attacked from behind and stabbed in the neck. He then staggered back, tripped against the edge of this table and fell through the glass top, shattering it and breaking off one of the legs. He was then cleaned up, removed from the hotel room and deposited in the alleyway beyond. The room was thoroughly cleansed, and the broken table placed here amongst the other refuse from the day-to-day operations of the hotel."

Holmes pulled out his crystal wand and wound the handle once more. He ran the wand around the edges of the table and found another bright spot on some of the glass on one corner.

"Is it the dead man's?" I asked.

Holmes shook his head.

"I don't think so, there were no other wounds on the body. Even the bloodstain on the front of his coat wasn't from him. I believe our assailant cut themselves before rummaging around in the man's pockets," he said.

He stood up, put his wand away and brushed his hands together to remove the dust and grime from the table frame.

"In my mind, it does confirm that the man was murdered inside the hotel. The question remains, did the assailant remove him or the hotel staff themselves?"

"Given Sir Rupert's predilection to protect his hotel's reputation, I would say the latter," I said.

Holmes nodded.

"Quite so, Watson."

We turned back towards the corner and the other alleyway when a voice piped up behind us.

"Oi," it said.

We turned and saw a man standing in the shadows a little further down the alleyway. I could just make out his features and realised it was the doorman from the roof. He shuffled his feet and looked around nervously as if expecting to be found out at any moment.

Holmes strode straight up to him.

"Hello Frankie," he said.

"Mr. 'olmes," he returned, tipping his hat slightly, "Sorry I couldn't say anything upstairs. Mr. Croan scares the bejesus out o' me."

"That's fine, Frankie, what would you like to say?" asked Holmes.

Frankie lifted his chin to indicate the adjacent alleyway.

"The body, round the corner, 'e's been 'ere before."

"News travels fast," I said.

"I keeps me nose to the ground, I do. Mr. 'olmes pays me to do it," he retorted.

"Yes, go on. Do you know who the man is?" Holmes asked.

"Nah, but 'e's been here a few times. Comes in an' meets with another gent and the boss, mostly up on the top floor," he said.

"That would be Sir Rupert's office?"

"Yeah, yeah. And then sometimes 'e stays after. Flashes the cash around. Sometimes brings the ladies 'ere. Mostly ladies of the night, if you know wot I mean," he grinned.

Holmes nodded, "Yes, I know what you mean. When did he come this morning?"

"Well, that was weird. 'e arrived about four o'clock. I was on duty upstairs, 'e brings in a tall, dark 'aired girl. Beautiful she was. Foreign though, but still beautiful. They booked into a suite and I suppose got down to it. Maid came about seven this morning with breakfast, went in and found 'im dead as a doornail on top of the smashed coffee table. Mr. Croan found out, all 'ell broke loose, and then 'e was dumped downstairs."

"I suppose if I asked anybody else, they would deny everything?"

"Yep, word's gone out. Immediate sacking or worse."

He looked around nervously again.

"I gotta go before it's me," he said.

I quickly butted in, "Can I just ask, you mentioned the other gent, who is that?"

Frankie turned to me; his expression showed that he had no idea who I was.

"It's alright, Frankie, this is Doctor Watson, my associate," Holmes said.

Frankie relaxed, "The other gent is the Scots man, Sir Stannis McDonald."

My mouth dropped open at the mention of that name.

"Thank you, Frankie, you've answered a few questions I had. There'll be something extra in your payment this month," Holmes said.

"Oh, fank you, Mr. 'olmes," he said and vanished through a side door.

"Sir Stannis?" I asked, "Head of the Watt Steam company? What would he be doing here?"

Holmes turned, "It's becoming clearer, Watson, but there are still several pieces missing."

***

We found Lestrade leaning against a wall, biding his time but becoming frustrated with inaction. He got to his feet as he saw us enter the alleyway.

"Well?" he asked.

Holmes strode up to the corpse again and indicated for both of us to join him. He hunched down and picked up the man's hands again. He turned them over and revealed numerous callouses on the man's fingers and palms.

They were not the hands of a man that the clothes he wore heralded. This man was a tradesman of sorts and a hardworking one at that. I tried to work out how someone in a trade, no matter how hard he toiled, could afford the lifestyle he seemed to be living.

Holmes noticed both Lestrade's and my confusion at the state of the man's palms. He pulled out a small tool and picked out some black matter from beneath the man's fingernails. He held the hands out.

"Smell his hands," he said.

In turn, Lestrade and I leant forward and sniffed at the proffered hand. We both reared back in revulsion at the horrid chemical smell.

“Good Lord,” said Lestrade.

“What say you, Watson?” asked Holmes.

"Some sort of oil or spirit-based chemical. It's not paraffin or alcohol," I said.

“No, it’s not,” said Holmes as he placed the man’s hands down again and stood, “It’s a new type of fuel called diesel. It is formed from a fractional distillation of petroleum. The black beneath the man’s fingernails is possibly asphalt or alkene, one of the by-products of the process.”

“A new fuel?” I asked, “Why would we need a new fuel? Coal is used in everything from cars, airships, heating, manufacturing, electricity. It will never be replaced.”

Holmes smiled, “True. We have coal, for now, but what if someone could find an alternative. Cleaner, more efficient, cheaper?”

“The human race would advance even quicker than it has so far?” I said.

“Ever the optimist, Watson, that’s one of your traits I do so admire. What about who that discovery might affect?”

I thought for a moment before realising where Holmes was going.

“Good Lord. The coal barons. The steam engine companies,” I said.

Holmes smiled widely and nodded.

“Yes. Exactly,” he said, “And I think they would pay quite handsomely for any information about the development of such fuel and any engines associated with it.”

Lestrade’s face was a mass of confusion.

“I have no idea what you two are talking about. Care to fill me in, or should I just take care of the body?” he said.

“I think we will require you for the next chapter in this adventure, Inspector. I believe that there will be a need for the yard’s services,” he said.

He stared off into the distance for a moment, as if recalling some memory from the great databanks of his mind and finally smiled.

"There is only one place that I know of that would require this type of fuel," he said.

***

Lestrade had a car parked nearby with two uniformed constables within. He directed one to secure the alleyway and wait for the coroner's men to arrive and remove the body.

The other man, Collins, was to drive us to a destination known by Holmes. He gave the address to the man, who then sparked the vehicle into action.

The ground car was a different beast to the airborne dirigible. Collins fired up the coal furnace below the small boiler, ensuring it was stoked with plenty of the black fuel and released the steam into the drive train when ready. The car lurched forward with a jolt as the inner turbine reached the required pressure. This form of transport had replaced the simple horse and carriage many years before and Holmes's idea that there was a simpler, ever more efficient system in the winds played through my mind, but I flicked it away with a healthy level of derision.

We took a brief stop at the nearest Police Station in Belgravia where Lestrade exited and strode into the station to organise some assistance for Constable Brown back at the Ritz. He quickly returned, and Collins had us away.

We headed south to the Thames and drove along the sprawling and bustling river, alive with boats and ships belching great gouts of black coal smoke and pure white steam, as they plied their trade along the river and supplied the great city with its needs.

We turned onto the Albert Bridge and crossed over the river. To our left was the expanse of Battersea Park, alive with people and their pet dogs. Children played in the bright sunshine and mothers sat in groups talking animatedly to each other.

I often forgot that the average person does not deal with the morbid and depressing sides of human nature that crop up in the life shared by Holmes and me. The only way that most of these people would learn of a body found in an alleyway, would be to see it appear in a column of the daily paper. Then most would glance at the article and turn the page to seek more light-hearted entertainment.

We entered a highly industrial area made up of large workhouses and warehouses. The area looked decidedly less salubrious than that which we had left in Piccadilly and Belgravia. The people walking the street eyed us both with envy, at the level of dress displayed by Holmes and myself, and with suspicion, as we were in a police vehicle with two officers.

We pulled in through a large set of wrought iron gates, with the sign "British Diesel Company" emblazoned above them. The three wings of the building formed a natural courtyard, and we parked before what was evidently the main entrance.

As we exited the vehicle, a loud droning noise greeted us from above. I looked up and saw a massive airship slowing down above the compound. It stopped in mid-air and hovered. Several men emerged from the nearby warehouse and stood looking up at the ship. A loud clanking sound followed by a whirring noise heralded the descent of the lower half of the aircraft's gondola.

The dirigible was one of the newer types of transport craft. A large zeppelin attached to a split-level gondola, the top half being used for controls and engines, the bottom being purely for cargo.

As I watched, the cargo deck was lowered on thick steel cables attached to winches, supposedly secreted in the upper deck. Within about a minute the lower level reached the ground. It was covered in large cylindrical drums with "North Sea Oil Company" logos plastered on them.

The men unloaded the barrels and rolled them to the bottom of a long flat roller system covered by a large continuous sheet of some strong material. Another man, standing to the side, turned a crank handle at the base of a strange-looking mechanical device. The contraption let out a few of what seemed to be mechanical coughs then began to run. It belched out huge plumes of black smoke and a deafening roar. My hands shot to my ears to protect them from the din.

The operator moved to a nearby switch, pulled it forward, and the whole belt began to move with a series of screeches and groans.

The other men started to load the barrels onto the belt, and they were ferried off into the bowels of the warehouse.

“Fascinating, isn’t it?” Holmes said next to me.

“Loud,” I yelled.

“Yes, but the power of that primitive engine is incredible,” he said.

I looked incredulously back at the contraption. I then realised this was one of the diesel engines that Holmes had been talking about. I noticed it was a lot smaller than some of the steam engines I was familiar with. Even smaller than the one in the Police vehicle that brought us here.

“Why do you say primitive?” I asked.

“By the looks, it’s one of Rudolf Diesel’s early prototypes. Nothing goes to waste it seems.”

He glanced up and spied the large smokestacks above us, plus another smaller chimney that had a constant flame pouring from it.

“Very impressive,” he said.

“What is?”

“They have their own refinery for fractional distillation of the petroleum in those barrels we saw. They produce their own diesel fuel here. Small quantities I imagine, just enough to power their prototypes and inventions,” he said.

I gaped at the chimneys myself, never imagining that such an operation existed in London.

It was then that several of the workers turned and noticed us watching them. They in turn stopped and stared at us. Some probably suspicious of the two police officers.

Another man stepped out of the warehouse and headed straight for the inactive men.

"Right, you lot, quit your lollygagging and get this lot unloaded. We can’t afford to have that ship sitting here all day,” he said.

They all snapped back to work. The foreman turned his attention to us and walked over, a stern look on his face.

“What do you lot want?” his question directed at Lestrade.

Holmes piped up before Lestrade could begin.

“If I may, my good man. We are looking for someone, and you might be just the person to help us. We think that one of your workers had a slight mishap at the Ritz Hotel last night. The Bar Manager was forced to have him thrown out. But before then he was yelling loudly about how he worked for this company and would have the owner come and buy the hotel. Well, you can imagine that Sir Rupert Linklatter was not very impressed when he found out and asked us to come and suggest that the chap stay away from now on."

"Seems a bit strange having the police do that," he said.

"Yes. Well, to be honest, it was either us or Sir Rupert's men."

The foreman's face changed to surprise. He nodded.

"Fair cop. Who was it?"

"We only have a description. Five ten. Brown hair. Dressed like a dandy."

The foreman nodded.

"Bloody Danny Green that would be. Came into some money of late. Big notes himself all the time."

The foreman stood up and yelled at the men unloading the dirigible.

"Oi, any of you lot seen Danny today?"

They all shook their heads. He turned back to Holmes.

"I ain't seen him all day either. He only lives around the corner, 13 Beatty Street. Lives with his Mum, the pillock."

The foreman seemed to think this was the end of the conversation. As luck would have it, the men finished their unloading and the raucous noise of the cargo bay ascending blotted out any hope of immediate conversation.

Holmes waited until the noise abated and the airship began to pull away before pressing the foreman.

"If you would be so kind, I think we should talk to Mrs. Fyord, just to warn her in case Sir Rupert decides to visit unannounced," he said.

The foreman smiled, "It's Miss. Miss Madeline Fyord. She's very particular. But, yeah, follow me, I'll see if she's available."

We headed through the main doors and into a brightly lit reception area. Even though we'd been outside in the sun, the light level within this room was almost disorienting.

The foreman laughed as he saw us shielding our eyes from the bright lights.

"Yeah, it takes a little getting used to," he said, "We generate our own electricity. The Boss likes to show off the capabilities of our engines. You don't get lights this bright with steam turbines."

My eyesight finally adjusted, and I could take in more of the details of the room. It was certainly not typical of the exterior of the buildings. The wood panelling had been painted in a clinical white and lacquered to give it a smooth almost glass-like appearance. Polished brass had been used extensively to accentuate the white.

At a desk in the centre of the room sat a young woman who eyed us off suspiciously before replacing the look with a well-practised but welcoming smile. I looked around and realised the foreman was gone.

"Gentlemen," the receptionist said, "Welcome to the British Diesel Company, can I help you in any way?"

Lestrade took the lead.

"I'm Inspector Lestrade of Her Majesty's Scotland Yard, we would like to see Miss Fyord, if you please," he said.

"Could I ask on what business?" the receptionist asked, her smile fading slightly.

"It's about one of her employees, a Mister Danny Green," he said.

The receptionist pushed a small switch which lit up. She reached for a black polished handset and turned a crank next to it.

Placing the mouthpiece to her lips she said, "Sorry to disturb you Miss, but there are several men from Scotland Yard here to see you."

A small indistinct buzzing came from the earpiece.

The young girl answered, "Yes, it's about Danny Green."

More buzzing and the girl eyed us with a slight tinge of concern on her face. She recovered and indicated the large ornate doors to our left.

"Miss Fyord will see you, please just through those doors."

***

Holmes opened the door to reveal a lavishly decorated office with a large wooden desk in the centre with brass and leather accents.

I noticed a door to the side closing and saw a hint of a long leather boot with a woman's hand sporting black nail polish drawing it shut. I turned towards Holmes and saw that he was apprised of the situation.

We both turned back to the remarkable woman that sat behind the desk. Miss Fyord was more than beautiful. Artists would vie for the chance to carve her in marble just for the chance to gaze upon her face. She sported long tresses of iridescent blonde hair that fell around her alabaster skin. Her piercing blue eyes gazed out below long black eyelashes.

She stood as Holmes approached, and I could see that she was also tall and slim. She wore long leather pants with knee-high boots, and her trim figure was compressed into a tight leather waistcoat over a flowing silk blouse.

She held out one immaculately manicured hand and took Holmes's hand in a firm and lingering handshake.

"I am Madeline Fyord, owner of this little enterprise, and you are?"

"Sherlock Holmes, madam," said Holmes, turning to introduce the rest of us, "My associate Doctor Watson, and this is Inspector Lestrade and Constable Collins of Scotland Yard."

Miss Fyord nodded to each of us in turn then sat down. We looked around for chairs but realised there weren't any. I admired that fact as this presented us in a reverse power game scenario.

"And how can I help you, Mr. Holmes?"

"I'm sorry to say, that we've come about the death of one of your employees. A Mr. Danny Green," he said.

Miss Fyord's expression remained impassive as she seemed to search her memories. Finally, she spoke.

"Green. Yes. Low-level Engineer. Working on the development of a new marine diesel engine prototype. We are hoping to use boats as our first move into the power unit market," she replied then continued after a pause, "Sad. How did he die?"

"He was murdered. Presumably at the Ritz Hotel, but his body was found in the alleyway next door."

"The Ritz, you say, I must revisit how much I'm paying my engineers. That's not an inexpensive establishment. Well thank you for informing me, I will have my receptionist contact his next of kin and pass on my condolences."

She stood again to bid us goodbye.

"I'm sure you need to rush off to apprehend the villain behind this, so I won't hold you further," she said.

All four of us held our places. Miss Fyord looked from face to face. Her stern look melted slightly as she realised we weren't going to leave. She sat down. The atmosphere had turned slightly.

Holmes continued, moving forward so that he towered over the desk and looked down at Miss Fyord.

"Mr. Green, a low-level engineer in your words, had been seen at the Ritz on a number of occasions. He held meetings with Sir Stannis McDonald in the office of Sir Rupert Linklatter."

A smile crossed Miss Fyord's face at the mention of those names.

"You know the gentlemen?" Holmes asked.

"Of course, Sir Stannis is my biggest competitor. The diesel engine we are developing is his biggest threat. We may only be a small company, but we have a mighty product on our hands. As for Sir Rupert, he has the largest controlling interest in the North Sea oil fields. He has been playing us off against British Steam for months. Hedging his bets so to speak."

Her demeanour changed.

"Are you trying to tell me that this Green was selling us out to our competitor?" she asked.

"I cannot say at this point, they may have just been old school friends for all I know," said Holmes, a little too quickly for my like. I recognised it as a tone he took when confronted over a point he could not justify with facts.

"Then what's the problem?" Fyord asked.

"Early this morning, Mr. Green was seen entering the same room as a tall, slender, woman of Indian appearance. The next time he was seen, he was dead in an alleyway with a puncture mark to the back of his neck. The puncture mark is reminiscent of a weapon used by a member of an elite all-female Indian assassin's guild."

Miss Fyord laughed out loud.

"And you think that was me?" she blurted out.

A small grin came to Holmes's face. He shook his head slightly.

"Oh no, madam, I don't think you had anything physically to do with this murder."

He walked across to the door we'd seen close earlier, grabbed the knob and wrenched it open.

Standing inside was a strikingly beautiful Indian woman, almost the same height as Holmes, with a slender, powerfully athletic build. She was dressed in a tight-fitting blue silk blouse, with a black leather bodice and black leather pants. I noticed that there were knife scabbards on the sides of her knee-high boots. I was relieved to find them empty. She also wore a black leather aviator's helmet with thick brass goggles. Her long black hair spilled out of the helmet and cascaded down to her waist.

This was not the look of a simple secretary or office worker. This woman was dressed for business. Bloody business.

"Madam, if you would be so kind, could you join us please," said Holmes.

The Indian woman stood in the small, white-tiled room that acted as Miss Fyord's private bathroom. She had a stern expression on her face with her piercing brown eyes trained on Holmes. She looked ready to pounce.

Her demeanour changed when Miss Fyord piped up.

"Parvinder, please do as Mr. Holmes says," she said, "I think we can clear this up quickly."

"As you wish, Ma'am," she said and walked into the office and took an "at ease" stance that would be the staple of any of the armed services.

"Let me introduce Miss Parvinder Singh, my associate and one of my closest friends. I think in future, Parvinder, it may prove prudent to lock the bathroom door," said Miss Fyord.

Holmes blanched a little with embarrassment at the suggestion he'd interrupted the woman. He recovered quickly. Miss Fyord took up the questioning.

"Parvinder, these gentlemen tell me that you were seen at the Ritz Hotel this morning. That you were meeting up with our Mr. Green from the new engine development team," she said.

The Indian woman turned to look at Miss Fyord with a questioning gaze. The blonde-haired woman looked directly into her eyes and nodded slightly. Holmes saw it all as well.

Parvinder turned her gaze forward and nodded.

"Yes. It is true," she said.

"You've been seeing Mr. Green for quite some time now, haven't you, but keeping it quiet, even from me."

Parvinder nodded again and spoke in a deadpan monotone.

"Yes. Daniel and I were in love. We have been together for several months. I think Daniel was going to propose marriage to me this morning. I was very excited," she said.

I almost burst out laughing at the woman's act. It was preposterous. I'm not even sure she knew who the man was, let alone being hopelessly in love with him.

Holmes simply smiled.

"I'm sure young Daniel would have been overjoyed with such a heartfelt response to his forthcoming proposal. Having you kill him probably came as an incredible surprise as well," he said.

Miss Fyord stood up at this suggestion.

"Kill him? Why would she kill him? It's obvious that she loved him."

Holmes turned towards her, his hand on his chin in contemplation of this strange conversation.

"My belief is that you, Miss Fyord, had your associate or should I say your hired assassin here, kill Mr. Green because he was selling your company's secrets to your competitor. You found out and wanted to make sure he died on the premises of one of your enemy's business partners."

"And what proof do you have?"

"For one, we have witnesses that place them both in the same location. We have reason to believe that my suggestion of industrial espionage is true. I will have to approach Sir Stannis to confirm it. He may not be happy, but the truth will come out. And one last piece of evidence would be …"

He turned and grabbed the Indian woman's right hand and turned it over. She sported a large bandage that covered the palm. Fresh blood had soaked through since the bandage had last been changed.

"The assailant cut herself on a glass-topped table, before reaching for Mr. Green's coat and taking whatever information he carried, plus the contents of his pockets."

Holmes turned towards Lestrade.

"Is this enough evidence to at least take Miss Singh here to the station house for further questioning?"

Lestrade nodded in agreement. Suddenly, his eyes grew wide, and he thrust a hand inside his coat. He pulled it out holding his pistol and trained it on Miss Singh.

I watched in shock as the tall woman stepped up behind Holmes, wrapped her injured arm around his chest and pulled her left hand out from behind her back.

She held what looked like a small brass pistol in her left hand and pressed the barrel against Holmes's neck. I looked closely and saw the plunger had been withdrawn and was cocked ready to fire.

I copied Lestrade and reached into my coat and withdrew my pistol. I noticed Collins standing nearby looking a little lost. Constables were only issued with nightsticks, not pistols. He drew his truncheon from his belt and held it at the ready.

"Ma'am, you have two guns pointing at you. We only want to ask you more questions to ascertain the truth. Let's not make this any harder than necessary," said Lestrade.

Holmes remained calm and spoke slowly with just enough volume for the Indian woman to hear.

"Hmmm, from the feel of it that would be a Bharat S13 Spring operated needle pistol, developed for the Bengal Infantry and used for close fighting and assassinations. Well that certainly confirms your origins, Miss Singh," said Holmes.

The Indian girl remained quiet. Miss Fyord broke the silence.

"What origins? Mr. Holmes?" she asked.

"Miss Singh here is a member of the Vishkanya. A secretive guild of female assassins operating out of India, primarily in the Punjab and Bengal areas," he said.

Miss Fyord laughed out loud.

"Nonsense. Parvinder's family has lived in England for decades. She was born in London and lived around the corner from my Grandfather's house. We have been friends for most of our lives," she said.

"Indeed," said Holmes.

"Is that true, Miss Singh?" I asked.

The woman's face remained impassive. Her hand tightened on the gun as she answered.

"Yes. I have lived in England all my life. Madeline is my best friend. We went to school and University together. I have worked with her company since I left school," she said in a dead monotonic voice.

I could see Holmes wasn't convinced. His face showed a slight tinge of anger at what he thought were obvious lies.

"Then perhaps, Miss Fyord, you could convince Miss Singh to unhand me and accompany the Inspector to the station so that this matter can be laid to rest. If Miss Singh was so in love with Mr. Green, then even a policeman of Inspector Lestrade's experience and expertise could not possibly charge her with Mr. Green's murder."

"Yes," said Miss Fyord standing up, "I think this has gone on long enough."

She raised her voice and directed her next sentence at the Indian woman.

"Parvinder, the time has come. You know what to do," she said.

I noticed a flash of confusion and incredulity race across the tall woman's face. She turned to Miss Fyord bowed her head slightly, then turned her face forward. Her face regained its impassive expression again.

"Yes. It will be done," she said.

Parvinder stared off into space and released Holmes who staggered away. He turned back to address the woman just in time to see her bring the needle gun up to her temple and squeeze the trigger.

The gun let out a stifled ringing noise and what sounded like something punching into meat.

The Indian woman's eyes rolled back into their sockets and she collapsed in an unceremonious heap on the floor. The gun slid away from her and stopped near Holmes.

I looked down at the gun and saw a long brass needle sticking out of the end. It was mottled with red blood.

I looked back at the woman and saw a small puncture in her left temple like the wound on Green's neck. A dribble of blood ran out of the hole and dripped onto the floor.

I couldn't help myself but blurted out, "Good Lord."

Holmes looked at the dead woman then turned to face Miss Fyord. The company owner was calm as if this was an expected occurrence.

Holmes cocked his head and spoke.

"Well, that was unexpected," he said, "Wasn't it, Miss Fyord?"

She turned and looked into Holmes's eyes, her face unmoved.

"Shocking, I would say," she said.

"You don't seem very upset," I said.

Miss Fyord turned to face me; a flash of anger ran across her features.

"My best friend just killed herself, in my office. I will not give you intruders the pleasure of seeing my distress," she said standing up and moving around to the front of her desk.

"Now, if you'll excuse me, I will go home so that I may mourn alone," she finished.

She turned to Lestrade and said, "I assume you will need a statement or something from me. I will remain at home for the next day or two. My receptionist can give you my address."

With that, she turned and walked through her office doors and into the reception area before anybody thought of stopping her.

I was flustered. I looked at the retreating figure, then to Holmes and Lestrade.

"What is going on?" I asked keeping my voice from rising to a shrill cry.

Holmes turned from watching Miss Fyord leave, a small sardonic grin on his face.

"What do you mean, Watson?"

"You're letting her go. You said all along that this was a case of espionage. That Green was killed because of what he knew and what he was selling to Sir Stannis," I said.

"Ah, yes, but I don't have any actual evidence. Only conjecture," he answered before turning to Lestrade, "I assume that you are content with the case at hand, Inspector?"

Lestrade looked at the body and then back at Holmes and me. He nodded.

"Sadly, yeah, I agree with Holmes. We've got enough evidence to put this down to a lovers' tiff or something, but not enough to lay any other charges."

He turned to Collins.

"Constable, can you go and organise a coroner's wagon to pick this unfortunate up? There's not much else to investigate at the moment."

"Yes sir, but…?" Collins said.

"I'm sure Mr. Holmes will be continuing the investigation from here on, but as far as the Yard is concerned, it's closed," Lestrade said.

He winked at Holmes, "Isn't that right?"

Holmes nodded.

"Yes. And to allay your fears Watson, I will indeed be looking further afield. There is a lot more to this, and it involves very powerful people, so care is needed at every turn."

He thought for a moment with a finger extended on his chin.

"I may have to consult with Mycroft."

He looked back at the open doorway into the receptionist area and smiled.

"I think, in Miss Madeline Fyord, we have a very intelligent and incredibly shrewd adversary. One that is not above hiring assassins whose code is one of complete loyalty, even unto death. One that is prepared to take on the most powerful men in the country without a drop of fear or doubt, and one that may involve us in many adventures to come. A truly formidable woman," he said.

I stared at the expression on Holmes's face. I shuddered a little as it was one, I hadn't seen since we first met a lady that he always referred to as "The Woman", a Miss Irene Adler.

The Adventure of the Sugar Merchant

It was early one cold autumn morning that Holmes and I were dragged into one of our strangest cases ever, an adventure involving Haitian voodoo and, of all things, zombies.

I was in the sitting room of 221b Baker Street on that cold morning, the fire ablaze to strip the chill from the air. I had finished off a wonderful breakfast provided by our landlady, Mrs. Hudson, and was relaxing with a second cup of coffee and the morning papers when I came across a late article, slotted in between the international affairs and finance sections. It detailed the account of a fire in a warehouse down in Canary Wharf. Many of the city's fire brigades were called, but their efforts were to no avail. The warehouse succumbed and crumbled under its own weight in the late hours of the previous evening. The article had been included so late that there was no more than the scarcest of details.

It was at that point that my erstwhile associate Sherlock Holmes arose from his slumber and sauntered into the sitting room, resplendent in a smoking jacket and looking quite awake for one who had arrived home in the early hours.

"Ah, Holmes," I said, "finally joining the living, I see."

Holmes smiled and helped himself to a coffee. "Obviously you are aware that I was home late."

I nodded.

"I was on the trail of someone that I had presumed to be involved in the affair of the disappearance of the eldest son of Lord Langley. Sadly, the trail went cold sometime in the wee hours of the morning. I returned home to re-invigorate myself for another long night ahead."

"A shame," I said. "Any other clews?"

He looked off into the distance through the window and absent-mindedly replied, "A few, but nothing substantial. The boy has simply disappeared from the face of the Earth."

He sipped his coffee and turned. Spying the open newspaper, he asked, "Anything exciting to relieve my mind of my disappointment?"

"A warehouse fire in Canary Wharf. Scant details. Could be arson. Could be an accident. Could be nothing really."

Holmes harrumphed, pursed his lips, sipped his coffee, and sat down in his easy chair. "Then I will cogitate further over the Lord's son." He placed the cup down, clasped his hands on his chest, and sat back, eyes closed. This was a natural meditative pose for him, or as I soon noticed, a comfortable pose where he could quickly drift off to sleep.

I smiled to myself and quietly finished the paper.

***

I snapped awake as the doorbell downstairs rang. I glanced across and saw that Holmes had left his chair and was nowhere to be seen. The clock on the mantel told me it had been an hour since I watched Holmes fall asleep.

I started to rise when Mrs. Hudson appeared at the doorway with Inspector Lestrade in tow. I shook the inspector's hand and thanked Mrs. Hudson. I also asked if she'd seen Holmes at all. She denied any knowledge of his leaving, so I hoped he was still on the premises. I led Lestrade into the sitting room, where it was a tad warmer. He shed his overcoat and gloves and placed them over the back of a chair.

"What brings you on this miserably cold day," I asked.

He looked a little embarrassed but went on with his request. "There's been a fire," he started.

"The warehouse?" I asked.

His eyes opened wide in surprise. I indicated the discarded paper on the settee. "There was a brief article in *The Times* this morning," I said, a wry smile on my lips.

"Ah, that would explain it," he said.

"What about the fire requires Holmes's involvement?" I queried, just as the man himself entered the room.

"Did I hear something about a fire?" he asked, "Not the warehouse fire that you mentioned, Watson?"

I nodded. "Seems to be."

Holmes indicated the seats and took his favourite chair. He sat back and looked at Lestrade across his steepled fingers. Lestrade sat and I made my way to the door to call down for coffee from Mrs.

Hudson. I returned just as Lestrade began and sat down myself, a little flush of excitement within me. I always hoped that Lestrade would bring some case that piqued Holmes's interest.

He began to relate the events of the previous night. "You're quite right, it was a warehouse fire – a big one, down in Canary Wharf. Arson as far as we can tell. It burnt the entire place to the ground. The brigade got it under control quickly. We were lucky it didn't spread any further."

"Any suspects," I asked.

"Just one."

"Oh, well do you need us to help track him down?"

"No," he said. "No need for that."

"Why?" I responded.

"He's dead. They found him in the fire."

"Oh."

Holmes unsteepled his fingers as a question formed on his lips. "What makes him so remarkable that you needed to come here?"

Lestrade wiped his brow with a handkerchief. "It's two things. The first is we know he was the arsonist because the flint box he used to light the fire was lying nearby."

"How very strange," I said.

"The other thing is, the Coroner reckons he's been dead for at least three days."

***

Lestrade's final comment urged the three of us to travel to the city morgue. There we found the coroner, Smithers, working away on the desiccated corpse of the poor unfortunate that had been found in the burnt-out warehouse. The poor man's hair had all but burnt off, and his face was blackened and slightly blistered. His hands were blackened, but the rest of his body was virtually untouched. From this observation, I assumed his clothing had taken the brunt of the flames.

The smell was horrendous, but Smithers had tried to temper it by placing small piles of rose petals around the room to release their fragrance. Holmes held any disgust at the smell in check and began to examine the corpse. He moved in a complete circle around the body, viewing it without touching. He hummed and murmured to himself, an indication that he was finding interesting observations.

"What's your opinion, Smithers?" he asked.

The coroner stood upright and thought for a moment. "He was in here three days ago," he said. "Same body, at the time he was in good condition, but now he's as you see him."

"How do you know it was the same body?" I asked.

Smithers moved around to the head. He pointed at a few wisps of unburned hair. "It's a male. The hair colour is the same. The height is the same. Weight is about the same, give or take what the fire took with it." He pointed at the corpse's mouth. A gold tooth gleamed dully from within the rictus grin. "Second upper pre-molar on the left has a gold cap. Not rare, but given the other features, it points to the same man." He nodded to a pile of scorched and burnt clothing on a nearby chair. "He's was also wearing the same clothing that he was when previously here."

Holmes was impressed. He peered at the gold tooth and the hair. "If this body was here three days ago, how did it get up and leave?"

Smithers turned to face him, his eyes glancing across to Lestrade who had obviously already asked this question. "He didn't. He wasn't here at the time. He was found down at the river's edge last Tuesday. The constables that brought him in said he was just another homeless person. His clothing said as much too. He was part of a group of men all found dead. Four in all. It was a very busy night."

He folded his arms and leaned against the autopsy table. "We've had recent instructions from the Health Ministry and Scotland Yard to process any vagrants as quickly as possible. The cold weather has started to run through the city's homeless population like the plague. Those in charge are worried that we don't have the resources to spend time on each homeless death."

His face grew grim. "I'm neither impressed nor in favour of such actions, but I have my orders." He waved a hand over the dead man. "I performed a cursory examination – heartbeat, temperature, and ligature resistance – to make sure I could pronounce him dead. He was then taken to a local funeral parlour in preparation for cremation. How he was taken from there is a matter for them to explain."

"And you have no reason to suspect the man was still alive?" I asked.

Smithers gave me a withering look. "Doctor, you as well as anybody should know that someone presenting with no heartbeat, a sixty-degree body temperature, and *post mortem* ligature stiffness shows all the hallmarks of a dead man."

Holmes smiled. "I think he has you there, Watson."

I kept my mouth shut at the rebuke.

Holmes continued. "I think your assessment is quite correct, Smithers, and I must commend you for it. The man is obviously dead now. Whether he was dead previously is down to your observations and, given we were not present, we must accept them." He moved around the corpse, his hand on his chin as he contemplated. "The main problem is that I believe this man to be Dominic Langley, the son of Lord Byron Langley, fourth Earl of Northbridge."

"Good God!" I exclaimed. "How do you come to that?" I knew that Holmes had been on the trail of Dominic Langley for a number of days and had been frustrated at every turn.

"Same height, weight, hair, and eye colour. The evidence of the gold tooth seals the deal. Plus . . . ." He moved over to the pile of charred clothing and leafed through the items. "Dominic Langley had a strange compunction to eschew the trappings of his wealth and station and to seek the excitement of the lower classes. He would often wear the clothes of the street and reside amongst the vagrants down at the river bank."

Holmes turned back to stare at the corpse. "Though there is something that troubles me," he said. "Do you object, Smithers, if I conduct my own examination?"

Smithers turned towards Lestrade who nodded. "Not if the inspector doesn't mind," he replied.

Holmes moved around the body and gently picked up its right hand. He bent down and sniffed it. His nose wrinkled at whatever odour wafted from the digits. He repeated with the left hand then placed both at the body's side. He then moved across to a nearby table covered with instruments and picked up two pairs of forceps, a pair of cotton swabs, and a small ceramic bowl. He moved back to the corpse's head and gently prized the man's jaw apart. A sickening cracking sound issued. I assumed it was the tendons stretching beyond their current capabilities.

Holmes placed a swab between the tines of the forceps and pushed it deep into the poor man's mouth. He moved it about then pulled it out again. He withdrew his magnifying glass and examined the swab. "Hmm," he murmured. "Most interesting."

I moved over and stared through the glass at the swab. It was relatively clean, except for the last vestiges of saliva from the corpse. "Clean?" I posited.

"Yes. I had half-expected it to have traces of ash and soot on it."

"A natural assumption if the man was still alive during the blaze," he said. "He would have inhaled the soot as he drew his final breaths."

"Exactly, but there is no evidence."

"So he *was* dead?"

"One would presume such, but I smelt traces of turpentine on his fingers – a powerful accelerant used recently in other cases of arson around the city."

"Perhaps the arsonist was sending a message. Trying to lay blame on the dead man."

"That is one line of thought. There's also this." Holmes pointed out some more observations to me. "Watson, if you would notice: The skin that was covered by clothing is virtually untouched. A little dirty, probably from the fire, but not burnt or scorched in any meaningful way."

He picked up the other swab, dipped it in some water, and ran it across the corpse's cheek. It left a bright area of unblemished skin. "The skin on the man's face is likewise relatively untouched by the fire. There is a little blistering on his scalp where, I assume, burning embers settled to ignite some of his hair, but the rest was only discoloured by the falling ash." He picked up the corpse's right hand and examined the fingertips, murmuring to himself as well.

"What does it all mean?" I asked.

"His fingertips are damaged and scorched, as well as smelling of turpentine, but the rest of him is relatively unharmed. In my opinion, this man, Dominic Langley, simply set fire to part of the warehouse, then lay down in a clear area of the floor and awaited his fate."

I was taken aback. "But he was supposedly dead. How, and why, would anybody in their right mind do such a thing?"

"That is what we need to find out. It is sad to think that young Langley died in this way, and I feel that there is something more to his fate. He was a healthy young man, not one prone to die of exposure, so why did he present as dead in the first place? And then why was his body stolen from the crematory, if indeed he didn't walk out on his own? Then, how did he end up in the middle of a burning warehouse? I am perplexed, and these questions pose the next part of the mystery that we shall address," he finished.

***

The carriage dropped Holmes, Lestrade, and me outside of a wonderfully appointed four-storey Georgian mansion nestled in a quiet street near Grosvenor Square in Mayfair. Holmes made his way to the front door while I paid the cabbie. Lestrade looked a little out of sorts at the opulence of the area. I admit I felt a little awkward as well.

A well-dressed butler in full formal dress answered. Holmes murmured something that I failed to hear, and we were shown into the immaculately presented main foyer where the man took our hats and coats. He showed us into a nearby reception room to wait until our introductions were made to the master of the house. I moved around the room, relishing the richness of the furnishings and decorations.

"Remarkable," said Holmes looking over my shoulder, "how much wealth a simple thing as sugar can produce, isn't it?"

"What do you mean?"

"Lord Byron Langley is the single largest importer of sugar to the United Kingdom. His father, the third Earl of Northbridge, was ambassador to Jamaica during Lord Byron's childhood. He grew up amongst the rich West Indian culture and decided to stay once his father returned to England. He married Myra, a missionary's daughter, who sadly died during the birth of Dominic Langley."

"How sad," I remarked.

"Yes. Dominic was sent to England to be educated while Lord Byron grew the industry that his grandfather had bought into, and expanded it to include the importation of sugar to the United Kingdom. He returned only a couple of years ago. My understanding is that was to be with his son during his final years of college, with the intent that Dominic would eventually take over the business. All this will be a bit of a shock to him, I imagine," he added.

As I was about to ask further questions, the butler returned and spoke. "Lord Byron will see you now. If you would follow me."

All three of us duly followed and were let into an ornately furnished study, with bookshelves lining all four walls and a massive oak desk in the centre. Lord Byron was a rather tall and rotund man, with a large beard and the look of someone that enjoyed life to the fullest. He walked around his desk and took Holmes's hand in both of his own.

"Mr. Holmes!" he said. "Welcome, welcome," He turned towards Lestrade and me. "And these gentlemen would be?"

Holmes introduced the both of us, then his face turned grave. "I suggest you take a seat, Lord Byron," he said. "I do not bring pleasant news."

Lord Byron's face dropped, a touch of fear flashed across his visage. "It's Dominic, isn't it?" he asked as he took a seat.

Holmes nodded. "Yes, I'm afraid it is," he said. "Very early this morning, your son was found in the remains of a burnt-out warehouse. I'm afraid that he had passed."

Lord Byron's face turned to shock and dismay. "Oh, my," he said. "How?"

"We are unsure at this stage, but it appears to be smoke inhalation from the fire."

Lord Byron looked off into the distance for a moment and murmured to himself. "Silly boy," he murmured. "What have you been up to?"

"I beg your pardon, sir," Holmes asked. "I didn't quite catch the question."

Lord Byron looked up in surprise. "Sorry. Nothing. Just thinking out loud. Do you have any clews as to why he was there?"

"None. I was hoping you might know, but didn't want to press, as I assumed the news would be upsetting enough for you."

Lord Byron took a deep breath to calm himself. He let it out in a relaxed and controlled way before speaking. "I won't lie. It is distressing, though part of me believed that Dominic's wild behaviour might result in such an eventuality." He stood up and strode around the room, waving his arms as he spoke. "I gave him everything. The best schools. The riches of Croesus. He has never wanted for anything, but he preferred to turn his back on all that at times to live with the down-and-outs in the slums. To learn what it was like to have naught, he would tell me."

He looked out a side window for a moment, gathering his thoughts. "I had assumed it would be in one of these slums that he would meet his end. Was it at the waterfront down Southwark way?" he said, turning back to face us and pressing up against the desk.

"No," Holmes said. "Actually, it was a warehouse in Canary Wharf."

Lord Byron's eyes lit up. "Where in Canary Wharf, exactly?"

Lestrade pulled out a small pad of paper. "20 Bank Street, on the South Dock."

Lord Byron's face dropped in shock. He sat heavily in his seat, deflated as if he had been struck in the face.

Holmes stood and moved to the desk. "Lord Byron?" he asked. "Is something wrong?"

"That's *my* warehouse," he replied.

***

Lord Byron insisted on joining our little excursion to his destroyed warehouse, explaining that he would have already gone there sooner, except that he was awaiting word about his son. He ordered his own carriage brought around, and within several minutes his driver had us wending our way through the centre of London, Whitechapel, Shadwell, and finally Canary Wharf. The driver pulled up before the awful sight of the devastated warehouse. We exited the cab and Lord Byron's face fell in a shock greater than the news of the death of his son.

The warehouse was beyond salvage. Three sides had been gutted, the wooden walls burnt to the ground. Only the fourth wall, made primarily of red brick, had survived. The contents, large bales filled with refined sugar, had been reduced to large puddles of thick, black sludge. The location of Dominic's body was evident from the lighter-coloured patch in the middle of the scorched cobbled floor. Holmes went straight towards it and began examining the area.

The remains of a wooden fire-lighting kit lay nearby. He bent down and ran a finger over the stones next to it and rubbed two fingers together. He scanned the rest of the area and stood as something in the far corner piqued his interest. He walked to the corner and bent down again. A small lumpy object lay in the soot. Holmes picked it up to examine it. He sniffed, and then pulled away in disgust.

"Something, Holmes?" I asked.

"I think I've found the source of the blaze," he said holding up the object. It appeared to be glass or ceramic but was blackened by the fire. "This was once a small glass vessel and held turpentine. Whoever set the fire, and sadly I believe it to have been Dominic, lit it near this part of the wall. As the liquid burned and became hotter, the surrounding wall ignited and the glass eventually melted. The rest is fairly obvious." He stood and wiped his hands on a handkerchief pulled from his coat pocket.

Lord Byron was flummoxed. He moved across, peering around the warehouse as he did. "Mr. Holmes, you said that you think Dominic lit this fire."

Holmes nodded.

"But why? Why would he do this? This was part of his legacy."

Holmes nodded again. "I must admit, Lord Byron, that I am at a loss as to the reason behind his possible actions. You mentioned he eschewed the high life to spend time with the lower levels of society. Perhaps that clouded his mind and led to this. He may have also fallen in with the wrong crowd, one that sees you as an enemy of society and convinced him to act in this way. At this stage, I have no evidence, and no clews, so I have only conjecture."

Lord Byron dropped his head in defeat. He made his way back to the carriage, turning back before entering. "I thank you for your service, Mr. Holmes. Please forward a letter of request to my accountant with your fee attached. You did as asked and found my son. His state of being was not part of the bargain. I will retire back to my residence for now and make the arrangements for his burial. Again, I thank you."

I could tell that he was on the verge of a breakdown and understood fully. In one fell swoop, he had not only lost his son but had found out that he had betrayed him and destroyed one of his greatest assets.

Holmes walked quickly to the carriage and placed a hand on Lord Byron's shoulder. "I will find out the reason, your Lordship. Until then, I would not even consider any recompense. There is something here that does not make sense, so I am just as invested in finding the solution as you are. I promise I will not let you, or the memory of your son, down."

Lord Byron patted Holmes's hand and nodded. "Thank you, sir. You are a true gentleman."

I noticed his Lordship stare off into the distance over Holmes's right shoulder for a moment before he turned and boarded the carriage. A moment later, with a snap of the reigns, the driver led them away from the desolation.

Holmes watched them go, and then he turned back and walked towards Lestrade and me. I was about to ask him whether he had noticed the Lord's last action, but he swept past the both of us and continued on in the direction of Lord Byron's gaze. I followed in his wake, intrigued as always.

On the far side of the warehouse, in a corner near the brick wall, was a large set of crates. They were scorched, but relatively unscathed from the fire. The contents not so much, however. They held a large collection of small glass vials with cork stoppers. The majority had cracked from the heat and spilled their contents, which had vaporised in the heat. Holmes reached out and moved the top crate aside, spilling a mass of broken glass and residual liquid. I noticed immediately a strong sweet odour wafting up from the spilt fluid.

Holmes found that the contents of the crate below were in much better condition and extracted an unmarked vial. He held it up to the light and showed that it contained a pale, clear yellow liquid. He popped the cork and sniffed at the contents.

"Any idea, Holmes?"

"Yes, Watson, some idea. It's certainly not sugar, that's for sure." He placed the vial into a pocket inside his coat and turned away from the crates, a look of excitement had crossed his face. "I will need to return to Baker Street. I have a long night ahead."

***

That evening I was called out on a late emergency and didn't return until the wee hours of the morning. I went straight to bed and awoke later that day. Still slightly bleary-eyed, I stumbled into the sitting room to find Holmes busily working away at some chemistry experiment. Coloured liquids boiled in beakers and piped up through a series of distillation tubes.

I stepped closer and spied a beaker of fresh blood sitting on the end of the table. "I'm sure you could ask Mrs. Hudson to fix you something more suited to sustaining yourself," I said pointing at it.

Holmes looked at the beaker and then at me. A wry smile came to his face. "How very droll, Watson," he said, "but regardless of what you think, I'm not a vampire. That is our young Dominic Langley's blood. I stopped by the morgue early this morning and convinced Smithers to withdraw some for me. I believe it may contain some vital answers."

"Have you managed to determine what the yellow, fragrant liquid is?"

He stopped. A look of excitement came across his face. He motioned to the bench and a large volume on botany. I read the entry aloud:

"Chrysopogon zizanioides, *or common* vetiver. *A long-stemmed grass that produces a fragrant oil when crushed in quantity.*"

"Yes," said Holmes. "It is used widely in perfumes and cosmetics. The liquid we found is the oil of the plant. On the current market, a single vial of one fluid ounce would be worth the same as about ten tons of sugar."

"A very valuable commodity, then," I said. "I thought that Lord Byron was purely an importer of sugar."

Holmes smiled. "Like any good entrepreneur, he has a diverse range of investments and means to derive profit. It seems, as my research has yielded, that two years ago, Lord Byron bought out a vetiver plantation and refining plant in the southwestern region of Haiti."

"Haiti?" I asked.

"Yes. It makes sense. The vetiver can be extracted, packaged, and shipped quite simply and quickly from Haiti to Lord Byron's sugar refining factory in Jamaica, and from there to be transported to the United Kingdom or Europe along with the sugar."

"All right, a good investment then. What of it?"

He held up the vial with the remains of the liquid inside. "At this stage, not much, but given Lord Byron's distant look in its direction yesterday, I think this means a great deal to him."

"What of the blood, then?"

Holmes placed the vial down and put on some thick leather gloves. He picked up a beaker full of a cloudy yellow liquid that had been heating over a Bunsen burner. He placed it down on an asbestos mat and, pulling off the gloves, withdrew a small dropper from a glass bottle. "Let's hope this works," he said, displaying the huge grin on his face that I had seen so often when some experiment had piqued his fascination for obscure chemistry.

He gently squeezed the dispenser's bulb and two drops of a transparent liquid fell into the beaker. The result was immediate. The cloudy liquid went completely clear. "Fascinating."

I leaned in closer to the beaker. He placed a hand on my chest. "Probably not a good idea, Watson. Best to stay a little back."

I stood up and moved back. Holmes wasn't usually the most careful man during his chemistry experiments, so anything that had him cautious was obviously far more dangerous than desired.

"What is it, Holmes?" I asked.

"*Tetrodotoxin*," he replied. "Rather quite deadly."

I was shocked. This was even more reckless than normal for Holmes. "Why in blue blazes are you messing around with that?"

The poison was a highly potent neurotoxin, occurring naturally in several deadly species of fish. It would attack the central nervous system and paralyse any person or animal that came in contact with it, within moments. "I found it in young Dominic Langley's blood."

"Is that what killed him?"

"It's incredibly potent. A tiny amount can disable, and larger amounts can kill. I can't reliably tell what concentration he had in his body, but there's a good chance it was the cause of death."

"Good Lord!" I said.

"And that's not all, Watson. I also found that our Dominic had a large dose of a hallucinogenic drug or a deliriant in his bloodstream. I haven't isolated it as yet, but it seems to be akin to that extracted from the common Devil's Trumpet, or datura plant."

"Strange," I said. "Where would that have come from?"

"Well, funny enough, the datura plant is quite common across Central America and the West Indies."

"Haiti?"

"Possibly."

Holmes paused in thought for a moment, his hand beneath his chin, his forefinger braced against this cheek. Finally, he moved towards his room. "I believe," said Holmes, "that we need to visit the last known location for young Dominic – the riverfront."

***

A hansom dropped us off on the high street in Shadwell. I paid the driver, who had eyed us with suspicion from the moment he had picked us up. I couldn't blame him really. Holmes had delved into his extensive collection of costumes and was dressed in the manner of a common street beggar, complete with makeup.

I didn't have the same level of costumery available to me. I sported my oldest pair of pants, complete with several small tears, a stained shirt and vest, plus my oldest coat. I found some dust, a remarkable feat given Mrs. Hudson's predilection for cleanliness, and mussed up the shoulders a little. I located an old pair of boots and dirtied them up in a small mud puddle on Baker Street.

As we made our way towards the riverbank, I felt very self-conscious, but Holmes took it in his stride. He slumped his shoulders to affect the caricature of an elderly street denizen. I tried to follow suit but felt even more uncomfortable. We reached a small alleyway that led to the river and my hackles were raised straight away. It felt very much like a perfect place for an ambush, and soon enough shadows appeared at both ends of the lane.

A tall man shuffled towards us. The light filtering through showed me his scarred face and a sneer full of blackened teeth. "What do we have here?" he asked. "If you want to use this pathway, you have to pay the tax."

I began to speak, but Holmes shut me up. "I'm looking for Snivellin' Pete," he said in his best East End accent.

"Who?" the man returned.

"Snivellin' Pete. 'E controls this area, I'm told. An 'e don't like it when others try to take over."

The man's face grew red with anger. He stepped forward, grabbed Holmes by the shirt front, and pushed him against the wall. "I'm in charge now," he said. "This Snivelling Pete is gone. Dead."

I went to move, but Holmes was much quicker. He grabbed the man's arms, twisted to one side, stepped forward, and slammed the taller man to the ground. All but one of the other shadows disappeared.

Holmes stared down at the man and spoke in his normal voice. "Are you telling me that Snivelling Pete is dead? How would you know that?" he asked.

The man stared up with incredulous eyes. It was obvious he hadn't been bested in this way for quite a while.

"I . . . I . . . ." he stammered.

A quieter voice piped up from behind us. "Is that you, Mr. 'Olmes?"

I turned and saw a diminutive little man. He stared wide-eyed in disbelief. Holmes looked up and smiled. "Tommy the Rat, isn't it?"

"Yes, Mr. 'Olmes, yes. I know what 'appened to Pete, I does."

Holmes looked down at the man on the ground. "If I were you, I'd find another area of the river to command, or else I might be forced to come back another day. Are we clear?"

The taller man, his eyes still wide in fear, nodded. Without looking back, Holmes stepped away and the man scampered to his feet and disappeared around the corner. Holmes turned to Tommy. "Let's get out of here in case he decides to disobey my advice."

***

We retired to The White Swan, two streets over, where our clothing and appearance fit, and we knew we were on neutral ground in case of any reprisals. It turned out that Tommy the Rat was a long-time cohort of Snivelling Pete, whom Holmes confessed was both the local tough who controlled this part of Shadwell, and, by chance, was also a member of the Baker Street Irregulars. Holmes had hoped to catch up with him to see if he had any information about Dominic Langley's demise. He had co-opted Pete into keeping an eye out for Langley two weeks earlier.

I brought three pints of local ale back to the table. Tommy took his and downed half of it without taking a breath. I sat, mildly amused, and took a draw from my own. Holmes waited until Tommy paused before asking him about Pete's disappearance. "You mentioned that you knew what happened to Snivelling Pete."

"That I do, Mr. 'Olmes, that I do," he said taking another sip of beer.

"Well?" I asked, growing a little impatient.

"Oh, yes, sorry. Is good beer this," he said. "It all happened about three nights ago. We was just 'angin' around down at the bank. There'd been a rumour of some roughs coming down from Whitby and trying to muscle into Pete's territory. 'E was going over a plan to find them and teach 'em a lesson." He stopped and took another sip of beer.

"Was there a young man in your group that didn't quite fit?" Holmes asked.

"The toff?" Tommy countered.

"I assume, yes," Holmes answered.

"Yeah. Pete 'ad brought 'im along a week before. Said 'e would be useful to us. I didn't like 'im one bit. Seemed a bit soft if you ask me."

"Fair call. What happened to Pete and the toff?"

"Right. Well, on that night, we was making plans and getting ready for a bit of a rumble, if it came to that, an then it all goes to 'ell."

"How?"

“Pete’s standing there, talking away, ‘is ‘and goes to ‘is neck and ‘e collapses. Pretty soon the other three, including the toff do the same.”

“How is it that you escaped?”

“I was in the shadows, like always. I don’t like the spotlight, me. Anyways, I waits for a bit then creeps out to check on ‘em. I couldn’t find no breath. They was dead as doornails. I got outta there as quick as like. Next day I comes back and they’s gone. Don’t know if the plods got ‘em or what.”

“You didn’t take long to find another gang to run with,” I said.

“It’s a dog-eat-dog world out there. Man’s got to do what a man’s got to do.”

“Quite so,” said Holmes.

***

The next morning, I was awakened by Holmes rapping on the door to my bedroom. “Come, Watson,” he said. “Time is wasting. We have far to go today.”

Moments later I shuffled down to the sitting room, dressed and ready for the day. Holmes was already at the door, waiting to depart. My stomach rumbled, but I spied a basket of fresh scones that Mrs. Hudson had made on Holmes’s orders. I loaded some into a tea towel and hurried after him. "What in blazes is the rush?” I asked as we stepped into a waiting hansom.

“Our first stop,” he said, “will be at the funeral parlour, the use of which has been seconded by the coroner. I wish to ask the proprietor some questions, and your presence will help in two areas: One to provide a numerical advantage, and two because of your medical knowledge.”

I munched on a scone, spilling crumbs across my front, and pondered his words. I hated to admit it, but on a number of occasions Holmes’s medical knowledge had outshone my own, but I hoped for my own sake that I could help.

We stopped outside of a building with “*Richard’s Funeral Parlour*” emblazoned above the door. I brushed a good number of scone crumbs to the street and shook out the flour dust from the tea towel before pocketing it. I made a mental note to return it to Mrs. Hudson when we arrived home.

Meanwhile, Holmes was examining a small window to the side of the double doors. There was a crack extending across the length of it. As I joined him, he reached out towards the doors and turned the handles. Even at this early hour, the business was open. We let ourselves into a small but well-adorned reception area. A sideboard held a jug of water and several glasses. I shrugged off my manners and headed for the water. The three scones that I had ingested had left my mouth rather dry.

As I drank, I watched Holmes examine the door through which we had just entered. I was about to ask why when a rather tall and gaunt man appeared in a doorway leading to a service room. He had a surprised but inquisitive look on his face.

"Gentlemen, I am Mr. Richard," he said, "the owner of this establishment. My condolences to you at this time."

Holmes smiled. "Oh, that won't be necessary. We aren't customers. My name is Sherlock Holmes, and this is my associate, Dr. John Watson. I am a consulting detective in the employ of Lord Byron Langley. We merely have some questions regarding a recent visitor to your establishment."

Richard's face changed slightly to suspicion. "Yes?"

"We are under the impression that you have been receiving the bodies of unidentified street denizens who have succumbed to the cold during this unseasonal weather. One such victim arrived three days ago, but we believe he may have not been disposed of properly and was taken away once more."

Mr. Richard look surprised at that last statement. "I assure you, all unfortunates that arrive here are accounted for on receipt, through to their final destination."

"In fact, it was only three nights ago," Holmes added. "The person in whom we are interested arrived at the city morgue with three others. They were quickly dispatched to your establishment."

"We tend to prepare the victims very quickly," said Richard. "He must have been cremated later that day. I could check the files if you like."

He turned to leave, but Holmes stopped him. "That won't be necessary, as we know that the man we are interested in was not cremated. He turned up at the city morgue again, yesterday morning."

Mr. Richard turned, a shocked look on his face. "Impossible. A theft of a body from this establishment has never happened. Not in the hundred years that my family has been running it."

"And I believe that to be the case. However, some evidence may contradict your assertion. If I may be so bold, where were you, exactly, last Tuesday evening?"

Without thought, Richard's hand rose to a small bandage on his neck as he thought up an answer. "I was here," he said. "All night."

"I believe you," said Holmes.

"What?" I asked.

"Quite so, Watson. I believe that Mr. Richard is telling the truth. He was here all night last Thursday. In body, but perhaps not in spirit."

"I don't follow," said Mr. Richard.

"That wound on your neck," questioned Holmes. "Have you had it since Tuesday evening?"

Richard was shocked. He nodded dumbly.

"Perhaps, you were leaving last week and felt a sharp pain in your neck? The last thing you probably remember before waking up the next morning?"

He nodded.

"How?"

"The pane of glass outside the main doors is cracked," he said. "I propose that you stumbled, put your hand out to brace yourself, and broke the glass." Richard raised his right hand. A small cut was visible on the edge of his hand.

"I believe that you were actually attacked as you left," Holmes said. "Where did you wake up?"

"In here," Richards replied, "but I have no idea how. I had locked the doors."

"And the lock," said Holmes, "as I observed earlier, has been broken, but from the inside."

Richard again nodded in agreement.

“From the inside?” I asked.

"Yes," Holmes said.

“By whom?” I was feeling very frustrated.

“Possibly by Dominic Langley. Possibly by Snivelling Pete. Possibly by one of the bodies brought here,” said Holmes.

“But,” I countered, “but, they were dead.”

“And that is the pertinent fact, isn’t it?”

***

That afternoon, we bought tickets and departed Paddington on the train to Windsor. Holmes had explained that we had an appointment at Lord Byron Langley’s country residence. He had gone there to prepare for Dominic’s funeral. I felt that there was something that Lord Byron was keeping from us. Holmes was of the same opinion, although I believed that he knew more than he was letting on. I hoped that he did. The whole question about corpses walking out of funeral homes was causing my doctor’s brain to have palpitations.

We disembarked and found a hansom to take us out to Dorney Court, a beautifully presented Tudor house about seven miles from Windsor Station. Holmes remarked that Lord Byron had purchased the manor house before he returned from Jamaica.

“I’m flabbergasted,” I said. “I didn’t think that the importation of sugar could be so lucrative.”

“I think it might be that, and also the other investments that Lord Byron has made over the years – especially the one located in Haiti.”

“Haiti?” I asked. “There’s that country again. You mentioned Haiti the other day. What about it?”

Holmes smiled. “This is one of the reasons we need to meet with Lord Byron again.”

We stepped out of the hansom, crunching gravel underfoot as we made our way to the main doors. I looked up as we walked and noticed the sun setting in the west. The night was going to be clear and I presumed very cold. I was glad I’d worn one of my thickest coats. The same butler met our knocking and, after taking our coats and hats, showed us the way to Lord Byron’s study.

The sugar merchant was seated behind an enormous carved oak desk with a pile of paperwork to one side. The desk sat in front of a large window that showed the last vestiges of light as the evening intruded onto the day. Lord Byron's face was grave. I put it down to the arrangements he was undertaking to bury his son. We took seats before his desk and I sat back in the comfortable folds of the well-padded chair. Holmes looked at Lord Byron through his steepled fingers.

"Again," Holmes said, "we are very sorry to intrude on you in your time of grief, but we have come across some very troubling clews and I believe that I need more information from you before I can make sense of everything that has happened."

"Anything at my disposal is yours," said the Lord as he leaned forward, "I just wish to bring the culprits for my son's demise to justice."

"Thank you. Many of the avenues of our inquiry seem to stem from the small Caribbean nation of Haiti."

At the mention of that country, Lord Byron stiffened. Holmes stood and moved across to a nearby cabinet displaying a variety of artefacts. He picked out one and studied it as he began to speak. It seemed to be a bottle made of translucent glass with a small cork stopper. It seemed old, and an inner feeling intruded on my consciousness that urged Holmes to put it back lest it be dropped and broken.

"Your son was in fact killed by a poison called *Tetrodotoxin* – a very rare chemical in this country, but one which is extracted from the common pufferfish found across the world – including the waters of the Caribbean. Another substance was found in his bloodstream that also seemed very curious, a hallucinogen or deliriant derived from the datura plant, or what you may know from your previous homeland as The Devil's Trumpet. Incredibly rare in England, and only a few specimens exist within the hothouse of the botanical gardens in London. The presence of the datura deliriant once again brings up the name of that West Indian country, Haiti. The plant occurs in abundance on the entire island."

"How would my son come into contact with such chemicals here in Britain?" Lord Byron asked.

Holmes turned and smiled at him. "Indeed. A very valid question that I have been pondering for some time."

He uncorked the little bottle and brought it up to his nose. Lord Byron's eyes grew wide. Holmes took the bottle away and studied it. "This is a very old artefact," he said as he turned to look back at Lord Byron. "I place it as mid-eighteenth century, by the looks of it. A perfume bottle I would say, possibly used by a lady of some standing. Perhaps it was one of your ancestors. Your mother, or even your grandmother perhaps? Your grandparents were residents of Jamaica well before your father became the High Commissioner. Isn't that right?"

"Yes. Yes. That is right. My family resided in Jamaica for well over a hundred years. We established the sugar plantations in the central hinterlands at that time and have been importing sugar to Britain and Europe since. How does that have anything to do with all this?"

Holmes put the bottle back then turned and moved closer to the desk. "It's not the sugar that is the primary matter in this case. It's the perfume."

Now I was confused, but then Holmes brought out the glass vial he had found at the warehouse. He held it up. Lord Byron's face went pale.

"You recently procured a plantation on the island of Haiti, did you not?" Holmes asked. "Just before you returned to England."

"Yes," Lord Byron replied. "What of it?"

"The plantation," he said, "grows a special type of grass called *Chrysopogon zizanioides*, commonly called *vetiver*. The plant's oil can be extracted and used in perfumes. From what I understand, the value of the oil is over one hundred times that of sugar by weight. For someone in the export business, this would have been worth its weight in gold. I also understand that in a short time, you have set up a very lucrative arrangement with Yardley and Statham here in London and *Houbigant Parfum* in Paris."

Lord Byron sat staring at Holmes. His face had become impassive as he listened to Holmes explain. "As you said, I'm a businessman. It was a great opportunity, so I jumped at the chance."

Holmes moved a step forward and placed his hands on the edge of the desk. His imposing height allowed him to stare down into Lord Byron's eyes with an intensity that I had always found quite disturbing. "How great was the opportunity?" he asked. "How far were you willing to go to complete the deal?"

Holmes let the question hang. The room became suddenly very quiet. The evening outside was incredibly still with no hint of wind or breeze.

Lord Byron finally broke eye contact with Holmes. He rose unsteadily to his feet and turned away to look through the window, out at the darkening night. "I only did it to ensure the future of my business and safeguard my legacy for Dominic," he said turning back to face Holmes, "The damned Government set up the British Sugar Company four years ago. They grow beets of all things and extract the sugar that way. It was becoming cheaper than importing the real thing. I had to find a way of expanding my operations. When I became aware of the plantation on Haiti, I acted on it."

"But something went wrong, didn't it?" asked Holmes.

Lord Byron's face went grim. "Yes. The local farmers weren't willing to sell. They revered the vetiver plants for some reason. They only farmed what they needed. Had no concept of industrial farming. Something about their heathen religion. I employed local militia to take over and expand the plantations. I offered recompense to the local chieftains, but there was trouble," he said as he turned back to look out the window letting the last statement hang. His head dropped as he fought his conscience.

"Trouble?" I prompted.

He peered back then dropped his eyes. Even a man this resolute in his station in life was disturbed by what he was about to say. "The militia that I employed overplayed their hand," he explained. "They virtually wiped out a local town. Killed the chieftains and members of the council. Any men that took up arms were killed."

He turned back to us. Tears had formed and run down his cheeks. He was truly distressed by the events undertaken in his name. "By the time I found out, it was too late," he said, "I had travelled to the plantation and made what restitution I could with the locals. I dismissed the militia and employed as many of the townsfolk that would work for me. I tried – honestly I did – but they had lost all hope. Their men were dead. Their women left as widows, their children orphans. I returned to Jamaica and started preparations to leave. My heart wasn't in it anymore. I left a manager to continue the operation, but I decided it was time to retire. I vowed to bring Dominic in to take over."

He was weeping profusely by now. "I was almost too late. One night they attacked."

"Who?" Holmes asked.

"*Zombies!*" Lord Byron whispered his face now a wasteland of fear and trepidation.

"Zombies?" I blurted out in disbelief, "Dead people? Re-animated?"

He nodded slowly. "Yes. The townsfolk on Haiti had employed a *caplata*. A dark witch of the Voodoo religion. Capable of raising the dead to do her bidding. That last night, before I set sail, the plantation was attacked. My staff were slaughtered where they stood. My only saving grace was that I was in Kingston awaiting the ship that brought me back to London. I found out after I arrived. That was two years ago. I haven't returned."

He pulled out a handkerchief and blotted the tears from his eyes. A strange resolve seemed to come over him. I'm still not sure if it was an acceptance of fate or a shimmer of courage to face the unknown. He stood to his full height and spoke one last time.

"I feel that she's here," he said. "I now believe that she killed my son, turned him into a zombie and bade him to set fire to the warehouse. I know that I cannot fight her plague of dead men, but I will not go down meekly. I ran before, but now I must face my accuser and plead my case."

I was impressed but confused at his stance. He was, of course, guilty of the deaths of many people, if not by his word at least by his deed.

Suddenly, Lord Byron's guilt was no longer a factor in this case. I started to form a question on my lips when all hell broke loose, and it was forever forgotten in the maelstrom that followed.

A scream issued from deep in the house. All heads turned towards the cry. The sound of glass breaking made Holmes and me turn back to face the sugar merchant.

Several panes on the window behind him imploded inwards. Pairs of arms reached in through the broken glass. My doctor's mind noticed the long gashes form down their length as the jagged glass shards bit deep into their flesh. Blood flowed as they reached for Lord Byron. He screamed as he was grabbed by many hands and wrenched off his feet.

I remarked in my mind's eye that the owners of the arms were incredibly strong, as Lord Byron was by no means a small man. He was dragged bodily through the broken window and disappeared, leaving only a scream hanging in the tumult.

I sprang to my feet, ready to run to Lord Byron's aid. Holmes had already vaulted the desk and was peering into the gloom beyond the window.

"What in blazes happened?" escaped my lips as I ran. Holmes continued to peer into the dark grounds outside.

"Zombies, it seems, Watson," he said, matter-of-factly.

"What?" I asked.

Before he could answer, the door into the study burst open. We both turned.

Standing in the doorway was a black woman. She wore richly coloured robes and had strange designs painted across her face in light colours. She stepped into the room and was followed by two slack-jawed men. They stood well over six feet tall, their arms hung by their sides and their eyes were glazed and unable to focus.

As I turned to look at Holmes, something struck my neck. It stung like an insect bite. I raised my hand and pulled the offending item from my throat. It was a small feathered dart.

My mind became clouded, my vision blurred. I managed to turn and stare at the woman once more. She held a long hollow tube to her mouth. A small sound of expelled air followed. Something flew past my face and the tiny grunt I heard could only have been Holmes.

Darkness began to cover my eyes. I fought to maintain control, but gravity won, and I fell to my knees. The wooden floor was the last thing that I saw before the shadows drew a close to my consciousness.

***

My eyes blinked open and drew focus on a white tiled ceiling. I lay for a moment gathering my thoughts and trying to determine where I was when a figure passed into my view. He wore a blood-stained white coat and mask and held a pair of forceps in one hand and a scalpel in the other. As the scalpel hand came closer, I thrust up my right hand up and stopped its descent.

He yelped and jumped back slightly. "Good Lord! Dr. Watson – You're alive!" he said, dragging the mask from his face.

I immediately recognised Smithers. I tried to sit up. Smithers aided me, and I realised I was sitting on an autopsy table in the morgue.

I looked around and saw Holmes lying on the table next to me. Thankfully he hadn't been the object of Smithers's occupation yet. The table beyond held a larger body, covered in a blood-soaked sheet.

Smithers noticed where I was looking.

"Lord Byron Langley," he said. "The constables said he was mauled by a wild animal or . . . something. I'm still trying to determine by what."

"Holmes?" I managed to croak.

"Dead. Like you – " he said, before rushing over to where Holmes lay.

He bent down and listened. He then stood and lightly slapped Holmes on the cheeks. A harder slap brought a groan from the recumbent form of my associate. His eyes flickered and opened. Within moments he sat up and looked around. The fog lifting quickly from his drugged mind. He focused on me and a wry smile came to his face.

"We survived," he said. "She mustn't have wanted us to join her zombie army."

"What?" Smithers and I both asked.

"The *caplata*," said Holmes. I sat staring at him with a confused expression.

"The *caplata*. The black woman. A female voodoo witch hired by the townsfolk in Haiti. It all makes sense now."

I didn't share his feeling of completion. "In what way?"

He took a deep breath, closed his eyes for a moment then continued. "Dominic Langley was hunted down and turned into a zombie by a voodoo priestess. Under the influence of *datari*, she was able to coerce him into lighting a fire in Lord Byron's warehouse. Not only did she want him dead, but she wanted to destroy his life as well. Very vindictive, but I suppose it sent a message. In the end, she led her zombies to Lord Byron's estate and finished what she had been employed to do."

I was still confused but had to know. "What about us?"

He smiled. "We were poisoned with *tetrodotoxin*. Not enough to kill, just enough to disable us. We were lucky. Any more poison and Smithers here would have needed to conduct real autopsies. As it is, we survive to fight another day."

"The zombies?" I asked, "What about the zombies?"

"Ah, similar to us, I suppose," he said, looking around the morgue. "The *caplata* poisons them with enough to disable and incapacitate. They appear to be dead but are in reality alive. She then administers the *datari* and bends their will to do her bidding. I wouldn't be surprised if Smithers receives several more clients over the next couple of days as the zombies are found. They will either recover or to cover her tracks, the *caplata* will probably administer more poison to finish the job."

I contemplated what Holmes had said, but one question remained. "Dominic Langley," I said. "He was dead *before* he entered the warehouse. You established that as there was no soot in his throat."

"Yes?"

"So . . . how did he set fire to the place?"

Holmes stared at me blankly as his mind tried to determine the answer.

The Adventure of the Disappearing Debutante

It was late spring in 1882 when a knock at the front door of 221b Baker Street presented my good friend Sherlock Holmes with an unexpected opportunity.

The caller was a simple messenger boy who delivered an expensively embossed invitation to Holmes on behalf of his old university friend, Roderick St. John-Smythe. I was the one to answer the door, partly to relieve our landlady, Mrs. Hudson, of the chore, and also because of a slight case of boredom.

I brought the envelope to Holmes, who proceeded to withdraw the card within, accompanied by a single-page handwritten letter. He began to smile a little as he read to himself, before explaining the details to me.

"It's from Roderick. It seems that we have been asked to attend a coming-out ceremony."

I was a little surprised, as it didn't seem the type of occasion in which Roderick or Holmes would have shown an interest.

"Any idea why?"

"No. There's no mention of a reason. I believe that Roderick may be trying to introduce me into polite society, or perhaps to pair us up with young ladies to take us away from this bachelor life of ours."

"That may be worthwhile then," I said. "I don't intend to stay single all my life."

"And good for you, Watson. I myself would need to meet someone extremely special before I shrug off my bachelor ways."

"Indeed," I answered with as healthy a dose of cynicism as one word could allow.

"Regardless of the bevy of young ladies on display, I believe that the event may prove useful from another front altogether."

"Such as?"

"There will no doubt be many affluent gentlemen at this event. Some there to display their eligible daughters, others there to examine the goods on offer."

I was a little put out by Holmes's graphic description of such a time-honoured event as a debutante ball.

"That's a little harsh, isn't it?"

He noticed my expression and smiled.

"I do apologise, but I find these sorts of evenings little more than a few steps above a slave auction in medieval Arabia. But I'll still go. It may be amusing. It may even be beneficial. I hope to make the acquaintance of some of the gentlemen there and, when next they are in need of services such as I can provide," he finished, "my name will spring to mind."

Three nights later, I stood in our sitting room, dressed in my finest black-tie ensemble. I was a little put-out, as I'd hoped to be allowed to wear my dress uniform and show off my medals. Ladies of all stations have always been drawn to the trappings of service, but Roderick's invitation and a follow-up telegram stated that the men must be attired in simple black-tie. Something about not taking the attention away from the debutantes, and especially the guest of honour. Who this guest was to be was a question to which I would seek an answer on arrival.

Holmes stepped out of his rooms resplendent in his own ensemble and immediately I felt rather frumpy. The long black suit highlighted the tall, slim stature of my friend, and even accentuated his aquiline features so that he appeared even more devilishly handsome than usual.

"Ready then, Watson?" he asked.

"Er, yes. Ready."

"Good, good. Let's be on our way then, shall we?"

Downstairs, we found that the night had set in, as the invitation was for nine o'clock, well after the dinner hour. Luckily, Mrs. Hudson had provided a sumptuous feast to keep us going. She had hinted it was to forestall any effects of the champagne that would certainly be on offer.

A hansom sat outside, ready to whisk us to our destination. We didn't have to travel far, as after a quick trot through Marylebone and Mayfair we arrived at St. James's Square. Before us stood Cleveland

House, the London townhouse of our host for the evening, Harry Powlett, the fourth Duke of Cleveland.

Cleveland House is a lovely four-storey Georgian mansion overlooking St. James's Park. My understanding is that it was used only rarely on such occasions, as the Duke spent most of his time in County Durham, at the family home of Raby Castle.

Our hansom was greeted by a footman and we followed the red carpet to the front door, where we handed our invitation to a doorman who announced us as Mr. Sherlock Holmes and Dr. John Watson.

A few heads amongst the assembled guests turned towards us, but failing recognition returned to their own conversations.

We stood on the small landing for a moment, peering across the assembled guests. I noticed a lovely melody creeping across the room from a string quartet nestled on a balcony above the main ballroom.

As Holmes and I stepped into the throng of people, one well-presented guest made his way over. I thrust my hand out to greet Roderick.

"Thank you ever so much for inviting us," I said.

"My pleasure. It was mostly as a favour to the Duke. He had asked for an assemblage of the most eligible bachelors in London."

"And you think we are included in that group," asked Holmes.

"I didn't really care. You two just happened to come to mind."

Roderick stopped talking as a tall, elegant man in full dress uniform, complete with feathered headdress, a line of medals, a ceremonial sword, and a blood-red sash across his chest stepped into the room. I was a little miffed at seeing the man, as I would have liked the chance to wear my own uniform.

The doorman announced, "Presenting his grace, Baron Sebastian Von Steurer of Bavaria."

"A German," I retorted out loud, receiving a slightly reproachful look from Roderick.

He waited until the Baron and his coterie had moved away before answering. "Yes. Another reason the Duke wanted so many eligible bachelors here," he said, "All will become clear in a few minutes."

I kept an eye on the Baron as he made his way through the crowd, stopping from time to time to make the acquaintance of someone he obviously knew. I had never heard of him, but admit it was probably due to the fact I rarely circulated in these sorts of social circles.

Eventually, the Baron stopped before an older but very proud and upright man who sported a healthy shock of silver-grey hair and an impressive lion's mane beard with no moustache. He was dressed in a tail suit, with a single pin on his left lapel showing three swords leaning in with their points almost touching. I assumed it was the family crest or arms.

Roderick noticed my fascination and spoke up. "Ah, you've spied our host then," he said.

I was a little taken aback. "That's the Duke?" I asked.

"Yes. This entire affair is to introduce his young daughter, Elizabeth, into noble society."

I then noticed a woman standing demurely behind the Duke. She was small and a little diminutive, but attractive. She appeared to be around twenty years younger than the Duke.

"The woman is his wife, Lady Catherine Stanhope. They married late, as the Duke was engaged with his business affairs abroad for much of his early life. The child was a surprise to both of them, I think, but now the Duke wants only the best for her."

"To a point," Holmes piped up. "She has been promised to the Baron, has she not? Not something I would prefer for my own child if I had one."

Roderick harrumphed under his breath.

"Well, yes. That is partly why I am here, after all. The engagement was coordinated by the Home Office, along with the blessing of the Duke, who will benefit remarkably from the business opportunities between the two countries that this match will bring about."

I was flabbergasted. "You mean to tell me that poor young girl is just a pawn in some diplomatic and business coup?"

"Well, if you put it that way," said Roderick, "yes. It's not any different to the proposals made between Royal families of old. It will be of great benefit to her family and to the country as a whole. The British and German governments have been negotiating a trading pact for some time now. The Baron here is a senior member of the

Emperor's cabinet. We wished to open up channels of communication between our two countries. The Baron will receive a one-off payment of fifty-thousand pounds, and the marriage between himself and Lady Elizabeth seals the deal."

It was my turn to harrumph. Holmes simply smiled. "Fear not, Watson," he said. "Some things have a way of working themselves out,"

A loud voice rang out from across the room. We all turned to find a footman in full Georgian dress standing before a doorway and reading from an unfurled scroll of parchment.

"My ladies and gentlemen, if you would give me your attention please."

I realised this was the moment that the debutantes were to be introduced, and joined the group around me in forming a small open circular area for them to enter and parade around.

The Duke and the Baron were accommodated with positions at the front of their group.

Two doormen opened a pair of ornate brass doors and a line of beautifully attired young ladies could be seen stretching off down the corridor. Each was attended by a maidservant, making final touches to their hair, makeup, and dress.

The footman began, "May I present Lady Josephine Swann."

A tall, slightly gangly girl strode into the room. She appeared quite embarrassed, probably because she was the first to be introduced. She found her confidence and made her way past the assembled guests, her eyes meeting each in turn and stopping on one fellow across the circle from myself. I imagined this was her particular favourite and would be afforded the first dance in short time.

The footman continued and presently announced the arrival of ten other girls who followed the tall girl into the room and milled around in the circle under the calculating gaze of all and sundry.

I noticed the footman peer over at the doorway as he was about to announce another name. The lack of a further debutante stopped him short. He strode across and checked with the doormen. They both shook their heads. One marched down the hallway but returned quickly shaking his head and speaking in hushed tones to the footman.

The footman's face flushed red and sweat popped out on his forehead. He resumed his position and addressed the gathering one last time.

"My ladies and gentlemen, the band will now strike up for the first dance," he said, peering up at the band leader, who nodded to the footman and then to the other instrumentalists. Soon a lilting melody filtered over the crowd and young men approached each of the debutantes, in turn, to ask for their hand in a dance.

The rest of the crowd withdrew to the edges of the room to allow the courtship ritual to continue.

I noticed a new commotion erupt near the entrance-way and caught sight of the Baron and Duke in animated conversation. The Duke's face was flushed red – possibly with anger, probably with embarrassment.

I realised that his daughter was not among the young girls introduced previously and that this was the cause of the Baron's protestations. I continued to watch as they both made their way from the room, through the debutantes' entrance.

I turned back towards Holmes and Roderick to see a young man approach from a side doorway. He stepped up to Roderick and whispered in his ear. Roderick nodded several times and waved the man away. He closed in on Holmes and me and spoke.

"If you would both be so kind to accompany me, I think your services would be of valuable assistance," he said.

We followed the young man and quickly made our way out of the ballroom and down a nearby corridor. He stopped outside of another doorway and indicated for the three of us to enter.

Inside, we found the red-faced Duke and the even redder-faced Baron, still embroiled in a heated conversation.

"I do not understand why you would embarrass me in such a way," the Baron said, his voice thick with a German accent.

The Duke was obviously trying to defuse the situation but failing miserably. He held his hands out in placation, but the Baron did not seem to want any consolation.

"Sebastian, I have no idea what Elizabeth is up to. I don't know what could have happened but can only think of the worst. Do you think I would expend so much money on this event if it was only to embarrass you?"

The Baron looked long at hard into the Duke's eyes and a slight hint of calm crossed his face.

"No. Not unless you wish to do yourself an injury. What do you intend to do about it, then?"

The Duke looked across at Roderick and sighed in relief. "Roderick, thank goodness," he said and indicated the three of us to the Baron.

"Yes, I know this Roderick," said the Baron then continued. "These two," as he indicated Holmes and myself, "I do not know."

Roderick quickly introduced the two of us and added, "I invited them along tonight simply as they are eligible bachelors, but Sherlock Holmes is also a renowned consulting detective and, by chance, can add a level of investigation that would be problematic due to my position within Her Majesty's government."

Holmes quickly took the lead, turning to the Duke and saying, "Can you please explain what has happened, from the start, and do not leave out any details, no matter how small."

The Duke pursed his lips and regarded him for a moment before starting. "My daughter, Elizabeth, has recently come of age. A pivotal time in any woman's life, but more so for Elizabeth, as it makes her eligible for wedlock. In this case, I negotiated her hand in marriage to the Baron."

The Baron stood prouder and puffed out his chest slightly, no doubt assuming to affect more of a presence. Personally, I was unimpressed and hopefully hid my views from those around me.

"And in return . . . ?" prompted Holmes.

"In return, there would be a discreet change in the way Bavaria exchanged business with my companies – a benefit to both my family and to England as a whole."

"The reason that Roderick was involved," he said.

"Yes, precisely," said the Duke.

"Was your daughter accepting of this arrangement?" Holmes asked.

"What does that have to do with anything?" the Duke replied. "She is of noble stock, and that has been an expected part of her future – to accept the contract of marriage as negotiated by myself."

I could hold my tongue no longer. "But surely in these enlightened times, such a forced proposal would be rejected by the younger members of even the most noblest of families."

The Duke blanched at my suggestion. A tiny smile crossed Holmes's lips.

"That is immaterial," he answered. "The arrangement was made. It is Elizabeth's duty to accede to it."

"That may well be so," Holmes countered, "but we should investigate all facets of this mystery. There is the *why*, plus the *how*, the *when*, and naturally the *where* to determine before we can close this case. Also," he added, "the *who*."

"The *who*?" I asked.

"Yes. *Who* stands to benefit from Lady Elizabeth's disappearance? *Who* does it most affect? *Who* could be responsible? Even *who* is the root cause?"

I nodded.

"I don't understand," said the Baron.

"Well, sir, we simply must establish various facts," Holmes continued. "Was this a kidnapping?" The Duke's face dropped in shock. "Is it an attempt at ransom? Or is it simply a sign of cold feet on behalf of the young woman? All ideas are relevant until we dismiss them one by one."

Holmes stepped towards the entrance to the parlour and then turned back. "First, shall we retrace young Elizabeth's steps?"

***

The Baron followed us for a while but decided to return to his lodgings. It turned out that he had been offered rooms within Cleveland House as a guest of the Duke, a fact that I found interesting in itself, and I noticed that it also piqued Holmes's curiosity.

The Duke led us to the first-floor bedrooms, and we stopped outside of Elizabeth's room. Holmes turned back to the Duke. "Do you know if anyone has examined this room?" he asked.

"I have no idea," he said. "I can only assume that one of my servants came here to confirm that my daughter was missing."

Holmes actually smiled. "Good," he replied. "That means it should remain almost exactly as it was when Lady Elizabeth left it."

He opened the door and peered in. The gaslight was still burning, casting a yellow pallor. It was a large double room with a free-standing four-poster bed along the centre of one wall. A wardrobe and tallboy sat opposite, with a dressing area complete with a mirror beside it. Nestled against the opposite wall sat a small dressing table and writing desk.

Holmes entered and glanced around. I followed close behind, not wanting to miss any of his investigative techniques. However, I purposely stopped in the doorway to restrict entry by the others in our party. A harrumph from the Duke greeted my actions. I stood my ground until he spoke. "I say, Doctor if you wouldn't mind moving aside so I may enter," he said.

Holmes spun and held up a hand. "If you would be so kind and please do not enter until I have finished my initial investigation."

This was greeted with another harrumph and an audible sigh. Holmes ignored both and continued to peer around, not touching anything while he perused the scene in its entirety. Finally, he moved across to the writing desk and peered down. I noticed a folded piece of parchment sitting in the middle of the desk.

Holmes reached for a small pencil and gently pushed the folded page open until he was able to read it. His expression was one of intense interest. I noticed a small smile play on his lips for a moment before being replaced by a more serious look.

He dropped the pencil onto the desk and reached inside his pocket for a kerchief. He used the small square of cloth to smooth open the parchment, then picked it up and brought it across to the doorway.

"What have you there?" asked Roderick.

"The first clew in this mystery," Holmes said, "though it may be all that is required for now."

Roderick withdrew a pair of gloves from his jacket and took the proffered note in hand. He read aloud for the benefit of the rest of us.

"*To the Duke of Cleveland*," he said. "*We have your daughter. There will be no marriage between a Bavarian prince and the non-Teutonic spawn of the Englander.*" Then he added, "It is signed by The Sons of Bavaria."

He handed the note back to Holmes before turning to the Duke. "I am so sorry, your Grace," he said. "It would seem that your daughter has indeed been kidnapped, and by some German resistance group. I've never even heard of these 'Sons of Bavaria'."

The Duke's face was a mesh of anger and fear and glowed bright red with it. "We must talk to the Baron, immediately," he said, "And have the local constabulary search high and low. My daughter must be found."

The Duke, Roderick, and the Duke's valet left at high speed, leaving Holmes and me alone. I was slightly mystified. It was then I heard Holmes chuckling to himself. I turned to find a grin across his face.

"You find the kidnapping of this young girl funny?" I asked.

Holmes opened the note which was the first chance I'd had to have a good look. The writing was a delicate flowing script. It occurred to me straight away that this was a woman's handwriting. When he saw that I'd finished, Holmes moved back to the writing desk and began to search the drawers. He finally found the object of his search and straightened up, holding a small diary. He opened to the first page and read the name inscribed there.

"Lady Elizabeth's journal," he said.

He placed it on the desk and opened to a random page full of a similar flowing script. He put the note above and compared the two writing styles.

He let out a little sigh of anguish as I noticed that the two scripts didn't match as he would have first imagined. He flipped through several pages until one particular passage stuck out from the rest. The writing on this page was almost identical to that of the note.

“What do you surmise?” I asked.

“Well the diary is most certainly Elizabeth’s – it has her name on the first page. I assume that the lighter, more-delicate script is hers. The single passage that matches the note must have been made by another.”

He flipped through the diary and found two more passages in the same style. “I would say these were written by a very close confidant of Miss Elizabeth. A close friend or . . . .”

He stood up and smiled at me.

"Or?" I asked. "A maidservant. Somebody that would be as close as a friend and always be with Lady Elizabeth.”

He read one of the passages and another laconic smile grew on his face. “Yes. This passage follows on from the previous one, but that was written in Elizabeth’s hand. I would say that it was dictated to somebody whilst she was predisposed, possibly while she was in the bath.”

He checked the pages closely and then showed it to me. His finger pointed to two small discoloured circles at the top of the page. “Water droplets,” he said.

“Extraordinary,” I replied. “But what does it mean?”

“Our young Elizabeth has either staged her own kidnapping, or this maid-servant was responsible.”

“That seems unlikely.”

“Indeed,” he said. “I would think that there is something more that has triggered Lady Elizabeth’s actions. We must ensure that she left of her own free will, and then determine why.”

“Should we tell the Duke or Roderick?” I asked.

Holmes grinned. “Why would we do that? They have their investigation to pursue, and it will keep them busy and out of our hair long enough that we might even solve this case without them.”

I nodded in agreement.

Holmes moved across to the wardrobe and opened it. The wardrobe was half full, with several bare hangers dangling from the rack. A couple had fallen to the base and lay abandoned. The remaining clothing was of a very high quality, suited to a woman of

Elizabeth's station in life. Satin and silk dresses for formal occasions, plus several cotton dresses for day-wear.

Holmes closed the door and moved to the tallboy. He opened and examined several drawers, finding a similar result with two of them being only half-filled with clothing and essentials. There was a drawer dedicated to Elizabeth's smalls, which I was a bit embarrassed that we were investigating, but Holmes in his wisdom simply opened it to check its emptiness before closing it once more.

Another held several exquisite silk scarves, neatly rolled up. Again, several were missing, not something that would require laundering all at once.

He closed the last drawer and stared at the four hat stands arrayed on the top. Only three held hats, and those were of the delicate type used for formal occasions.

"What do you think, Watson?" he asked.

"Someone has packed for a trip, perhaps," I replied, "or it's washing day, though given that there are scarves and a hat missing, I would be surprised if those items are located in the scullery."

One of Holmes's eyebrows raised. He moved across to a small wicker basket and glanced inside. I checked as well. It was empty.

"Could still be washing day, I suppose," Holmes said as he headed for the doorway.

"Where to next?"

"The laundry, of course. Not just to check on the young lady's clothing, but below-stairs is always a good place for gossip and hearsay."

***

As we descended the stairs to the basement, the noise of suppressed conversation was palpable. It was obvious that word of Lady Elizabeth's disappearance had reached the underground world of Cleveland House.

As we stepped out of the stairwell shadow and into the dimly lit passageway, two maids, engaged in a deep conversation, immediately straightened up, almost dropping their loads of plates and towels. They scurried off before we could even apologise.

We made our way down the long passageway towards the bowels of the basement. Tiny snatches of conversation ceased as soon as we were in eyesight of the speakers.

Finally, we reached the kitchen and stepped through into the scullery. A large, formidable-looking woman was busily running a tablecloth across a washboard. A large red stain spoiled the appearance of the normally crisp white linen and seemed to be drawing its own ire from the woman.

After a moment of patient waiting, Holmes let out a small cough. The woman jumped and dropped the cloth into the bucket in her fright. She turned around a hint of anger on her face which disappeared as soon as she saw us.

Immediately she stepped down from her stool and wiped her sudsy hands against her apron. “My word,” she asked. “Are you two gentlemen lost?”

“Not at all,” replied Holmes. “We seem to have found the person we were seeking.”

“Me?” she asked. “Why?”

“If I am not mistaken, you would be the person most skilled in the laundering of this household’s clothing.”

Her chest puffed up at the slight compliment. “Why yes, that would be me,” she said. “What can I do for you then? Have you soiled your lovely suits?”

Holmes smiled. “No, nothing like that, but thank you for offering. We are investigating the location of the Duke’s young daughter.”

The woman’s face dropped. “That poor dear. If those Germans harm one hair on her head, then they’ll have to deal with me.”

I felt that I wouldn’t want to be in the kidnappers’ shoes – if there were kidnappers.

“And that is a sentiment shared by me and my associate here, Dr. John Watson.”

“Oh, a doctor, aye. Well, I’m Mrs. Havsham, if you have a mind to know. Been in this house for nigh on twenty years. Seen that lovely lass grow up, and would never wish any harm to her.”

"Quite so," said Holmes, "You are the perfect person then to help our inquiries. Would you know if young Elizabeth has any clothing that has been brought here for laundering?"

"That's a very personal question," she said, tensing a little before smiling, "But you seem to be a lovely gentleman, so I will tell you. No. I'm surprised, but there's naught been brought down here for a day or so."

"Interesting," said Holmes.

Mrs. Havsham was about to speak when a very loud voice cut through from the folding room next door. We turned to see an attractive flame-haired young woman dressed in a kitchen hand's uniform float down the stairway into the room carrying an armload of tablecloths. She directed her speech to a straight-backed man who stood at the shoe bench, polishing a pair of knee-high boots.

"Hello, Fritz," she said. "What's up with your master this evening? I haven't seen him since before luncheon."

The man stopped working, a look of intense hatred bordering on fury crossing his face. "My name is Friedrich, not Fritz," he said in a very thick German accent before diverting his attention back to the boots.

"Doris," said Mrs. Havsham. "Leave the Baron's man alone and get those over here."

Doris smiled, walked into the scullery, and across to the washing barrel. She dumped the tablecloths onto the ground and clapped her hands together, releasing a cloud of white powder.

"Don't know why they needs me to go up and get these. Those maids upstairs are just lazy good-for-nothings."

Mrs. Havsham face showed a look of indignation. Her reply was a little sharp. "The maids have guest rooms to prepare and beds to turn down. You were asked to help out, so there should be no argument."

"I have pastries to bake for the morning," she said, turning around and heading back to the kitchen.

Mrs. Havsham shook her head. "Don't know what gets into their heads nowadays."

We bid her a good evening and Holmes stepped into the folding room, with me close behind. Friedrich was busy with his boots and ignored us. He was wearing a starched white shirt with a dark tie with a vest, matching his black trousers. I noticed a small red-and-white pin in the lapel of his vest. It had the look of a pin given for having been in military service.

Meanwhile, Holmes was scrutinizing a nearby pile of laundry, topped by a jacket that clearly belonged to the Baron. He leaned in and pulled a long red hair from the shoulder. It was then I noticed a small smear of white powder on the arm. My eyes grew wide.

"Can I help you?" came Friedrich's voice from behind us.

Holmes turned towards the valet and studied him for a moment. The valet began to become very agitated before Holmes spoke to him in German. "*Sie sind der Mann des Barons*?" he asked. (You are the Baron's man?)

Friedrich straightened. I spied a military background just by his posture. "*Ja. Seit vielen Jahren bin ich mit ihm zusammen*," he said. ("Yes. For many years I have been with him.")

Holmes returned to English, much to my happiness, and continued. "Ah, born in Saxony, I think?"

Friedrich's eyes opened wide as if he had seen Holmes perform an unexpected magic trick. I was growing used to the way that Holmes could pick apart a person's life solely through observation.

"Yes, but how?"

"And from your posture, I would say Army – First Royal Saxon Corps, perhaps?"

Friedrich's face softened slightly. He appeared intrigued by Holmes's remarks. "Yes, but – ?"

Holmes cut him off. "Is this your first time in England?"

"No. Ve have come here a number of times. The Baron has interests in this country. He keeps a close eye on them."

"And the Duke?" Holmes asked.

"Yes. The Duke and the Baron have long known each other. The Duke has companies that deal vith the Baron's as vell."

"Interesting. And the Lady Elizabeth? She has known the Baron for a while?"

"Not really." He stopped and put the boot brush down. An exasperated look appeared on his face, and he looked like one under some internal torment. He stared off into space and began to speak more to himself than to us. “It’s these Englanders. They have changed the Baron. He vas never interested in politics, just business. Then they arrange this marriage to the young Lady Elizabeth. The Baron has always liked the ladies. Especially the young ones. He has never vanted just one, so I don’t understand it. It does not make any of the sense.”

He suddenly caught himself and realised what he’d been saying. He remembered his chores, picked up the boot brush, and began polishing the boots once more. “If you’ll excuse me, I am the busy,” he said.

Holmes turned and moved back into the scullery. He stepped up to Mrs. Havsham again.

“I beg your pardon again, madam,” he said.

Mrs. Havsham stopped her washing, happy to have Holmes’s attention once again, and dried her hands on her apron. “Not a problem, sir.”

“The young Lady Elizabeth, and the Baron?” he asked.

Mrs. Havsham’s face went very serious. She checked on Friedrich, then looked from side to side before leaning in closer to us.

“All arranged without young Elizabeth’s consent. The Duke has sold her off to further his business interests, and that old lech just wants to get his hands on a young filly, if you know what I mean. He’s never been able to keep his hands off them since he’s been coming here.”

She stopped herself when she realised what she’d said. She started to turn, but Holmes asked one more question. “Lady Elizabeth would have needed a maidservant, would she not?”

Mrs. Havsham nodded, “Yes, that would be Caitlin. Caitlin Brown.”

“Where could I find her?”

“She should be around unless she’s gone for the day. She has family over in Lambeth. Since we’ve come back to London, she’s been going home regularly to see them. Check with Mrs. Scunthorpe, the housekeeper, just down the hall,” she said pointing off down the corridor.

Holmes smiled and said, “Thank you, Mrs. Havsham. Sorry to have taken your time.”

“It’s all right,” came her reply as she turned her attention back to the washing.

Holmes took my arm and led me away. We moved through the kitchen where Doris was busy making pies, her arms dusted in flour up to the elbows. She noticed us and smiled coyly. I nodded in reply as we moved on.

***

Luckily for us, Mrs. Scunthorpe was in her room, readying herself for the servants’ evening meal. Our appearance brought an interested look to her face. “Are you gentlemen lost?” she asked. “The party is still going upstairs. I can take you back if you wish.”

“No, that will be quite alright, Mrs. Scunthorpe. I am Sherlock Holmes, and this is my associate, Dr. John Watson. We are assisting with determining the location of young Elizabeth, and were hoping that you could help us.”

Mrs. Scunthorpe sat down heavily, almost in a faint. She put a hand to her forehead in anguish. “Oh, my, this has been a night. I think we’ve kept it from most of the guests, but it won’t be long. I’m happy to provide any help to find that young girl, and soon.”

“I understand that her maid’s name is Caitlin Brown,” Holmes said.

“Yes.”

“She would probably have been the last person to have seen Elizabeth, and presumably would have been helping to ready her before the introductions. Has she been around since then?”

Mrs. Scunthorpe thought for a moment, a quizzical look on her face, and then shook her head. “No. I haven’t seen her since earlier. The guests finished dinner around seven o’clock, and the young ladies went back to their rooms to prepare for the ball. Elizabeth and Caitlin went past me as I was coming upstairs to supervise the removal of all the dinner dishes, but since then I haven't seen hide nor hair of her.” She sat bolt upright. “You don’t think that she was kidnapped as well, do you? Or worse, that *she’s* the kidnapper?”

Holmes held his hands up to calm the housekeeper. "No, no, nothing like that, I assure you. We just need to retrace Elizabeth's steps and talk to Caitlin. Could you give us her home address?"

"Certainly," she said and quickly pulled out a piece of paper and a pencil, jotting down a Lambeth address.

Holmes smiled and took the paper.

Mrs. Scunthorpe looked up at him, her eyes full of anguish. "Please find our young Elizabeth. She's a good girl. She doesn't deserve any of this."

"You mean the kidnapping?" Holmes asked.

"Oh, and that as well," she said, his question drawing a look of surprise.

***

As we climbed the stairs back to the ground floor, I had to ask Holmes a question. "The First Royal Saxon Corps? It was the pin on Friedrich's vest's lapel, wasn't it?"

"Why, yes, it was. Well done."

"Is that how you determined his accent?"

Holmes smiled. "Actually, no. I met a fellow student at University who was born and raised in Leipzig. I polished my very basic German by conversing with him from time to time. Some of his pronunciation was vastly different to what I'd learned, and we decided that it was because of the local dialect influences."

"Outstanding," I said. "Where to next?"

"Well, I believe a short trip is in order," he said, holding the small scrap of paper in his hand. "I feel that the current occupants of this address will reveal a lot more about this mystery than anything else."

We walked a short distance down the corridor before hearing stern voices coming from a room nearby. We stopped and crept up to the doorway. They belonged to the Duke, the Baron, and Roderick. From the tone and volume, the Baron was enraged.

"This disappearance is a ruse! You are just trying to humiliate me. What more do you want? More money? More business contacts? I'm very close to forgetting everything and returning home. The Emperor will not be amused."

Roderick piped up, “I assure you, your Grace, there has been no intent by either the British Government or by the Duke himself to undermine this deal. For all we know, Lady Elizabeth has been kidnapped and is in great danger as we speak.”

“The police have been informed,” said the Duke. “The Government has dispatched agents to search as well. I am at my wit's end. This is my only daughter we are speaking of here. I can only assume that we will receive a ransom note soon. I will pay whatever they ask to get Elizabeth back.”

“That may be so,” said the Baron, “But what if the Lady Elizabeth is soured by this experience? What if she returns damaged? I was promised a young beauty. If that is no longer the case, then where is my recompense? In fact, I may simply walk away from this deal altogether. It seems very slovenly for the British Government to have let these brigands snatch the Lady from under their noses.”

We could hear the Duke simply bristling in rage. “See here! That’s my daughter you’re talking about!” he said, his voice rising in volume along with his anger.

Roderick stepped up and diffused the situation. “I’m sure that Her Majesty’s Government was not responsible for this act, and I’m also sure they would be happy to provide compensation, or indeed improve your situation, should anything untoward arise.”

“Very well,” said the Baron. He suddenly appeared at the doorway, causing us both to jump back in surprise. He had a wry smile on his face which didn’t fade when he came upon the two of us. He quickly looked each of us in the eye and continued on down the corridor. I felt that he would have been quite happy to whistle a jaunty tune as he did. I started to have severe doubts about his innocence in all this.

Roderick appeared at the door. “There you are. Anything new?” he asked. “We need to find this lass as soon as possible. The favourability of this deal for the Government is degrading by the minute.”

Holmes replied, “I understand your concern, but there was nothing new in her room. We questioned a few of the staff and nothing either. I plan to journey home and contact my Irregulars. They have an ear to the street and may have come across these so-called 'Sons of Bavaria'."

Roderick thought for a moment and then nodded. "Agreed. I have men working on it as we speak, but they don't have as close an insight into the criminal underbelly as your urchins do." He pulled out a pocket watch and we realised it was well past eleven o'clock. "Hmm. I daresay there will not be much sleep gained in this house tonight, but that will only lead to more anger and indecision. Meet us back here in the early morning – say eight o'clock. Hopefully, there will be more information by then. With any real hope, we may have even found the Lady Elizabeth."

"Indeed," said Holmes.

With that, Roderick went back into the room to inform the Duke. We turned on our heels and proceeded to the front door.

***

As we alighted from the hansom that dropped us in front of 221b Baker Street, Holmes stepped to the side of the footpath and spied up and down the street. He focused on a shadowy spot a couple of houses away, held up his hand, and clicked his fingers. I swore that the shadows dissolved and a figure moved quickly away.

The hansom drew away and I turned to enter our house just as a young boy in filthy clothes ran up to Holmes. "Wiggins," Holmes said.

The boy, Wiggins, removed his flat cap and addressed Holmes. "'Ello Mr. 'Olmes. Sorry, I took so long. What can we do for you this fine evening?"

"Small job for you. I need someone to keep a watch on Cleveland House at St. James Square. Pay particular attention to a German called Baron Von Steurer – tall, fifty, grey hair, moustache. I want to know what his movements are." He turned towards me, "Watson, do you have a crown on you?"

I fished around in my purse, drew forth a silver coin, and dropped it into Holmes's hand. He turned and gave it to Wiggins. It disappeared into a pocket as quickly as it appeared in his hand.

"Here, this should cover any expenses you'll have. Whoever goes will be there all night. Stay out of sight and send word if the Baron leaves"

"Is the prize on offer?" Wiggins asked.

Holmes smiled, "Naturally. Anyone who brings me a vital clew will receive a guinea, as always."

Wiggins gave a mock salute, placed his hat on his head, and said, "Right you are Mr. 'Olmes. We are on the case." He turned and hightailed it down the way he'd come with increased speed.

"I'd hate to say it," I commented, "but I think that the police will still be putting their boots on by the time your Irregulars have come up with solid clews."

"Quite so. It's amazing what can be achieved with an eager force of invisible urchins and a little cash incentive. Now let's change. We have another address to visit before this night is out."

***

By the time the hansom dropped us outside the Lambeth address supplied by Mrs. Scunthorpe, it was well into the wee hours of the morning.

There was a light still burning in the front parlour window – a good sign for us and one that bode well for a quick conclusion to our search.

Holmes stepped up to the door and rapped lightly with the knocker, trying hard not to cause too much ruckus for the neighbours.

For a moment there was an immediate hive of activity inside the terraced house before a shuffling could be heard just inside, and the bolts were drawn on the entrance door.

A grey-haired, stoop-backed man opened it and peered up at Holmes's tall imposing figure through watery eyes.

"Yes?" he asked, "Do you know what time it is?"

"I do apologise, sir. I assume that you are Mr. Brown? Father of Caitlin?" Holmes said.

"Grandfather actually," the old man said.

"Ah, good. I am Sherlock Holmes, and this is my associate, Dr. John Watson," Holmes said.

The old man looked Holmes up and down then repeated the gesture with me. "What's that to me?" he asked.

"Well, your granddaughter was in the company of Lady Elizabeth Powell, the daughter of the Duke of Cleveland, earlier this evening, and now both have disappeared. We have been tasked with ascertaining their whereabouts," Holmes added.

The old man looked us both up and down again. He seemed very determined to stop us from entering his house.

Suddenly, a softer voice came from within. "Father, let those gentlemen in. It's cold and you'll pay for it tomorrow, I tell you."

The old man turned for a moment and then looked back at us. He shuffled backwards to allow us to enter.

It was much warmer inside. While we divested ourselves of coats and scarves, The man wandered back into a nearby sitting room. I looked for somewhere to hang my coat and noticed that there were no free hooks. All four were taken up with coats, all of which had scarves draped over them as well.

In the end, Holmes and I simply folded our coats over our free arms and stepped into the parlour.

A woman of about forty years of age sat in the warmth of the little room. A cooling pot of tea was in the middle of the room on a small table. A quick scan showed a total of four teacups distributed on either the middle table or the two other side tables.

Holmes sauntered up to the woman. "Mrs. Brown, I assume? As I mentioned, I am Sherlock Holmes, and this is my associate, Dr. John Watson."

"Yes," she said. "I'm afraid that you've wasted your time, Mr. Holmes, Caitlin hasn't been home for weeks. We are so proud of her. She's fallen on her feet with Lady Elizabeth. The two are inseparable."

"That is my understanding as well," said Holmes, "So much so that in such a time as this, when young Elizabeth has been driven to her wit's end, she seeks solace in the only other place available."

Mrs. Brown's face creased up in confusion. "Where would that be?" she asked.

"Why, *here*," said Holmes, "Amongst the family of her closest friend."

"But I just told you, Caitlin is not here, and Lady Elizabeth has never visited before."

"I admire your audacity in protecting the young lady," he said, "as well as your daughter, but we both know full well that they are within,"

Mrs. Brown's face showed a distinct flash of anger. "I said they aren't here," she said, her voice rising in volume. "This is my house, and you should believe what I say."

Holmes paused to let the irritation in the air dissipate for a moment, before continuing. "And that would be fair, except for the evidence."

"What evidence?" said Mrs. Brown.

"Four coats hanging in the entranceway – one with an exquisitely expensive-looking silk scarf. No offence to you or your father, but I would think such an item to be quite an indulgent addition to your wardrobe. Plus there's the matter of the four teacups scattered around this room," he said.

Mrs. Brown looked deflated by the simple logic. "Come in here, Caitlin," she said, not even needing to raise her voice.

A door at the other end of the room opened and two shamefaced girls in their late teens entered the parlour. Elizabeth was immediately recognisable by her more opulent attire.

"Sit," said Mrs. Brown.

Holmes and I shifted around to allow the two to take their seats.

Lady Elizabeth sat straight-backed and stared up into Holmes's eyes. "I do not think we've had the pleasure, sir."

Holmes bowed slightly and said, "No, we haven't, Lady Elizabeth. I am Sherlock Holmes, and this is my associate Dr. John Watson. You may have met Roderick St. John-Smythe. He works for Her Majesty's Government and has been assisting your father broker the deal with the Baron regarding your hand in marriage."

At the mention of the Baron, Elizabeth stiffened and drew in a sharp breath. "Something that brings you concern, it seems," Holmes added.

Elizabeth was close to tears, Caitlin, sitting next to her, took her hand and tried to console her. Elizabeth regained her composure before continuing, her voice slightly shaky. “Are you here to take me back?” she asked, her tone tingling with nervousness.

“I believe that you are of age. Therefore I, and no other person in authority has any right to do so. I am also happy to keep your secret until you are prepared to return. I would say, however, that your father is extremely worried. They believe the story that you and Caitlin fabricated regarding your presumed kidnapping.”

“But you didn’t,” she said. “Otherwise you wouldn’t be here.”

“True. I generally look beyond the obvious. My purpose here is to establish *why*. Why would you steel yourself away at the instant of, perhaps, the most important moment of your life so far?”

At this Elizabeth lost her control. Tears flowed freely down her cheeks as Caitlin pulled Elizabeth’s head to her shoulder and allowed her friend to weep. She turned her head towards Holmes and spoke, her accent much broader than the gentle speech of Elizabeth.

“It’s all because of that rotter, and that red-haired tart,” she said.

Holmes smiled at the descriptions. “The Baron and – I presume – Doris, the kitchen hand?”

Caitlin nodded. “Yes. She’s been gettin’ above her station with the Baron. It started with a little flirtin’, and then suddenly she goes missing late at night and slopes in just before dawn. I knows she ain’t been out the house. You can talk to Friedrich – he knows all about it. Poor lad. He has to keep a lid on it. And then she parades around like she owns the place. Sayin’ she’s gonna move to Germany and work in the Baron’s house and all that.” She turned back and patted Elizabeth’s head, cooing softly to her.

With her head still buried in Caitlin’s shoulder, Elizabeth sobbed. Caitlin patted her head and continued, “I takes her back to her bedroom and we worked out a way for Elizabeth to disappear.”

“Did you plan to go back at any stage?” Holmes asked.

“We hadn’t thought that far ahead,” she said.

Holmes turned towards me and spoke. “Watson, I think we can leave these people in peace. We shall retire for the night and return to Cleveland House in the morning.” He turned back to face Elizabeth and Caitlin. “Lady Elizabeth, I will not reveal your whereabouts until I have resolved this matter. I feel that there is a lot more to the Baron’s activities than a simple tryst with a servant girl. I wish you luck with the future, but I feel by nine o’clock tomorrow everything will be in order.”

We bid *adieu* to the four, replaced our coats, and stepped out of the house, closing the door behind. Moments later the bolts were drawn.

***

On Holmes’s instructions, I made my own way back to Cleveland House the next morning. He said he would be leaving early and would meet me there.

As I stood outside the grand mansion, another hansom arrived, depositing Holmes and Roderick to the footpath beside me. Roderick was in a less-than-hospitable mood but contained it behind his normally stoic façade.

Holmes greeted me and we made our way into the house. We were shown into the drawing-room where the Duke and Baron were having a stern conversation. It finished as soon as we entered, and the atmosphere remained business-like. I then noticed Friedrich standing to one side, not far from the Duke’s own valet.

Roderick withdrew two sets of papers from his satchel and placed them on the desk, along with a beautifully crafted fountain pen, laid at the head of each contract. The Duke and Baron immediately set about poring over the documents. The Baron then turned towards Holmes and Roderick. “No word on my beautiful Elizabeth?” he asked.

Holmes and Roderick shook their heads and dropped their gaze.

I noticed a slight smile cross the Baron’s face before he removed it. He turned his attention back to the contract. “One-hundred thousand,” he said. “Well, this should more than compensate my broken heart for the loss it feels.” He picked up the pen, signed both contracts and pocketed the pen in one fell swoop.

He turned to Friedrich and spoke in German. “*Mach die Taschen fertig*,” he said. “*Je eher wir uns von diesen Engländern und ihren blöden Frauen trennen, desto besser*.” (“Get the bags ready. The sooner we get away from these Englanders and their stupid women the better.")

Friedrich looked shocked at the Baron's words. He shot a furtive glance towards Holmes, knowing full well his grasp of German. Holmes simply smiled back and nodded. Friedrich's eyes grew wide and he quickly left the room.

The Baron was oblivious to everything and hovered over the Duke, waiting for him to sign.

"If I may be so bold, your Grace, you may wish to read the contract a second time to be clear on the terms," said Roderick. The Duke regarded him for a moment and went back over the details of the contract.

Suddenly a shrill voice entered the room from the doorway. "You pigeon-livered flapdoodle!" it cried.

We all turned to find Doris, her angry face almost the same colour as her flaming hair. Her eyes stared daggers at the Baron. He stood up straight and was taken aback by the vitriolic delivery of the young kitchen maid.

She stepped into the room and headed straight for him. "You used me! All that sweet talk about taking me with you was just bollocks!"

She walked up to the Baron and slapped him hard across the cheek. He was left stunned and unsure how to continue, his hand going to his jaw.

She continued to yell into his face, punctuating each word with a finger jab to the chest, "I'm not just some common strumpet looking for some well-heeled johnny to sweep me off my feet! I got talents, I do, and I'm not gonna waste 'em on some foozler like you!"

She stared deep into his face for a moment before letting out an enraged howl and storming from the room.

The Baron stood, stunned. The Duke placed his pen on the unsigned contract, turned towards the Baron and asked, "Would you care to explain?"

The Baron stammered for a moment before Holmes interrupted. "I believe the Baron is trying to apologise. It seems that ever since this deal began to be brokered, he has been playing the field, as it is called, with your staff. The primary reason has been to undermine his relationship with your daughter."

The Baron began to grow angry. "How dare you!"

Holmes ignored him and continued, "The unfortunate Doris there was just the main player. My informants, who were watching the Baron, saw him leave your presence with a young blonde girl late last night. She was wearing simple brown street clothes with a brown bonnet. Her hair was quite long, braided into in a single plait.

The Duke's eyes lit up. "That sounds like Audrey, my chambermaid," he said. He threw a stern look at the Baron. "How could you, sir? She is barely sixteen!"

A voice with a thick German accent came from the doorway. "I know how."

We turned to find Friedrich standing there. He stepped into the room and spoke. "It vas always his plan. The young ladies who consented vere a bonus, but he only vanted to make the young Lady Elizabeth grow jealous and enraged so that she might do something silly and help the Baron change the deal in his favour."

"What are you doing?" yelled the Baron, stepping up to his valet and staring straight into his eyes.

"I am fed up vith this charade. I was born a man of honour. I am a Saxon. I vas an army officer. I cannot condone vat you had planned, and I vill not be a part of it. You bring dishonour to my country, and all for a little money. Your bags are packed. I quit."

The Baron's rage knew no bounds. He seethed at his valet and brought his hand up in a fist ready to lash out at the younger man.

The Baron's fist flew, but Friedrich simply stepped aside and the Baron tumbled to the floor. Friedrich looked down at him and shook his head.

"Baron, you really are a petty little man. I vish I had never come into your service."

The Duke stepped up to him and placed a hand on his shoulder. "You will always be welcome in my employ, dear boy. Go back to your room and I will find you later. We can discuss it then."

Friedrich nodded, said, "Thank you, your Grace," and left.

The Duke looked down at the Baron and shook his head in dismay, he then peered across at Roderick.

"Why didn't you know about this charlatan?" he asked.

"I do apologise, your Grace, I will be sending out some severe reprimands when I return to my office."

The Duke turned back to the desk, picked up both contracts, and tore them to shreds. He threw them at the Baron as he picked himself up and tried to regain his dignity.

"To think I almost let my daughter marry you," he said. "Get out of my house!" He turned on his heel and left the room.

The Baron started to move from the room. "Would you like a hand with your bags?" Holmes asked.

The Baron stared back at him with a steely gaze that could melt ice. He ignored the question and left.

"Obviously not," I said.

***

Back at Baker Street, we enjoyed a mid-morning repast of scones and coffee.

"I think that went quite well," I said.

Holmes took a sip of coffee, a pleased look on his face. "I'm not sure what was better, seeing the Baron's comeuppance, or watching Roderick embarrassed and grovelling to the Duke."

"Don't be too harsh on Roderick," I said, "He obviously doesn't have the quality of informants in his network like you do."

"Perhaps," he said. Then his face changed as he remembered something. "You wouldn't have a guinea on you, would you? I'll need to pay Wiggins for his information."

Grumbling, I reached once again into my purse.

The Adventure of the Edinburgh Professor

After all these years I can truly say that life with Sherlock Holmes never presents a dull moment. Even a simple train trip has the opportunity to turn into a case of life or death.

Such was the situation I once again found myself in as we returned from a trip to Edinburgh on the East Coast express. Though some would argue that the ten-hour journey, with multiple stops along the way, could be called anything but an express route.

The occasion had seen us journey north to visit my cousin, Dr. Patrick Watson, a renowned surgeon who emigrated to Scotland ten years previously. It was there that Holmes and I became embroiled in an investigation of an apparent haunting of a young family. The case was cleared up quickly and as with most supernatural occurrences was explained away, by Holmes, in an utmost rational solution.

We had booked a first-class sleeper, even though we did not envisage needing the beds. It gave us the comfort of knowing we had somewhere safe to store our belongings and seek refuge if the situation required.

The train itself was quite full. It was mid-January, and many Scots sought out the warmer climes of the south of England at that time of year, plus the service only ran once or twice a day, putting immense pressure on the limits of the train. We were very lucky to have retained our sleeper, as we were almost required to postpone the return trip due to the haunting.

All that aside, we managed to enjoy the first half of the journey, spending the majority of our time in the club car after a delightful luncheon. It was there that we met up with Professor Bernard Lumley. A fellow first-class traveller from Edinburgh who was travelling in the sleeper three doors down from our own.

He was a jocular fellow in his early sixties, that thoroughly enjoyed the sound of his own voice. We found that he was an emeritus professor of Eastern European anthropology at the University of

Edinburgh. His work centred on the early Prussian kings and the influence of the last vestiges of Charlemagne's rule on them. He was very coy about the purpose of his journey, but it seemed to involve the transportation of a very important relic to do with his work. He was bringing it to the University College in London as they were undertaking their own studies in that same area.

Holmes was entranced and engaged with the good Professor in a thoroughly detailed conversation about Prussia and Charlemagne. I'll admit that I was completely lost and as time drew on began to grow extremely tired and quite bored. I decided I needed to stretch my legs and possibly take in some of the cool evening air to reinvigorate my senses.

I stood and bid adieu to Holmes and the professor before striding from the carriage. I found the gangway between the club car and first-class sleeper occupied by several smokers. Even though I enjoy the odd pipe and cigar, I didn't wish to partake in their second-hand smoke and pushed through into the sleeper car.

As I rounded the corner, I noticed two gentlemen further down the corridor. One was leaning over, the other seemed to be keeping watch. I ducked back and stood with my shoulder pressed to the wall listening intently.

They spoke German and the coarseness of their hushed tones precluded me from translating anything I could hear. I could, however, hear the rattling of a sleeper door which seemed to indicate that they were struggling to open it. I deduced that they were either breaking into the sleeper or had forgotten their keys. My suspicious mind told me the former.

I decided to play dumb and simply stroll down the corridor to take in as many details as I could.

Upon seeing me they both straightened up and tried to look as innocent as possible. Failing dismally on all accounts.

I genially said, "Good evening," to them as I passed. Taking in the number of the sleeper, and as many details about the two men as I could. They mumbled a similar reply to me and fidgeted about until I was well past.

I noticed that they turned back to the door as I rounded the far corner.

I quickly found the guard at the far end of the next sleeper and told him what I'd seen. It was his duty to move them on, so I made a note to check back with him later.

I soon found myself in the second-class coach. Almost every seat was taken. The racks above were full to overflowing with suitcases and bags, and at either end, several people milled around. These were the poor unfortunates that either didn't manage to book a seat or were left adrift when the earlier train was cancelled.

I made my way down the centre aisle, feeling a little self-conscious as I was wearing my travelling suit which was a more expensive style of dress than most of these passengers could afford.

As I moved along my eyes were drawn to a most lovely face. She was young, in her early twenties, had shortish brown hair and a rather dark and swarthy complexion. Very out of step with the lighter skin tones and reddish-brown hair of the passengers around her.

I also noticed she was reading one of my own treatises of Holmes's cases. A shimmer of pride ran through me to think that a young girl, such as this, would take the time to read my work.

It was at that moment that she looked up and caught my eye. A small smile played across her lips before she took her attention back to the story.

I carried on and eventually found myself in the guards' car at the very rear of the train. I had a quick chat with the guard and said I was just trying to find somewhere to take in some fresh air. I noticed his straight-backed demeanour and managed to prize the name of his regiment and the rank he had held. Upon hearing of my own service, he relaxed, and we quickly swapped a few war stories and remembrances.

At one point, he even pulled out a bottle of whiskey and offered it to me. I thought better of it for a moment, but then the chill made its presence known, so I thankfully took the bottle from him and gleefully downed a short swallow.

It was as I handed the bottle back, that there was an almighty thump from the front of the train.

The carriage swayed dangerously as the driver applied the emergency brakes. I was thrown forward and the bottle slipped from my grasp and broke upon a large steel box hidden in the corner. I landed in an unceremonious heap at the guard's feet. He managed to hold on to one of the railings nearby.

Screams and shouts of dismay could be heard running up and down the carriages. I rolled over and looked up the aisle. Suitcases were strewn all over. Several people had been cast from their seats and lay atop the cases or vice versa.

A few people had suffered small cuts and abrasions either from striking the seats nearby or from the baggage that rained down on them.

When the train finally came to a standstill, I regained my feet with the help of my newfound friend and moved forward to provide any level of assistance that I could.

Luckily, most of the injuries were light and superficial. Most of the passengers were simply in a state of shock. I told those suffering to sit still in their seats and relax themselves until more information arrived. I did not have any supplies to treat the wounds, so told the guard to stay with the injured passengers and I would come back with my medical bag.

I worked my way through the next carriage, attending any unfortunates that I found and telling them to remain seated and relaxed until I could return. In the back of my mind, I started to worry about whether I had enough supplies on hand.

It is my habit, especially when travelling with Holmes, to bring my medical bag, but it is only ever lightly packed with bare essentials for emergencies. This was an emergency, but the scale was probably beyond even my foresight.

I reached our sleeper and unlocked the door. On returning to the corridor, bag in hand, I began to make my way back to the second-class car when a voice called out from behind.

"Watson? Where the devil have you been?" it said.

I turned to find Holmes moving up the corridor towards me.

"I was taking some air with the guard at the back of the train, just before this calamity," I said, "There are injuries to many of the passengers, I was returning to give aid where I could."

"Good man. I wanted to check that you were uninjured then lend a hand outside. This may be a simple problem with the train, but there was a loud thump before we braked that has me puzzled," he said.

"I heard that too, I presumed we'd hit something on the track."

"From the forward compartments it sounded a lot like an explosion," said Holmes, his face becoming stern as the thought of an investigation loomed.

***

I managed to dress the majority of wounds very quickly within the second-class carriages. They were only superficial, and my assistance was more or less comfort to the passengers rather than a medical need.

As I was finishing up with one patient, the head conductor entered the carriage. He addressed the assembled passengers and said that the train had been damaged and would require repairs before there was any chance of proceeding through to London.

He stated that the train had stopped about ten miles north of Grantham, near the small town of Hougham. Two porters had been sent to a nearby farm to procure some horses and ride on to Hougham to organise transport and accommodation.

The conductor said that all passengers would be lodged for the night or could be transferred to Grantham where they could make alternative arrangements.

A passenger raised a hand and asked, "Can we not sleep on the train?"

The conductor said that suggestion had been brought up, but that all the sleeper cars were full of first-class passengers and it was considered unfair to subject others to the inconvenience of sitting for the entire night. He added that there were also standing passengers and did not consider it appropriate that anybody sleep on the floor.

There was a general murmuring and mumbling of voices as the passengers gathered their things and prepared to leave the train.

I quickly tidied up my medical bag and made my way back towards the first-class sleeper carriage. As I stepped into the corridor, the door of the compartment near to ours, opened and a man stepped out. I once again found myself face to face with one of the German gentlemen. He was as surprised as I was and quickly ducked back inside.

I made a note of the compartment number and stopped by my own to retrieve my suitcase in readiness to leave. I noticed that Holmes's case was still present, which seemed odd as he'd had much more time to pack than I.

I decided to find him first so that we could join the procession of passengers together rather than become separated.

As I reached the end of the corridor, I turned back just in time to see both Germans leaving their compartment. They looked around suspiciously then headed towards the second-class carriage. I noted they only had a small valise between them. I thought about calling out to them that the train was being evacuated but they were away before I could gain their attention. I stared after them for a moment before carrying on to seek out Holmes.

***

As I entered the club car, I found the majority of first-class passengers milling around with their belongings. A porter was checking names and allocating people to small groups for the onward journey.

I asked what the current plan was, and he told me that they had managed to acquire two small wagons that were able to transport four passengers at a time on to Hougham. There they had managed to find accommodation in the Inn, and a nearby manor house, for the first-class passengers. The townsfolk had rallied and set up temporary beds in the town hall for the remaining passengers.

I gave my name and Holmes's and we were allocated to a twin room at the Inn. I noticed that the Professor was in the same place. I was a little inwardly disturbed by the prospect of spending an evening talking further about mid-sixteenth century Prussian politics but decided if there was brandy involved then I would be fine.

I pushed on further, searching for Holmes but finding nothing until I came upon the open doorway leading down to the trackside. A chilly breeze wafted in through the doorway, so I pulled my collar up and left the train.

Darkness had well and truly set in, making it very difficult to see anybody outside. A few paraffin lanterns marked a bustle of activity further up the track. Just the sort of thing that would draw Holmes, so I pushed on through the cold to see what was happening.

A group of men milled around the train engine, pointing and waving hand-held lanterns at parts of the train.

From what I could see, the driving mechanism on one of the great steel wheels, located towards the rear of the engine car, had been damaged.

From my rudimentary knowledge of trains, I realised that the pin that held the crank in place was missing. There was just a hole with buckled metal, and the crank itself was bent and broken and lying askew.

It was that crank that drove the wheels, which meant this engine was going nowhere on its own.

“Damnable luck, ay, Watson,” came Holmes’s voice from behind me.

I turned and saw that he was smoking a cigarette and viewing the broken engine next to me.

“What would have caused something like that?” I asked.

“I can only assume we either hit a rock or tree trunk, or it was poorly maintained and broke from overuse," said Holmes.

I found his explanation a little below his usual enthusiasm for solving the unknown but forgave him as this didn’t appear to be anything worthy of his skills.

Then a new voice piped up from the gloom behind us. It had a much higher pitch than either of ours.

“I reckon I know what’s happened?” it said.

We both turned to see a young woman sitting on a tree stump in the gloom out of reach of the paraffin lamps. She stood up and stepped towards us.

It was then I realised it was the young lass I'd spied in the second-class car reading one of my pamphlets.

"And what do you think caused this?" Holmes asked, his interest now piqued. I was unsure if it was because of the attractiveness of the woman or from boredom.

"A bomb," she said.

I admit I guffawed out loud at the claim.

Holmes simply smiled and asked, "And why would you say that?"

"Two reasons," she said, "Don't you think there's an interesting smell?"

Holmes leaned in towards the wheel and sniffed.

"Oil, coal smoke," he said and sniffed again. It was then his face changed to surprise.

"That's it," she said.

"What is it, Holmes?" I asked.

Holmes turned and peered at the girl.

"Smells sweet. I'd say it's Nitro-Glycerine, mostly likely from dynamite. They still use it in Scotland. Easy to get," she said.

"And your second reason?" asked Holmes.

"This," she said and brought something out from behind her back.

Holmes reached down and grabbed one of the paraffin lamps to allow us a better look.

The object that the lass held was simply a mess of wires, metal strips and pieces of wood. It looked nothing like any type of bomb that we had ever dealt with before.

"Perhaps it's just some trackside rubbish that fell from a previous train?" I said.

She stared into my eyes with disdain. I immediately felt like retracting my statement just on the piercing derision contained in that stare.

"I think you sell the young lady short, Watson," said Holmes. He handed the lamp to me and took the object from the girl. Then proceeded to study almost every part of the mess.

After a moment he said, "Ingenious."

He looked up at the young woman and said, "Not just this device, but the fact you recognised it as such."

He began to point out parts of the contraption and explain what they did.

"These two flat panels would have been placed over two consecutive pieces of track. When the train wheel ran over both it completed an electrical circuit. The current ran down these wires that would have been inserted into a bundle of dynamite. It would have taken less than a second for detonation to occur. The fact that the main pin on the eccentric crank, which sits on the third to last wheels, was affected explains that. With the pin blown out, the wheels could no longer turn; therefore, the train was disabled. By design not accident."

He leaned in and sniffed the device.

"The same sweet smell as the train wheel. This device was definitely in contact with nitro-glycerine," he said.

He looked at the girl and handed the device back to her.

"Have you told the engineers?"

She nodded, "Yeah, they took one look at me and fobbed me off. I'm a girl. They know better."

She indicated the tree stump behind us.

"I've been sitting there, hoping you two would turn up," she said giving me a scornful look, "Thought you might at least listen."

I dropped my eyes to the ground, a little shameful of my own dismissal of her claims.

"Where did you find that?" Holmes asked nodding towards the device.

She turned her head and looked up the track.

"About seven hundred yards that way," she said, "When that bang went off, I started counting. We came to a standstill around thirty seconds after the bang. One of these trains goes about fifty miles an hour. I did the math."

"Extraordinary," I said.

"Then I walked off seven hundred steps and started looking. Found that about a minute later and hightailed it back here."

I found that I was regarding this young lady in a whole new light. Not only was she rather attractive, she was incredibly intelligent and resourceful.

It was then she held her hand out to Holmes.

"I'm Lois Cayley," she said shaking his hand and smiling.

"Sherlock Holmes," Holmes replied.

"Oh, I know who you two are," she said.

"Really?" I questioned.

"Yeah. I've read all your stories, Dr. Watson. Love them. I couldn't believe my eyes when I saw you walk through the second-class carriage."

She pulled a pamphlet out of her vest pocket and unfolded it. A small drawing of my likeness sat in the centre of the back page. I couldn't even remember sitting for the portrait but was most approving.

She looked at the drawing and said, "The picture doesn't really do you justice Doctor, but when I saw you here with Mr. Holmes, who looks exactly like his drawings, I knew it was you two."

"We are very flattered to have such a public knowledge of our appearance," said Holmes with a reproachful tone to his voice, mostly aimed at me, "But the question remains Why?"

"Why?"

"Yes, why, did someone wish to stop the train? What is their motive? Has there been or will there be a crime? If so what is it?" he said.

***

A group of engineers appeared to take another look at the broken wheel and crank. Holmes showed them the broken device and tried to convince them that the damage was possibly due to a bomb. None of the men seemed to be imbued with any level of humour and refused to even give any credence to the notion. After several moments of interchange between Holmes, Lois and the engineers, the three of us gave up.

Holmes said, "There's nothing more we can really achieve until we determine why someone wanted to stop this train. I think the only avenue open to us is to journey into Hougham with the rest of the passengers and take stock of those present."

"Ask around?" I asked.

"Precisely," he said.

Holmes handed the device back to Lois and said, "Yours I believe."

She simply looked at the mangled mess of wires and metal and tossed it to one side. Its usefulness had passed.

"If you think you're ditching me to take over this investigation, then you've got another thing coming. You're first-class passengers, so I'll meet you at the Inn," she said and walked off into the gloom towards the second-class carriage.

We both watched her leave, then I remarked, "My word, what a remarkable young lady."

Holmes simply watched her leave, a small grin on his face.

"She is that," he said.

We made our way back onto the train and found it remarkably empty. The other passengers had been ferried off to the nearby town whilst we had investigated the damaged train.

We headed back towards our sleeper and as we approached our own room, I noticed the door to the cabin the Germans had occupied was slightly ajar. It shouldn't have been of any interest but being a part of Holmes's life instils a heightened level of curiosity in one's soul.

I stepped up to the doorway and knocked. There was no reply, so I pushed the door open and looked inside. It was empty, the Germans and any luggage long gone.

It was only through sheer luck that I heard a groan as a started to close the door. I pushed my way into the room and noticed the connecting door was open.

From what I had gathered so far, the connecting room was Professor Lumley's room. I ducked in and was stunned at the scene.

The room had been ransacked. The contents of drawers and cupboards were strewn across the place. The professor's suitcases were open, any remaining items tossed aside.

Another groan echoed up from the floor.

There lying amidst the detritus of his suitcases, several items of loose clothing draped across his supine frame, was the professor himself.

I dropped to one knee and examined him. He had a nasty gash on his forehead and bruising around his chin and cheek. I was certain that the poor man had been assaulted.

"Professor?" I said, "It's John Watson. Can you hear me?"

Holmes poked his head into the room and looked around.

"What have you found, Watson?" he asked.

I looked up.

"The professor has been assaulted. My initial reaction is it was those Germans who were using the room you're standing in."

I looked back at the professor and lightly tapped him on the cheek.

"Professor? Professor?"

His eyelids fluttered slightly then opened.

"Professor, thank Lord," I said.

His face showed abject terror. He grasped my arms with his thin, scrawny fingers.

"I didn't tell them where it is. I didn't. It should still be safe."

"What is?" I asked.

He pulled himself towards me.

"You must protect Charlemagne," he said, his eyes wide in fright.

His eyes slowly shut again, he let out a final breath and relaxed his grip on my arms. I eased him back to the floor and gently tapped his cheek once more.

"Professor? Professor?" I asked.

I felt his neck, searching for a pulse or any sign of life. There was nothing. My shoulders slumped.

As I turned away, my knee caught some of the clothing and dragged them off the Professor's body.

"That explains it then," said Holmes.

I peered back and saw a large bloodstain on the professor's midriff. I could see an inch-wide wound, with blood still seeping from it.

"Murder," I muttered under my breath.

I turned to Holmes and asked, "But what was he muttering about?"

Holmes simply shook his head. I turned and began another scan of the room.

"The simple answer would lead to the reason the train was stopped," said a voice from behind Holmes.

I looked over Holmes's shoulder and saw Miss Cayley standing behind him. I was stunned that she could have crept up on him without notice.

Holmes pondered for a moment before posing the question.

"What was so important that the poor professor gave his life to protect it? And what was that about Charlemagne?" he asked of no-one in particular.

Miss Lois took that as a request for information and began to speak.

"Well, the professor and I were undertaking a similar journey, I presume. I am transferring from Edinburgh University to Cambridge. The word across campus was that Professor Lumley was taking a leave of absence to undertake some study in London. He was an expert in modern anthropology, specialising in early Prussian monarchy and politics. One of the rumours that has haunted the university, since I joined at least, was the existence of some rare artefact in the anthropology department. Nobody knew what it was, but all the gossip led back to Professor Lumley," she said.

"Well we'll never know now," I said.

"Have you found his journal?" Lois asked.

I turned back towards the comely girl.

"What?" I asked.

She pushed past Holmes and came into the professor's room. I thought it most impertinent of her at the time but was beginning to gather this was her normal attitude.

"His journal? He's a professor of history, surely he would have some form of diary or journal in his possession," she said as she began to rummage through the spilled contents littering the room.

I turned to Holmes, a questioning look on my face. He simply smiled and watched the young woman at work.

“She has a point, Watson,” he said.

I spun back just as Miss Cowley stood up with a thick leather-bound volume in her hand.

“I’d say this would be it,” she said handing it across to Holmes, “It’s locked. I reckon you’d have a better chance of breaking it open than me.”

Holmes reached into a pocket and extracted a small set of picklocks. He had the diary open within a matter of moments and flipped straight to the last entries.

All three of us crowded in to see the pages. Holmes flipped backwards and found one that had a rather detailed hand-drawn diagram of an ancient crown. It had none of the delicate beauty of Queen Victoria’s crown jewels but was more of a simple affair. There were eight golden panels each in a rectangular shape with a curved top. Each panel was adorned with large, somewhat gaudy jewels. I assumed that the artisans of the day did not possess the quality of implements to cut the gems to a smaller more ornate size. Four of the panels contained pictograms surrounded by jewels, the front was topped with a large golden cross and an arc of gold ran from front to back to strengthen the whole thing.

“The crown of Charlemagne,” said Holmes, “Formally used to crown the kings of France and believed to have been lost during the revolution.”

“It must be priceless,” I said.

“That would be an understatement,” said Holmes, “But the monetary value is negligible compared to the intrinsic heritage value to any of the Prussian, German or French states that Charlemagne once ruled over.”

“Do you reckon that’s what the Professor was bringing to London?” asked Lois.

Holmes flipped to the last entry, read it to himself and nodded.

“That’s exactly what he was doing,” he said.

“Does it say where he hid it?” Lois asked.

“No, but any person of intelligence would have left it in the safest place possible," he said, "And that would be the strongbox in the guards’ carriage.”

“You met the professor, didn’t you?” asked Lois, “He was very intelligent, just lacked a bit of common sense.”

“We can check the baggage car as we go through then,” he said.

***

As we exited through the connecting sleeper and into the corridor, Holmes ducked back into our room and moments later returned cradling our guns. We had taken them with us to Edinburgh in case any rum business arose. Thankfully they weren’t needed.

He handed mine to me and the weight of the cold metal in my hand brought back a flash of memories from the action I had seen in Afghanistan. I felt the phantom pain from my bullet wound again and winced.

Holmes saw my look and said, “These are just for protection. I don’t envisage we will be needing them.” He patted me on the shoulder and placed his own gun away. I followed suit and proceeded after him towards the rear of the train.

Lois piped up behind me.

“You don’t have a spare do you?” she asked.

I shook my head.

“Damn shame,” she said, “I suddenly feel a little vulnerable.”

I turned to her and said, “I’m sure that’s a new position for you, not something you would feel very often.”

“It’s a modern world, Dr. Watson, a woman has to have confidence and be prepared to survive in it.”

I nodded and smiled. We hurried on after Holmes.

As we made our way through the next first-class carriage, we could hear grunts and muffled curses from ahead. Holmes slowed and eased himself against the wall leading to the gangway between cars.

I could hear the noise of several large suitcases and trunks being tossed around and finally, a curse in German wafted out. The owner of the voice was evidently looking for something as he mumbled to himself, “Wo ist es? Gottverdammt.” (Where is it? Goddammit)

The sound of another loud thump against a sidewall announced another suitcase flying across the car. Holmes placed his right hand in his pocket, grasping his gun, and walked out into the gangway. We followed close behind. I had my hand on my gun as well.

"Hello there," he said, "We've just come to see about our bags. I see you're having a little trouble yourself, perhaps we can help?"

We stopped as the tall, ugly faced man, stared at us with intense hatred and pulled a knife from his pocket.

"Niemand wird dir helfen, Englander," he said and launched forward with the knife. (No-one will help you, Englander)

Holmes batted the blade away and stepped to his left. He immediately jabbed at the German's jaw with his left hand and followed through with a right punch.

Dazed, the German reeled back, before refocusing and launching forward with the blade once more. Holmes managed to grab his leading arm and brought it down on his knee. The blade dropped from his hand and skittered across the floor of the baggage car, disappearing under a discarded suitcase.

Holmes and the German squared up and began to trade blows. I pulled my gun and tried to aim at the German. I intended to wing him, but such a shot was difficult to pull off in the circumstances.

The two combatants finally parted, and just as I was about to pull the trigger, Lois stepped in front of me. I cursed under my breath and dropped my gun hand.

The young lady kept moving and it was then I noticed she held a portable fire extinguisher. She hefted the shiny cylinder above her head and waited for the right moment.

Suddenly, the German was forced back towards her from one of Holmes's left crosses and she struck. Lois brought the extinguisher down onto the German's head with a resounding crack. He dropped like a stone and lay still.

Worried that she'd killed him, I dodged around her and knelt to check the man's vitals. I let out a sigh as I realised he still had a pulse.

Holmes said, "Good work young lady, though I would have had him eventually."

"I figured we didn't have time for macho heroics. We need to find the other one and rescue the crown," she said.

Holmes nodded in deference, "Quite, so."

He turned and led the way through the second-class carriage. I sidled up to him and whispered.

"We should have tied him up," I said.

"No time, Watson, plus the young lady is right, we need to get after his friend," he replied.

***

Just as we entered the final second-class carriage, we spied a shadowy figure moving about in the Guards' carriage.

"There," shouted Lois.

I drew my gun, as the three of us hurried our way down the aisle. Holmes managed to outpace both Lois and myself and reached the final car first.

He suddenly turned, a horrified look on his face, and rushed back towards us.

"Back," he cried. I soon knew why.

An explosion in the guards' car rocked the carriage, throwing the three of us backwards. I landed heavily against a row of seats and struck my head. I understand that I passed out and only have the recollections of Holmes and Miss Cayley to piece the rest of my narrative together.

Holmes landed near me and was rendered unconscious also. Lois was the lucky one. She was shielded from the blast by the two of us but was thrown backwards. She landed heavily but remained relatively unscathed.

She got to her feet, her head still a little groggy, and looked towards the guards' car. The shadowy figure crept back into the burning carriage and picked a cube-shaped object from within the ruins of the strongbox. The figure turned and looked once towards her before darting out of the back of the wagon.

Lois picked her way past our reposing forms and hurried towards the rear. As she reached the exit she spied the man running up a nearby pathway towards a waiting horse-drawn cart. She jumped down and gave chase, catching up with the man just as he placed the small box into the rear of the cart and jumped up onto the trap.

In the most unladylike fashion, Lois leapt onto the trap runners, grabbed the man by his lapels and pulled him bodily from the cart. They both landed amongst the dust and stones by the side of the road.

Lois regained her feet first and strode to the cart and pulled out the metal box. She turned to the man and said, "I will return this. It's not your property. It's the property of the University and the Queen herself."

The man began to chuckle as he got to his feet.

"Oh, but there you are right and very wrong, Fraulein. True, it is not my property, but neither is it the property of your Queen. In fact, it is the property of Kaiser Wilhelm, the Emperor of Germany and modern Prussia," he said.

"If that is the case then he should talk to the correct authorities, not send a pair of common thieves to steal it for him," she said, "I'm sure they would listen."

"You are still yet young. The power and prestige possessed by such as that crown, are not given up lightly. Your Queen, your Prime Minister, your Government, would never submit to such a request. We thought it much easier to take matters into our own hands," he said as he brushed dirt from his coat.

"You killed an old man," she said, her voice filled with vitriol.

"He would not cooperate. Damn fool. Gunther overstepped the mark, but," he held out his hands in a plea of innocence, "if the professor had complied he would still be alive."

Lois stared at the German. Her anger simmering and ready to boil. She took a step forward.

"I will take this, and the proper authorities will deal with you," she said.

"I think not, Fraulein," the German said.

Lois stopped when she spied the gun pointed at her.

"Are you going to kill me too?" she said as her anger began to subside, and she tried to maintain her composure.

"I wish not as you are a lovely creature, but you know too much and that could embarrass the Kaiser," he said, "Now please put the Crown back onto the cart. There's a good girl."

"Don't good girl me," Lois screamed, her resolve flooding back in waves.

She hefted the box and threw it towards the German. It struck him in the chest, knocking him slightly backwards. The box continued its journey, falling to the ground with a dull thud.

The German's gun hand rose and aimed at Lois.

"Thank you, Fraulein, and Auf Wiedersehen," he said.

The sound of the gun cocking filled Lois's ears. She turned away in an attempt to avoid the bullet.

The sound of a gunshot rang out into the still night.

After a moment, Lois's eyes opened. Her brain searched through every nerve ending but failed to feel any pain. She straightened in time to see the German's stunned expression as he stared at her, his finger still poised on the trigger of the gun.

He gagged several times, trying to form words but failed. A dark stain spread out across his shirt. His hand relaxed and the gun fell to the ground, no longer a threat to anyone. The German dropped to his knees then fell face-first into the dirt.

Standing behind him, smoke trailing from the barrel of his gun, was Holmes.

***

I awoke to find Holmes kneeling over me, a concerned look on his face. As I blinked my eyes to allow them to focus on his aquiline face, I saw a smile bloom on his mouth.

"How are you, old friend?" he asked, reaching out a hand to help me into a sitting position.

I noticed Lois standing nearby holding a solid-looking metal box.

"Is that?" I asked.

Lois nodded.

Holmes cocked his head and said, "Actually we haven't checked yet."

I managed to regain my feet as Lois placed the box on a nearby seat. The strong padlock on the front proved to be no hurdle for Holmes as he quickly went to work with his picklocks.

The padlock dropped to the floor of the carriage and we all congregated around as Lois slowly opened the lid.

I think all three of us were rather relieved when we saw the circular gold shape within the box. Lois reached in and withdrew the crown. It was almost exactly like the drawing in Professor Lumley's journal.

It was a very chunky and overtly ornate piece of jewellery, but it had a certain regal look about it and I could well imagine it sitting on the head of the once king of all of western Europe.

My thoughts were broken by Lois.

"Good Lord it's ugly," she said.

"It has a certain charm though," said Holmes.

"I believe it would have looked magnificently majestic on top of Charles the Great's head," I said in defence of the crown.

Holmes smiled and said, "I do agree with you there, Watson. Maybe not the style of crown to adorn our own Queen's head, but a ninth-century warrior king? Yes, I believe so."

Lois turned it around to examine every side of the crown, before returning it to the box.

"Well, what do we do with it now?" she asked.

***

We quickly found the chief engineer who was still surveying the damaged engine and consulting with his crew to determine a way of moving the train. After briefing him of the whole affair he located the conductor and left us to it.

As luck would have it the next carriage to Hougham was just leaving, we sent word with them to alert the local sheriff. With nothing more to do we settled into the club car and awaited the arrival of the authorities.

The bar had been vacated, so I fixed some drinks and we sat down to allow Holmes and Lois to run through their version of the evening's events. I pulled out my notepad and took down copious notes, surprised and alarmed by the various actions of my cohorts.

When both stories were finished, I reread and asked questions to garner extra details. I was amazed at the audacity and athleticism of the remarkable young lady. I peeked across at Holmes from time to time while she told her tale and saw a smile and a look of admiration on his face.

"This was probably not the gentle journey you had expected, my dear," said Holmes, "Where will you go to from here?"

Lois took a sip from her gin and tonic and told us how she spent two years at finishing school in Switzerland, before returning and entering University in Edinburgh.

"I'm afraid that I didn't enjoy the courses on offer, so am heading south to Girton College in Cambridge. I hope to finish my course over the next two years," she said.

"Admirable," said Holmes, "What is your desire for career and life?"

Lois thought for a moment, staring off into space as if to gather her thoughts.

"Adventure," she replied, "I think not the dull life of a married woman for me. My father was a soldier, he always told me to take life by the throat and wring as much out of it as possible."

"And good for you," said Holmes, "Too many a good-spirited woman succumbs to a life of servitude. There needs to be more of your ilk in this world."

I thought on the mention of her father for a moment then asked, "Your father. Where did he serve?"

"He was in the Forty-second Highlanders," she said, "Sadly he died in the war with Afghanistan."

"My word," said Watson, "Captain Thomas Cayley."

She cocked her head at the name.

"Why yes," she said.

"One of the bravest men I've ever met," I said. We had crossed paths during the war. It was one of the biggest regrets of my life. I met him several days before his final campaign. So, full of life and a larger character than even his imposing frame could promote. The next time we met he was carried in on a stretcher. His flesh rent by wounds and bleeding profusely. I had neither the skill nor tools to aid him and he passed under my care.

I related this all to Lois whose face dropped, showing a mix of sadness and admiration. She held back tears as she leant forward and took my hand in hers.

"Thank you, Doctor," she said, "He obviously made quite an impression on you in such a short time, and I can only express my gratitude that you tried to save him."

She leant back and took a long draw on her drink. I repeated her actions. I rose and fixed another round. After my little story, I think we all needed it.

After a brief pause, Holmes finally spoke up.

"I think, Miss Cayley, should accompany us to London for the time being. If I understand correctly, the next semester does not start at Cambridge for at least another week," he said.

Lois nodded. Holmes pointed to the metal box.

"We need to see that the cause of all this fuss is taken on to its intended destination. I also believe that my brother should be informed of these events," he said, "And I strongly believe that Miss Cayley here should be rewarded for her part in the recovery of the crown. I will be putting that to Mycroft as well," he said.

He smiled at Lois.

"My brother works for the Government, so I am sure they will be filled with gratitude and can be convinced to convert that gratitude to some form of compensation," he said.

Lois's face lit up with that thought.

"I was only doing what I thought was right, but could always manage better with extra funds," she said.

"Couldn't we all," I remarked.

The Adventure of the Double Cross

It was a lovely late summer afternoon in 1890 when the shrill cry of our doorbell broke the serenity. I was reposing in our small garden with a cup of iced tea and the Sunday papers. Mary stepped out onto the patio and handed me a folded telegram.

"I think it's from Sherlock," she said, adding with a wry grin, "Should I prepare your travelling case?"

Perplexed, I stared at the proffered telegram and then back at my wife and shrugged.

"Oh, I shouldn't think it will immediately come to that," I said.

Mary chuckled to herself, "No, it never does," and retired back into the house.

I watched her go for a moment then turned my attention to the paper. Unfolding it, I read the words with a touch of trepidation and excitement.

It asked for my attendance at a meeting between Holmes and Lestrade at 221B Baker Street, at ten o'clock on the morrow.

"The game is afoot?" I asked myself in hope. Secretly, I admitted to myself that life had grown a trifle dull these last few months. Any chance of an adventure with Holmes was a chance worth taking.

***

I stepped from the Hansom onto the footpath outside the dwelling that Holmes and I once shared and welcomed the glorious morning sun on my face.

Part of me still missed my time in this house, but another part reminded me of who waited for me in my own home. I smiled at that, proceeded to the front door and rang the bell.

Mrs Hudson's face was awash with delight as she saw me standing there. Forgetting herself for a moment she threw her arms around me and welcomed me inside.

"Oh, I'm so happy to see you, Doctor, his nibs hasn't been himself for so many weeks now. Only the odd bit of adventure for him from time to time, the rest he spends alone up there. I takes him food, but most nights it comes back uneaten. I've been ever so worried," she said.

I comforted her and apologised for my absence. I explained that I had been extremely busy with my practice and had failed to call upon my old friend and cohort. I promised to make amends, starting with this current endeavour.

She smiled and seemed satisfied.

At the top of the stairs, I knocked once and entered.

I found Holmes sitting in the sunlight filtering into the parlour. He was dressed ready to leave at any moment and was perusing the morning paper. I realised immediately that it was more from impatience than interest, as he bolted to his feet and shook my hand as if we hadn't crossed paths in years. In truth, it had been a few weeks, but I appreciated his welcome all the same.

"What ho, Holmes?" I said, "Have you any clew as to the Inspector's request?"

Holmes shook his head.

"No, Watson, nothing. I've read all the papers and there has been nothing reported of note, so I can't imagine it is a high profile case of any sort, which is a little disappointing, but I admit I have been rather bereft of anything of concern for a while now, so I am very interested in what he has on offer."

He stepped across to the coffee table and poured two cups from the steaming pot.

"Coffee?" he asked in hindsight.

"Thank you," I answered, not necessarily needing another, but not wanting to cause any offence or break in concentration on my friend's part.

I blew on my coffee to cool it slightly and sipped. Remembrance filled my mind; Mrs Hudson did make a good brew. As I took another sip, the doorbell rang.

"Ah, that would be the Inspector," said Holmes placing his cup down and pouring a third, adding a single spoonful of sugar and some milk before stirring it while we heard the sound of footsteps climbing the staircase outside.

Holmes stood with the cup in hand as there was a knock on the door and Inspector Lestrade stepped in.

"Lestrade," said Holmes, "Good to see you." He extended his hand and, surprised, Lestrade took the proffered cup.

"And you Holmes," he took a sip, and let out an audible sigh of pleasure. "Perfect."

He turned towards me and nodded, "Doctor."

I returned the motion. Holmes left a pause of silence hanging in the air while we all became attuned to the same level before speaking.

"Now, Inspector, you have a problem," he said, before taking his seat. I mirrored his actions and Lestrade set his cup down, removed his hat and coat and sat on the third corner of a triangle between us.

"Yes, yes, I do," he said, a slight expression of embarrassment or concern crossing his face.

"I presume it's not a Yard request, as there has been nothing reported this morning," said Holmes, waving a hand across the small pile of newspapers nearby.

"No, nothing like that," said Lestrade, picking up his cup and sipping it again. "It's personal."

Holmes brightened, "Oh, yes?"

Lestrade's face grew darker.

"It's about my cousin. Foolish girl," he said.

I stifled a smirk at the outburst from the Inspector, a man I had known for many years and one who held his emotions and opinions in check at all times.

"Go on," said Holmes.

"A couple of years ago, she went off and got herself married again."

"Nothing strange in that."

"To an American," he spat, a hint of inter-country animosity underpinning his speech. I was even more surprised. Holmes's face remained impassive.

"No. It's nothing like that. I don't care that he's from the States, it's just that I don't know anything about him."

"I assume you checked his background," said Holmes with a grin.

"Of course, I did. My family would have been disappointed if I hadn't. I love my cousin. I've known her all my life. Last thing I want is for her to be hurt. Now, this berk has gone and run off, or disappeared at least, according to her."

"Well, it could happen. Many a man disappears in this city over the course of a year," I said in the unknown man's defence.

"Yeah, but, they are usually low-lifes," Lestrade said.

I nodded. It was true, the underworld of the city was a ruthless place.

"Do you have a name?" asked Holmes.

"Goes by the name of William Middleton. Well-built fellar, about as tall as you, Holmes; dark hair, neatly trimmed beard. Runs a tailor shop down Camden way. I couldn't find anything about him. It's almost like he just appeared five years ago. Claims to have come over from Georgia, to ply his trade in the great metropolis. I've always had my doubts. I mean who would leave America to come to this place? From what I hear the roads are paved with gold and the weather's always marvellous," Lestrade said.

"There is a lot to love about London and England for that matter," I said trying to lighten the mood, "It's not all darkness and crime."

Lestrade glanced at me, then turned back to look into the distance while he sipped his coffee.

"Anyway, Francine drags me around and says that Bill was gone. Four days ago. It's too early to bring it up at the Yard, so I thought I'd come here. I've tracked his trail and there's nothing. Like his past, really. Just nothing. I've got a bit saved up so I can pay you."

"Don't be silly, Inspector," said Holmes, much to my own relief, "I wouldn't dream of ever asking you for money."

Lestrade looked relieved as well.

"Finish your coffee and then you can escort us to this man's shop," he said.

Lestrade nodded and drained his cup. He placed it on the tray and stood up.

"Best get going then," he said.

Surprised, I quickly drained my cup and repeated Lestrade's actions. Holmes simply smiled as he sipped and glanced up and down at the agitated vision of the Inspector.

***

The Hansom dropped the three of us at the corner of Camden High street and Pratt Street. Holmes stopped for a moment and peered around. I followed his gaze, which stopped on a young street urchin holding out his cap to passers-by in the hope of receiving a few coppers. The urchin looked across at Holmes, nodded and replaced his cap. Holmes nodded in return and I watched as the urchin hurried off and disappeared into the crowd.

I realised that this must have been one of the Baker Street Irregulars, the little band of urchins and street people that Holmes employed as a sort of spy network spread across greater London.

We walked down Pratt Street and Lestrade stopped before a three-story Georgian terrace. The ground floor was a small shop with the name "The Yellow Rose Tailor" proudly displayed on the front hoarding. A door to the side of the shop indicated that the floors above were dwellings.

Holmes studied the shop frontage for a moment before addressing Lestrade.

"I thought you said that this Middleton fellow was from Georgia?"

Lestrade nodded, "Yes, that's what he told my cousin."

"Why, Holmes?" I asked.

"Well Watson, the yellow rose is a name often given to a young slave girl named Emily West, who was captured by Santa Anna, and taken with him when he invaded Texas in 1835. The stories say that she was a spy who helped the Texan army defeat the Mexicans at the Battle of San Jacinto. She is somewhat of a hero and legend in Texas. I don't believe that her name would even be known amongst the people of Georgia."

"Remarkable what snippets of information you retain Holmes," I said.

"Thank you, Watson."

He stepped towards the front door, "Shall we go in?"

Just at that moment a cry of, “Hello,” echoed out from behind.

We turned to see a small group of people hurrying towards us. One taller gentleman stepped forward and addressed us directly.

“I say,” he said, “Do you gentlemen have any idea where Middleton has got to?”

Lestrade took the lead and replied, “That’s partly why we’re here. I’m Inspector Lestrade of Scotland Yard. We are investigating Mr. Middleton’s apparent disappearance. Any information that you could provide would be most appreciated.”

The face of the man at the front dropped in agitation. He pointed at the shop and said, “I’ve no idea where the fool has gone, but he’s still got my suit in there. I haven’t got another, and I needed it yesterday, for Sunday service.”

Another man piped up behind him.

“And he owes me money for groceries. I’ve tried his wife, but she’s skint, an’ din’t know where he was.”

Lestrade held up his hands before the mob began baying for blood.

“I am sorry, but we are as mystified as you all seem to be. Our only hope is to trace Middleton’s last steps and see where they lead. We can surmise all we like, but until we find evidence there’s not a lot we can do.”

Holmes smiled.

“I think you are starting to come to my way of thinking,” he said before turning towards the crowd. “Might I ask who here last saw Middleton?” he asked.

A woman’s voice piped up from the rear, “I dropped off my skirt on Wednesday around two,” she said.

Another said, “I saw him leave not long after that.”

“Me too,” said another man.

Holmes looked at both.

“In which direction did he go?”

“He was headed to the high street,” said the first pointing in one direction.

“No, I saw him going towards College Street,” said the second pointing in the other.

Holmes stared at both men for a moment and was about to open his mouth to ask something when the woman spoke up.

"No, he was on the high street. I passed him around two-thirty. I asked him when my skirt would be ready, and he ignored me completely and breezed by without a by-your-leave. I was ropeable. Though he did seem very troubled."

"And which way was he headed then?" asked Holmes.

"South, down towards Euston Road," she said.

Holmes smiled. "Thank you all." He pulled out a small notebook and pen and handed it to the man at the front of the group. "Can you all please put your names and addresses down in this notebook? We may need to come and see you again."

The man took the book and quickly scribbled his name inside. He handed it to another who simply stared at the writing implement before the woman grabbed it off him.

"You really must learn to write one of these days, Fred," she said and entered both her own and Fred's details. The other two followed suit and handed them back to Holmes. As they bustled away we turned back to the shop. Holmes barely glanced at the list of names before returning the little pad to an inner pocket.

Lestrade pulled a ring of keys from his pants pocket, selected a large brass mortice key and unlocked the front door. Struggling, he pushed the door, only to have it stick. Lestrade jiggled it back and forth a few times before he managed to push it wide enough to enter. He ducked behind and picked up a pile of mail and parcels that had gathered.

Finally, the door opened fully with Lestrade holding his find.

"That's quite a bit of mail for only a few days," I said.

Lestrade looked at the items. There were two large ones that appeared to be fabric, with a number of envelopes as well.

"It would appear that business is healthier than my cousin lets on," he said.

"Is that something your cousin has mentioned?" asked Holmes, ever alert for clews.

Lestrade looked up at my friend, "She has mentioned it on and off for the last few months. Middleton always seems busy, but there's only ever enough money to make ends meet, never any more for luxuries."

"Interesting."

"Why?"

Holmes peered around the front of the shop. A polished wooden counter greeted all customers, with a set of changing rooms sitting off to the side. The frontage was furnished with exquisite fabrics and drapery, with two dressmakers' dummies sporting elegant suits on view in the front window.

"One wouldn't think that business was slow, given the style used in this area," he said.

Lestrade peered around and nodded in agreement.

I admit that I was quite taken aback by the ornate dressings of the shopfront and would happily have given my business to the owner.

Holmes walked towards a covered area behind the counter and flung back the drapes revealing a doorway leading to the rear of the shop. He pushed through and Lestrade and I quickly followed.

As expected, the rear of the shop was a plainer, more productive environment. Two sewing machines sat on benches to one side. Several dressmakers' models wearing unfinished suits and dresses stood nearby. A large flat table took up most of the middle of the room; this was obviously the cutting and preparation table, as a half-finished garment adorned the surface.

"It would appear that our Mr. Middleton left in quite a hurry," Holmes said, peering around the room and stopping his gaze at the unfinished suit. To me, it looked the type to be worn to Sunday service.

A small desk sat in the corner, next to a sturdy looking safe. A pile of letters and bills of sale sat upon the desk, reflecting Holmes's question concerning the state of the business.

Lestrade dumped his armful of letters and packages upon the cutting table. They spilled across the surface. My eyes were drawn to a small light-coloured envelope that was slightly thicker than the other larger envelopes containing bills and orders.

The sound of a drawer sliding open drew my attention away from the mail. I looked up and saw Holmes rifling through the desk. He pulled out a foolscap leather-bound volume and placed it on the desk.

Intrigued I stepped up and looked over his shoulder. The pages within the folio showed columns of figures with annotations as to the source.

"The accounts?" I asked.

Holmes nodded; his attention directed at the figures. He proceeded to flip through to the end and made several murmurs as something gelled in his mind.

"Anything, Holmes?" I asked.

"Yes, Watson, quite." He pointed at the final few figures of the accounts book. I saw that they were quite large. By my simple reckoning, Middleton's business was doing rather well for itself. I peered up the column and noticed several figures in the debit column. The scrawl next to them was a simple repeated line exclaiming, "XF to JC," each was a sizeable figure and reduced the running balance to almost zero at every occurrence.

"Do you think XF means transfer?" I asked Holmes, pointing at one of the entries.

"I would think it is something like that. From what I can tell, the money coming in is substantial. The business is doing well, but almost every month or so, a large sum is transferred out with no real identification as to the destination. This JC seems to be code," he said.

I turned to Lestrade, "Middleton's not a religious man is he?"

Lestrade's eyes widened in surprise, "I don't think so why?"

"Just a hunch," I said, "JC, Jesus Christ, it may have been a tithing payment or some such to the church."

Holmes smiled, "Very good Watson, I like your thinking. This is not a religious donation, but I believe you may be on the money, so to speak, this JC may actually be a person or a group of some sort. Perhaps, they were Middleton's benefactors and these payments are to pay down a debt."

He stood up and looked at the safe.

"Inspector, do you think that ring of keys has one that fits this safe?" he said, bending to peer at the engraved plate above the lock.

“It’s a Harold Haworth, 1850C.” He moved the small brass cover plate aside to reveal the keyhole. “Ah, yes, it would be a standard double mortice lock.”

Lestrade walked over and held the ring of keys before him. Even I could tell there was nothing that qualified for the correct key.

“Hmmm,” said Holmes and moved back to rifle through the desk drawers again. After a few moments, he stood and withdrew his lock pick set. I could tell from a slight grin on his mouth that he was hoping they would be required.

He knelt down, laid out the kit on the floor beside him and set to work. Within a minute or two we heard the satisfying click of the lock mechanism and the thick metal door opened silently on its well-oiled hinges.

The interior was littered with papers, envelopes and more books. Holmes examined each in turn, before standing up with what looked like a small bank account book. He flipped through the entries, then stepped over to the ledger. After a moment of reading both books together, he said, "Ah-ha."

“Holmes?”

He turned the bank book around and showed us the entries within.

The bank book simply showed a series of deposits. I peered down at the accounts book and made the same discovery. The amounts and dates were identical with each of the accounting entries marked “XF to JC.”

“Who’s the account for?” asked Lestrade.

Holmes turned the book around once more and opened to the first page.

“It says, John Calder,” he looked up for a moment searching his memories, “I don’t know that name, but it’s the address that is interesting. This account is with the Bank of Cornwall, Penzance Branch. I assume then that Middleton has been making entries into the account via a local branch, or even a different bank altogether, and they are transferred to this Penzance branch. It would seem his benefactor comes from Cornwall.”

"That's news to me, Francine has never mentioned anything about Cornwall or Penzance. I figured Middleton had come straight to London from Southampton or Portsmouth. Well, I never," said Lestrade.

While Holmes checked the safe again, I wandered over to the cutting table and rifled through the mail. As I had expected, apart from the two bolts of material, the rest were bills and invoices. Then my eyes fell on the buff-coloured envelope.

I picked it up and turned it over. To my surprise, it was not an official letter at all. There was no stamp. No postmark. Not even an address. Only a single word was scrawled on the front in a very jagged form of handwriting. I said the name out loud.

"Mudge."

"Who?" asked Lestrade.

I turned and saw both looking at me. I held the envelope before me.

"This envelope was amongst the mail, it simply says 'Mudge' on the front. What or who 'Mudge' is, I have no idea."

Lestrade picked up a letter opener from the desk and joined me. He took the envelope and carefully slit along the top.

"Police business. I'll explain to Middleton when I see him next," he said with a sly grin.

He opened the top of the envelope and upended it over the table. A small folded piece of similarly coloured paper slid out and I gasped when the rest of the contents spilled onto the table. They tumbled out one at a time until five stared up at me.

Holmes looked up and saw my expression of horror.

"Watson?" he asked as he moved across and peered down at the table. He was silent for a moment, then simply said, "Interesting."

The three of us stared down at the small dried objects on the table.

Lestrade said, "Lemon seeds?"

"Orange pips," said Holmes, "Five orange pips."

He reached for the note and opened it. Inside, one name was written in red in the same handwriting: *Calhoun*. Below the name was a crudely drawn glyph with one horizontal and two vertical lines, all within a red circle.

"Not again," I said.

"I think so," said Holmes.

"I'm confused," said Lestrade.

***

It was a whirlwind of action that found me early the next morning sitting in a first-class sleeper across from Holmes wending our way to Penzance deep in the south of Cornwall.

I replayed the last few hours of the previous afternoon in my mind as we pulled out of Paddington station and began the journey westwards.

Holmes explained to Lestrade the significance of the five orange pips. A sign that the nefarious organisation known as the Ku Klux Klan had a vendetta against the addressee of the note. Holmes, however, added that the person of interest was not the name on the outside of the envelope, this Mudge, but the name scrawled inside, Calhoun.

He stated at the time and backed it up once we returned to Baker Street in the early evening, that Calhoun was indeed the Captain of the ill-fated Lone Star, a bark, registered in Savannah, Georgia, that we believed to hold the murderers of Joseph and John Openshaw. They had never been brought to justice as the Lone Star was believed lost at sea not long after the younger Openshaw's death.

Lestrade was now extremely interested. This was no longer just a case of his missing cousin-in-law, but a case of unsolved murder from many years previously.

Back at 221B, Holmes quickly pulled down his notes from the previous case that concerned the unfortunate demise of members of the Openshaw family, supposedly at the hands of the Ku Klux Klan.

Stuck between the pages was a loose leaf of paper. Holmes pulled it out and read. It was the crew manifest for the Lone Star. Three names were underlined in red. James Calhoun (Captain), William Mudge (mate) and George Savage.

The facts of the case came to mind. These three were the only Americans on the ship at the time. The Lone Star was registered in

Savannah, Georgia, but I remember Holmes stating that the name probably originated from Texas, it being called the Lone Star state.

"I thought this was all done and dusted when the Lone Star was lost," I had said.

Holmes held up the small envelope with the pips inside and the note.

"Given the names on this letter, I can surmise, but not prove, that there were at least two survivors of that shipwreck," he said.

"What does the symbol mean?" Lestrade asked of the three-lined sigil above Calhoun's name.

Holmes looked at it for a moment.

"The Ku Klux Klan is known for using a version of the Greek cross, which has a shortened vertical line, with a small picture of a drop of blood in the centre. During the Openshaw case, I sent for a volume related to this newly established group and using that, I found that they also have a version with two vertical stems that signifies vengeance. Simply, a double-cross."

"So, this Calhoun has double-crossed the Ku Klux Klan?" asked Lestrade.

"It would seem that way," said Holmes, "Given our experience with them, I can only hope we find him before they do."

"What if they finish the job for us?" I asked.

"I would rather we brought him to justice, at least only to give closure to the Openshaw family," he said, "What's left of it."

I had nodded in agreement.

Holmes was quiet for the first part of the journey, his mind seemed ablaze, but his demeanour was dour.

He finally turned to me and said, "Facts, Watson, facts and data. I have too little of both to predict an outcome. That frustrates me no end."

His only deductions to date were that Calhoun and Mudge must have survived the sinking of the Lone Star. The "JC" that supposedly received monies from Middleton was most likely the Captain, James Calhoun. The location was interesting, but as it was the most westerly part of the United Kingdom, the survivors probably washed up there. One possibility was also that this Mudge had journeyed to London to set up a business and raise funds for their return to America and was sending money back to Calhoun either to stockpile or as restitution.

I had asked why Calhoun wasn't in London. To that, he had no direct answer but admitted that Calhoun was in his early sixties, and may have been injured or incapacitated as a consequence of the Lone Star's demise.

Holmes admitted that was why he wished to go to Penzance. From the apparent quick disappearance of Middleton and the last known sighting, he surmised that our quarry headed towards Euston station. Either to escape altogether, or more likely, head to his benefactor in Penzance in person, rather than simply send a telegram.

That was our reason for heading with such haste to the far-flung reaches of the country.

In my lovely wife's defence, she has more insight than I could hope to have at times. I returned home late and informed her that I was to be off early the next morning. She presented me with both a late and nutritious supper and a packed valise ready for at least four day's travel.

Her justification was that I had been out for longer than expected, and the fact that Inspector Lestrade had sent a note directly to me. She handed it over with a slight grin.

I read the contents. Lestrade apologised to me for not coming with us but gave me the name of a trusted officer in the Penzance police station.

I slept a little easier than expected with the knowledge we would have some form of constabulary backup.

That relief was dashed with what Holmes said when we had settled down in our compartment.

He simply leaned over and said, "We are being followed."

Shocked, I asked for an immediate explanation; then Holmes's actions the previous day came to mind.

As soon as we exited Middleton's tailor shop, we were approached by a very young street urchin. If not for the caked dirt on his face I would have called him rather handsome or even cute for his age.

Holmes had taken a shine and talked to the boy, before reaching into his pocket and dropping a guinea into his outstretched cap. The boy had scurried off without another word. On the train, Holmes had confessed that the boy was one of the Baker Street Irregulars and had been put on the case.

It was Holmes's belief that the fact we found an envelope with pips in it, meant that the sender was still around and apparently unaware of Middleton's departure.

It seemed likely that the person would be keeping watch on the tailor shop and had undoubtedly seen the three of them enter the previous day. Holmes had told the young urchin to spread the word and have himself, Lestrade and I, watched and followed.

I then remembered another urchin approached Holmes as we made our way into the Paddington Station proper. I smirked to myself that Holmes was a soft touch, recalling how he entered into a long exchange which ended with another guinea changing hands.

Holmes now confessed that he and I had both been followed by two men. One a dark-haired, swarthy gentleman with a large bushy beard, the other a tall, fair-skinned, powerfully built blonde man.

"Good Lord," I exclaimed.

"Yes," he said, "I do hope you brought your service revolver as I requested."

I patted my pocket, one to signify to him, the other to calm my nerves and reassure myself that it was still there.

"Who are they?" I asked.

"They are either members of the KKK, as it is called, who are desperate to know the whereabouts of Calhoun, or, and this may sound very strange, they are other crew members from the Lone Star," he said, "And if I was to make a conjecture, I would say they are Savage and one of the Finns."

My eyes grew wide. "How could you tell that?"

He smiled, "Simply from the facts. We presume that only the Americans on board were in league with the KKK; Savage is the only American we aren't sure about; and the large blonde fellow sounds like someone of Finnish extraction."

I nodded. It made sense but was still a supposition until proven.

***

The sudden jolting of the train snapped me awake. I looked around the compartment and noticed Holmes was missing. The bathroom door slid open and an elderly gentleman, replete with grey hair and large pair of wiry grey sideboards stepped into the compartment.

I almost stood up at the audacious intrusion of the fellow.

"I say, Sir, I think you have the wrong compartment," I blurted out.

The man simply smiled and shook his head.

"Holmes?"

"Yes, Watson, of course it's me."

"Why the devil are you dressed like that?" I realised he was wearing attire more suited to second or third class than the first-class carriage which we occupied.

"I'm going to do a little investigation and track down our friends," he said, "Give me an hour and I'll meet you in the club car. It is time for luncheon, and we can discuss what to do on arrival."

With that, he unlatched the door and was gone before I could say another word.

I checked my pocket watch and realised we had been gone from London for a good two and a half hours. I decided to wait for another half an hour before making my way to the club car. I calculated that I should be able to enjoy a small meal and drink in peace before Holmes joined me.

As it was, I had finished my meal of smoked trout and vegetables and was sitting back with a brandy and reading the paper, which I had saved for such a moment, when Holmes, dressed in his normal attire again, joined me.

I folded the paper as he said, "Watson!"

"Anything to report, Holmes?"

He smiled and was about to speak when the waiter arrived. Holmes ordered the same as I and waited for quiet once more.

"There are two of them, just as my spy reported. I was detained for a while as I sat behind and waited for them to speak. The swarthy bearded man is an American. He has a broad accent, from the south, possibly Texas or Tennessee. The other is definitely a Finn. He has very little English, and a very broad accent to go with his northern European looks."

"Very good, where does that leave us? Obviously, they are following us, which means they are after our quarry."

"If the American is this Savage fellow, then it indicates that our quarry is indeed Calhoun, or at least that's what Savage thinks as well. We will need to lose them on arrival in Penzance."

He smiled.

"I believe another little disguise may be of advantage."

It was then I told him about Lestrade's contact. I had avoided the fact until we knew of what lay at the end of our journey.

"Excellent. I think the constabulary will be of use if we find Calhoun and need him arrested. Until then I would prefer to lead the investigation. I think the best course of action is for you to proceed to the hotel. That way you can lead Savage and the Finn away from me. I understand that there is a café nearby. If you return there and wait, I will approach the Bank to obtain the address associated with this account, then return." He held up the passbook.

I nodded in agreement. "But, won't they be watching? They'll see you approach me."

He smiled widely, "Oh, I don't think that will be a problem."

When Holmes's lunch arrived, we lapsed into silence while he ate. I stared out of the window and enjoyed the sight of the countryside as it passed by. The next thing I knew, Holmes stood by the table in readiness to leave.

"We have an hour before we arrive. Remember all I've said, and I'll see you at the café," he said before leaving the car.

I went back to my paper.

***

I arrived back at our compartment shortly before the train was due to arrive at Penzance. Holmes was gone but had left his valise behind. I assumed it was to allow him ease of movement once the journey was finished, so I voluntarily dragged the bag out, ready to be collected by the porter.

Try as I may, I kept my eyes to myself as I alighted from the train and waited to collect our luggage from the porter's station, but every man with a beard or every tall man that passed by grabbed my attention as our potential mystery spies.

When finally, the luggage arrived, I picked our cases from the porter's trolley and made my way to the exit. There I managed to flag a Hansom and journey on to the hotel. I was unaware of any tail I may have picked up, though I didn't attempt to hide in any way.

When I arrived at the Queen's hotel, I was delighted to find that our telegram had been received and two rooms awaited us. I informed them that my colleague would be along momentarily and asked them to hold his key but deliver his valise to the room. I quickly went to my own room, laid out my things and hurried down to the café.

It was a very European affair, with a number of tables outside in a small courtyard at the front of the hotel, making the most of the fine summer weather.

The patronage was light on, so I was able to attain a table nearest the street itself. I had picked up a local paper and sat back to wait, whilst enjoying an afternoon pot of tea and scones. My eyes searched over the top of my paper from time to time, but I couldn't identify or locate the suspects.

I lost track of time, once again, and when I picked up my cup and found it empty, I realised that a good hour had passed. My pot was likewise empty, and the small plate held a few scattered crumbs.

My paper chose that moment to lose its rigidity and toppled forward revealing the most unpleasant face I've ever had the horror to behold.

I began to fold the newspaper in readiness to swat the man away when he spoke in hushed tones.

"Watson, it is I. Be quiet and stay surprised. I've found Calhoun's address. He's staying in the Tolcarne Inn, a little pub down by the docks. Seems he can't keep away from ships. Go to the police station and bring Lestrade's contact to the inn within the hour. I'll meet you there."

I whispered back, "But what about Savage?"

"I know where he is, I'll make sure he doesn't follow. Yet."

To make our meeting look legitimate, I fished out my coin purse and gave the horrible beggar a copper and then shooed him away.

"Go away you smelly thing," I said, standing up and waving my arms around in an overtly animated gesture. I smiled inside at my own little piece of acting. I caught sight of the grimace on Holmes's face. A harsh critic of actors at the best of times, our Holmes.

He shuffled off and as I went to pay my bill, I caught sight of movement across the street through the front doors. I kept my eyes forward and saw two gentlemen approach the edge of the road. I ducked into the hotel foyer and heard a slight commotion behind me.

As I walked to the front desk, I glanced through the entrance and saw Holmes between the men and the hotel. He was using his stooped bulk to his advantage and overplaying his hand at begging. The men tried to push past, but he had them at a disadvantage.

I quickly asked the Concierge where the police station was. He gave me the directions to an address only three streets away and pointed me to a doorway towards the rear of the hotel. I scurried off before Savage and his Finnish accomplice could break away from Holmes. As I reached the doorway I glanced back, Holmes and the other two were gone.

The police station was a tiny affair, a small entry foyer allowed for only two people to wait. A wooden counter greeted anyone requesting assistance.

I rang the bell and waited. As luck would have it the only officer on duty was the one I was after. I introduced myself and held out the card that Lestrade had left for me. Inspector Ransome smiled as he saw the name. He shook my hand jovially and mentioned that Lestrade and he had started out as bobbies in the East End. Ransome, it seemed, had moved to Cornwall when he attained the rank of Inspector. He laughed that he was done with the rough streets of London and was much happier in the quiet of Penzance.

"The most we have to deal with here is arguments over whose dog has invaded whose front yard," he said a broad smile on his rotund face.

I returned his smile, before signalling that the quiet of Penzance may be about to be broken. I explained what we knew so far, which I admit wasn't much, and that we had an address.

Ransome nodded at the mention of the Tolcarne.

"That's a bit of a rough part of the town. The docks can get a might rowdy on a Saturday night. They usually sorts themselves out, and the publican is a good sort. He don't truck with no trouble," he said.

He invited me through to the back rooms of the Police station. The area opened up into a small office, with a door leading through to what I presumed would be the holding cells. I wondered which members of this little adventure might be held up there before the day was out.

We stepped up onto the front seats of a large trap with a covered wagon at the rear, used for transporting perpetrators of crime back to the station.

The docks area wasn't very far at all, then again Penzance is not a large town by any means, especially when compared to London. The whole place would fit comfortably just in the East End.

Ransome, showing signs of his former street-smart self, parked the trap down a side street, well away from any view from the Inn itself.

We alighted and stepped onto the broad esplanade that ran along the seafront. The inn sat about a hundred yards down the road. It was an old two-storey whitewashed building. There were a few patrons sitting on benches outside enjoying the diminishing sunshine and nursing the dregs of their drinks before last call sang out from inside.

I was pondering what to do next when a voice spoke up behind us.

"Watson!"

We both turned and found Holmes striding up the side street towards us. He held out his hand and took Ransome's in his own.

"Inspector Ransome, I presume," he said, "Sherlock Holmes, thank you for joining us, and for bringing the wagon with you. I hope we'll be in need of it. I assume Watson has filled you in."

Ransome nodded and spoke, “Yes, but I still don’t see any crimes committed.”

“Ah, yes, not in this matter. But, if things progress as I believe they will, we should be able to indict this Calhoun character with the murder of young John Openshaw, some five years ago, and his father Joseph before that,” he said.

Ransome nodded.

Holmes peered around the corner towards the Inn and took in the layout of the land for a moment. He ducked back and said, “I think it would be best if you stayed here, Inspector, while Watson and I enter the inn and determine whether we indeed have Calhoun and Mudge and whether there is enough evidence that your intervention will be required.”

Ransome leaned back and patted his formidable midriff and said, “I could always take a table at the inn itself. I would be closer to the action, as they say, and it would be a matter of mere seconds before I could come to your aide.”

Holmes smiled, “Perhaps, but we have another pair of miscreants that might be a little unnerved by your presence. I am hopeful that they will play their hand once we have entered the establishment.”

“I thought we had lost Savage and the Finn?” I asked.

“You had,” he said with a broad smile, “I made sure to re-engender their interest and lead them here on foot. They are skulking nearby.”

I glanced around.

“But not if you give away the fact that we know they are nearby,” Holmes said, admonishing my actions. I dropped my gaze to my feet, like a naughty schoolboy.

As we walked to the inn, I asked Holmes how he came by Calhoun’s address.

He smiled and said, “I went to the bank and found a young, impressionable teller. I showed him the passbook and said I had found it on the seat in the London to Penzance train. Instead, of handing it in to the station master where I believed it would become lost amongst the large amount of misplaced items, I thought it my civic duty to track down the owner and hand it back.”

"Did the teller not suggest that you leave it with the bank?"

"Yes, yes he did. I admitted that I thought the same but determined that if the owner realised they had lost it on a train, he would give up all hope and forget about it. The teller did suggest that they could re-issue the passbook. I answered that the effort required to prove identity and create the records once more were worrisome in the least, and besides, it may be days or weeks before the owner came forward."

A slight smirk came to Holmes's face.

"I put on my most innocent air and finally the teller gave in and provided me with the address. I thanked him roundly and asked his name so that I might advise this Calder, as I was sure he would be most appreciative and may even pass on his gratitude to the branch manager. The teller naturally brightened at that suggestion."

"You are wicked Holmes, really," I said.

"Yes. It's the actor in me. I will, however, write to the bank manager myself and commend the teller, especially if this little adventure resolves itself the way I believe it will."

We reached the inn and entered the front bar. There were quite a few patrons outside, but not that many within. The day was nice, so sitting in a dark, smoky room was not high on most peoples' minds.

Holmes walked up to the bar and gained the attention of the burly barkeeper who was drying glasses with his apron.

"I am here to see a Mr John Calder. I believe he is staying in one of your rooms," Holmes said.

The barkeep looked Holmes up and down.

"Why?" he asked.

Once again, the little bank book came into play. Holmes held it up before the landlord.

"I found his passbook and I wish to return it to him," he said.

"You can give it to me," the man said.

"Forgive me sir, but I think I would be more comfortable returning it in person," he said.

The barkeep looked him dead in the eye for a moment. I truly believed he was contemplating whether to wrest the book from Holmes's hands. I hoped it wouldn't come to that.

I was, however, relieved when the man nodded to the staircase nearby.

"Room 2, top of the stairs on the right," he said.

Holmes placed a guinea piece on the bar.

"I thank you, that should pay for two pints of your finest. My colleague and I will have them when we return momentarily," he said.

The barkeep disappeared the coin so quickly I wasn't even sure I'd seen Holmes place it down.

"Right you are then," he said, a smile suddenly crossing his face.

We climbed the stairs and found a small landing that serviced the only two rooms available in the inn. Due to the age of the building, the ceiling was so low that Holmes had to stoop a little to avoid striking his head on the exposed oak beams.

Holmes presented himself before the door to Room 2 and knocked. I took up a position slightly behind him, unaware that my hand had drawn itself to my pocket and clasped the heavy metal of my service pistol.

The door opened, revealing a moderately tall man who, much like Holmes, stooped to avoid the low ceiling. He sported a well-trimmed beard and had the slightly weathered features of a man who had spent time at sea. I realised it was our quarry from Lestrade's description of him. Holmes knew instinctively.

"William Middleton, or should I say Mudge?" he asked.

"Who the hell are you?" Mudge asked, a look of surprise springing to his face, "How do you know me?"

"Your cousin, Police Inspector Lestrade sends his regards. I also have this," Holmes said, pulling out the small buff-coloured envelope with Mudge's name scrawled on the front and holding it forward.

Mudge stepped back in shock.

"It's you? What do you want from us?" he asked.

Holmes took this as an invitation and followed Mudge into the room. I ducked in and shut the door behind me.

Mudge cowered in the corridor, blocking our view of the main part of the room. He finally moved when another voice broke out tinged with a thick American drawl.

"Get out of the way William, I can't see who it is?" the voice said.

Mudge moved to the side, revealing an older man with a shock of grey hair. His face showed deep lines and the skin was tanned a deep brown. He sat in a chair against the far wall, and strangely for the temperature of the day, had a blanket thrown across his legs. Holmes deduced his identity just as quickly as I had.

"Captain James Calhoun, late of the Lone Star, I presume," he said stepping into the room.

"You have me at a disservice, sir. I have no idea who you are," said Calhoun.

"I am Sherlock Holmes, this is my associate Doctor John Watson," he said.

"And that means what to me?" Calhoun said with an air of dismissal.

"Our paths have never crossed, but I was employed by John Openshaw before his untimely death five years ago, to which I lay the blame at your feet," he said.

Calhoun broke out in a fit of laughter and threw the blanket aside. I looked in shock at what the rug had covered. Both of Calhoun's legs were missing below the knee, both ending in ugly stumps.

"Good lord," I said under my breath.

"You can throw what you like at my feet, they're at the bottom of the Atlantic. Lost when that damn ship fell apart and I dragged this big galoot up from below decks. Main mast snapped off and smashed them to nothing. We washed up on the south coast, everyone else went down with the ship."

He looked us both up and down and thought for a moment.

"You don't look like Klansmen, so, why are you sending young William here those orange pips?" he asked, "You've scared the bejeesus out of him."

"And that's where you have us at a disservice. We didn't send them. I think I know who did, though. Your partner in crime George Savage."

He extracted the letter and held up the double-cross symbol so that Calhoun could plainly see it.

Calhoun's face changed to confusion then relaxed back to slight anger.

"That idiot, he thinks I double-crossed him. Last I saw of him, he was diving overboard like the coward he is. You can tell that slack-jawed chowder headed rum gagger that if I sees him again I'll fix his flint for good."

"I don't know the fellow, so I won't, but why would he accuse you of double-crossing him?"

"That I don't know."

"The gold, I reckon," said Mudge.

Calhoun turned and stared daggers at Mudge, shutting him up.

"Gold?" I asked.

Mudge glanced at Calhoun, then at me before overcoming his answering.

"We were smugglers, that's all, I don't know nothing about murder. I only joined the Klan cause the Captain said I should. We were taking a load of gold back to the Klan in Tennessee," he said, letting it all out, his demeanour brightening as he cleared his conscience, "That's what I thought this was all about. I owe the Captain for saving my life, but don't owe the Klan anything."

"Shut your pie hole, you fool," said Calhoun.

He turned towards us.

"You've got nothing on us or else you would have brought the law with you," he said, "Now get out before things go South."

"Fine," said Holmes turning towards the door, "I have proved that you were behind the Openshaw murders. I will return shortly with the police and have you dragged away."

I turned as well but was brought up short by Calhoun's voice from behind.

"Yeah, I don't think so," he said.

We both turned to find the Captain pointing a gun towards us. Holmes raised his hands slowly, I followed suit keeping my right hand lower.

"What are you doing?" Mudge asked Calhoun.

"I didn't want it to come this, but I've lived too long to end up in a noose," he said.

I slowly dropped my right hand towards my pocket.

"Uh, uh, aah, sonny, I don't think so," Calhoun said, indicating my hand with the barrel of the gun. I raised it quickly.

I kicked myself inside for being so foolish and dropped my head slightly. There we all stood silently, while Calhoun figured out who to kill first. The next few moments are still a blur.

Suddenly, the door burst in. A tall, bearded man stepped into the room. He brought up a small revolver and pointed it towards Calhoun. I could see the taller blonde-haired Finn hovering on the landing outside.

"You owe me," he said, "I killed two fellows on your orders, you promised me, so you owe me."

"Savage!" replied Calhoun, a broad smile on his face, "I thought you were dead."

I saw his gun move slightly then an explosion rang out through the room dulling all further sound.

Savage dropped his own pistol and clutched at his chest. A dark stain spread across the dirty white shirt. He dropped to his knees, his face a mass of shocked terror, and fell forward with a dull thud. The thumping of feet on the stairs told me Savage's Finnish partner had given up on the whole venture.

I dropped to my knee and checked Savage for any signs of life. When there were none, I looked back at Calhoun who wore an expression of pure delight. I knew then that this was a man with no scruples. There was only one place on Earth for such as he, and if I lived another day, I would see him hang there.

Calhoun smiled and said, "I told you I'd fix his flints." He turned the gun towards Holmes and said, "You're next."

Holmes simply smiled and replied, "I think not."

Calhoun's face finally dropped. Holmes knelt down, picked up Savage's gun and directed its barrel towards the old man.

"Poor choice of weapon, Captain, that's a Stevens .22 calibre pistol, if I'm not mistaken. A lightweight firearm much favoured by sailors and seamen. Unfortunately for you, it has a single shot, which you have used, and it must now be reloaded to be of further use," he said.

Calhoun's face screwed up as he realised he'd been found out.

"Damn you," he said and dropped the pistol.

***

Ransome entered the apartment with remarkable speed for such a large man. I found out later that he had observed Savage and the Finn entering the inn, so had taken it upon himself to relocate to the front bar. He was taking his first sip of ale when Calhoun's gun went off and almost collided with the Finn as he made good his escape.

The Inspector entered the room and with the wide-eyed expression of one unaccustomed to dead bodies took in the scene. I took him gently by the arm, pointed out the gun, Calhoun and the fact that Holmes had the culprit covered. I suggested that he bring the wagon to the Inn door and send for an ambulance to take Savage's body away.

We stayed for two more days to assist Ransome with the finer details before travelling back to London. I was relieved. Holmes had solved two cases in one single moment. I could update my notes on the original five orange pips adventure and had enough fodder for an entirely new adventure.

The first question I raised with Holmes was what to do with young Middleton, or Mudge, or whatever he wished to call himself.

Holmes was circumspect in this matter.

"For all intents and purposes, Middleton has committed no crime. He was an accessory to smuggling, but that would only apply if the gold had made it onto American soil. It now lays at the bottom of the ocean, so technically no crime has been committed. By his own admission, he was not involved in the Openshaw murders. We can only take his word as we have no further evidence to convict him. We heard Savage admit to the murders on Calhoun's orders, so we have the culprits. Middleton is Lestrade's problem now. I will tell the Inspector all I know, and he can keep an eye on him. It is up to Middleton to confess to his wife. Regardless, it should all make for some interesting family dinners around Christmas time," he said a broad smile on his face.

"And the Openshaw family?" I asked.

"Sadly, John was the last of his line. I shall inform the estate, but that will only give them a procedural closure of sorts after all these years. There are only a few scattered cousins left in the family. So, there is nobody emotionally attached in reality. I have probably had the most investiture in this case, so it brings a very high level of relief, I must say," he said, sitting back and sipping his coffee.

I took the opportunity to glance out the window at the countryside rushing past. The day was bright and serene, and I was eager to be back with Mary. By the time I glanced back at Holmes, his head had sunk to his chest and he was snoozing restfully.

I smiled, happy that another successful adventure was finished.

The Adventure at Dead Man's Hole

It was a dreary day in mid-October that found Sherlock Holmes and me standing on the northern bank of the Thames. To our backs the great stone walls of the Tower rose up, blocking out what little light there was, casting us into a perpetual twilight and robbing us of any heat that the sun might provide. To our left, the mighty north tower of the bridge loomed above us.

Although the bridge's construction had officially finished several months before, there was still a certain amount of work that continued to be done. Shouts rang down from above as the workers went about their business. The clanking of metal and striking of rivets rang out across the slowly moving river as the final construction of the bridge went ahead, heedless of our activities.

The object of our visit lay below, the stinking silt and mud of the riverbed. I could see numerous deep holes in the mud, which could only mean that Lestrade and his men had combed the area for clews before we had been called.

I imagined the fuming anger brewing within Holmes's mind as he surveyed the destitution that was the supposed location of a crime. And it was no surprise when he said, "You would think, Watson, that by now Lestrade would understand not to utterly destroy the evidence of a crime before he calls upon me."

"I do agree, but as I understand it, he wasn't even here when the body was removed, so in his defence, he had no control over the matter." My reply met with a solid and angry harrumph, which brought a slight grin to my face.

The body had been found earlier that morning by one of the workers as they arrived for their shift. There had been no surprise or hurry for that matter in recovering the corpse. This area was renowned for trapping anything that floated down the mighty river. The tides of late had ebbed and flowed with remarkable heights as a full moon smiled down on the city at night, bringing with it the waters, but taking them away once morning broke.

In a city of the size and with the vitality of life that London possessed, it was little wonder that numerous cadavers washed up on her banks during the course of a year.

The area was also the daily home to hundreds of workers employed on building the mightiest bridge to ever grace the cityscape. Accidents happened, far too regularly for my liking, which had forced the creation of what came to be known as Dead Man's Hole.

The designers of the bridge had included a small thoroughfare through which pedestrians could quickly circumnavigate the northern tower and gain access to the nearest bank of the Thames. Sadly, as more and more workers succumbed to gravity and other accidents associated with construction on such a large scale, a place needed to be set aside to house the bodies of these unfortunates until they could be collected by the coroner or a mortician. The pylons and footings of the new bridge also provided an unforeseen hazard, whereby they became a catchment area for all and sundry that floated down the river. Many times, that included the corpses of animals and humans. The watchmen who patrolled the shoreline were tasked with releasing animal bodies to the mercy of the river and to ensure that any humans were taken into the Dead Man's Hole to await their fate.

It was to the Hole that Holmes and I had been drawn by an early morning telegram from Inspector Lestrade of Scotland Yard. I was shaken awake by Holmes's entreaties and virtually dragged from my bed chamber and piled into a hansom even before I broke my fast. I think that Holmes had been a little bored of late, and any evidence of a crime worthy of his attention was a singular delight to his mind.

The dour overcast day and chilling breeze did nothing to enliven my spirits, which continued to claw at my conscience with cries for coffee and breakfast.

The hansom had dropped us off near the corner of the Tower, and we'd made our way across the small rutted track that serviced the construction site and towards the North Tower of the bridge.

Lestrade met us, looking almost as tired and worn out as I felt.

"Sorry to bring you out this early, Mr. Holmes," he said, "but this one's got me puzzled."

“I do hope so,” said Holmes as we clamoured our way across the mud track and onto the small concourse at the base of the bridge.

The Dead Man’s Hole, as I would come to know it, was little more than a covered tunnel, but had been shut off from public access by a series of wooden barricades. I was unsure if they had been there before or were for the benefit of the current occupant.

Inside the temporary room, we met with a young man who went by the name of Byron Smith. He introduced himself as the coroner’s assistant and shook each of our hands. Dispensing with any small talk, to Holmes’s apparent delight, he showed us five lumps lying on the floor covered in stained white sheets.

Smith quickly explained that they had found four bodies in the last three days, three of which were obviously street people that had fallen into the Thames. He pointed to a fourth body and explained it was an unfortunate worker that had fallen from the South Tower rigging just the day before. The last body was the reason for our visit.

Before Smith could unveil it, Holmes turned to Lestrade.

“You haven’t explained why this one has you flummoxed,” he said.

“No, I haven’t,” he said, nodding at Smith, who quickly drew back the sheet. “See for yourself.”

“Good Lord!” I gasped.

Holmes simply stared at the body, a hand cradling his chin, and murmured to himself.

Before us lay an extremely sorrowful sight. It was difficult to tell the actual age, but it looked at first sight like the body of a young man or more of a boy, but that would need further confirmation. His skin was sallow and puffed, indicating a prolonged amount of time beneath the surface of the water. It glistened in places from the presence of adipocere, a waxy substance that forms from the fat on bodies in water and protects them from decay. His hair was matted and dark, his eyes closed shut from engorgement. He was completely nude, showing the brutalisation that he had suffered at the hands of the elements. To add to the peculiarity, a thick strand of rope was still tied around his ankles.

I made him to be around five feet ten inches tall. His weight was obscured by the bloating, but my instincts told me that he had been between nine and ten stone.

Holmes dropped to his knee to make a closer inspection of the corpse. I stepped closer, mindful of the dim light in the tunnel, and gasped again when I made out the scarring on the body.

"You see it then, Watson?" Holmes said.

"What do you make of it?"

Holmes pointed to the marks on the body's chest. They weren't deep, merely superficial, made possibly with a knife or other sharp-bladed instrument. The edges had been puckered by the exposure to water. A long line ran from the throat to the navel, a smaller line ran across the chest just below the pectorals.

"That looks like a cross, but the horizontal line is too low, it's unsymmetrical," I said.

"Or inverted," Holmes said.

My eyes widened. I had seen that symbology before, but never in this way. It was then I noticed a single deeper wound on the left-hand side, slightly above the horizontal line. It too was puckered but was certainly not superficial.

"He was stabbed?" I said.

"Indeed he was. These lines were carved before he died. This," Holmes said pointing to the deeper wound, "was what killed him."

I took a deep breath. It was murder then, and not just some poor vagrant who had died of the cold.

I noticed a pattern of cuts on the forehead and pointed to them. "What are those?" I asked.

Holmes pulled out his glass and leaned in closer. I looked around and found a small portable gas lamp nearby. I brought it across and bent down to shed more light on the subject.

"My word," I mumbled in surprise at the strangely intricate pattern.

"Yes," murmured Holmes. "It's a pentagram. Inverted from the traditional Wiccan form."

"Witches?" I asked, a hint of unreality in my voice.

“No, nothing like that,” Holmes said. I breathed a sigh of relief. Witchcraft in any form was a strange world, especially if some were now delving into ritual sacrifice, as this seemed to indicate.

“This is worse,” Holmes finished, before standing up. “This is Satanic.”

I almost dropped the lamp in surprise.

“Satanic?” I asked.

Lestrade pitched in, “Satanic?” Even Smith’s face dropped in shock.

“I do believe so,” said Holmes, “The inverted cross. The inverted pentagram – both symbols of Satanic cults. The deep wound above the heart indicates how this man – ” He stopped himself and peered at the corpse for a moment. “How this *boy* died.”

“You think he was a boy as well, then?” I asked. He nodded. “My estimation is he was in the water for a good six months.”

“I agree," said Holmes, "The level of water absorption, the amount of adipocere, and the lack of overall decay would suggest that sort of timeline.”

Lestrade spoke up. “Do you think he’s from London?”

“That is impossible to tell,” he said as he dropped down to his knees once again and pointed to marks on the corpse’s wrists and neck, and to the rope tied around his feet. “These marks are burns from a rope tied around them, just like the type around the feet. They indicate that the corpse was tied and probably weighted to keep it from floating away.”

He stood again and turned, gazing off into the distance as if looking through the nearby tiled walls and out across the great river.

“The recent rains and the abnormally high tides have swelled the Thames upriver. Perhaps our friend here resided upstream and his bonds broke, sending him south and towards the sea. I wonder . . . .”

And that was how I found myself observing Holmes as he mud-larked about in the deep, stinking silt of the great river.

We had borrowed long leather waders from the site foreman and long leather gloves. I had to admit to a feeling of foolishness as I stood on the edge of the stone wall that formed the bank of the river.

The waders came up to my chest and the gloves covered my hands and forearms. I felt like an out-of-place farmer or steelworker.

Holmes carefully trudged his way across the little area, stopping every so often to plunge his hand deep into the muck and fish around for any clews on offer. His efforts had elicited nothing but more mud. In fact, as I became more bored and my unsated hunger grew I began to question my erstwhile colleague's actions.

Finally, I cried out, "Holmes, what the devil are you searching for?"

He stopped and peered up at me, a familiar look on his face. "Why I'm searching for clews," he said as if in answer to everything.

"Any clew in particular?" I asked, through my thinly disguised impatience.

At this, he gave me his aggrieved look. "Well, we have nothing to tell us of this boy's origins. Is he from London? Is he from farther afield?"

I nodded, I already knew that, but still wondered.

"We have the rope," he began.

Again, I nodded. The rope was made of plain hemp, available in any store.

"To what was it attached?" he said.

At that, I shrugged. "Some sort of weight, I imagine."

"Yes, excellent," he said, drawing breath to give me time to reply. When I didn't, he continued. "The body had to have been weighed down at some stage, for at least six months. It was so bloated that it would otherwise simply float on the surface, much like a cork or leaf, and not as subject to the tides. But if weighed down a little, the undercurrent would snatch it and drag it swiftly downriver."

I nodded. It made sense – simple physics that I had seen during my own trips to the seaside.

"The weight itself could provide additional information," he said.

"Possibly not," I countered.

"That is also true," he said, a slightly annoyed tone to his voice.

He ducked down and drove his arm up the shoulder into the dirty brown water. He struggled slightly, then peered across to me.

"Watson, I don't suppose that you could assist me," he cried.

Not disguising my look of disgust, I moved towards the thin iron railings that acted as a ladder down to the riverbed. I reached the bottom and gingerly stepped off, my foot disappearing into the putrid mud. I stepped towards him amidst the most disgusting *schlooping* noises. Just as I reached him, he stood upright with his prize in hand. He smiled and turned towards me, surprised to find me only a few yards away.

"Never mind now," he said. "I've found it."

I bit my tongue to suppress any remonstration.

***

It wasn't until mid-morning that we returned to 221b Baker Street. Once she realised that we hadn't eaten, Mrs. Hudson was quick to bring up a sumptuous brunch with coffee. I thanked her effusively over the noise of my grumbling innards and set about demolishing the fare, whilst perusing the morning paper.

A sketch of the latest player on the political scene smiled up at me from the front page. Sir Geoffrey Warrington was a rising star in the ranks of the opposition party. He had previously made a name for himself as an industrialist trading in goods between the Continent and the United Kingdom, and now that he had entered politics, the thinking was that he would soon lead the Liberals into power at the next election in a couple of years. I turned the page over to find something less boring to read and soon lost track of time.

Holmes was concentrating on something in his chemical corner. I brought over a small plate of food and a cup of coffee, which he unconsciously ate and drank whilst studying the object of his attention. To me, it was just a bunch of stones, wrapped in a small hessian sack. A short trail of broken rope was attached, but Holmes had verified that it was the same as that which bound the corpse.

"I don't understand what's so fascinating about that," I said.

Holmes grinned. "And that is a little disappointing," he said. "What we have here is evidence."

He carefully emptied the stones onto the table and spread the hessian sack out next to them. He pointed at the sack and said, "This small sack has been cut from a larger open-weave bag and roughly sewn together with hemp twine. This type of hessian is used for the holding of root vegetables rather than grains – hence the open weave. It is still strong, but won't allow the vegetables to escape. The twine is ordinary, which is a shame."

He reached over and picked up one of the stones. It was round and smooth and consisted of a white stone, marked with specks of black and brown.

"This is interesting in two ways. First, it's smooth," he said, rotating the stone between his fingers, "but not perfectly spherical. It was smoothed by nature, rather than the hand of man. I would suggest from a running river."

He picked up his glass and peered closer at the stone itself. "The specks of black and brown rock within the conglomerate indicate that it is a type of white granite – not a very common stone, but one that is well known in particular regions."

He placed the stone down and moved across to the bookcase. He extracted a large volume of Ordnance Maps and plonked it down on the workbench. He flipped to London and placed his index finger on the Thames.

"We can assume that the body came downstream, probably due to the recent rains in the West Country which have filled the local streams and rivers and flushed them into the great river."

He came to the edge of the map near Hounslow, quickly turned the maps, following the river through Slough, up past Maidenhead, eventually stopped and placed his finger on Reading.

"Reading," I said, "Nothing ever happens in Reading. Why do you think this boy is from there?"

"He may not be from there, but that is where his body came from."

He pointed to the River Kennett and traced it upstream.

"The Kennett is one of the fastest flowing rivers that feed the Thames. It just so happens that the area near Main Lake is home to several quarries that specialise in white granite. One could surmise that the corpse would have been placed into one of the quieter ponds in that area."

"How, exactly?" I asked.

"The poor unfortunate boy has been underwater for at least six months. Therefore, he was placed deep in a quiet body of water." I nodded. "The stones are from a river, probably just picked up from the bank as needed. The hessian material is from a bag used in a more rural area."

I nodded again. It all made sense. "So what now?"

Holmes looked blank for a moment. He stared at me, then his eyes dropped to what remained on his plate. He picked it up and replied, "Food. I think that I need to have a bite to re-invigorate my mind."

***

I was called away in the early afternoon and didn't return until the evening had settled in. I found Holmes and his brother Mycroft in the sitting room, engaged in a deep debate. Holmes looked across at my entrance with a dour expression on his face. I knew immediately that some new piece of information had come to light in my absence.

"You look exceedingly downcast."

Holmes nodded, as did Mycroft, "Yes, we are. Typically two events occurring on separate days would play no part in the same investigation, but when they transpire within hours of each other, the linkages blaze across my mind like fireworks."

"What's happened?" I asked, looking first at Holmes then at Mycroft, who simply raised his eyebrows and shrugged.

"Mycroft," he said, "has come with a request from a senior member of the House of Lords, Lord Howard Moncrieff."

I searched my memories and reminded myself. "Moncrieff? Isn't he the Earl of Dorchester or some such?" I asked.

Holmes nodded, "Well done, Watson. Precisely."

Still confused I pressed for more information, "And what has happened to him?"

"It seems that Alexander," said Mycroft, "the Moncrieff's teenage son, has vanished. Two days ago."

"But that isn't a long time – especially for a teenager. Perhaps he's run off on some lark for a few days with his friends."

"Perhaps. He disappeared from the school grounds of Pangbourne College. No-one has seen hide nor hair of him since."

The name Pangbourne rang bells within my mind. "Pangbourne College. But that's – " Then it hit home. My eyes widened, "That's just outside of Reading."

"Precisely, Watson, precisely."

"What did he look like?" I asked, my mind on fire.

Holmes held up his hands.

"Calm down, old friend. The body we examined is not Alexander Moncrieff. He is blonde-haired, very slightly built, and has crystal blue eyes. Very different from the boy that was pulled from the river. And remember, the Moncrieff boy has only been gone two days, while the other spent six months in the water."

I relaxed but was still very intrigued. "But you think these two are related?"

"I do. At this stage, it is supposition, but the closeness of location, and the age of both, lead me to believe that there may be a connection." He stared at Mycroft for a moment, before saying, "Dear brother, is the Government keeping any files open on the activities of Satanic Cults within England at the moment?"

Mycroft's face remained stoic. "Why do you ask?"

"The boy found in the River had markings that suggest such. He was also killed by a single wound to the heart by a wide-bladed knife. It may have all been a prank gone wrong, but given this second boy's disappearance, I'm leaning towards the conjecture that he was sacrificed and that there may be more."

"I do not know off-hand if there is anything, but I will make some inquiries. If I find anything, I will return. Until then, what do you plan to do, Sherlock?" asked Mycroft. I could tell he was aching to be gone. His face had shown a hint of disgust at the mention of Satanists, but from experience, I knew that he was more than happy for his brother to undertake the more visceral detective side of such an investigation, and would rather hear of the success or failure at a later date rather than be involved in the deliberations.

"In the morning, I feel that Watson and I will away to Reading." He stepped across to his worktable and stared at the maps. "These drawings do not do justice to the physical locations. There should be more data that I can collect that will lead me to a more concrete conclusion. I don't like supposition *per se*, and would rather that my ideas be dashed with evidence than linger in my brain longer than necessary."

"Well, I wish you all the best. Keep me informed. If you find the boy alive, I'm sure the boy's parents will shower you with riches. If not, then at least they shall be at peace."

With that, he left.

***

The constable at Reading Police Station read the letter from Lestrade again, just to make sure that he had our details square in his mind.

He peered up at Holmes, a quizzical look on his face before he surprised both of us with his next utterance.

"What I'd like to know is, how do two gentlemen from London know about the disappearances?" he asked.

I was shocked. Lestrade had said that Moncrieff hadn't mentioned his vanished son to the police.

"Disappearances?" asked Holmes, placing a heavy inflection on the last syllable. I detected a slight tilt of his right eyebrow as the only evidence of his own surprise.

"Yes," said Constable Corden, eyeing each of us again. "Disappearances."

Holmes continued. "I only mentioned the one body found in the Thames. I don't think that I said anything about any others."

Corden realised he'd made a mistake. He stared at Holmes for a moment, possibly running the conversation back through his mind before nodding.

"So you did," he said finally, "So you did." He reread Lestrade's letter, averting his gaze for a moment before re-locating his confidence. "Well, that's settled then." He looked around. The only other person in the station was a drunk, lying prostate in a cell at the rear of the building. I doubted if the man could hear or even if he would have cared, but Corden leant forward and whispered, "There have been four so far. Regular as clockwork, near the end of the month. All young boys, around mid-teens. Their distraught parents or friends come in. They can't find little Johnny – he's run off or something. I've had no evidence of any foul play, and I'm at my wits' end, but I try to reassure them as best as I can."

He moved across to a nearby desk and brought back a thick file, full of loose papers. He opened it and picked up the top page.

"Neville Borthox: Fourteen, five-foot six-inches tall, dark hair, brown eyes, around ten-stone nine-pounds. Went missing one month ago. Last seen on the Abbey School grounds close to sunset."

I look at Holmes, he shook his head.

"Not our boy," he said.

Corden picked up another sheet.

"Reginald, or Reggie, Hyde-Northam: Fifteen, five-foot eight-inches, nine-stone six-pounds, fair hair, green eyes. Missing for two months. Last known location, Leighton Park Public School."

He flipped to another sheet.

"Clarke Greggson: Thirteen, five-foot two-inches, seven-stone nine-pounds, red hair, green eyes. Missing for almost three months. Last seen at St. Josephs College."

He picked up the final sheet, read his own report and nodded several times, whilst murmuring under his breath.

"I remember this one. Garrison Wainwright: Sixteen, big boy, five feet ten inches tall, ten-stone, dark hair, brown eyes. Reported missing four months ago but hadn't been seen for two months before that. Parents thought he'd just run off. Weren't that worried, to be honest."

"Where was he last seen?"

"He was from Farley Field, down south. Out of school. Worked on his father's farm. The parents are salt-of-the-Earth types. Not too bright, but hard working. As I said, they weren't worried. He'd run off before. The father's a bit of a drinker and gets a might handy. When he hadn't come home for two months, the mother started to get worried and reported it."

I said, "It sounds like our boy then."

Holmes nodded. He reached into his pocket and brought out the Ordnance Map of the area. He quickly plotted the last known locations of each boy. They were scattered around the area, but even with five points, they formed a slight ring around the town of

Reading. The location of Pangbourne College was outside the defined area. The Thames ran through the very centre of the ring.

Holmes pointed to a series of ponds and lakes that flanked the River Kennett upstream from its confluence with the Thames near Reading. He peered up at Constable Corden and said, "Could you take us to this area?" Then, after the officer had walked away, he added, "I'll also send a telegram to Lord Moncrieff. I think that we might need to visit him this afternoon."

***

The police station had access to a simple cart that they used for carrying several men to situations when required. Corden enlisted one of the junior constables to drive, and the three of us sat in the rear. The station wasn't far from the banks of the river. We crossed a large bridge and continued to follow the southern bank towards the series of lakes that had interested Holmes so much.

The area near the river was lined with deep thickets of trees, the land opening up to farms and fields on the south, with dry stone walls bordering each allotment. The river still ran quite strongly. I could hear the constant bubble as water washed across the small rapids created by the build-up of rocks and stones. It was a totally different sound to the slow languid pace that the Thames achieved even during an exceedingly wet spring.

Holmes had his Ordnance Map open in his lap and was keeping track of where we were in relation to the geographical points of interest marked by the cartographers. To the south, I could see the large granite quarry that serviced Reading and provided her with stone and lime for building works.

As we approached a point on the river where it split into two, Holmes called out to the driver, "Take the south fork, please."

We turned and picked our way slowly along the disused rutted track. To our left passed a series of large and small ponds. I glanced at Holmes's map and saw that they were all connected by a network of small streams.

Holmes noticed my interest and said, "This whole area is a major wetland consisting of ponds and lakes, all joined by tiny rivulets that become raging torrents during the wet season."

“I don’t understand where you are taking us, though,” I said.

Holmes pointed to a small pond at the end of this particular branch of the river.

“Here. From the facts I have at hand, my deductions have led me to this spot.”

He looked up from the map and pointed. “In fact, we are here,” he said. Corden and I looked in the direction of his finger.

A small calm pond sat at the end of the southern branch of the river. The driver circumnavigated the bank and pulled up on the western side. We stepped out of the cart and onto the muddy ground. Luckily, Holmes had the foresight to insist that we both bring heavy boots. Corden knew the area well and had brought his own from the station.

I peered around. The pond was small but very still. A tiny inlet on the northern side was the source of water from the larger branch of the river. The water drained on the eastern side, running down that branch until it re-joined further east.

Holmes glanced around for a moment then headed towards the tiny inlet. Corden, the driver, and I hurried after him, struggling to keep up with his rate of stride through the boggy ground.

“A-ha!” he said once we reached the inlet. It was there I saw the object of his attention. The inlet joined the pond to a sharp bend in the river. The bank of the river was littered with masses of round white stones of the same type as we had seen in London.

Holmes studied the area for a moment before peering across the pond. He glanced down at the muddy ground, shaking his head slightly and making *tsk*-ing noises. He gently stepped along the banks of the pond, hunched over and examining the ground as he moved.

Finally, he stood and let out a small triumphant shout.

I walked up next to him, mindful of staying close to his own footsteps and asked, “What have you found?”

He pointed at the sodden ground and I could just make out several of the small round stones, half-pushed into the mud. Several deep holes, which I presumed to be footprints, ran down to the water’s edge.

"I assume you detect the presence of bootprints amongst the mud and grasses?" Holmes asked.

I was astonished all the same but had to nod at Holmes's remarkable find. "How?"

Holmes turned to me with a wide grin on his face. "Simple deduction. This little pond is regularly kept filled from the river itself via that inlet. Normally it is as we see it, extremely still. The flow out of the eastern side is the same as the flow from the north. The current runs across the northeastern section of the pond." He pointed to the area before us. "Anything in this area will remain still."

"But the body in London?" I asked.

Holmes turned to Corden. "Constable, when was the last storm?"

Without hesitation, Corden responded, "Five days ago. A mighty storm it was, too. I had to bring the lads out to assist the fire brigade with a few rescues that night. Shocking it was."

"That storm stirred up this little pond somewhat. The river would have flooded, and the current would have disturbed anything lying within these muddy waters. The body we observed was wrenched from its mooring and taken downriver on the crest of the torment."

I pointed at the impressions in the mud. "But these are footprints aren't they? Surely, they would have been washed away."

"Which means they are much fresher. Possibly only two or three days old. The ground is still so damp that access without leaving any mark is impossible."

"If they are that fresh, then that means – " I said, realising that someone had possibly left something – or someone – behind.

Holmes's expression turned grave. He nodded. "Yes, Watson, I feel that there is at least one more body in these waters. Somewhere in that direction." He pointed towards the outlet and then turned to Corden. "Constable, did you bring what I asked?"

Corden nodded and trudged back to the cart. He returned quickly with a small four-pronged anchor attached to a long length of rope and handed it to Holmes. "I noticed this anchor at the station. It's used by the canal barges that work the river. The constable was good enough to attach a long length of sturdy rope."

I followed as he made his way to the edge of the water. He unfurled some rope, then swung the anchor around in a wide circle before letting it fly out into the middle of the pond.

The water broke up in a large splash, sending ripples out to all sides of the bank. Holmes waited for the anchor to settle on the bottom then slowly wound the rope back in.

His first try resulted in nothing but an anchor full of dense weed and thick mud. After several more tries in different directions, I was about to comment that maybe he was wrong when the anchor stuck fast.

"I have a bite," he said, as would a fisherman with a live fish on his hook.

He struggled with the rope, slowly dragging in both the anchor and its catch. Bubbles erupted on the surface of the lake as the object at the end of Holmes's rope was dragged towards us.

After a few minutes of a tediously slow battle with his sunken prize, Holmes pointed at the pond surface. A pale white object could be seen through the murk. I didn't need to observe it clearly to know what it was.

Corden, the driver, and I stepped into the water as far as our boots would allow and grabbed at the thing, dragging it up to the bank. I let out an exasperated sigh as we stared at the bloated and sodden body lying on the bank.

Holmes dropped the rope and stepped towards the corpse. It was a boy, of that there was no mistake. His hair was filthy, but even so, I could that it was blonde. Two large hessian bags full of stones were tied around his throat and feet. Holmes placed a hand on a shoulder and rolled the body onto its back. The boy was slightly built, possibly around five-foot-six inches in height.

"It's Moncrieff," Holmes said. I nodded.

Corden simply said, "Who?"

"Another boy that went missing a couple of days ago. Son of Lord Moncrieff, up in Pangbourne," I said.

"Oh my," said Corden. "Why didn't they report it to us?"

"They went straight to a higher authority," Holmes said, "Sadly for Alexander here, someone else was trying to do the same thing."

With the boy on his back, we could clearly see a deep wound on the left side of his chest. The two sets of markings on his forehead and chest were the same as those on the body at Dead Man's Hole.

With a slight look of disgust on his face, Holmes pointed out across the water and said, "I think you'll need to drag this pond, Constable. If I'm right, there are at least another three bodies in there."

***

We were let into the main entrance of Moncrieff House by the butler and shown into a small parlour off to one side of the elaborate foyer. A maid brought tea and scones and, realizing that we hadn't eaten for quite some time, I tucked in while we waited for the Lord and Lady to arrive.

Holmes stood to one side of the room, examining one of the many paintings, but I could tell that his mood was quite grim.

"Would you like a scone?" I asked, holding a small laden plate towards him.

He turned, the darkness on his face. "Yes, thank you," he replied, moving across and taking the plate from me. Just as he took a small bite, we heard movement outside. He set the scone down and prepared to meet our hosts.

Lord Moncrieff entered first. He certainly was a presence with a stout frame, his piggy face sporting a shock of white hair, and with ruddy cheeks and a double chin. He was followed by a diminutive woman who trailed in his wake and was almost unseen behind her larger husband.

"You'd be Holmes then?" Moncrieff said.

Holmes nodded and shook the Lord's proffered hand. "Yes. I hear that you've met my brother."

"Ah, Mycroft. Yes, good man. I assume you have news then if you're here."

I noticed Lady Elizabeth and offered her my seat. She shuffled across to me and sat down. Her face was a mask of timidity and fear. She stared up at her husband with the haunted look in her eyes of a mother who has lost a child.

"I'm afraid we have nothing concrete at this stage, but a body has been found," Holmes said. Lady Elizabeth let out a gasp and raised a hand to her face.

Lord Moncrieff faltered slightly but caught himself and remained steadfast. "Is it Alexander?" he asked.

"That can only be determined by yourselves, I'm afraid. The poor unfortunate was taken to the Reading Coroner's building. They will need one or both of you to attend and determine whether it is your son."

Moncrieff nodded, his face grave. "An accident?"

"I'm afraid not," Holmes said. "The indications are far worse, but inconclusive. We still have much investigating to do before this can be laid to rest. Which brings me to the main reason that we are here. I understand that your son was last seen at his school. Is that correct?"

Moncrieff's face turned towards anger. "Yes. Damned foolish place. What am I paying for if they just let these boys loose on the local towns?"

Lady Elizabeth looked aghast. "Howard, this isn't the time to be going into that," she said, her eyes bordering on tears, but her heart remaining as stoic as she could.

"I apologise, dear," he said, "but really, this isn't the first time."

"First time for what?" I asked.

Lady Elizabeth peered up at me and said, "There was a boy, two years ago, who left the school one summer's evening and never returned. We heard about it from an acquaintance. It was never reported by the school itself. He was one of Alexander's closest friends. We almost withdrew him because of it."

"And now it's happened to our Alexander," Moncrieff said. "There will be hell to pay when I see that Principal."

He took a deep breath and drew himself up to full height.

"If you'll excuse me, it seems I have a trip to make to Reading," he said and disappeared. "Dear?" echoed back from the nearby hallway.

Lady Elizabeth sprang to her feet, obviously used to being ordered around. She stopped and turned back. "I assume that you were about to ask for permission to talk with the schoolmasters?"

Holmes nodded. “Yes, I was.”

“Ask for Mr. Reginald Brown. Alexander liked him.” I noticed a tear form and run down her cheek. Her strength was beginning to fade. “Alexander wasn’t a strong boy. He inherited my frame and lack of athleticism. He was also a very emotional boy and easily led. Again, my traits.”

She took my hand in her own and stared deep into my eyes. “My husband had always hoped that Alexander would be more like him, but that didn’t happen. Still, I think that he loved him. I know my life will never be the same. All I can ask is that you find out what happened. It will never relieve the pain, but it may bring us a little bit of peace.”

She released my hand and was gone before I could reply.

Holmes stared at the empty doorway, contemplating.

“A trip to the school then,” I said.

***

The main building of Pangbourne College was a towering Georgian edifice built with orange-red brick and grey stone. The window frames and guttering were all white and stood out in stark contrast to the walls.

Holmes and I passed through the main entrance and were greeted by a rather ornate foyer. The school had been refurbished in recent years, possibly due to the input of funds from parents such as the Moncrieffs. A matronly woman with severely tied-back grey hair took our request to see Master Brown and disappeared quickly when we added it was to do with Alexander Moncrieff’s disappearance.

Soon we were met by a tall man in his mid-forties with thinning blonde hair. Reginald Brown was an affable man, and I could tell that he held a deep concern for his students’ welfare. He plied us with questions of his own to elicit details about Alexander. Holmes gave him several vague answers which either caused him to stomach his unease or told him that no further information would be forthcoming.

Upon hearing that Holmes was a detective, Brown suggested that we should examine the boy’s bedroom. The master seemed to brighten at the prospect of watching Holmes at work. I was unsure whether he knew of Holmes’s reputation or was merely intrigued. As we walked along the shadowed corridors, Brown stopped a young student passing by and whispered to him. The boy took one look at Holmes and me and scurried off.

We finally stopped at one of the non-descript doors that lined the corridor. Brown turned the knob and ushered us inside. The room was small and brought back remembrances of my own during my time in public school housing. I admit now that those remembrances were not always pleasant.

"Good Lord, these boys," said Brown hurrying over and opening a window. Out of the corner of my eye, I noticed Holmes wince in almost physical pain, no doubt imagining the evidence that could be destroyed by such an act.

Brown turned and took a breath of the fresh air flooding the room. "That's better," he said.

Holmes peered around the room. "If you don't mind, sir," he said, looking Brown directly in the eyes. The Master quickly ducked out of the way and joined me near the entrance.

He pointed to the unmade bed on the right and said, "That's Alexander's bed and his side of the room."

Holmes stood stock still, initially only moving his head for a moment. I could only see the detritus of a teenage boy's life in disarray across the area, but I knew that Holmes was searching deeper.

Finally, he reached forward and picked up an open newspaper from the desk. It took me a moment to form the question internally.

Why would a teenage boy have a copy of the newspaper?

I could make out a black outline surrounding a small square of print on the paper.

"What is that?" I asked as my companion read the page carefully.

He simply ignored me and turned the paper over. A small card dropped from within the pages and fluttered to the floor. Holmes quickly bent and picked it up. A small smile crossed his face.

"Interesting," he said, turning to Brown, "Do you have much interaction with the local girls' school, or is there any interaction between these boys and the fairer sex?"

Browns' face became stern. "Certainly not," he said, a slightly angry tone on his lips, "We have a strict policy on that. There are no organised or even casual activities where students can mix. This school has a strict Catholic philosophy and a matching set of policies."

Holmes nodded.

"Why?" I asked.

He held up the paper. "This is an advertisement regarding a group from the Reading Girls' School," he said. "They want to meet up with boys from the other schools. There's an address to forward an acknowledgement." He held up a card. "This has details regarding the consequent meet-up."

"He was always going on about meeting those girls," said a voice from the doorway. I turned and saw a young boy of about fourteen with a shock of curly red hair and a pasty white face covered in freckles.

"He was supposed to meet up the day that he went missing," the boy continued.

Reginald Brown looked shocked, "Hamish, why didn't you say anything?"

"Alex told me to keep it to myself. He didn't know how long he'd be gone. I didn't want to ruin it for him – it seemed to be important to him."

"Well it may have been very important," said Holmes with a slightly sinister tone. "Did he mention anything further?"

Hamish shook his head. "No. He skipped out in the early evening. Said that he was meeting someone outside the gates, and was heading over to Reading, although he wasn't very specific."

"Did anyone else go with him?"

He shook his head again, "No. No one else knew anything about these girls. I just thought it was all a joke, but Alex just kept going on about it, always bragging to anyone that would listen. No-one did. No one thought much of Alex anyway. He was always bragging about something or other. Most people just ignored him when he started talking."

I looked at Brown. He nodded, "It's true. I think that his father was the main problem. Alex tried to be like him, but he was just a braggart with nothing to back it up."

"What do you think?" I asked, looking across at my friend, but his attention was solely on the personal advertisement and the little card. I leaned in and whispered, "Wasn't that the night of the full moon? I was under the impression that was important to these Satanist blackguards."

Holmes lifted one eyebrow and looked at me out of the corner of his eye. I took it to mean be quiet and promptly shut up. After a moment he finally spoke.

"Watson, I think another trip to Reading is in order."

***

The building that housed the offices of *The Reading Chronicle* was a simple two-story Georgian affair, made of blocks of the same black-specked white granite with which we had become all too familiar.

Holmes and I entered the main entrance, which served as both a reception point and a place for dealing with customer enquiries and requests for advertisements. A young woman of about twenty sat behind the long wooden counter and seemed genuinely pleased at our arrival. It was possible that the day had been rather slow, and any interaction was to be welcomed. A small nameplate told us her name to be Bess Frampton.

Holmes produced the copy of *The Chronicle* that we had found in Alexander Moncrieff's room and showed it to Miss Frampton.

"Good afternoon," Holmes said. "My friend and I are interested in the origins of this personal advertisement,"

Miss Frampton read it thoughtfully and was silent for a moment and then began to nod. "Yes, I know this one. We've had similar requests around the second week of the month for the last six."

"Do you have copies of the others?" Holmes asked.

She nodded and disappeared into the large area behind the counter. I peered through a gap in the frosted glass wall and noticed rows of wooden desks with several people were busily writing. After a few minutes, the young lass returned carrying a bundle of newspapers.

She dumped them on the counter and proceeded to open each, laying them out side-by-side.

Holmes and I searched each page for the advertisements and found that they were all of a similar structure, except that the address changed in each.

"It seems as if they are covering their tracks by using a different return address," Holmes said. He thought for a moment before picking up a form and filling it out with his name and our Baker Street address. He pulled out a guinea and placed it on the counter.

"Miss Frampton, if you would be so kind, can you arrange for the delivery of the *Chronicle* to this address?" he said pushing the slip of paper forward, "When the next one of these advertisements appears, and each month onwards until I advise otherwise."

She read the slip and nodded. "I can do that. I'll put it through to deliveries. We already have a few customers in London, but it won't cost a guinea, even if you get the paper every week for a year," she said.

Holmes smiled, "That's fine. You can keep the rest. I don't think that we'll need more than one copy, in any case."

Bess looked delighted and took the guinea from the counter, slipping it into her pocket. "You'll have your paper within a week or two," she said with a wide grin, "if this person is punctual."

"Excellent," Holmes bowed. "And thank you for your service, Miss Frampton."

***

The following weeks were spent back at 221b Baker Street. Holmes and Mycroft had managed to keep the discovery of the other bodies out of the news. In the meantime, we received two pieces of information that were of the most horrid nature.

The first was that Constable Corden and his men had dragged the little pond off the main part of the River Kennett and sadly found not three but four bodies. Three matched the reported boys, but a fourth was unknown. Each boy had the same markings carved into their foreheads and chests and had been killed by a single wound to the heart from a wide-bladed knife.

The second was that Lord Moncrieff had visited the Reading Coroner and identified his son, Alexander. I could only imagine the grief that had overtaken Lady Elizabeth. I hoped that she had someone to support her, as I didn't believe her husband to be that person.

Early in the week after our return, we had received a summons from Mycroft Holmes to meet him in the Stranger's Room at the Diogenes Club, in order to discuss Holmes's findings so far. It was there that my friend explained the five dead boys identified so far and the unknown sixth. Mycroft was appalled by the loss of life.

"Satanism," said Holmes with a dour look on his face.

Mycroft's face was almost as dark as his brother's. "Not good, Sherlock, not good," he said instead, "Britain is too important on the world stage to have this sort of . . . of . . . pagan ritual going on. I would dearly love to put the full force of Her Majesty's law on to this matter, if just to help Lord Moncrieff, but it is a purely civil matter. What do you plan to do about it?"

Holmes sipped his coffee and thought for a moment. I knew that he'd been working hard in the background, formulating some plan, but the details hadn't been forthcoming. I was on the edge of my seat, waiting for him to continue.

"I expect the delivery of a newspaper from Reading within the week. In there, I hope to find a personal advertisement calling for boys of a – How should I say it? – a *virginal* aspect, to make contact with the girls from a nearby college. It seems to be a simple fishing exercise, but the catch rate has been rather astonishing."

"I don't follow," Mycroft said.

"It is my belief that these cultists are using the newspaper to find the young boys whom they use as sacrifices in their detestable rituals."

"Why boys?" Mycroft asked.

"From my research," Holmes said, "it seems that virgins feature prominently in the more esoteric and graphic rituals. They believe that the devil requires them to be pure of sin."

I took a sharp intake of breath. It did make sense.

"But why not girls?" Mycroft asked.

"Boys disappearing at that age is less obvious, and not liable to attract as much attention from horrified or distressed fathers."

Mycroft nodded. I was quite disgusted at the thought of what had been going on.

Holmes continued, "When I receive the advertisement, I will answer from an address in Reading. I've already arranged for one of my young cohorts to spend the next fortnight there. He will make the contact and ensure that he becomes the next object of the cult's obsession."

He turned and indicated me. "Watson and I will journey back to Reading and join the young lad. I would hardly allow any harm to come to one of my Irregulars."

Mycroft nodded. "Good, good. You have it in hand. I may be able to provide a tiny bit of assistance, but it will have to be discreet," he said touching an extended forefinger to his nose.

***

It was early the next month that Holmes's copy of *The Reading Chronicle* finally graced us with its presence. There, as bold as life on the personal pages, was the latest advertisement. It asked for young boys from the local area to meet with the girls of The Reading Girls' School. Those interested were to send a telegram to the listed address, different from the previous six. Holmes read it with a sly smile on his face.

"What do you think?" I asked.

"Marvellous," he said. "The exact same format, but a different reply address. The *modus operandi* is perfect to weed out the chaff, but we need to make sure our response attracts their attention."

Holmes disappeared into his room and returned several minutes later, sporting his travelling coat and hat, and carrying a small valise. He handed a small note to me which had an address in Reading written on it.

"Join me in three days at that address. By then, I feel that the game will well and truly be afoot." He then promptly left, leaving me slightly aghast.

***

When I finally set foot at the Reading abode that Holmes had organized, I'll admit that I had been busy with patients and other trivial tasks for the last few days, but throughout my mind raced with questions regarding events that would unfold.

I was greeted at the front door by a young man of around thirteen years, with neatly combed jet-black hair and dark brown eyes that glinted with recognition when they fell upon me. I was taken aback for a moment as the boy drew no remembrances from my mind – that was until he spoke.

"Dr. Watson?" he said.

I stammered slightly, "Aiden?"

When I had seen him previously, he sported torn and dirty street clothes, with a filthy flat cap hiding his mussed and mud-streaked hair. The boy that stood before me was the total antithesis of that. He was remarkably well-appointed and could have passed for any public schoolboy of good upbringing.

"Yes, sir," he replied politely, before bowing slightly and stepping back to allow me in.

I found Holmes in a small reception room. He was dressed very smartly, and I realised that he was affecting the guise of young Aiden's father, or at least guardian.

"Ah, Watson," he said as I entered, before giving Aiden an order to take my coat and valise to the back of the little house. As Aiden left he simply said, "Just in case anyone calls, we must retain the impression that Aiden and I are family and have been here a while."

I nodded and then asked, "What progress have you made?"

Holmes indicated a small chair and I sat, ready to hear all. "We've done very well," he said, "I sent the telegram prior to arriving here in Reading, and young Aiden and I moved straight in. It was only the next morning that a knock on the door revealed an answering telegram. Aiden has been invited to a *soirée* for members of the girls' school and their guests tomorrow night."

"Do we know where?" I asked.

"They're sending a hansom for him tomorrow at six o'clock. We'll follow in our own cart, parked around the corner."

"Good. Do you know anything else?"

"Of course," he said, smiling in that inimitable way of his, telling me almost as much as anything that he would say. "I went to the address and waited to see who, if anyone, of note, visited."

"And?"

"It was a small house off the High Street. The only occupants that I could see were a young girl of probably Aiden's age, and a matronly woman that may be her mother – or like me, is posing in that role."

"Interesting. Any idea what they are about?"

"Window dressing," he said, "because it wasn't they who were of interest, but those that visited later in the day. We answered their first telegram with a request for more information. I was present outside when it arrived. The visitation occurred later in the day and proceeded the reply with Aiden's transportation details."

"Who was it?"

"A beautifully appointed black brougham pulled up outside, and a tall man in a dark suit and top hat paid a visit to the two women. By the way, he carried himself, I don't believe that he was the owner of the carriage, but rather a servant. I wouldn't be surprised if the same carriage is used to pick up young Aiden tomorrow night." He took a breath before continuing. "I waited until the man had left, then followed the carriage at a good distance, until we left the town and they headed into the countryside. I dropped back and used the dust thrown up by the brougham to track them. After a time, they finally pulled off the road and went up a lane that led to a rather well-maintained manor house."

"Do you know whose?"

"I didn't at the time. They used a side entrance, so I circled around until I found the main gates. The name of the house and the owner were proudly displayed. The house is one you would know – Southcote Manor."

I was puzzled. The name certainly rang a bell. I searched my memories. "You're correct. It seems very familiar," I said.

Before I could find the information, Holmes said, "It's the home of Sir Geoffrey Warrington."

"Good Lord! You don't think that the potential leader of the opposition is involved in this Satanist crowd, do you?"

“I hope not,” he said, “but I’ve sent a telegram off to my brother, who seemed very perturbed by the prospect. We shall have some of that help he promised, tomorrow night.”

I snuck my hand into my coat pocket and felt the cold comforting sensation of my service revolver. The fact that we were about to confront a deranged sect that not only worshipped the opposite force of all that is good and wholesome in this world but one that also had powerful political allies, filled me with the deepest dread.

***

Several minutes before the allotted time for young Aiden’s transport to arrive, Holmes and I left via the rear door and then through the back fence gate into the service alley, and around to the nearby side street where Holmes had parked his hired dogcart. We brought it around and sat almost fifty yards from the front door to keep watch.

The dark black brougham arrived directly at six o’clock. A tall man with the top hat disembarked, knocked on the front door, and a moment later returned with Aiden. The door to the brougham was opened from within, and Aiden’s face lit up with a wide smile. I presumed that the young lass was inside.

When the brougham was over a hundred yards away, we fell into the same pace behind it. We turned towards the southwest and I assumed that we were heading towards Southcote Manor. I amused myself by viewing the houses and landmarks that we passed on the way. Most were of Georgian age, with several newly added terraces, along with many grand neo-gothic buildings from a long-ago age.

I noticed that another carriage had fallen into lockstep with us and maintained a distance of fifty yards from our rear. I turned to Holmes and mentioned it, asking whether it might belong to Sir Geoffrey Warrington.

Holmes smiled, “No, but it does belong to Her Majesty’s Service. Mycroft has sent us some help. There will probably be more trailing further behind that one.”

I took one quick look over my shoulder and studied the cart. It was a large four-wheeler with a pair of well-built men in dark coats in the driver’s seats.

After nearly half an hour of travelling well into the countryside, Holmes spoke up. “We aren’t heading towards Southcote Manor.”

When the brougham took a left-hand fork in the road, Holmes pulled the dogcart to the right fork and stopped after fifty yards. Several other carts, including the large four-wheeler, pulled up near us.

Holmes spoke to the driver of the first cart. “Jansen, they’ve headed towards to the Padworth Quarry,” he said. “That’s slightly unexpected. We’ll need to approach with care and surround it. I suggest sending one group to the western side, while Watson and I and the other group go to the east.”

The young plainly clothed man nodded and barked orders at the other carriages. They rumbled off past us. Holmes pulled our cart around and headed down the other trail.

Within a few hundred yards we came to another fork and took the left, I noticed that the right-hand trail dipped as it disappeared amongst the trees. Our track soon opened up and I saw the wide expanse of the quarry lying to our right. Holmes pulled up in a small layby, dropped to the ground, and hurried across to the edge of the pit.

I was shocked at the sight before me.

Down at the bottom of the quarry, in a large open, flat space, a circular area was lined with blazing braziers. The bright full moon bathed the circle of people, their faces hidden by hooded robes. They stood surrounding a central figure dressed in a dark brown robe standing next to a wide flat stone, which had all the hallmarks of an altar. The central figure’s hood was thrown back and I recognised him immediately as Sir Geoffrey Warrington.

The black brougham stood off to the side, and as I watched, Sir Geoffrey motioned towards it. Two men quickly broke off and hurried to the carriage. They man-handled the supine form of young Aiden from the carriage across to the altar. There they stripped him and lay him on the large flat stone. Sir Geoffrey drew a large wide-bladed dagger from beneath his robes and held it aloft. He began to address the assembly. “Lord Satan, we, your faithful servants, gather beneath the full moon to present to you this poor offering, so that you may bless us with another month of continued success in our endeavours.”

I gasped and heard Holmes swear under his breath. Any chance of harm coming to one of his Irregulars was anathema to him. He turned towards Jansen and spoke.

"Get some men down to the entrance!" he hissed and then pointed to the man in the centre of the circle, "I suggest we let the majority of the people escape, as they will want to soon enough, but make sure Sir Geoffrey is detained."

Jansen and his men moved off.

"Why will the other people try to escape?" I asked.

Holmes smiled. "Because of this."

Suddenly, he moved forward and slid and skipped his way down a steep path to the quarry floor. I was taken aback but quickly joined him. He raced towards the circle of adherents, pulled out his revolver, and fired into the air.

The effect was incredible.

The group scattered like a flock of pigeons, running to-and-fro as if the devil that they had so wished to meet had, in fact, arrived. Holmes ignored them and moved towards Sir Geoffrey. The politician simply stood and eyed Holmes, a grin on his face.

"Drop the knife," said Holmes. "This disgusting play-acting is over."

"You have me at a disservice, sir," said Sir Geoffrey.

"I am Sherlock Holmes."

Sir Geoffrey's smile grew. "Ah, Mycroft's little brother. The detective." He waved the knife before him. "What gives you the right to confront a Member of Parliament embracing his religious freedoms? You aren't the law. You are nothing."

Holmes stepped forward. His face was alight with an anger I had rarely seen. He opened his mouth to speak but was cut off as Jansen stepped in front of him, a pistol trained on the politician.

"He may not be the law, but I am," Jansen said. "Inspector Michael Jansen, Intelligence Branch, and you are mine now."

***

It was a dismal day that found Holmes, Mycroft, and me back in the tiny town of Pangbourne for a memorial service. It was a sombre occasion for Lord and Lady Moncrieff to say farewell to their son, Alexander.

The rain pattered on the ground as we gave our condolences to the family, who thanked Holmes for both discovering their son's body and his killer. Lord Moncrieff kept his stoic visage as always, but my heart sang for Lady Elizabeth who seemed on the verge of a breakdown.

The three of us moved to a sheltered patch where we could watch the rest of the assembly and speak.

"What of that degenerate, Sir Geoffrey?" I asked, noting my voice was full of disgust.

"He will hang," said Mycroft, "The Prime Minister is adamant of that. He has placed the full force of the Attorney General's Office onto it."

"What of the others?" asked Holmes.

His face soured slightly. "The Security Service is scouring the country for them. Sir Geoffrey has kept his mouth shut, and will probably take their identities to the noose."

"Damn him," I swore.

"Yes," said Holmes. "I think that's what he wanted all along."

"Why would someone in his position do such a thing?" I asked.

"Regardless of any supernatural connotations," said Holmes, "I suppose it was that inner belief in the Devil's works that gave him a level of inner superiority and confidence which enabled him to achieve such a high office. History is replete with many an evildoer that has possessed such an aura, and I'm afraid that it is in the nature of man to bolster his inner worth through such fictitious means."

I nodded and peered out at the rain pattering down as the last of the mourners disappeared from view.

The Case of Vanderbilt and the Yeggman

As I drew the curtains on another mid-spring evening, I couldn't help but shiver. The temperatures during the day had been mild to warm, but the chills of winter had not yet removed themselves completely from the night.

Turning back to survey the mess I'd made of the day's *Telegraph*, I realised that a stranger could only draw one conclusion from reading its contents: A heatwave was blasting the great city, given the panic contained in every story. Such was the dread that gripped the media and political class over incidents occurring thousands of miles away in Afghanistan.

The outcome of another skirmish between Russian and Afghani forces threatened to bring British forces into play. Such an expansion was too close to the Indian border for the locals to accept.

Coupled with veiled threats emanating from Russia, the events had placed the British Defence Forces, both home and abroad, on notice for immediate deployment to the region. Contracted arrangements to finish several new British Ironclads had been brought forward. The Prime Minister had formed a war committee and was in the process of requesting additional funding for defence spending.

I shook my head as I gathered up the scattered pages of the newspaper. The sabre-rattling affairs of state always brought back flashes of my time in Afghanistan. I tried to dispel such remembrances, but a small squeal of pain in my shoulder answered the siren song.

I stretched to full height, trying to ease the throb through movement. Placing the newspaper on the settee, I paced about the sitting room in an attempt to stop the ache. I put it down to the chill or the silly way I had stooped down to pore over the newspaper.

Holmes was out on a case to which I hadn't been made privy, so I had occupied my time with the news, attempting one of his techniques of cross-matching articles to build a deeper picture of the story –

something for which I now berated myself as I stepped around the room, bringing the fire in my shoulder under control.

I paced past the door to Holmes's bedroom and then the fireplace, and found myself at Holmes's chemical bench. It was there I saw some of His private paraphernalia: Two slim glass syringes were filled with brown-tinged liquid, resting in an open red silk-lined case.

"Oh, Holmes," I said out loud, a hint of exasperation on my lips. I picked up one of the syringes and looked closely at the contents. Pursing my lips, I peered around for any other evidence of Holmes's cocaine habit. Finding none, I replaced the syringe and snapped the case shut.

I've failed to stop you in the past, but at least I can delay any future use for a little while.

I stepped away from Holmes's table just as the door to the sitting room opened. Surprised, I quickly slipped the syringe case into my jacket pocket and promptly forgot about it.

The tall aquiline features of Sherlock Holmes poked through the doorway and glanced across at me.

"Ah, Watson, good man," he said. "Grab your coat. Lestrade needs us at the Yard. *Tout de suite*, it seems."

***

Even though the traffic at that time of night was rather light, it still took the hansom a good twenty minutes to cover the distance to the Yard. I had lost count of the number of times Holmes and I had journeyed along the same route over the last few years. The hansom pulled to a stop outside the front entrance, where we alighted. As always, I turned and paid the driver before joining Holmes.

"What is this about?" I'd waited to ask, as Holmes was disinclined to converse during our journey.

"Lestrade's telegram was non-specific on that point."

He pulled out a small, folded paper and read aloud. "*Come now. Have arrested supposed friend of yours. Will only talk to you.*"

"Very strange," I said.

"Hopefully," answered Holmes. I caught sight of a slight smile on his face. He did love a good mystery, and given the amount of information he had to hand, I hoped this one kept him intrigued.

"What friend of yours could he have arrested?"

Holmes turned towards me, that grin still in place, "On that note, Watson, I can honestly say I have no idea. The telegram didn't give me enough information, and I certainly have no knowledge of any friends or acquaintances that have come under the suspicions of the police of late."

I looked up at the imposing edifice of Scotland Yard, the nearby gas lamps casting a pallid glow across the orange-and-grey bricks. We stepped through the great oak doors and stopped in the small reception area. The gap above the small wooden counter provided the only view into the inner workings of the Metropolitan Police.

At that time of night, only a few bobbies were on duty, either moving around with sheafs of paper or sitting at their desks and filling out reports.

We stepped up to the counter and rang the small metal bell.

A young constable looked up and approached the counter. He recognised us straight away and nodded to the door to the side of the counter. Stepping through as he opened it, we followed him through the uniform work area and into a corridor beyond.

"The inspector's down in the basement," he said. "We've got a right strange one this time."

"The basement?" I said to Holmes in surprise. He simply smiled and held up a single finger to silence any further questions.

We went down a short flight of steps just outside the workroom and walked along a long corridor that ran past storage cupboards and finally into the area reserved for small holding cells. From our past experience, I knew that there were also some unfurnished rooms specifically set aside for interviewing suspects.

I'll admit that I've never enjoyed entering this part of the building. It reeks of misery from an older time, almost as if we had entered a medieval dungeon complete with torture chamber. Admittedly, the only criminals brought here are those charged with crimes against the Crown. The Yard's location means that miscreants captured near the Houses of Parliament, or worse, Buckingham Palace itself are most likely to be brought there.

Finally, the young constable stopped and knocked on a solid wooden door. The knob turned and the door opened a crack, revealing the familiar face of Inspector Lestrade.

"Excellent," he said before stepping back and opening the door fully, allowing us to enter. The constable withdrew, and Holmes and I stepped into the sparsely furnished room.

The only other occupant of the room was a rat-faced little fellow who looked to be in his mid-forties. I could add or subtract a decade though due to the light. He sat on a chair in the middle of the room, his hands shackled behind him.

His features were amplified by the fearful look on his face and the way his eyes darted around the room and across both of us as we entered. A hint of recognition dawned on that face as he saw Holmes and he broke into a wide grim.

"Mr. 'Olmes," he said. "God bless you, sir!"

Holmes peered down his long nose and returned the smile. "Hello, Nobby," he said, "What trouble have you got yourself into this time?"

Nobby looked mortified. "Oh, no, sir, I done nuffin', 'onest. I've been tellin' the inspector 'ere just that. It's all a stitch-up."

Holmes turned to Lestrade, whose expression held the look of someone that lived his life being lied to by criminals.

"What is Nobby here meant to have done?" Holmes asked.

Lestrade pulled out a small notepad and made a big deal out of flipping to the requisite page, whilst eyeing the man in the chair with a healthy level of disdain.

"Arnold Brown, known on the street as 'Nobby', was caught coming out of the back entrance of Number Ten Downing Street – an address I'm sure you are familiar with."

I was aghast. My eyes darted back to look at Nobby again. I studied him more closely and realised that beneath his slightly grubby coat, he wore a neatly pressed dinner suit, with a white low-cut waistcoat and matching white bowtie. If I were to have met Nobby in a mansion house, I would have mistaken him for the butler or a simple valet.

Lestrade continued, “Two uniformed constables were on duty patrolling the grounds when they came upon this fellow skulking across the rear lawns.”

“I wasn’t skulking,” said Nobby, “I ‘ad an errand to run for my master.”

Lestrade harrumphed. He’d obviously heard this before we arrived.

“And who would that master be?” asked Holmes.

“I shouldn’t really say,” said Nobby.

“Fine, then. It’s the cells for you,” said Lestrade, fed up with Nobby dodging the question, "You wanted Sherlock Holmes. Well, here he is. If you're not going to answer the questions then you'll spend time in the lockup.” He stepped towards Nobby, whose face lit up in fear.

“All right, all right,” he said, peering back at Holmes hoping for some sympathy from my friend. When Holmes remained stoically still, Nobby relented, dropped his head and continued. “I’m workin’ as man-servant to Mr. Johan Vanderbilt.”

“Who?” asked Lestrade.

“Johan Vanderbilt,” repeated Nobby, “He’s an attaché to the German ambassador. I been workin’ out of the London residence. It’s a good job, been there for the last six months. On the straight and narrow, me.”

“Well that’s very good to see, Nobby,” said Holmes.

I was quite intrigued. From experience, I knew that Holmes had a large sphere of acquaintances across London, and indeed the country. I assumed that Nobby fell into one of the various coteries that circled Holmes, or vice-versa.

“How exactly do you know Nobby here?” I asked.

“I’d like to know as well,” said Lestrade.

“Ah,” said Holmes, a wry smile on his lips. He stepped closer to Nobby, stared down at him for a moment before turning back to us. “Nobby here taught me everything I know about safe-cracking. He’s been at it for well over twenty years. One of the best in London.”

Lestrade’s face lit up. “A yeggman, aye.” He rubbed his hands together in glee. “Must be good at his job, ‘cause I don’t know him, but a yeggman caught coming out of the Prime Minister's residence – you might be going down for a long time, my boy."

Nobby cried out in terror, "I done nuthin'! I was working for Vanderbilt, 'onest, I was. Talk to 'im. He'll vouch for me!"

Holmes remained stoic, surveying the scene, searching for clews and digesting all. I'll admit my heart went out to the little man. His demeanour suggested sincerity, but I could tell that Holmes, himself, wasn't convinced. Lestrade was ready to hang the safe-cracker.

Holmes pondered for a while longer, leaving the room in silence, before he turned to Lestrade. "I assume, Inspector, you haven't searched Nobby as yet?"

"No. When he started going on about only talking to you, I thought I'd better wait."

"I've got nothin' on me, 'onest, Mr. 'Olmes. We've known each other for years. I wouldn't ask for you to vouch for me if I'd done somefin' bad, now would I?"

Holmes stood, peering at Nobby's face for several moments before turning to Lestrade. "Inspector, if you would be so kind, could you please undo Nobby's handcuffs?"

Nobby's face lit up. I was taken aback. Grumbling to himself, Lestrade stepped behind Nobby and undid the cuffs.

The yeggman rubbed his wrists to restart the blood flowing. "Thank you so much for trusting me, Mr. 'Olmes. You're a saint, I've always said that," he stated as he stood and headed towards the exit door.

Holmes waited until Nobby put a hand on the doorknob before speaking.

"Ah, not so fast Nobby." The former safe-cracker stopped in his tracks and turned slowly to face Holmes. "It might be prudent to inspect your garments before you head off. Just to satisfy the inspector. I wouldn't want him to think that there was anything untoward about this affair," Holmes said. I felt that there was something unsaid in his statement that would become evident quite soon.

Holmes held out a hand, I could tell he was holding his smile in check, "I'd like to have a quick look at your coat if I may." He shrugged, "Just as a matter of course."

Nobby's face was aghast. He slowly peeled off the coat and handed it to Holmes. My friend took it without taking his eyes off Nobby's expression. My eyes flicked between them, and I finally saw what Holmes saw. As Nobby's eyes dropped to the bottom of the coat, Holmes nodded, turned the coat around, and examined the lining inside. He let out a small, "A-ha!" and stepped over to the chair. Laying the coat across it, with the inner lining revealed, he ran a finger down the stitching in the centre and found a small unsewn section.

"If I'm mistaken, Nobby, I apologise in advance and will repair your coat," he said, before jamming a finger inside and pulling at the thread. It came away easily, revealing a larger section that had evidently been unpicked. The hole created was large enough for his entire hand. Holmes stood and reached into an inner pocket of his own coat and slipped out a pair of fine kid-skin gloves.

Wearing them, he thrust a hand deep inside the lining of Nobby's coat and fished around for a moment. A smile crossed his face and he brought out a folded sheaf of stiff parchment held together with a bright red ribbon. I caught sight of a seal on the outer page. I'm sure that there was a crown, and possibly a lion or unicorn.

"Good Lord!" said Lestrade. "What in the blazes is that?"

Holmes straightened and examined the papers for a moment, mumbling to himself before looking at Nobby and shaking his head.

"Nobby, you've been a very bad boy," he said.

The (now it seemed) active safe-cracker, looking much more presentable in full valet uniform, dropped his head in shame.

***

As Mycroft Holmes looked up from his work, his mouth dropped open in surprise as he spied his brother's silhouette in the doorway. "Sherlock? What in blazes are you doing in here? And how did you get in?"

A pale face at Holmes's shoulder looked past us and addressed Mycroft. "I'm sorry, sir. I did recognise your brother and was about to come for you, but it's what he was holding that made me bring him straight to you."

Mycroft stared at the man, a flush of anger ran across his cheeks. "Fine, Johnson, but that's not the proper process is it?"

Johnson's face went bright red. "No, sir. Sorry, sir." He backed away and virtually ran away down the corridor.

Holmes moved across to the large oaken desk and *plonked* his prize on the desk before his brother's eyes. Mycroft peered at the parcel of parchment wrapped in red ribbon. He looked from the papers to Holmes, confusion writ large his face. Slowly he pulled at the bow of the ribbon and freed it. He unfolded the sheaf of papers and read the opening words on the first page.

His face turned from confusion to horror.

"Sherlock, where did you get this? You could be in serious trouble."

Holmes took one of the chairs before Mycroft's desk and motioned for me to join him. Mycroft watched in silence as I walked over and sat down.

"I'll admit, dear brother, that I didn't open the papers. I realised as soon as I saw the seal, and was informed of the original location, that it would be tantamount to treason. I could have left the papers with the constabulary, but we agreed that it might be best to bring them to someone of your – how should I put it? – *station* within the Government."

Mycroft pursed his lips and read the first page again. He shook his head. "Where did this come from?"

"I think you already know that."

"Yes. I do."

I piped up, "Well, I don't, so please explain to those of us who are still in the dark."

Mycroft glanced at Holmes for a moment, then turned his face towards me. As always, he treated me with respect. "Well, Doctor, I would think you already know this came from the Prime Minister's residence." I nodded. "Neither of you could have known though, that these are the PM's personal notes to be read out in Parliament on Monday morning. Once presented, they will be taken away and typed up to form an appropriations bill to be tabled at Parliament later in the week. The final bill," he patted the sheaf of papers, "is set to rock the country to its core."

"Why?" I asked, leaning forward in an attempt to make out the wording and figures evident on the parchment.

"This country is on the brink of war – with Russia of all places."

I nodded. "It's all through the newspapers."

Mycroft harrumphed. "Reporters," he spat, "Until they got wind of it, there was nothing but a simple border skirmish. It would have resolved itself in a week and England would have had no reason to be involved. Our papers have blown it up to the point that the Russians have been emboldened and are pushing ever further into Indian territory. This," he smacked the papers, "is the result. Our pacifist Prime Minister is suddenly egged on by his constituency and taking us towards conflict. This outlines the amount of money he will request from Parliament and the armaments and troops that it will pay for. All to be sent into Afghanistan and into this conflict."

"But surely we have learnt from the past," I said, imploring Mycroft.

He smiled back at me. "Doctor, you should know better than any of us here the futility of combat – combat that results when our ill-informed superiors begin to rattle their sabres."

Holmes finally spoke up. "I'm surprised, brother. I thought you fully supported the decision-making processes of our Government."

Mycroft sighed, "No, I fully support our Government. It just leaves me a little exasperated when those decisions go awry through unsupported opinions rather than actual facts."

He looked down at the parchment and thought for a moment before peering up at us once again.

"Enough of my own opinions, I can only assume that this parcel came from the safe in Number Ten." Holmes and I nodded. "Given the lack of excitement, I can also assume that it hasn't been found to be missing."

"Worse than that," Holmes said. "It has been replaced." He pointed towards the desk. "It seems that the miscreant that stole the original was also tasked with substituting another set of papers. I haven't seen them yet, but I assume they have revised figures created to mislead the Prime Minister and possibly embarrass him, or at worst, lead us to implement an incorrect regime of military acquisitions."

Mycroft thought for a moment, flipping through the notes and murmuring under his breath before looking back at us. "You may be right, Sherlock, but as to misleading the Government, that won't happen. The PM's figures would have been distributed to the Ministries of Defence and Finance already, plus to the Under-Secretaries to prepare the actual bill for tabling in Parliament. This action could embarrass the Prime Minister if he was to read them out in the House, but I feel that there is something far more sinister behind this." He stared at Holmes for a moment before the younger brother answered.

"Espionage," he said, a slight smile on his face.

"Why are you smiling?" Mycroft asked. "You could have just admitted that you already knew. I assume you know who then?"

"The Germans, it seems, but I'm unsure why. The man who stole these papers was doing so under contract to a member of the German diplomatic corps."

"Who?" said Mycroft, a look of confusion on his face. "I'm quite familiar with the Ambassador, Baron Egor."

"The papers were purloined by one Arthur 'Nobby' Brown, a yeggman from Soho," started Holmes.

Mycroft interrupted, "Sorry, did you say that he was an '*eggman*'?"

"No, *yeggman*," said Holmes, placing particular emphasis on the first syllable, "It is street slang for a safe-cracker. Anyway, Nobby Brown was hired by Johan Vanderbilt, an assistant to the Ambassador. Nobby was arrested outside of Number Ten whilst the Prime Minister was entertaining several European ambassadors, including Baron Egor Staal. Nobby went in with Vanderbilt, slipped away from the dining room, opened the safe, switched notes, and exited the building. It was only through sheer luck that a pair of bobbies were checking the rear of the property when Nobby crossed their path."

"Vanderbilt? I don't think I've met him."

"Well, you might have an opportunity tomorrow. He's to meet with Nobby to lay claim to these notes."

"It will be no good if it's on the Embassy grounds."

"With that, we are quite fortunate. Our captive yeggman was to meet this Vanderbilt in a small pub in Covent Garden to hand over the papers."

"What time?" asked Mycroft.

"Twelve-thirty, a half-hour after opening. Good idea, that. They should be able to hide amongst the lunchtime crowd," said Holmes.

Mycroft stood and picked up the parcel of papers and walked around the desk. "I need to get these back into the PM's safe before he becomes aware and – " He stopped and tapped Holmes on the shoulder. " – I don't understand what interest these Germans have in our defence movements, but we should use everything at our disposal to upset their attempt."

"What are you thinking?" I asked, my eyes darting across to Holmes and seeing a familiar sly grin on his face.

"Who would have written up the PM's notes in the first place?" Holmes asked.

"That would be Miss Marsden, the PM's personal assistant," Mycroft said shaking his head, "She would be long gone."

"Do you have anyone else on staff that can draft up a set of mock papers?" asked Holmes.

"Perhaps, but I think we need to keep the number of people within these walls that know about this to a minimum," Mycroft said.

"I believe I may know someone that can help. We'll need to borrow those," Holmes said pointing at the sheaf of papers, "Or at least an example of Miss Marsden's handwriting, for authenticity's sake. We will also, of course, need some official stationery, including some more of that ribbon."

"More than easy to arrange," said Mycroft.

***

Within half an hour, Mycroft had the wheels turning throughout the Houses of Parliament. At Number 10, Mycroft himself led us down a corridor and into the Prime Minister's outer offices. Using his own key, he rummaged through the personal filing cabinet of Miss Marsden and retrieved another batch of the PM's reading notes.

Back in his office, all three of us crowded around his desk to view the spoils.

Miss Marsden's notes were written out in a spidery thin scrawl, very reminiscent of the delicate hand of a woman. The fake notes consisted of similar penmanship but had a slightly heavier look to them.

Mycroft read through the faked papers, murmuring and mumbling to himself as he did so. Finally, he burst out, "Preposterous! Whoever wrote this has no idea about the workings of Parliament, or indeed the Defence force."

"Would the PM have gotten far into the figures before realising?"

Mycroft thought for a moment and shook his head. "Sadly, he would have probably read them all out and only realised once the guffaws broke out from the cross-benches."

"As I thought," said Holmes. He then pointed to the script and commented, "This was drafted by a man. The downstrokes on the pen are much heavier than Miss Marsden's, but overall, it is a very good likeness. The forger obviously had access to a set of notes such as ours."

"I agree," said Mycroft. "That worries me quite a bit."

"Why?" I asked.

"It would appear that the forger is working within these walls."

My eyes opened in surprise and I nodded in response. Such an act by a member of Parliament or the Civil Service was tantamount to an act of treason in the eyes of the law.

Finally, Mycroft sat back and closed the papers. He looked exhausted. I think it was mostly due to the gravity of the situation, rather than any physical exertion.

"Would it have been as bad as you thought?" Holmes asked.

"If the PM had read this out without examining it first, which is most likely, he would have seemed a fool, and would certainly have stumbled within a couple of pages. The scandal surrounding the theft and replacement that would soon erupt would be far worse." Mycroft peered up at his hawk-faced brother. "I can't thank you enough, I really can't."

"It's not us you have to thank," Holmes said, "I think you should send your regards, and possibly something a little more substantial, to Inspector Lestrade and the two bobbies that caught Nobby."

"Yes, yes, you're right. I will see to it. But first – " He pulled a few sheets of paper from his desk drawer and scrawled several lines whilst flipping through the sheaf of fake papers. I looked across at Holmes, a perplexed look on my face. He simply smiled and shrugged.

Mycroft laid down his pen, gathered up his notes and the fake papers, and stood up. He strode from the room with a rare sense of purpose. Holmes kept pace with him easily, but I found myself falling back. Luckily, the journey downstairs and into the sub-basement area was short.

We entered a large room packed with shelves and cupboards. A lone desk sat near the doorway and acted as a counter. A young man of barely twenty years sat behind the desk. He was working away on a sort of long handwritten document when he noticed us. His eyes went wide as we entered, he dropped his pen and shot to his feet.

A nervous voice peeped out of his mouth. "Mr. Holmes, sir. What can I do for you?"

"Ah, Atherton, good lad," he said. "Surprised you're here."

"Um, I took the opportunity to learn more about work, sir," he answered with a smile.

Mycroft returned his smile and nodded, "Good man. You'll go far with that attitude. Now, back to business, I need ten pages of the PM's stock paper, a length of red ribbon, a pen, and ink."

Atherton looked confused for a moment. "I'm only meant to give that out to Miss Marsden," he said.

"And normally that would be fair," said Mycroft, "But I have been asked to prepare some reading notes for the PM on Monday and know that he prefers all his notes to be on the same paper stock."

The young man nodded. "I can't argue with that." He turned and disappeared into the depths of the rows of shelves. The sound of his rummaging filtered back to us.

I pivoted and noticed Holmes taking a special interest in what Atherton had been working on. From where I stood, I could see that it was writing, some large, some small, some heavy, some verging on spidery. It was then I noticed Atherton's jacket hanging on a coat rack near the aisles of shelving. My eye was drawn to the pin on the lapel. It was composed of a small silver bar on a red and green striped ribbon. If I wasn't mistaken I would say it was the Afghanistan medal, I had a similar one myself for services in the war. I thought to myself that the lad was far too young to have served and assumed it was a father's or grandfather's pin.

I was about to comment to Holmes when the young lad returned. He *plopped* the supplies down on the desk and handed a wooden clipboard with an attached sheet of paper to Mycroft.

"Just need you to sign for these, sir. Normally, I wouldn't need to ask, but I've been told to keep a close watch on our more special items."

Mycroft nodded and signed. Atherton took the clipboard away and handed over the stationary. He nodded slightly, before saying, "A good night to you, gentlemen."

"And you to Atherton, and thank you," said Mycroft before ushering us out of the room. I looked back as I exited and noted Atherton's gaze intently fixed on the three of us. I was confused as to his expression – it appeared to be part concern, part fear, and part suspicion.

***

Within moments we had been ushered back into the cold London night. The fake notes, loose sheaf of papers, pens and ribbon – all contained in an official leather satchel.

Mycroft had expressed his concerns about our next steps but wanted to be kept up to date as things progressed. I admit I was still at a slightly loose end. I had faith that the Holmes brothers knew what they were doing, but as always would have liked some inkling of the plan going forward.

Holmes hailed a hansom and as we climbed aboard I peered back to find that Mycroft had already disappeared back inside the building. By the time I turned forward, Holmes had given the driver our destination, so I simply sat and watched as we navigated the virtually empty streets.

After about fifteen minutes of travelling along the edge of the river, we turned right then onto the King's Road. I felt it was time to ask, "Holmes, where the devil are we going?"

"To visit an old associate," he said in that enigmatic way of his.

"Another one?" I asked, the question disappearing into the ether. Grumbling to myself, I sat back in the seat and remained silent. After another few minutes and we turned into the Fulham Palace Road and headed towards Hammersmith. I was certainly intrigued by now, even more so when we pulled up in front of a dark four-storey Georgian building on the Hammersmith High Street. Holmes leapt from the hansom and made his way towards the ground floor entrance, leaving me to pay the cabbie.

"You might want to get him to stay for a while," Holmes said over his shoulder. "Say two hours."

I heard the heavy knocker hammer away as I was negotiating the fee with the driver and managed to join Holmes just as the door was opened by a crook-backed old man who looked to be in his seventies. He peered up at Holmes's darkened face and I saw a grin appear on his face.

"Sherlock Holmes! My word, it's been well over ten years, hasn't it?"

"Yes, Clive, yes it has," Holmes said.

The old man stepped back and allowed us both to enter. He looked me up and down before Holmes introduced me. "Ah, this is my associate, Dr. John Watson. Watson, this is Mr. Clive Trimble."

I held out my hand, but Trimble shied away, preferring to nod instead.

"Ah, yes, Clive doesn't shake hands. Do you, Clive?" Holmes asked as the old man nodded. "He is very protective of his hands. Any damage may affect his craft."

"Craft?" I asked.

Before I received an answer, Holmes strolled down the corridor, followed by the old man. I closed the door and chased after them, catching up in a room at the back of the house consisting of several draughtsman's tables, each with a gaslight situated above them. An ornate table sat at the end of the room, with two lights shining nearby.

Holmes and Trimble stood next to a normal flat table. Holmes withdrew the sheaf of parliamentary stationery, notes, and other paraphernalia from the satchel and placed them on the bench.

Holmes pointed to the figures that Mycroft had drafted, then the fake notes and Miss Marden's scribbles.

"Clive, I haven't asked for a return of the favour I gave you all those years ago, but tonight I am."

Clive's face dropped into a stern expression. "Nothing illegal is it?" He shook his head and backed away a step. "I don't want to be doing nothing illegal again. I've left all that behind. I'm too old to go back inside Wandsworth. It'd be the death of me."

"It's all right Clive. Nothing about this is illegal. In fact, you would be helping your country." Holmes pointed to the fake notes. "I need you to write up a set of notes like these – " Then at Mycroft's figures. " – using these numbers instead – " Finally, he pointed at Miss Marsden's writings. " – in the handwriting style of this young lady."

Clive looked at each in turn, his eyes lit up at the prospect of what he was to do. "And this is nothing illegal?"

"I assure you, this is all above board. Would I lie to you?"

The old man peered up at my good friend, a small smile crossed his lips and he shook his head. "No, no, you wouldn't lie to me, Mr. Holmes." He picked up the pages and moved across to the ornate draughtsman's board and began to delve into his craft. I was intrigued and watched from several feet away as he practised the strokes from the PM's secretary's scribblings before creating another set of notes with Mycroft's figures.

I almost started when I heard Holmes's voice in my ear. "The man is an artist. He is renowned for recreating historical documents and notations in almost the exact replication of the original's hand-writing and calligraphy."

"But that could so easily be seen as fraud or forgery," I said.

"Ah, yes. Sadly, Clive did stray onto the other side of the law on one occasion. We crossed paths when I was asked to help investigate a case of illegal forgery."

I must have looked confused, as Holmes smiled and said, "Oh, before your time, Watson, before your time. Not an overly exciting adventure, but I'd be happy to relate it to you at another time. Anyway, I tracked the original documents and the miscreants that had ordered the work to be done, and I managed to convince the police that our Clive here had been duped into committing a crime. They reduced his sentence by five years, which – given his age – probably saved his life."

"Was he innocent?"

"That question requires further discussion, as there was a lot of additional information that you would need to make your own judgement, and this isn't the appropriate time or place to expand fully."

We went silent as we saw Clive turn towards us with a disparaging look. I wandered away and perused the works on the other draught boards. One towards the far end of the room held a large sheet of parchment upon which were the letters *A*, *J*, and *S*, written in various styles and sizes. As I studied it, I noticed Holmes standing beside me.

"Ah, Clive has himself an apprentice, it seems," he said.

Confused, I asked, "How so?"

"Well the first thing one is taught is to practice your calligraphy using familiar text. The letters of the alphabet, your name, address, things like that. Most students use their own initials the most," he said, before turning away and rummaging through a large pile of seemingly forgotten sheets of parchment in the far corner. Finally, he stood and brought across a single but very dusty page. He placed it on the draught board next to the object of my interest.

It was a similar page, but it was covered from edge to edge with variations of the letters *S* and *H*. As I stared at the lettering, the penny dropped. I turned to face Holmes.

"You were a student?"

He smiled., “Why yes, Watson, I was. Clive never throws anything away. After he was released from Wandsworth, I helped him to set up this shop, and then engaged his services to learn the art of calligraphy and script replication.”

“Forgery, you mean.”

Holmes chuckled, “Well, yes, forgery if you like, but it was all in the interests of education. One must understand the criminal mind and their techniques to be able to interpret and judge the distinction between real and fake.”

Before I could reply, Clive looked up from his work and harrumphed. “I believe I have finished.”

We hurried over and glanced at the finished notes. I was amazed. To my layman’s eye, the delicate feminine scrawl of the PM’s assistant was reproduced as if by the same hand. I glanced at Holmes. A small grin told me that he seemed just as impressed.

“Excellent work, my good friend,” he said. “Excellent work.”

***

Holmes, Lestrade, and I arrived at The Lamb and Flag pub dead on midday. The wonderfully bright sunny day did nothing to heighten the drab look of the external façade of the building. It was nestled down Rose Street in Covent Garden, a street by name only, as in reality it was little more than a dimly lit back-alley that curved around connecting Floral to Garrick street.

The three of us had affected the look of everyday workers, shunning any trappings of finery and dragging out our oldest, shoddiest clothing. Holmes had any number of costumes from which to choose. I simply picked my oldest clothes that I had kept on hand in case Holmes dragged me off on another undercover adventure. It was Lestrade that looked the most out of place amongst the three of us. He obviously had to delve into the back of his cupboard and drag out some very old and well-worn clothing that must have been in everyday use once due to its wear, but they hadn’t graced his body in years.

The interior of the pub was no different from the outside in terms of décor and refinement. It was a simple room with a series of booths along the walls, consisting of hard wooden benches and tables, and a scattering of small wooden tables and stools across the central area. A bar ran along one wall, with the dour-looking landlord the only worker in sight.

This was simply a drinkers' pub, servicing the workers from the nearby markets, and one could assume, at night, the more questionable local trade.

As we sat nursing our pints of watery beer and avoiding the suspicious eyes of the landlord, Holmes and Lestrade told tales of their knowledge of the place.

"There's a room upstairs," began Lestrade, "that they call 'The Bucket of Blood', on account of the bare-knuckle fights they hold on the first Saturday night of every month."

"That's barbaric," I said, "Surely the constabulary should shut it down."

Holmes harrumphed to remind me to stay in character, while Lestrade chuckled. "The local bobbies know well to leave this place alone. The locals keep each other in check. The law only steps in when someone gets well out of line. It's a balancing act, but it works."

I crossed my arms at the thought.

Holmes piped up, "From my reading, this place has an even longer and stranger history. It was once a more genteel establishment attracting some of the local poets, such as Dryden and Wilmott. In fact, poor John Dryden was attacked by ruffians not far from here, supposedly in revenge for a satirical poem he wrote about Charles the Second's mistress at the time."

"I thought you said that it was more genteel?" I asked.

"Yes, but one must not vilify the King or his mistress. The intriguing fact was that Dryden didn't even write the poem. It was John Sheffield, the Third Earl of Mulgrave."

"So, he was assaulted for no reason, except mistaken identity," I said.

"As it would seem. Very difficult to bring a grievance against the King – especially someone held in such high regard as Charles the Second."

My comment was stopped short as the front door opened and in stepped a tall, slender figure. He was immaculately dressed in a morning suit, with a calf-length frockcoat over it. He took off his top hat and tucked it under his arm. His hair was dark and neatly trimmed, as was his full-faced beard.

He took one look around the room, regarding the three of us briefly before stepping over to the landlord. He held up his index and middle finger and placed some coins on the bar, before moving to the rear of the room and taking a seat in a booth that looked directly at the entrance.

Holmes stared down at his beer and spoke under his breath. "I do believe that is our man."

I directed my own comment at Lestrade. "I do hope you have things in hand outside?"

"Don't worry about that. I've got some of the best keeping their eyes on this place – one either end of Rose Street, and one across the road on Floral Street." He nodded towards the man we believed to be Vanderbilt. "Just in case he goes out the back."

"And Nobby?" Holmes asked.

"He has his own minder, making sure he plays his part."

"Good," said Holmes.

"I assume that you have your own helpers well advised," I said.

"Of course, Watson, of course. Wiggins and Tommy are on the case, with a couple of extras thrown in for good measure. They have Nobby's description, and using his depiction of Vanderbilt, they should have no problems picking up the trail, just in case."

"Surely," Lestrade added, "he'll be headed back to the German Embassy."

"That would be the logical choice, but something disturbs me about all this. The whole German connection, for a start. The Germans have had no interest in Afghanistan, or the sub-continent for decades, so I'm confused why they should show interest now." He took a sip of his beer before looking up as the door opened. "Ah, here we are now, I believe."

The small stature and rat-like features of Nobby Brown entered the pub. He stood in the entranceway while his eyes grew accustomed to the gloom before looking around the room. His eyes fell on the three of us and grew wide in fear. Holmes simply nodded at him before resuming his examination of the tepid contents of his glass.

The landlord piped up from behind the bar. "Hello, Nobby! Usual is it?"

I watched as Nobby peered over at him, before spying the man in the corner with the two beers before him. "Nah, thanks Harold," he said. "I have an appointment." Harold simply nodded and went back to drying glasses. Nobby made his way to the smartly dressed man's booth and sat opposite. The man we presumed to be Vanderbilt, and whom Nobby knew, leaned forward and spoke in a tone too quiet to hear. Nobby was galvanised into action and quickly reached into his coat pocket, extracting the sheaf of pages wrapped in the red ribbon and sliding them across.

The man drew the ribbon, unknotted the bow, and quickly perused the documents. I noticed a small smile come to his face before he closed the documents, retied the ribbon, and slipped them inside his own jacket pocket. From the other side, he withdrew a small envelope which he slid across to Nobby. I barely had time to register the colour of the envelope before Nobby had performed a disappearing act with it.

I leaned into Lestrade and spoke, "You might want to make sure to relieve Nobby of that."

"Already on it," he replied.

The two men held up their beers and clinked glasses before taking long draws in celebration. Their rejoicing was short-lived as Vanderbilt rose, put on his coat, and strode towards the entrance.

The three of us remained unmoved until he had left the building, and then we were a flurry of activity. Holmes and I headed towards the entrance doorway, while Lestrade moved towards Nobby, nabbing him by the collar just as the little yeggman was hightailing it towards the rear exit.

"Not so fast, my lad," I heard Lestrade say before following Holmes into the bright sunshine outside.

Vanderbilt was rapidly disappearing down the right-hand alleyway, heading towards the hustle and bustle of Floral Street. I noticed Holmes peer down the left-hand alleyway and cock his head for a moment before striding after the tall German diplomat.

"Intriguing," I heard him mutter under his breath as I struggled to keep up with him.

As we reached Hart Street, we saw the tall figure of Vanderbilt climbing into a hansom cab. Holmes turned to his right and waved. Immediately, a similar vehicle wound its way through the traffic toward us. We quickly climbed in as Holmes addressed the driver.

"Granton, you saw him?" he asked.

The undercover police officer nodded. "Yes, Mr. Holmes. He fits the description that Brown gave us. Don't worry, I won't let him lose us."

"Good man," said Holmes sitting back and relaxing only slightly.

"What troubles you?" I said. "The man grabbed a cab. Nothing unusual in that."

"Ah, but it is, Watson. Prussia House, which now serves as the German Embassy since unification in 1871, is located in St. James Square. It's barely half a mile from Covent Garden. A tall man such as Vanderbilt could walk it easily in ten minutes. I don't believe that's where we're headed," he said.

As I looked out of the cab, I realised we were passing along Piccadilly, well north of St. James.

"Where could we be heading then?" I asked.

Holmes had a broad smile across his face.

"Care to enlighten me?"

"You'll find out very soon," he answered. "It will be more interesting to see how Mycroft takes the news."

Still intrigued, I glanced outside and realised that we were then passing Wellington Arch and heading towards Belgravia. The houses and buildings had an air of elegance and expense about them that was a world away from The Lamb and Flag.

We passed many buildings proudly displaying flags of other nations outside. I recognised Austria, Hungary, and Italy before we turned into Chesham Street and stopped facing an ornate building that displayed a flag with yellow, black, and white horizontal stripes.

"The Russian Embassy," Holmes said before I could blurt it out myself.

We watched as Vanderbilt stepped from his cab and walked to the front entrance. I was shocked to see the two guards, standing at the front, step back and allow him unmolested entry to the building. This was a diplomat from another embassy – surely they would need some form of identification.

"Well, that was interesting," said Holmes, almost speaking for myself.

"They didn't even stop him. It's as if they know him," I said.

"Yes, so it would seem," Holmes agreed. He reached up and knocked on the roof. "Granton, pull up behind that other hansom. We're about to set a trap for this Vanderbilt chap."

As Granton pulled the hansom up in front of the embassy, Holmes and I alighted. Holmes strode over to the other cab and chatted with the driver. The driver peered back at Granton, who undid his coat and showed the police uniform beneath. The other driver needed no more convincing and left quickly.

Holmes and I moved away from the building but stayed within sight of both the cab and the entrance. The two men stationed on either side of the front entrance eyed us suspiciously for a few moments before turning away.

I leaned into Holmes and asked, "Why would Vanderbilt be allowed such unfettered entry to the Russian embassy? He's a German diplomat, isn't he?"

"That seems to be his station, but then we must delve into his history. Something is unknown to us," he said in that annoyingly deceptive way of his, "but becoming quite apparent." Before I could ask another question, Vanderbilt emerged from the building and strode straight to Granton's cab. We peeled away from our position and hurried after him.

"*Dobryy den' Gospodin* Vanderbilt," said Holmes (Good afternoon Mr. Vanderbilt), as we squeezed in either side of the shocked man, "I assume you are more familiar with your native language." Holmes rapped on the roof and the cab drew away and joined the light traffic.

"Vat is the meaning of this?" Vanderbilt blurted out. Holmes and I placed our arms across him bodily to restrict any chance of his escape. "I will call the police. This is an outrage. I am a German diplomat. Let me go at once."

Holmes smiled, "Sit back and relax, my good man. A policeman is already here, driving the cab. As for you being German – we will get to the bottom of that soon."

When Vanderbilt resisted once more, I pushed my hand into my pocket and pressed the barrel of my service revolver into his side. His eyes went even wider, but all fight quickly left him. Resigned, he sat back and awaited the journey's end.

***

The taller, straight-backed figure of Vanderbilt presented a far different sight in that small sparsely furnished room than did the object our earlier attention. Lestrade mentioned that Nobby had been sequestered to his own cell in Wandsworth for the time being. Holmes reminded Lestrade that Nobby had been helpful in snaring our new culprit, and with passing on the forged notes.

Regardless, he mentioned to me in passing that Mycroft would be informed of everything, which would hopefully have more weight with the judiciary.

Vanderbilt eyed us with both disgust and vile hatred. He retained an upright posture, in spite of the discomfort that he must have felt. I sensed it was more of an act to sway our opinion of him than anything.

"Who are you?" Lestrade asked him for the fourth time.

The familiar response followed, "I am Herr Johan Vanderbilt. I am a member of the German diplomatic corps. I ask for diplomatic immunity and wish to speak to my consular attorney."

Holmes, apparently fed up with the misdirection, finally spoke up. "But that's not altogether true is it, Ivan? I assume it's Ivan, as that is the Russian equivalent of Johan."

Vanderbilt's face turned to rage as he stared towards Holmes.

"I am Johan Vanderbilt. I am German. I was born in – "

Holmes cut him off, "Again, that isn't true, is it? I've been patient, but let us look at the facts, shall we?" He counted off on his fingers, deliberately using his thumb to start with. “One, you employed a local safe-cracker, Nobby Brown, to break into the Prime Minister’s personal safe and replace private papers detailing troop numbers and financial information for an ongoing operation on the Afghanistan border between English and Russian troops.”

He extended his index finger and tapped it. “Two, you personally delivered those papers to the Russian Embassy. Three, you understand Russian. Four, you wear a close-cropped full-faced beard, very rare in Germany, but very common in western Russia at this time. Five, in The Lamb and Flag, you signalled the number two to the bartender using your index and middle fingers. Any purebred German, worth his salt, would use his thumb and index finger for such a gesture. A mistake like that could get you shot amongst the spy community.”

Holmes waited for any reaction. When there was none, he continued. “All we’re interested in is who you gave those papers to among the Russian staff, who your accomplice is inside the Government, and how long this has been going on.”

“I will never speak. I have diplomatic immunity. You can’t prove anything.”

“To be honest, we don’t need to prove anything. Once those forged papers reach Russia, the fallout will unveil the agents within their embassy, and they will deal with them accordingly. As for you, we have accepted your diplomatic immunity and you will be handed over to the German Embassy staff, who I’m sure will have many questions of their own.”

At that moment the door opened and two tall, well-built men in ill-fitting suits entered. They had the square-jawed, blonde hair, blue-eyed look of Continental Germans. They took one look at Vanderbilt and stepped forward.

“Ah, they seem to have arrived,” said Holmes.

Vanderbilt’s eyes widened in fear and his mouth dropped open. He quickly thrust a hand toward his mouth. I was closest and threw out my hand, knocking whatever he’d held to the floor. It was a capsule of some sort. By now two burly men were holding Vanderbilt, but he kept lunging toward the object. Holmes reached down and picked it up. Sniffing it, he quickly turned his head away. Then he held it toward me and I took a careful smell as well. Bitter almonds. *Cyanide.* Vanderbilt had attempted to avoid our questions, but fortunately, he had been prevented.

"Well done, old chap," said Holmes.

***

It was an early morning a few days later that found Holmes and me perusing the papers whilst finishing off another sumptuous breakfast prepared by our wonderful landlady, Mrs. Hudson.

As I sipped my morning coffee, I mused out loud that the last word we had received from Mycroft was over three days previously.

"I'm still a little shocked at the identity of the German agent within the Home Office," I said.

Holmes looked up from his paper. "Well, the lad had a grudge against Her Majesty's Government."

"I can understand, given that his father died in Afghanistan. Losing one's father so early in life leaves scars, as it did young Atherton."

"Sadly, yes. He brooded on it for years. He wasn't working late to improve his prospects – he was copying classified documents, as I saw on his desk when we surprised him the other day. He'd managed to position himself somewhere that nobody would take any notice of him, learning the ins and outs of the Home Office and the Prime Minister's office, because nobody would think twice about talking around the person in charge of stationery. Such a person is always invisible in such an organisation."

"What will happen to him?"

"Hopefully he will only be treated as a dissident, and not charged with treason," Holmes said, "Well, that's to be hoped for anyway. His biggest mistake was falling in with Vanderbilt. Young minds are so impressionable, especially when they bear a grudge against authority. It will be for Her Majesty's authorities to decide." Holmes turned back to his newspaper.

I did the same and began to read *The Times*, coming across an article that smacked of a result of our recent adventure. The headline read *Russia Calls for Talks*. The article indicated that sources within the Government stated that the Russian ambassador to England had visited the Foreign Secretary to begin talks aimed at easing tensions on the Afghanistan-Indian border.

I peered across at Holmes and held the paper so he could read the headline. "It seems as if Mycroft's little ploy worked."

Holmes looked up from his own reading and smiled. "He will be pleased."

Our attention was diverted by the ring of the doorbell downstairs. A murmur of conversation filtered up to us, which gave me the impression that Mrs. Hudson knew our visitor, followed by a series of heavy footfalls on the steps that led from the entrance to our door.

"I believe we will be able to ask Mycroft all about it," Holmes said.

The door opened and admitted Mycroft with a slightly red face, but possessing a very pleased expression.

"Good morning," he said, removing his coat and placing it on a nearby chair. His eyes darted towards the open newspapers on our table and he nodded. "Ah, so you already know then. Remarkable that something so simple could have such an impact."

"What did you write in those notes?" I asked.

"Nothing ground-breaking," he said, "I merely doubled the number of ground troops, and added a second division of artillery to the figures that the Prime Minister was already requesting. His original numbers were drawn from the intelligence gathered on the Russian's available forces in Afghanistan, and I simply made it appear that England was prepared to overwhelm them with troops and engines of war."

"The bluff worked," said Holmes.

"Yes, yes, it did," Mycroft added, "All I really wanted was to paint a picture that said we were prepared for a protracted campaign. It's something that neither side would really want, and obviously, the Russians wanted it even less than us." He shook his head at the futility of it all. "Especially when one considers that there's nothing there. It's all just ground that even the locals don't really care that much about."

"And Vanderbilt?" I asked.

He nodded towards Holmes and said, "Ah, yes. Everything that my dear brother deduced was correct. The Germans were able to sweat a lot of information out of Mr. Vanderbilt. It seems he had been working under a false name with a false identity for quite a number of years. His real name was, in fact, Ivan Letorovski, born in St. Petersburg. He moved to Germany twenty years ago and worked his way into the diplomatic corps over that time."

"Do we have any agents of that type?" asked Holmes, a sly grin on his lips.

I knew he was having a dig at Mycroft, and his brother didn't disappoint. "If I told you that, you would end up in the same place as Vanderbilt," he said.

"And where is that?" I asked, a sudden prickle of fear rising up my spine.

"Ah," said Mycroft, "the Germans told me that once they had finished interrogating him, he was going to be returned to Germany." He paused for a moment. "In the diplomatic bag."

I winced. "That sounds nasty."

> *I leaned back and took down the great index volume to which he referred. Holmes balanced it on his knee, and his eyes moved slowly and lovingly over the record of old cases, mixed with the accumulated information of a lifetime.*
>
> *"Voyage of the Gloria Scott," he read. "That was a bad business. I have some recollection that you made a record of it, Watson, though I was unable to congratulate you upon the result. Victor Lynch, the forger. Venomous lizard or gila. Remarkable case, that! Vittoria, the circus belle. Vanderbilt and the Yeggman. Vipers. Vigor, the Hammersmith wonder. Hullo! Hullo! Good old index. You can't beat it . . . ."*
>
> – Dr. John H. Watson and Sherlock Holmes
> "The Adventure of the Sussex Vampire"

The Adventure of the Second Body

As the years drew on in the lives of myself and my greatest friend in the world, Mr. Sherlock Holmes, it seemed that the gaps between our visits grew as well. Holmes had retired in the early part of the century to a tiny country cottage near Beachy Head in Sussex. There he continued to enjoy his research into all things esoteric, whilst also keeping bees as a form of relaxation. I, however, maintained a life in the busy metropolis of London, though my days of medical practice were well behind me.

It was on one of the rare occasions that I journeyed south to call upon Holmes that he was once more dragged from his self-imposed retirement and into the world of crime.

We had been simply catching up over a sumptuous afternoon tea, with me showering Holmes with questions about past cases in an attempt to fill in some of the gaps in my notes. I still maintained a healthy number of papers relating to our past cases in my tin dispatch box. Though sadly, Holmes had taken it upon himself to put a stop to the publication of his tales, I hoped to at least compile as complete a record as possible, either to be published by myself or to leave them to a potential future biographer.

I could tell that Holmes knew of my intent, but rather than denigrating my exploits played along to his own amusement. He seemed to enjoy my company, and my questions sent him back to a more exciting time in both our lives.

It was during my questioning over the lost details of the mystery of the banker's wife, that a knock on the door broke our concentration. Holmes's housekeeper answered and within a few moments showed a rather young and slightly scruffy-looking constable into the parlour.

The young man just out of his teens, I could tell, held his helmet in his hands and glanced around with an expression of awe mixed with fright.

Holmes simply waited until the man composed himself enough to make his introductions.

"Hello, Sir, my name is Kendrick Kesson. Ah, Constable Kendrick Kesson, that is," the young policeman said.

After a moment, Holmes spoke. "Well met Constable. I assume you know that I am Sherlock Holmes." The man nodded. Holmes held out a hand to indicate me. "This is Doctor Watson."

Kesson's eyes lit up as he looked across at me. He nodded. "A pleasure Sir, I never dreamed I'd get to meet both of you. Together."

I nodded my thanks and let Holmes finish his assessment, which I assumed was coming. Kesson opened his mouth to speak, but Holmes held up a finger to silence him, before steepling his fingers before his face as he observed the young man.

"So, Constable, you have obviously come in a hurry. You have mud splashed on your boots and lower pants leg. Given the weather has been rather dry these last few days, I assume you were in a boggy field or a forested area which shielded the ground from direct sun."

The constable's mouth dropped open and he nodded.

"You have a small twig gripping the back of your coat and two dead, but wet leaves stuck there as well, so I can presume it was a forest."

Kesson nodded again. "Yes, Sir."

"Now, the darkness of the mud suggests a sizeable forest with a lot of leaf litter to break down. The only sizeable forests in the area are Westdean, which is hardly far enough for you to have worked up such a level of perspiration." Kesson's face remained impassive. "Or, perhaps you've travelled quite far from somewhere like Ashdown?" Again, the young constable's eyes widened in disbelief. "Yes. That's it. Ashdown forest." I saw a small smile come to Holmes's face. "You'd be from East Grinstead then? Working for Captain Neafsey?"

Kesson nodded, his mouth still agape and unable to form words.

I turned to Holmes. From his expression, I could tell that Holmes was holding back a slight chuckle. "Alright Holmes, how?"

"I do apologise to the both of you. Captain Jules Neafsey has done this before. He once worked with Lestrade and moved down to East Grinstead about ten years ago. He takes great delight in sending his junior constables to me when asking for my assistance. He confessed that it was to engender in them a sense of wonder at the art of deduction. In this case, that foreknowledge has simply helped me to ascertain the location of our next adventure together Watson."

***

The drive north took us through the edge of nearby Eastbourne, then Halsham and Uckfield before finally turning west towards Ashdown forest. Kesson's slightly nervous demeanour kept up throughout the journey, answering Holmes's questions with barely more than one or two words. He kept very quiet about the purpose of the trip until Holmes posed a taunting question to the young Constable.

"I do assume that the Captain and the Coroner will meet us at our destination?" Holmes asked, a wry grin on his face. "I haven't had the opportunity to talk with Dr. Grey for quite a while, it will be nice."

Kesson turned around, a puzzled expression on his face. "How did you know?"

I glanced at Holmes, the same question on my lips.

"Oh, that was simple. You have been charged to collect me. Therefore, this is a very irregular crime."

Even I nodded at that piece of deduction.

"We are heading to the midst of a great forest. Not the normal site for a robbery, or any form of fraud, therefore I can only assume there is a body of some sort to be examined."

"Amazing," said Kesson, turning back in a nick of time to realign the car with the road ahead, much to my relief.

Holmes continued, "If there's a body, therefore the Coroner, Dr. Grey, will need to be involved at some point."

As Kesson shook his head, I could see a smile grow across his features. A smile I had seen on many a young policeman's face as they became astonished at Holmes's abilities.

"You are simply astounding Mr. Holmes. Yes, yes, Dr. Grey will be there, and you are quite correct. A body was found deep in the forest. I won't say any more as the Captain expressed his wishes for you to form your own opinions once you arrive."

I became increasingly intrigued by these events and could see another publishable story building as we drove. After another mile,

Kesson turned north once more into a small rough trail and travelled for another minute or so before stopping next to two other cars.

We stepped out and found ourselves deep amidst a heavily wooded area. With only small dirt trails providing any navigable pathways.

Kesson indicated a winding pathway leading West. "Along this way gentlemen, please follow me."

The trail led deeper into the darker area of the woods, and within a few minutes, we found a large congregation of people milling about amongst the trees.

The two policemen were easily identified. One possessed a visible level of authority higher than the other. I assumed this was Captain Neafsey. Spying Holmes, he smiled and moved in our direction, thrusting a hand towards my good friend. As Holmes shook the Captain's hand, he introduced me and then asked about the goings-on. "Apologies if I've interrupted anything, but this one seemed intriguing enough to interest you." Neafsey then turned and indicated a balding man, hunched down with his back to us. "Dr. Grey should be able to fill you in on what we know so far."

As we approached the Doctor, I looked around and was surprised at the ages of the other folk scattered around. Only one other was an adult, while the rest, about ten in all, were all children.

Holmes leant in at that moment and spoke softly to me. "I have been wondering about the scout troupe, myself. Looking at the well-worn path through this area, it may be a regular trail that they follow."

Before I could say anything, we reached the Coroner, who stood to face us. A broad smile broke out across his face as he saw Holmes. They shook hands like old friends, and Holmes introduced me as another medical professional.

Dr. Grey had a warm, friendly handshake and spoke enthusiastically about all the adventures of my erstwhile friend that he had read in the Strand over the years. It was then I finally noticed the body, or at least what was left of the body.

Standing near an open grave, the Coroner moved away, to allow Holmes and I, full view of the object of their attention.

Lying, before us, about a foot below the level of the surrounding ground, was a dirt-stained skeleton. The skull and bones of the shoulders and upper chest had been uncovered, the rest still covered in dirt and forest mulch.

"The scouts found this earlier today, as they were on a trek through the forest. Some of the poor mites are still a little shell-shocked by the whole incident."

Glancing around at the young boys, I noticed a couple had that hollow look I'd seen on the faces of boys, not much older than they, coming off the field of battle. Death seen at a young age can have a profound effect on the mind.

Holmes's voice snapped my attention back to the skeleton. "Is this how it was found? Or did somebody unearth more of the body?"

"As far as I know, no one else has touched it."

"Good," Holmes said, stepping closer and hunkering down for a closer look. He pointed at the edge of the hole. "The sharp edge indicates that this was achieved with a shovel or more likely the square edge of a spade. It does leave one main question open."

"What's that?" I asked.

"Was the purpose of this to uncover the body or to bury something else?"

I was surprised by Holmes's question. "What do you mean?"

Standing and moving to the end of the shallow trench, Holmes pointed to the starting point, then at the skeleton. When I realised there was a vacant gap of some three feet, my own mind became confused.

"Good, you see it too then Watson?" said Holmes nodding at my perplexed expression. "Whoever dug this hole either didn't know the precise location of this body or didn't know there was a body here at all." He crouched once more and looked along the edges of the trench. "In fact, I would submit the latter."

"Why?"

Pointing along the edge of the small trench, Holmes indicated the line and made a small deviation to his right when his finger came in line with the skeleton. "This hole has all the hallmarks of someone digging a grave, but then finding it already occupied."

I stepped next to him and glanced along the same direction. Indeed, the trench deviated slightly to the right as it reached the skeleton.

"I would conjecture that our gravedigger began his excavation, possible to bury a body he had brought along given the dimensions of the hole at this point," Holmes said pointing nearest to us, "then unearthed the skeleton. Being intrigued, he continued to uncover more until either, time grew short or he was disturbed, possibly by the scout troupe. Which leaves …"

His voice trailed off as he scanned the area, before moving deeper into the underbrush. I examined the ground myself, but could not see what Holmes had, so waited until a familiar tone of enlightenment echoed back. Dr. Grey, the Captain and I followed after Holmes and found him standing by a pile of dirt.

"What have you there Holmes?" I asked.

Holding a handful of dirt, he let it run through his fingers and examined the grains as they fell back to Earth. "This is freshly dug. The looseness of the dirt suggests it hasn't had time to settle and become hard-packed once more." He scanned the immediate area, glancing down at a disturbed patch of grass and what appeared to be two ruts leading up to it. "The body was dragged across to this area, then lay here while the culprit dug a new grave. There is a second body here Captain, you'll need to dig out both the skeleton and this one to give us more clews to go on." Holmes continued to walk around the area, murmuring to himself and studying the ground.

"Something disturbing you Holmes?"

As he walked, he thrust a finger up and waggled it in the air. "Yes, Watson, yes there is. This is far too much of a coincidence. An unknown person, chooses a secluded part of a forest, such as Ashdown, to bury a body, only to find another body already buried there." He stopped and stared at me for a moment. "What do you make of it?"

I thought for a moment. "Either a wild coincidence as you say, or this was the most logical spot to bury a body in this location."

"Or?"

I tried to read Holmes's face, but he retained that stoic almost smug look that I sometimes found irritating, but knew it also meant he was well advanced in the solution than I. "It's not the first."

Holmes smiled widely. "Well done Watson, well done."

The Captain standing nearby looked completely puzzled by our dialogue. He didn't possess the pseudo-telepathic link that Holmes and I did. "What? I have no idea what the two of you are talking about."

"You can tell him, Watson," Holmes said as he continued to examine the ground throughout the surrounding area.

I turned to the Captain and his confused constables and said, "This area is well suited for nefarious means. It is secluded, probably rarely visited, and the ground seems quite pliable and easily dug." Their puzzled looks remained, so I finished with, "It would make a prime location to hide a body, as we have already seen. Therefore, there are probably more buried around here."

As I finished, Holmes let out a familiar "Ah hah," from deeper in the trees. We hurried over and joined him as he pulled branches and leaves from another patch of ground. The fresh brown colour of the dirt had faded back to a deeper, less vibrant brown, but the unveiled patch was slightly elevated from the darker, more settled Earth around it.

"I do believe this area marks another shallow grave," Holmes said.

"Blimey," said the Captain, turning to his nearest Constable, "Dickerson, spades, now." The young policeman sped off without another word.

***

The next hour was a whirlwind of activity, with Holmes moving around the area, uncovering two more possible gravesites. Kesson and Dickerson followed him around and gently excavated the area until it was confirmed a body lay beneath each. The constables refrained from unearthing more than was required to determine there was a body buried there. The light was starting to fail, and Holmes wanted to concentrate on the number of sites rather than their contents at that stage.

As fascinating as the uncovering of the mini cemetery was, I did notice out of the corner of my eye that Captain Neafsey took it upon himself to speak once more with the Scout leader and within a few moments the scout troupe left the area and, I presume, headed back to their campsite.

I'm happy to admit that my interest began to wane, just as the light in the forest, it was then that Holmes joined me. "From what I can see Watson, that is all of them." I glanced around and realised there were now five sites that had been found to contain buried corpses.

"Good Lord Holmes. This is horrible. A serial killer I presume?"

"I'm not overly convinced of that Watson. I have asked Dr. Grey to oversee the exhumation of the corpses. I don't believe there is much more I can deduce from their interred state. The ones we have unearthed so far are similar in so much that they are laid out in the same posture. The age of the bodies differs by only weeks or months, giving me the impression that whoever has been using this area to dispose of these bodies has done so for possibly only the last year."

"And the skeleton?"

"Ah, now that's the most interesting. I think that is still the outlier and may be the clew that breaks this riddle apart."

I had no idea what he was on about but considered that to be a return to our time together many years previously. It was at that point that the Captain stepped over to us and suggested he drop us back at Holmes's house.

Holmes agreed but said he wanted to meet with Dr. Grey in the morning to examine the bodies. The Captain motioned for Dr. Grey to join us and explained Holmes's request.

"This many bodies will need to go to the hospital. I simply don't have the room at the morgue. We'll use one of the wards, there haven't been many patients of late, so it should be fine."

"Excellent," said Holmes. Turning to the Captain, he continued, "One thing troubles me Captain, and that is the skeleton. I don't have enough data and hope that an examination of all the bodies will confirm, but something tells me that there should be more poor unfortunates buried here of the same period as that skeleton."

Glancing at me he asked, “Watson, in your opinion, how long would you say that skeleton has lain here?”

I looked back at the first open grave, more as a way of focusing on the question rather than searching for information. "Given the lack of flesh and no obvious clothing, I’d have to say over ten years, possibly more.”

Holmes nodded. “That was my deduction as well, which piques my interest even more.”

***

The Captain drove us back to Holmes’s cottage assuring us that the bodies would be extricated and moved to the hospital by morning. It had been my intent to head back to London the next day, but I decided to change my plans and stay until this little adventure played out.

That evening we enjoyed a sumptuous meal prepared by Holmes’s housekeeper, and I had hoped to sit with Holmes and continue our discussions well into the evening, but he busied himself amongst his old files, while I wiled away the hours, until bedtime, reading a novel I’d brought with me.

It was over breakfast the next morning that I asked Holmes about his previous evening’s studies. As he sipped his coffee he said, “Our initial idea that this was all to do with a serial killer disturbed me somewhat. I wanted to delve into my files to find an occurrence of any other killers that took means to hide their victims’ bodies in such a remote location.”

“What concerned you so?”

“Serial killers, by nature, act mostly on impulse. Those that find they need to hide their victims will do so in locations nearby, or highly accessible to them, sometimes by necessity, sometimes so that they can visit their handiwork. The presence of that many bodies in such a location means that there was a large amount of forethought put into the act of murder and disposal of the corpses.”

“Perhaps the perpetrator is a local? And the forest is quite close to their home. That would solve both problems.”

Holmes thought about my statement for a moment. "That could be it, I suppose. We will need to establish the identity of the victims or at least the area of their origin."

I started to speak again when the phone tingled in the other room. Holmes almost leapt to his feet and hurried to answer. I followed, quite intrigued by his determination to hear from the caller.

The conversation was rather short but consisted of many nods and affirmative mutterings from Holmes. Within a few moments, he hung up. Turning to me, I could see a glint in his eye and a wry smile on his face. I was confused.

"Watson. The game is indeed afoot."

***

It was once we had driven North through the Sussex countryside and onto the growing town of East Grinstead, and finally entered the Hospital that Holmes's excitement began to make sense to me.

As he had suggested, Dr. Grey had sequestered an entire ward to house the unearthed bodies from the forest graveyard. There were six in all. It turned out another skeleton had been uncovered as part of the constables' excavations the previous evening. The other four bodies were all much more intact and to Holmes's earlier observation possibly only up to twelve months old.

My eyes scanned the bodies and skeletons and finally fell upon the object of Holmes's current scrutiny. Although the man's clothes were filthy with the dirt from his unchosen gravesite, I could tell that he wore the deep blue, almost black, uniform of a London policeman. I gasped with the realisation. Suddenly, what had started as a possible localised serial killer was now a case that would attract a much higher level of scrutiny from Scotland Yard.

I noticed Holmes take out his glass and begin a close examination of the policeman and stepped over to observe. A stern voice from behind, caused both of us to stand and glance around.

"I would much prefer if you would leave these bodies well alone."

At the doorway to the ward stood a tall, well-built man in a day suit. The stern look on his face, and the way he stood, betrayed his profession. A smaller man in a constable's uniform stood behind him, his expression was less grim and more full of wonder. A reaction to the display before him, I supposed.

Captain Neafsey stepped between the plains clothed policeman and the bodies. “And you are Sir?”

A greeting card was thrust in Neafsey’s direction. “Inspector Jackson. Scotland Yard. I have been sent to take over this investigation.”

“On whose authority?”

“Deputy Commissioner Andrew Black. London Bureau.”

Neafsey nodded, and I noticed a wry grin come to his face. “Ah, Blackey aye? We go way back, I’ll have a word with him later then and sort out the lines of authority.”

“And why would this concern you?”

“I am Captain Neafsey. Commander of the local precinct. Until these bodies are identified, this is still my case.”

The two policemen locked eyes for a moment. The tension building between them, until Jackson finally spoke. “Understood, Sir.” He indicated Holmes. “And why are these civilians here?”

“This is Mr. Sherlock Holmes and Doctor John Watson. They are helping with this investigation and have already provided undeniable assistance.”

“Doctor Watson is also assisting me with the preliminary autopsy examinations,” piped up Dr. Grey, winking at me as I glanced in his direction. I smiled at the wily old country Doctor’s quick thinking.

Jackson looked from face to face, scrutinising each in turn before relaxing slightly. “Fine. Then you can bring me up to speed on what has occurred.” He pointed at the dead policeman, starting with him.

Holmes and I backed away from the corpse as Jackson approached. It was then that the young constable accompanying him had his first good look at the body. I expected a touch of horror, but instead, his entire body seemed to deflate as his eyes fell on the dead man’s face.

“Oh, God, that’s Smithy,” he said.

“Out with it man, who’s Smithy?” asked Jackson.

The young constable stepped up to the gurney with the policeman’s body and stared down at what seemed to be a close friend. “Albert Smith. We signed up together. Smithy was a bit older than me, and a bit more streetwise. He grew up in the East End, so it was only natural they give him that beat.” He shook his head in sorrow. “Last I knew he’d gone missing. About a month ago. He’d done it before though, usually turned up again after a week or two. Pissed out of his brain. The Sergeant didn’t really care. He’d dock him his pay for the time and then put him back to work. Apart from his drinking, Smithy was a good policeman. Knew the East End docks like the back of his hand.”

“Interesting way of running your force up there in London,” said Neafsey, his statement directed at Jackson who harrumphed in reply.

“Well that leaves me to wonder then,” said Holmes, “Whether we have another killer running around the East End or is this something far more insidious.” He turned to Dr. Grey. “Considering this case is still in your hands, good Doctor, I would think it an appropriate time to begin a deeper investigation into the causes of death.”

Doctor Grey nodded then spoke to me. “It may speed things up if you could examine the skeletons first, then join me once I’ve finished with the first couple of fresher bodies.”

I nodded and moved across to claim an apron and some gloves before stepping over to the first of the skeletons. Holmes joined me, I thought in part to avoid the tension exhibited between Jackson and Neafsey, but he mentioned in passing that the crux of the matter lay, not with the fresher bodies, but with the older.

To begin I simply stood and examined the remains with my eyes, murmuring some audible notes as I went. “Male. Approximately five feet eight inches tall. Solid frame given the width of the shoulders.” There wasn’t much else left of the body. The skin and flesh had rotted away, along with the clothing. The skeletal junctures were still in place, but in moving the body it seemed that the constables had caused them to break as one of the arms and a leg lay separated from the main frame.

As I examined the arm I noticed the first peculiarity about the skeleton. All of the distal phalanges were missing. I quickly checked the hand on the attached arm. The same. I turned and called to Kesson to join us. As he approached I pointed to the hand and asked, “Did you find any free bones in the grave? The fingertips are missing.”

Kesson’s eyes grew wide as he studied the bones, but then he shook his head. “Not that I know of. We can go back out and look though. Take a couple of hours.”

Meanwhile, Holmes had retrieved a pair of gloves and was studying the ends of the fingers with his glass. “What do you make of this Watson?” I leaned in and stared at the magnified ends of the finger joints. Small scrapes ran along a couple of the knucklebones.

“I don’t know, what do you think?”

“We’ll check the other skeleton, but those marks may be consistent with a common carpenter’s chisel.” He placed the free arm down and picked up the other, checking each middle phalange, and the proximal on the thumb. Again, a couple had distinct score marks across the knuckle, as if something sharp had gouged the surface.

“Why would they cut off the fingertips?”

“To make future identification of the corpse almost impossible, or perhaps as a way of claiming a bounty, or even as a token to add to a collection.”

I screwed my face up at the last suggestion. “Oh, that’s disturbing.”

“Quite so, but it gives us a starting point.” Holmes led me by the arm to the second skeleton and we immediately examined the fingers.

“It’s the same,” I gasped.

“Excellent,” said Holmes. “A strong clew.” A smile grew on his face, as confusion grew on my own.

“Care to enlighten me?”

“From your observations, you believe these corpses to be around ten years in the ground, yes?” I nodded. “Good. So, we are looking for someone who operated around that time, and perhaps had a signature such as the removal of the fingertips.” I nodded again.

“Someone like Mad Dog Murgatroyd?” said a voice from behind us. We turned to find Captain Neafsey looking at the skeletons, with a wry grin on his face.

“Who?” I asked.

“Yes,” said Holmes, “James Mad Dog Murgatroyd. He was put away about eight years ago. Hanged not long afterwards, just before the end of the war. His execution was expedited to free up space in Wandsworth, I think.”

Neafsey nodded. “Oh, yeah, that it was. The Yard felt that we were going to get a few coming back from Europe that might go straight to Wandsworth, so anybody that wasn’t in for a long time was shuffled off, so to say.” The Captain stepped around the gurney and approached the left-hand side of the skeleton. “Now, if this is the work of Mad Dog, there’s one more piece of evidence to prove it.” Motioning for Holmes to join him and smiling at me, he continued. “If you would be so kind Doctor, could you turn this poor unfortunate on his right-hand side?"

As I did so, Neafsey pointed at the skeleton’s rib cage and said, “There, do you see it Holmes?” Holmes nodded. I strained to see and was surprised by a pair of deep gouges on the edges of the fifth and sixth rib bones on the skeleton’s left-hand side.”

“He was a vicious blighter was old Mad Dog. Used to carry around a nine-inch-long dagger, with a one-inch wide blade. Favourite method of attack was a sharp thrust up into the heart from behind. He was left-handed too, made it so much easier for him.”

“I actually read the Coroner’s reports of the day when Murgatroyd was arrested. He was consistent and quite accurate, each victim had identical scoring on the ribs. Made it so much easier to convict him.” Holmes looked across to the first skeleton. “Now, if you are correct Captain, as I presume you are.” Moving across to the first skeleton, he let the last word hang, before carefully manoeuvring the corpse onto its right side. "Ah, hah.” I hurried across to join Holmes and was greeted with a similar set of score marks on the rib cage. "What say you, Watson?"

I nodded. “Both remains exhibit almost identical injuries. From these marks, I would surmise that a sharp, wide-bladed instrument was driven upwards between the ribs and into the victim’s heart. Death would have been virtually instantaneous.” Turning to look across at Dr. Grey, I muttered, “Do the modern victims bear the same wounds?”

Holmes, Neafsey and I joined Dr. Grey as he examined the body of the unfortunate Smithy. The policeman's remains seemed fairly intact. No fingertips were missing, and there was no evidence of death by knife wound. Instead, Dr. Grey pointed to severe discolouration and bruising around the man's neck.

"Strangulation?" I asked.

He nodded. "It would seem so Doctor."

"Have you found similar on the other victims?" asked Holmes.

Dr. Grey nodded and pointed to the nearest body. A rather pudgy man in his early fifties. "Yes. Notice the severe bruising on the throat of that man. Our perpetrator was incredibly powerful, with large hands, and with what seems to be an almost animalistic delight in inflicting harm."

"Why would you say that?" I asked.

"The large man's windpipe was crushed, and there are several bruises on the back of his head. He was either forced against a wall as he was strangled, or his head was hammered to engender his compliance in the act. The strangler kept the pressure up well after the man was dead, hence the damage to the internals of the throat."

"But it ain't Mad Dog," said Neafsey, "It wasn't the way he'd do it, plus he was hanged back in 17, so not a copycat either."

Holmes nodded, but I could tell the wheels of his mind were spinning at a fast rate. He stood, staring at the corpses arrayed before him, a hand resting under his chin with one finger extended up his cheek. Neafsey stared at him for a moment, expecting a comment, but when none was forthcoming wandered away. I knew better than to break his concentration and did the same.

***

Several hours later, once we had finished a wonderful meal and were settled in Holmes's parlour, he with a pipe and me with a cigar, that I finally decided to ask his thoughts.

"Holmes, you've been withdrawn and pondering on this case since this morning. What is worrying you so?"

He drew deep on his pipe, then blew out a deliberately long and slow cloud of white smoke. "The facts aren't fitting into the narrative. The new bodies were found over forty miles from their supposed origin. We know this from the lone policeman, who still being in uniform was possibly snatched while on duty in the East End. We will have to wait for the identities of the other three before confirming that assumption." He took the pipe from his mouth and used the stem to punctuate his points. "Only someone who has applied a level of premeditation to their murderous activities would use such a remote location for disposal. But, the style of death indicates someone with an almost palpable psychosis entrenched in their mind." I nodded in agreement. The level of aggression was disturbing. "As to the two older bodies, and I am confident there will be more if the Captain continues to search, they are the end result of a concerted effort at hiding the evidence of crime. Our probable perpetrator, this Murgatroyd, was a known factor, with a repeatable modus operandi, which resulted in his own demise. I presume these bodies were from his work as an enforcer with the Hoxton Mob."

He suddenly rose and moved to a nearby bookcase, extracted a thick volume and walked to a nearby table. I jumped up, quite intrigued and stood nearby as he opened the book. It was a series of news clippings and annotations in Holmes's own spidery scrawl, about the goings-on of gangs and mobs in London. I hadn't seen these pages before and realised they were part of Holmes's later researches and studies.

"This, Watson is a volume of information I've been building that concerns the growth and activities of criminal gangs in London and the surrounding areas. It seems that since the end of the war, the number of recruits has grown with the returning soldiers, and the boldness of activities is increasing as well. As we enter deeper into the new decade, I believe it will only increase further. These gangs have been building in confidence in line with the activities of their spiritual brothers in the United States, ever since prohibition began."

"That seems to be a longbow you're drawing there, Holmes."

He stopped, look at me with a wry smile, before turning back to the tome on the table. Flipping through several pages, he stopped at one with the name Hoxton Mob written boldly across the top. Holmes pointed to a grainy photograph, clipped from a newspaper, at the top of the page. The photograph featured a bald man, in a suit, being helped into a black car. His helpers had been removed by Holmes's clipping.

"This is Ken Porritt, also known as Curly." I chuckled, as the nickname was an allusion to his obvious lack of hair. "Yes, it's cause he's bald, very dry humour these thugs have." Further below were two names, but no photographs. "Porritt has two known lieutenants, Rene Gibbison and Herbert Marginzer. Now, this gang became quite prominent across the East End before and during the early part of the war. They concentrate on running illegal betting rings out of few local pubs, and of course at some of the nearer racecourses."

"I'm assuming then that Murgatroyd was used to reclaim debts, or at least close them out anyway."

"Precisely, he was a little too enthusiastic, shall we say, and hence why he was eventually hanged."

"That perhaps explains the older bodies, but what of the newer ones?"

"And that has been puzzling me also. I dislike the idea of a random killer utilizing the same dumping ground as an earlier murderer out of pure coincidence, especially considering the size of Ashdown forest. For now, I'd like to believe that our new man must have had prior knowledge and perhaps is working in concert with our long-gone Murgatroyd, almost unwittingly."

"You believe he may be employed by the Hoxton Gang?"

Holmes held up a single finger. "That is one theory."

"The open grave then?"

He held up a second finger. "And that brings us to another set of theories. Our mystery man's purpose was to bury a body. He unearthed a second body, but instead of covering it up again, he left it alone." He stood and began to pace around the room. "Was that act on purpose? If so, why? If he were working for the Hoxton Gang, he would not wish to draw attention to his activities." Holmes stopped and stared at me, a wry grin on his face, then stepped back to the table, flipping over several pages until another account of a London gang was shown. "What if our perpetrator wanted that second body to be found? What if he wanted to draw the authorities to that site so that they would end up unearthing the other victims?"

"But why? I'll admit that in hindsight the newer graves were not very well camouflaged, but surely a murderer would wish to remain hidden."

"Yes, but what if this new murderer was working in competition to the original users of that dumping ground?" Holmes pointed at the page before us. It was similar to the Hoxton Mob page but was headed with the name Sabini Gang. A similar photograph sat at the top of the page; the name Charles Sabini written beneath it. "Then there may be more to this whole adventure."

***

The next morning as I entered the kitchen in search of breakfast, I found Holmes sat in the corner of the parlour, listening intently to a conversation on his phone. I refrained from questioning him out of respect and instead helped myself to the simple fare prepared by the housekeeper.

Luckily, there was coffee, toast, marmalade and the morning's paper. Resigning myself to wait until Holmes joined me, I simply ate and read the news. I was slightly relieved to find that nothing of our grotesque find had found its way to any local reporter's ear. I was sure that Holmes would be of the same opinion.

The local affairs reported in the paper were of a very trivial nature, which made for a much lighter read than those generally reported by the London press. I had almost finished the whole thing when Holmes finally joined me at the table.

He quickly poured himself some coffee and buttered some toast. Before I could inquire about his phone call, he said, "I presume you are heading back to London today?"

To be honest I hadn't even thought that far ahead. I had no train ticket booked as I was under no pressure to return. "I am willing to stay with you whilst this adventure is still underway," I answered.

"Oh, that's precisely why I asked. I just spoke with Neafsey, it seems that our Inspector Jackson has returned to London, with three corpses in tow, including the poor unfortunate policeman. The others will be ferried North during the day. I then made a phone call to a former colleague of Lestrade's. Chief Inspector Sheldon Wengert. He is now charged with keeping an eye on the criminal gangs running loose around London. I have arranged to meet with him later this afternoon."

I almost spluttered out my mouthful of coffee. "You're going to London?"

"Oh, yes, that's why I asked whether you planned to leave today. I thought we could journey together, and I was hoping I could reside in your abode tonight, and possibly tomorrow night."

"Well, of course, that would never be a problem. I just didn't realise you meant to leave almost this minute."

"Oh, there's no need for such haste," he said taking a sip of coffee before continuing, "The train from Brighton doesn't leave for another hour."

It was then I noticed that Holmes was already dressed ready to leave the house. I was still arrayed in my pyjamas and dressing gown. "Well in that case." I quickly downed my coffee and left to pack my bags.

***

Many hours later we were introduced to Chief Inspector Shelden Wengert, a tall slender man with blonde hair and prominent cheekbones. He did not look like a policeman in any way, which I assume helped him no end if he was required to assume an undercover identity.

Greeting us both with obvious enthusiasm, but holding his eagerness in check, he expressed his desire to work with us in any small way possible. It was obvious that our reputation had preceded us, a common occurrence especially since Holmes's retirement from active investigations.

"Have you heard about the six bodies found in Ashdown Forest?" Holmes asked.

Wengert nodded. "Yes, the news went through the Yard like wildfire. Jackson's handling that isn't he?" We nodded in unison. "Hmmm. Strange fellow. Very determined." I stifled a small chuckle. "Where do I fit in then?"

"Ah, we have one major clew that needs to be confirmed. The two skeletons show signs of death consistent with the activities of a local gang soldier from about ten years ago."

A shocked expression ran across Wengert's face. "Do you know who?"

"Yes, James Murgatroyd."

"Mad Dog? Good Lord. He was hanged four years ago wasn't he?" Spent most of the war in Wandsworth."

"That's our understanding."

A broad smile crossed Wengert's face. "I heard there were six bodies found, you mentioned two, you can't believe Murgatroyd had anything to do with it? I didn't see him hang, but I know some who did."

"No, no. The cause of death is completely different. My theory, and it's only a theory at this stage, is that another person became aware of Murgatroyd's dumping ground and used it for his own purposes."

"Interesting. I still don't see why I'm important here."

"I wanted to investigate the growing gang activities in London since the end of the war."

"Ah, yes, precisely why I have my own team."

"Mostly I wanted to find out any recent activity amongst the Hoxton Mob or their contemporaries."

Smiling, Wengert led us to a large map of London. Several areas had been marked with different coloured pens. Two small areas were shown in the East End of the City of London, with the adjacent borders coloured in a thicker amount of ink. The Chief Inspector pointed at it. "The Hoxton Mob and the Sabini Gang both lay claim to this disputed area. There have been some assaults, arson and even a murder or two in that area over the last two years."

"Surely you've made a large number of arrests then?" I said.

"Ah, that's the main problem." Wengert's smile slid from his face, as he became more serious. "It's amazing how few witnesses one finds in these matters. And those that come forward shut up or disappear before a trial can be held."

"What about the local bobbies? Do they keep a close eye on things?"

"Yes. Yes, they do, but a lot of them remain tight-lipped as well. We have another team working on that worrying little aspect."

"What about Constable Albert Smith? He was one of the first bodies we found."

Wengert's face lit up in surprise. "Smithy, aye? Now that is interesting. He was high on the list of suspicious constables. I didn't even realise he'd disappeared, but again that's not my area. I'll have to check with the other team."

"What about the soldiers? Are there any in the Hoxton Mob that would be able to, say, strangle a man with his bare hands?"

The policeman laughed. "Oh, most of them. These soldiers or enforcers are chosen for their particularly large build. Though most prefer to resort to their fists or other weapons. For the most part, murder is bad for business. The soldiers' duty is to act as a warning system to the populace."

"I assume the Sabini Gang has a similar predilection for well-built enforcers?"

"Yes. Again, they tend to only concentrate on threats and intimidation. Any violence is generally done through the use of cutthroat razors or knives. Sort of a signature to maintain their posture." He thought for a moment. "Murgatroyd was an interesting case, if I remember correctly, he overstepped the mark on several occasions. It was his boss that finally set him up, I believe, though it was never proven just assumed."

"Interesting," said Holmes, "That's very interesting."

***

Departing Scotland Yard, we caught a cab back to my abode and I settled Holmes into the spare bedroom that my housekeeper had prepared. I took the liberty of phoning her earlier in the day to give her plenty of notice.

I gave Holmes the grand tour of the place and left him to his devices, while I bathed and retired to the parlour for a late afternoon cigar and perusal of any items of mail that had arrived in my absence.

When my housekeeper informed me that dinner would be soon, I realised that Holmes hadn't made an appearance and, presuming him to have fallen asleep, went to his room to wake him. To my surprise the room was empty, the bed made and unused, except for a small depression where Holmes had obviously sat whilst putting on his shoes.

I smiled to myself as memories of old times flooded my mind. He may have retired, but when the smell of an adventure reached his nostrils there was no stopping him.

After a wonderful repast, I once again returned to the parlour to read the papers and write up some notes surrounding our current endeavour, with the full hope that Holmes would fill me in on any future developments. I knew that I wouldn't be able to publish anything but held out hope that I would find a suitable candidate to carry on in my future absence.

I obviously fell asleep in my chair and was shocked awake as footsteps plodded on the wooden floor into the parlour. My eyes fell on the slightly bedraggled figure before me, fear rising within me before I realised it was Sherlock Holmes. "Good Lord, Holmes, you look dreadful." His face looked sunken and sallow, and his normally tall frame stooped from fatigue.

"I do apologise Watson. I wish this was a disguise, but I am getting old and quite unused to traipsing all across this large metropolis like my younger self once did." I rang the bell, mindful of the late hour, but hopeful that my housekeeper had yet to retire. Holmes took a chair near mine and visibly deflated into it.

I waited until he regained his composure before pressing him for details. "Well, was the effort at least worth it?"

He glanced over and smiled. "Oh, yes, it was Watson, it definitely was." He sat up just as my housekeeper entered. I asked for coffee and brandy. She took one look at Holmes and nodded. Holmes waited until she left before sitting a little more upright and relating his tale.

"Watson, my first stop was to an old friend that served as a guard at Wandsworth up until recently. I plied him with questions concerning Murgatroyd. His actions in prison. His cellmates. His acquaintances. Any enemies he may have had. He was very forthcoming and spun a very intriguing story about this Mad Dog, as he was known."

"Yes?" I said, sitting up, my own interest rising.

"Mad Dog Murgatroyd was indeed extremely upset with his employers. It was well known through Wandsworth that he felt stitched up. The boss wanted a few people disappeared, so Murgatroyd murdered and buried them in Ashford Forest. My contact reckons that he only told a couple of people the actual location."

"Did you find out any of their names?"

Holmes smiled, "Oh, yes, yes I did. And one of them left Wandsworth several months ago and now works in the East End, for one of the gangs."

"Not the Hoxton Mob?"

"No. The Sabini Gang. For one of the Lieutenants. That's why I'm so tired and grimy, I spent a couple of hours wandering around the Sabini's territory looking for our possible culprit."

"And?"

"Oh, I found him. A huge man. With massive hands. And from the way he dealt with several people over that time, quite the temper."

It was then that my housekeeper returned with the coffee and brandy. I poured us both a good shot of both, and as Holmes was reviving himself asked, "Where does that leave us?"

"I think once we've finished this wonderful coffee and brandy, and retired for a well-rested night, we can contact the Chief Inspector and see where that leads us."

I was relieved, I half expected Holmes to be off again into the night to confront this potential murderer, but as it seemed age had slight wearied him and made him more mindful of his own limitations.

When I looked back I realised he'd fallen asleep, with his head resting on his breast. Another reminder of days gone past.

***

The following morning was a whirlwind of activity once Holmes's plans were enacted.

Upon awakening, I strode into the parlour to find it now empty. I presumed that Holmes had moved to his room at some stage during the night, only to be taken by surprise when I found him at the kitchen table taking some breakfast, whilst chatting amiably with my housekeeper.

As I sat and partook of my own breakfast, Holmes informed me that our first port of call would be back to see Wengert to take him through the information gathered the previous night.

We were given entry purely through the officer on the front desk's recognition of Holmes and me. A young policeman was called to escort us to Wengert, it turned out to be Constable Green, whom we'd met with Jackson. Holmes and he chatted amiably during our walk, with Holmes stopping our progress for a moment to have a more in-depth conversation with Green before we reached Wengert's rooms. I couldn't hear what was discussed but presumed Holmes wanted to know more details about Jackson's investigation.

"You're talking about Duncan Hullar? He's just a minor soldier in the Sabini Gang, works Raymond Mowler's part of the crew, who himself is just a minor lieutenant. They aren't even the main part of Sabini's organisation," Wengert said as Holmes laid out his information.

"And that seems to be perfect for what they have planned."

Wengert moved across to his board with the Sabini Gang's names and hierarchy mapped out. He wrote Hullar's name well below Mowler's, stepped back and studied it, glancing across at the Hoxton Mob board from time to time.

"And you're old friend places Hullar in Wandsworth at the same time as Murgatroyd?"

"Yes, in fact, they shared a cell for a period of three months, before Murgatroyd was moved into isolation in the weeks before his execution. I feel that he would have been at his lowest point at that time and would have vented out as much information about the Hoxton Mob as he could, to all and sundry."

"And that's where Hullar comes into it?"

"Yes. Hullar was released only a year ago. He had been imprisoned for a violent assault, that sort of record would have left him with very few options when he was released."

"Wouldn't he have used his information to gain a higher-level position in the Hoxton Mob?"

"Or, on Murgatroyd's insistence, he used that information to wangle his way into an opposing gang."

Wengert nodded, "Yes, that makes sense. Even though there is an uneasy peace, these gangs wait for the chance to tear pieces out of each other and gain more territory." He glanced around at Holmes. "You want to talk with Raymond Mowler?"

"Oh, I believe we should try to go to the top of the organisation. If nothing the fact we have uncovered this information will unsettle Mr. Charles Sabini and make him think harder before attempting anything like this in the future."

A smile grew across Wengert's face and he nodded. "If I know Charles Sabini, he will be furious. This could be quite interesting."

***

In my long experience walking in the shadow of Sherlock Holmes, I had been exposed to many a criminal element, and at times been fearful for my life. That afternoon, however, was something completely different.

After the great war ended, a void remained in London. A void created by the removal of so many good young men, also an economic void caused by the closure of many businesses due to their owners and employees going off to war, and many not returning. And a more recent void triggered by the number of men and women, who had been diverted to the cause of war, finding themselves suddenly unemployed while the remaining businesses realigned their efforts back to normal service.

As in nature, humankind abhors a vacuum, and that void was quickly filled with a new style of business. One based on various nefarious activities. Gambling, alcohol, drugs, sex, in a more coordinated and focused way than prior to the war itself.

Criminals banded together into gangs to run these new enterprises. The heads of each taking on almost the same allure as movie stars.

One of the most notorious in London was the Sabini Gang, whose leader, Charles Sabini, had grown up in the East End and now ran several nightclubs and oversaw a large number of bookmakers at racecourses across the south of England.

Wengert informed us that, even though Scotland Yard knew much of what the gangs were up to, there was an uneasy accord in place. The Yard's forces had been decimated by the war, and they were still recruiting. Much slower than the gangs it seemed, so a level of tolerance was applied that dictated where the gangs could operate.

I personally didn't like the idea that criminal gangs were basically operating unhindered in my beloved London, but I understood the pragmatic approach that the Yard took.

It was to one of Sabini's nightclubs that Chief Inspector Wengert took Holmes and me. It was only early afternoon, but the place was a hive of activity as preparations for the evening were underway.

The large man on the door knew Wengert and after a quiet word was sent deep into the establishment, we were led to a large smokey room in the back that operated as Charles Sabini's personal office.

I was surprised, as Sabini's reputation hinted at the glamourous, but he was a simple-looking man, albeit well built from the cut of his modest dark suit. The man standing behind and to his right was similarly dressed. I assumed this was his assistant or a bodyguard.

As we entered, Sabini remained seated, but obviously knew Wengert quite well. "Chief Inspector, to what do I owe this pleasure?"

"Thank you for seeing us at such short notice Mr. Sabini. May I introduce my companions."

Sabini cut him off, looked us up and down and said, "Good lord, Sherlock 'olmes and Dr. John Watson, I presume."

Holmes replied, "I'm impressed. I thought the years of my absence would have dulled any recognition."

"It's the 'at and coat, Sir. I 'ave also read every single adventure that Dr. Watson 'ad published in the Strand magazine. I'm quite the fan you known." He leaned back in this chair and took a deep draw cigar, blowing out a pall of smoke in one long languid release. "What can I do for one of my actual 'eroes?"

"I think it might be more of a question about what we can do for you," Holmes said.

"Oh, yeah, and what's that then?"

"The body of a policeman was found in a shallow grave down south in a very remote forest."

A puzzled expression crossed Sabini's face. "And that 'as what exactly to do with me?"

“The policeman’s beat was around this area, and across into Finsbury, Hackney and sometimes Hoxton.”

I watched Holmes’s eyes glued to Sabini’s face. I glanced across at the gangster, hoping to see what Holmes sought. Sabini simply shrugged. “Yeah, lots of coppers on that beat, what of it?”

“This one was taking money from one of your lieutenants. Mowler I think his name was.”

“I’d ‘ate to tell you ‘ow often that ‘appens.” Sabini held his hands out to emphasise his innocence. “It’s the way of the game, isn’t it? We keep our bobbies ‘appy, and they don’t make too many waves for us.” He glanced at Wengert. “Isn’t that right Chief Inspector?”

“We have an agreement, yes. We turn a blind eye, also yes, but not when you murder our constables.”

“Woah, woah, murder? You can’t blame my organisation for murder.”

Holmes piped up. “You have a Duncan Hullar working for you? Do you not?”

Sabini grimaced and spoke towards one of his assistants standing nearby. The assistant nodded and whispered back. A surprised expression broke out on Sabini’s face. He smiled and glanced back at us. “It seems I do. ‘e just so ‘appens to work for Mowler.” His face then turned sour. “’ere, what are you suggesting? Mowler put ‘im up to it?”

“Perhaps. I don’t suppose we could talk with this Huller?”

Shrugging, Sabini picked up his phone, dialled a number and waited. “Doris, can you track down Mowler and tell ‘im he needs to be ‘ere now and to bring Duncan Huller. Yes, tell ‘im I said now.” I noticed Sabini lose the thick accent when pronouncing Huller’s name. He replaced the receiver and held out his hands. “Well, we’ll see won’t we.”

It took only ten minutes for Raymond Mowler, with Duncan Huller in tow, to enter Sabini’s office. During that time Holmes and I were plied with all sorts of questions about our adventures over the years. For the most part, Holmes simply smiled and allowed me to answer those that pertained to points of clarification. Several though were aimed at the deductive methods applied by Holmes and seemed to have relevance to our current situation. I kept an eye on Holmes and realised he was enjoying the intellectual jousting with Sabini.

When Mowler and Huller entered, I was amazed. As had been described to me already, Huller was a large man, towering well above six foot six inches. I glanced at his hands and realised they were of such a size that they could easily surround a man's throat.

Sabini watched the two men enter and held up a hand as Mowler began to ask a question. "All in good time, Raymond. Mr. 'olmes and Chief Inspector Wengert 'ere 'ave some concerns about a particular Bobbie that's come to some 'arm."

"A Bobbie? We don't do nothing to no bobbies. That's bad for business ain't it?" answered Mowler.

"I've already alluded to that point of view, but a dead body's a dead body and the Yard don't like no dead bobbies."

"Who was it?"

"Constable Albert Smith. Known as Smithy. Been around these parts for years," said Wengert.

"According to one of my sources, he was receiving monies from both the Sabini Gang and the Hoxton Mob. Sort of playing both sides," said Holmes.

"Then it must 'ave been the 'oxtons," said Sabini, "Case closed. Good night."

Holmes smiled. "You would think, wouldn't you? Especially when the policeman's body was found in a shallow grave, in an area of Ashdown Forest that was previously used by a Hoxton Mob enforcer."

Sabini held his hands out in surprise, he glanced at Wengert. "Again, case closed." He reached over to pick up the phone. "I can call Curly Porritt for you if you like. 'e'd be just as fascinated as me, possibly a bit more."

Holmes held up his hand. "There are a few more interesting points that need to be said."

Removing his hand from the phone, but keeping his eyes fixed on Holmes's face, Sabini leaned back in his chair. "Go on then."

"There were other bodies in that location. Five more in all. Two were over ten years old, but three were just as recent as the unfortunate policeman. All men. All strangled. By someone with larger than normal hands and incredible strength."

That's when I saw it, and I could tell that Holmes saw it as well. Sabini's eyes flashed to the right, in Hullar's direction. I glanced at Hullar and saw his face take on a worried look.

"According to one of my sources, James Murgatroyd, who was responsible for the older bodies and worked for the Hoxton Mob, shared a cell with a young man for several months just before his death. Murgatroyd instilled in that young man a hatred for the Hoxton Mob, and information about the dumping ground."

Hullar began to grow fidgety as if he would have preferred to be anywhere else other than that room at that point in time.

"That man, I have been told, and after following him around the East End last night, can truly believe he would be capable of such violence, is your soldier Duncan Hullar." Holmes turned and stared straight at Hullar. The man's face dropped in abject horror.

"No. I never." He stared at Sabini, his eyes pleading for support or an alibi. Instead, he received only accusations.

"Is that true Hullar?" Sabini asked. He looked at Mowler. "Raymond 'ave you brought a killer into my organisation?" Then back at Hullar. "Well, what 'ave you to say?"

"You, you told me to kill 'im. I only done it on your orders."

"Oh, come now," he turned towards Wengert, ignoring Hullar's stare, "You know me Chief Inspector, I'm an 'onest businessman. I wouldn't do nothing like that."

I could tell Wengert struggled to contain his mirth at the suggestion, but Holmes added more. "Given that these bodies were placed in a location once used by James Murgatroyd, and the last body was located near a well-used pathway, I put it to you, Sir, that by your orders and Hullar's actions you were trying to implicate the Hoxton Mob as a way of undermining them and gaining territory."

It was Sabini's turn to laugh. "Nonsense. I'd never do that sort of thing. We've got an understanding, the 'oxton boys and me." He glanced back at Hullar. "I don't know what this blighter's been up to, but it 'ad nothing to do with me. If you want 'im Chief Inspector, then take 'im with you."

It was then that everything went crazy.

Hullar howled in rage at Sabini. His face turned to pure frenzy. He stepped forward and brought up those massive hands, grabbing Sabini around the neck and dragging him from his chair before anyone could react. Sabini was thrust against the wall, gasping for air as the tall man crushed his throat.

Mowler leapt at Huller, but a simple shrug saw him thrown aside. Sabini's assistant ran from the room. I presumed he went for help, but it could have been out of simple self-preservation. Wengert moved forward to grab at Huller, but received an elbow to the midriff, knocking the wind from his lungs.

Out of pure instinct, Holmes and I reached for our pistols, but we both realised that those days were gone, and we hadn't brought them with us.

It was the sudden shock of a gunshot in that small room, that stopped us in our tracks. All eyes fell on Hullar's back. The large man's hands dropped away from Sabini's neck and he slumped to his knees before collapsing to the ground.

Sabini held a small revolver in his right hand, a slender trail of smoke rising from the barrel. He looked from myself to Holmes. "I always keeps this on me, you just never knows when you'll need it. I picked that one up from you and the good Doctor."

***

Back at my house, Holmes and I reposed in the parlour with coffee and a mid-afternoon brandy, something I think was well deserved after the day's events.

"That didn't quite go as planned, did it?" I asked Holmes.

Taking a sip of coffee and placing the cup down, he smiled in my direction. "No, frankly Watson, it didn't, but the outcome was as expected."

"How so?"

"Sabini is no fool. He may not have damaged the Hoxton Mob's hold on any territory as he hoped, but he did remove a troubling element within his ranks. Both Hullar, who verged on the uncontrollable due to his anger problems, and Smith who was playing him against the Hoxtons."

"But, Sabini got away with murder."

"Did he?" Holmes said. "We believe he did, but we only have circumstantial evidence to tie him to the murders. In the eyes of the law, he is free. Hullar's death was self-defence. All the murders can be attributed directly to him. The Sabini Gang is renowned for the use of knives and blunt force trauma via hammers, but never strangulation, therefore there is no direct correlation to their methods."

"I still feel a little unnerved by all this."

"As you should Watson, as you should. Theoretically, we uncovered a strange plot to undermine one criminal gang by another gang and put a stop to it. We found a murderer and he found his just deserts. Sabini and his crew are well in the sights of Chief Inspector Wengert, so will have to play it safe for a while yet. Overall, actually a quite successful adventure."

"If you say so Holmes if you say so." I thought for a moment and asked anyway. "I don't suppose I can write this up for the Strand then?"

"No, Watson, you may not. I'm still retired. This was but a momentary reprieve, and to be honest, a most enjoyable if not a tiring one."

The Tranby Croft Affair

It was mid-morning on a quiet Saturday in September of 1890 that I sat silently in my study, perusing my latest pile of medical journals, when I heard the doorbell chime. The ring was followed by the sounds of my wonderful wife Mary shuffling down the hallway, unlocking and opening the door.

I could hear the sounds of surprise at first, followed by a muted conversation before two pairs of footsteps moved down the hallway towards my study. My concentration ruined, I simply stared at the door leading into my private sanctuary as the footfalls came to a stop just outside.

The door opened and, instead of the wayward patient I had expected, in stepped my good friend Sherlock Holmes.

As he laid eyes on my dressing gown and pile of unread journals, he said, "Sorry to disturb your personal pursuits on this fine morning, Watson, but I have received a rather intriguing telegram." Stepping forward he slid the closed paper towards me.

"Good to see you too Holmes," I answered, still a little stunned by his presence. Opening the telegram, I read its contents. It was addressed directly to Holmes. The message read.

> *"Sherlock. I need your brilliant mind. I am host to a royal guest for the Doncaster races. At night we play Baccarat. I suspect a guest of cheating. Not normally a real problem, but worried about involving HRH. Arthur Wilson."*

Reading through the message again, I refolded and handed it back to Holmes. "This Arthur Wilson, a friend of yours?"

"Oh, yes, our families have been intertwined for generations."

"He's from Yorkshire then?"

"Yes. With his brother, Arthur co-owns the Thomas Wilson shipping company. They inherited it from their father and operate out of Hull. Arthur owns the Tranby Croft estate outside of the city, where it seems he entertains many high-profile guests."

"I assume you know who he speaks of in this missive?"

"Oh, yes, the *royal* and *HRH* references, when coupled with the name Doncaster, which can only mean the race meeting, leads me to surmise that my friend is playing host to the Prince of Wales and his coterie."

"A very fortunate acquaintance on the part of this Wilson fellow, I would think, and one that he would wish to protect at all costs."

"Quite so, Watson, quite so. As the media play it out, the Prince is drawn to any manner of suspect activity. Baccarat is technically illegal in this country and given the company the Prince is known to keep; I presume that the amounts of money involved in these nightly card games would be rather impressive. With such amounts, any form of cheating by any party would be seen as both criminal behaviour and grounds for social exclusion."

"Surely it's not the Prince himself?"

Holmes held up his hands, "I can't say, Watson, I can't say, but never eliminate a suspect until you have all the facts."

"My word," I said, thinking that such a trivial little puzzle had the potential to be explosive, especially if the papers were to find out about it. Standing and moving around my desk, I asked, "Can we make it to Hull by this evening?"

"Yes, if you make haste and get changed. The next train from Kings Cross leaves at twelve," consulting my mantle clock, Holmes continued, "Which gives us less than an hour."

Flustered, I headed for the door, muttering to myself, "I'll have to consult with Mary." Flinging the door open in my haste I was met by my lovely wife holding a heavy-looking valise.

Mary took one look at my reddened face and said, "Well hurry up John, there are travelling clothes laid out on the bed for you, and this case contains two day's change of clothes, plus a dinner suit. You may have to have your shirts laundered by the staff if you are to stay for longer."

I was stunned but assumed that Holmes had pre-warned my wife, who in her infinite patience and acceptance of our lives had taken an active stance. Kissing her on the cheek, as I passed, I muttered, "Thank you."

"Never mind that, begone," she replied, a wry grin on her lips.

***

Despite our concerns, we made the train north with plenty of time to spare. Our luck ran true as we were able to procure a first-class compartment and quickly settled our luggage in place before setting off for the club car for luncheon.

Our time on the train was mostly spent catching up on our own recent doings, plus discussing other items of interest from the news of the land.

I probed Holmes on the possible identities in the Prince's entourage, but he was both unsure and unprepared to surmise.

After our post-lunch coffee, we returned to our car and settled in for the last couple of hours. I returned to the unfinished journals from my morning, whilst Holmes took the opportunity to catch some rest in preparation for whatever awaited us.

It was as we were wending our way East along the Humber River that I noticed the rolling green fields give way to the city itself. Although I knew Hull, or Kingston on Hull as it was properly named, was a bustling port city using the natural shelter of the Humber River inlet to access the trade routes into the North Sea, it still retained the spread-out look of a small village rather than the densely, nestled buildings of the capital.

Our exit from the train at Paragon Station was quick due to the volume of passengers having disembarked in Sheffield and Doncaster, and we soon found ourselves outside the sandstone façade of the station building. As I searched for a hansom or carriage capable of taking us the relatively short distance to Tranby Croft, a tall gentleman in a morning suit stepped towards us.

"Mr. Holmes. Doctor Watson?" I gaped at the man, shocked that anyone would have known us by our appearance, or even that we would be there. Seeing my discomfort, the man bowed slightly before continuing to speak in his deep, commanding voice. "I do apologise, I am Smithers, Mr. Wilson's butler. He asked me to meet you and bring you to Tranby-Croft." Smithers held a hand out towards a beautifully crafted Brougham, replete with a similarly dressed driver who hopped down and snatched up our bags before we could reply.

"Thank you, Smithers. It's been a while," said Holmes as we stepped into the covered part of the carriage.

“That it has Mr. Holmes, that it has. Mr. Wilson was very effusive about your imminent arrival,” said Smithers before closing the door and climbing up next to the driver.

“But you didn’t reply did you?” I asked Holmes.

“No, I didn’t, but Wilson knows that I would never think of disappointing him.”

***

As the sun was starting to dip below the horizon, we turned into the drive that ran to the front of Tranby Croft. The manor house was a three-story edifice built-in white brick, though the sun at that hour set the building aflame in a yellow glow. The size of the house and its surrounding grounds suggested the owner was affluent and my own knowledge of Wilson’s business pursuits told me he was indeed doing well.

Such a person was a natural magnet for the Prince of Wales, who enjoyed the company of the rich and powerful and had a strong preference for the more enjoyable pursuits in life, some of which, as rumour had it, his mother looked upon with sharp disdain.

Stopping near the main entrance, Smithers stepped down and led us straight in through the front doors and into a private study on the ground floor. There a slightly stoop backed man in his fifties, with a well-groomed head of faintly greying hair, paced back and forth.

Upon seeing Holmes enter the room, the man’s face brightened, and he strode across the room and took my good friend in a firm embrace.

“Sherlock, so good to see you. Thank you so much for coming. I know it’s a long arduous journey, but I will be forever in your debt.”

As they parted, Holmes simply patted him on the shoulder and said, “Arthur, you would never be in my debt, such is the bond between our families.” Motioning to some chairs near the fireplace, Holmes continued, “Should we discuss what has happened. I presume we only have a short while before your guests return.”

“How? Oh, never mind, I’ve never understood how you do it.”

Smiling, Holmes couldn't help but explain. "Simple really. You were here awaiting our arrival, so therefore you were alone. You mentioned Doncaster in the telegram, so I can only assume that the Prince and his entourage have attended the races and will return tonight for dinner and other pursuits."

Wilson nodded, "Yes, precisely."

"Who are the other members of the Prince's group? That may give me more information to peruse."

"Apart from his three servants, he is only travelling with his good friend Lieutenant Colonel Sir William Gordon-Cumming."

"Ah, the Baronet, formerly of the Scots Guards. The papers make it that they have become quite good friends over the last year," I said. At which point Wilson laid eyes on me as if for the first time. I could only assume it was because his mind was preoccupied with the goings-on and with Holmes's presence.

"Did I not introduce my friend?" asked Holmes, "I'm so sorry, this is Dr. John Watson, my close associate on my many adventures over the last few years."

Wilson shook his head and held out a hand for me to shake. "I'm so sorry Sir, I have been so preoccupied with this little problem, it has so consumed me all day and all last night that I haven't slept and cannot concentrate on anything else."

"No need to apologise, I completely understand," I answered.

Holmes took the reins and led the next phase of the conversation. "Now, Arthur please explain in precise detail, don't leave anything out, what has happened."

Wilson took a deep breath and began his tale. "It started the moment we had word from the Prince that he had chosen Tranby Croft as his residence for the Doncaster races this year. My wife, bless her, went all into a tizzy over the preparations. I think I have been dragged along in her whirlwind of activity, such that my own nerves and emotions are heightened beyond the norm."

It was at that moment that the door opened, and Smithers entered with a tray holding a coffee pot and three cups. "I thought you gentlemen might need refreshment after your journey." Placing the tray on the small table before us, Smithers leant in towards Wilson and said, “Might I remind you, Sir, it is past five o'clock. His Highness is expected soon, and dinner will be served at seven, with drinks in the parlour at six-thirty."

Wilson nodded. “Thank you, Smithers, you are a blessing." With that, the butler left. I poured out three cups, Wilson blowing on his before taking a long draw. Placing his cup down, he took another long slow breath before continuing his story.

“Yesterday was the Prince’s first day here. As you can expect the whole place was on tenterhooks. A Royal visit does not happen every week. All went well, and if I was to be honest, I don’t think the Prince has the level of pretension that is expected. He is a simple man, used to a lavish lifestyle, but one who is more interested in Earthly pleasures and pursuits rather than pomp and ceremony. The cook prepared a wonderful meal. My wife was cognizant enough to organise for several young ladies to attend the dinner, to provide a level of distraction for the Prince above and beyond simple conversation, shall we say. It was later, once the post-dinner entertainment was underway that he became bored and looked for more serious distraction. It was Gordon-Cumming that suggested we play cards. The Prince had grown to enjoy Baccarat, even though it has been illegal by High Court decree for several years.”

“I can only surmise it is that fact that makes it more appealing to the Prince,” said Holmes, “Given his documented proclivities.”

“Quite so, anyway, there were eight of us in all that moved into the smoking-room where a table had been set up. I, the Prince, and Gordon-Cumming, included. I had also invited several of the Prince’s friends, such as Lieutenant General Sir Owen Williams and Lord Somerset. Knowing that Gordon-Cumming was to be at dinner, I invited another Scots Guard, Lieutenant Berkeley Levett as well. My own son Stanley joined them at the card table, as did my wife Mary. I wasn’t interested in cards, but I stood nearby, intrigued by the game.”

“What happened during the game that convinced you someone was cheating?”

“I hope it wasn’t the Prince,” I said.

“No, no it wasn’t,” assured Wilson, “It was that Gordon-Cumming scoundrel. Or at least I think it was. He led the way, betting more than any other, and I was sure that at one stage, the number of counters before him increased after he had won the hand."

"Ah," said Holmes, "The French call that *la poussette*. Many a man has found himself in dire straits on the continent attempting such a fraud."

"But I can't prove it. I kept my eyes on him for the rest of the night, but I could see nothing untoward. It just seemed that my eyes were playing tricks on me. Afterwards, I took some of the participants aside and asked their opinion. A couple of other guests agreed with me, but most others simply thought he had a lucky night. I believe he walked away from the table with several hundred pounds, mostly obtained from the Prince."

"And that is the main problem here? Not just the cheating, but the target of that cheating?"

"Yes. I know the Prince would not miss the money, but such an act against the probable future King is something that just cannot go unnoticed."

Holmes thought for a moment, his hand on chin, a single finger raised along his jawline. A wry grin came to his mouth as a plan formed in his mind. "I think tonight, we should increase the numbers at the table, if possible. That way more eyes can be kept on this Gordon-Cumming. If you are fine with it, I will sit in on the game."

Wilson looked a little confused, "If you think so, but I don't understand the reasoning."

Holmes simply waved his concerns away. "Oh, don't worry about that, leave all to me."

***

Smithers took us to our rooms where we had just under an hour to dress before drinks in the parlour downstairs. When Holmes and I returned to the ground floor, we found the parlour virtually deserted.

The stoic expression on the butler's face told us nothing, but a few questions informed us that the Prince's retinue had returned only just shy of six o'clock. Wilson finally arrived with his lovely wife Mary, followed by several other guests over the next few minutes. Holmes and I were introduced to several of Wilson's friends, including those from the previous night, and some newcomers including another Scots Guardsman Lieutenant Lycett Green and his wife Ethel, and Lord and Lady Coventry.

I immediately fell in thick with the uniformed officers and exchanged notes on our postings overseas and any shared acquaintances we might have. Holmes quickly became the attention of several guests, just from the virtue of being Holmes.

It was well past seven o'clock when the Prince and his party finally entered the parlour. The Prince had a beaming smile on his face, which turned out to be due to his horse winning the Clumber Stakes. The assembled guests unconsciously formed themselves into a line against one wall, awaiting the Prince to greet each in turn. He simply waved a nonchalant hand at all of us and said, "Don't be silly. I'm not the King yet, this is a simple informal affair. Treat me like a friend, not a ruler."

With that, the dinner gong was rung in the dining room and we filed through to take our seats. I found myself between Stanley and Mary Wilson, and Lieutenant and Ethel Lycett Green, Holmes became positioned near the Prince and Arthur Wilson.

The fare on offer was of excellent quality, but in my opinion gone much too quickly, even though I felt my waistband straining in appreciation.

After dinner, we retired to the parlour once more where Ethel Lycett Green serenaded us for several songs after a period of quiet conversation between the guests. My eyes fell on the Prince who seemed quite flushed, possibly from his delight at winning the horse race, or more likely from too much wine consumed at dinner. Even though he talked with a young girl whose acquaintance I had not made, he fidgeted and squirmed in his seat. It was only when Gordon-Cumming stepped across and whispered in his ear that he became motivated.

The Prince called for Arthur Wilson and spoke while motioning around the room. Wilson replied and pointed to a door that I knew led to the drawing-room.

It was then that Holmes stepped up next to me and said, "I feel that the game is on, Watson."

Surprised, I couldn't work out what clews Holmes had found to lead to any furthering of our little mystery, but soon realised he meant little more than the approaching game of cards.

Several of the guests remained in the parlour, while over a dozen of us moved into the drawing-room. Several tables had been pushed together and covered in green baize, in preparation for the card game.

A dozen players quickly drew their chairs from beneath the table and sat. I deliberately held back, so that I could observe unmolested. Arthur Wilson stood nearby me as well.

The players that sat were, the Prince and Gordon-Cumming, the Lycett Greens, the Coventrys, Lord Somerset, Mary Wilson and her son Stanley, General Williams, Lieutenant Levett and Holmes. Money was quickly exchanged for small, coloured counters by all players, and the game began.

I must admit that I only had a passing idea about Baccarat, but quickly picked up the idea. In the form played, each person played against the banker who also dealt the cards. The person playing the bank shuffled the decks of cards and proposed a stake that they would play for. The bank stayed with that player until all cards had been dealt, or their stake ran out.

It was up to individual players to choose how much they wagered against the banker on each hand, but it seemed that the Prince and Gordon-Cumming were outbidding the rest of the players by a considerable amount.

The game itself was simple. Two cards were dealt to each player and to the bank. The total of the cards was their face value, except court cards or ten which were worth zero. The player tried to get closest to nine with those two cards, they were then allowed to draw another if desired. The bank was similar but had more complicated rules as well.

As I watched the first few rounds, I noticed that the Prince and Gordon-Cumming were both winning and losing at the same rate. Their piles of chips seemed to remain stable.

It was when the Prince became banker that things changed. Gordon-Cumming's rate of winning and losing remained the same, but he seemed to have more counters before him on hands he won, than on those he lost. Within a few hands, this caused the Prince's stake to diminish rapidly.

Glancing at Holmes, I noticed his eyes fixated on Gordon-Cummings as well. It was then I saw that the small pile of counters before Holmes had grown markedly, which was helpful as Holmes was next in line to be banker, when the players decided to take a break.

Coffee and port were served, and the group of card players milled around with those of us who had chosen to observe. I sidled up to Holmes and had a word. "Have you determined whether he's the one?"

Holmes replied, but even now, his eyes were fixed upon Gordon-Cummings, who was in polite conversation with the Prince. "Oh, yes, he's definitely cheating. But he is mainly targeting the Prince for some reason."

"How is he doing it?"

"I believe I know how, but I need to be sure. He is utilising some of the best sleight of hand that I have seen in a long while. Even Maskelyne would be envious of his talent."

"What do you plan to do?"

Smiling at me, he patted my shoulder. "Now Watson, that would be telling, wouldn't it?"

I shrugged and followed as he strolled across to where the Prince and Gordon-Cumming chatted. Standing to his full height, ramrod straight, he deftly butted into the conversation. "I do beg your pardon, your Highness, but I don't believe we were formally introduced earlier."

A stern look crossed the Prince's face as he stared at Holmes. I became nervous that perhaps Holmes's impertinence had offended the Prince but was relieved when a broad grin split his countenance and a hand was thrust towards Holmes. "Mr. Sherlock Holmes. I am absolutely delighted to meet you. Your exploits are legendary." They shook hands like old friends, the Prince then indicated me. "And I believe this is your associate Dr. Watson." I took his proffered hand and bowed slightly as I shook.

"Your Highness."

“I have read many of Mr. Holmes’s adventures, thanks to your deft writing hand. I do hope there will be nothing worth sending to the Strand from tonight’s little soiree.”

“So, do I, your Highness, a quiet night in Holmes’s company is a rarity in itself.”

Turning to Gordon-Cumming, Holmes held a hand out. “Sir William, you play an admirable game of cards.”

“Of what I have observed, so do you, Mr. Holmes. A challenge in itself and you present as a very worthy opponent.”

“Thank you. Though these simple parlour games do tend to be a little on the conservative side, with a lack of any real contest.”

“Oh, I’m sure we can see whether that can change in the next half. At least between the two of us, hey?”

“I think that would be marvellous,” Holmes finished as he moved away and reclaimed his seat at the card table.

“Good Luck,” I said over his shoulder before moving back to my own seat.

“Oh, there’s nothing here that involves luck,” he quipped, shuffling the cards before him as the other players returned to the table.

Then the game really started. With Holmes as banker, his stake was considerably larger than many of the others at the table. Dealing out and playing the first two hands, he was on a steady win-loss ratio, with Gordon-Cumming winning each against him. It was on the third hand that I noticed something interesting.

Gordon-Cumming drew a king and a three on the first round, then a five, giving him a total of eight. Virtually unbeatable. Before him stood a small pile of six counters, equivalent to around thirty pounds.

Holmes dealt out the other hands until it finally came to his turn to reveal his cards. I glanced back at Gordon-Cumming and noticed his pile of counters was now eight. The rules of the game state that a stake cannot be changed once the player’s hand has finished. I kept my emotions in check, but I did notice Holmes’s eyes glance down at the chips, a small grin leapt to his lips.

He turned over his own cards, revealing a four. The rules were that he should draw another card. Watching his hands, I noticed a peculiar movement of the fingers, which amounted to a five of spades appearing on top of his two cards. He had nine. Unbeatable.

A gasp went up around the table. Gordon-Cumming's face dropped in horror, even more so as the two piles of counters was raked in by Holmes.

"Frightfully bad luck there William," said the Prince, "I thought you had him."

The Baronet's face remained passive, his eyes boring straight into Holmes's.

The next two hands were without incident. Gordon-Cumming winning one and losing the other. It was the next that proved more eventful.

Gordon-Cumming, once again, drew a handy four and a five, giving him nine straight away. This time, I counted eight counters before him. He had opened with a higher bid and I was unsure if he was confident or just plain foolhardy.

Turning his cards, Holmes revealed a queen and a three. By the rules, he was forced to take another card. Glancing at the spot before Gordon-Cumming I was shocked again to see more counters than before. This time twelve red disks sat before the Baronet. Sixty pounds. Twenty more than I had already seen.

I noticed Holmes's eyes flash across to the pile. His hand hovered around the deck, before a deft movement once more drew a card and flipped it over onto the top of his hand.

It was a six. Holmes and Gordon-Cumming had tied. A gasp rose around the table once more. They would require a playoff. The discarded cards were quickly raked in, and Holmes dealt two to Gordon-Cumming and two to himself. The Baronet's cards amounted to five.

"You may raise your stake, I believe," said Holmes.

His lips twitching slightly, Gordon-Cumming replied gruffly, "My stake stands, I draw one."

"Very well," said Holmes, flipping a card over. It was a jack, worth nothing in this game. The Lieutenant Colonel remained on five.

Holmes quickly flipped over his own cards. He had drawn a two and a six. Giving him a total of eight. He did not need to draw another card.

“Bank wins, it seems,” Holmes said, reaching across and picking up the pile of counters.

Gordon-Cumming stood up.

“Why William, what is the matter?” asked the Prince.

It was then I noticed that the green baize before the Baronet’s place was empty.

“I must retire, I have exhausted my funds,” looking around the room, his eyes fell on me, “Perhaps the good Doctor would like to replace me.” I took one look at Holmes, who nodded slightly.

“Thank you, Sir,” I said, quickly taking the Baronet’s seat and exchanging several notes for counters. As Holmes was substituting my money for counters, I glanced over my shoulder and saw Gordon-Cumming making for the drawing-room exit. His face was red. I was not sure whether from rage or embarrassment. He stopped momentarily and motioned towards Wilson, who followed him from the room.

After another hand, Holmes passed the bank to his left. His excuse was that he’d held it for far too long, and it would be unfair to keep it. Just as I was starting to enjoy myself, the Prince yawned widely and stated that he was going to retire for the evening. The party had one final day of races on the morrow, and he wanted to enjoy every minute.

As the guests cashed in their counters and left the drawing-room, Wilson stepped up to Holmes and spoke. “I have only just finished a long and heated discussion with our dear Lieutenant Colonel. He wishes to make accusations against you.”

“Against me? Whatever for?” asked Holmes, feigning innocence, but wearing that sly grin.

“He has suggested that you cheated him out of almost a hundred pounds,” Wilson said, “I pleaded ignorance, stating that your good name is enough for me and that he would need solid proof."

"Well, he is correct, though I would suggest that tonight he has cheated the Prince out of much more. Perhaps I should talk with him?"

"He wanted that. I have him waiting in my study and have consoled him with a brandy for the time being."

"Good, good, then let's away."

***

Gordon-Cumming stood up as we entered the large study. His face was flushed red, and I was in no doubt that it was anger. He slammed the empty brandy glass down on a side table and stalked across the room towards Holmes.

"Now look here Sir," he said, almost shouting and pointing an accusatory finger at Holmes, "I demand an apology, and you're damn lucky I don't expose you to the entire household, his highness included."

Smiling sweetly, Holmes held out his hands to express his innocence. "I do apologise, Sir," he said, reaching into his jacket and removing his pocketbook. He fished out five twenty-pound notes and placed them on Wilson's desk. "I make it one hundred pounds, forty for the first hand, sixty for the second."

Stunned, Gordon-Cumming stared at the money before quickly snatching it up. "Yes. What in the blazes? You go to all that trouble and then simply pay it back." A smile stretched across his face as he glanced around at Holmes. "You must really value your reputation if you are so fearful and try to hide the facts so easily."

"Well, that may well be, Sir, but I think it would be you that should be afraid for his reputation," said Holmes.

"What do you mean?", asked the Baronet, a suspicious expression crossing his face. He glanced at the money as if to make sure it hadn't disappeared.

"I should think that the money I took from you pales into insignificance compared to the amount you have swindled off of the Prince over the last two nights."

"What?" shouted Gordon-Cumming, "How dare you, Sir? The Prince is a very good friend of mine, and as such, there is no reason that I could even contemplate what you suggest."

"The Prince is as you say, a good friend, but I think it is that friendship that has driven you down a dark path."

"I don't follow."

"No, you wouldn't, but might I suggest that since falling in with the Prince, your service pension and your other investments have not furnished you with a level of income that maintains a lifestyle reflective of your circle of newfound friends."

"How dare you, Sir? My income is none of your business."

"True, very, true. Normally that would be so, but it is my business in this case. The evidence is there, such as your evening suit, though expensive and fashionable, has grown beyond its time."

"What? How?"

"The ends of the sleeves are scuffed, showing a touch of white at the very edges. A sign of age and wear. The jacket's seams have been let in and out on several occasions, causing multiple creases down the sides. That jacket has seen you grow and shrink on far too many occasions. In fact, I'm sure that same could be said for the pants. Even your shoes are suffering from age, only the most diligent level of buffing can cover the multiple scuff marks on the toes and heels. Normally a man in your position would never allow himself to be seen in such a state."

"So, I have an old suit. I wasn't sure how long I'd be away."

"But it's not just that is it? You haven't any servants, in fact, you have been using one of the Prince's men as your own valet. A sign that you may not be keeping a full-time staff at home."

"I...I didn't wish to add to the overall entourage. The Prince has never complained."

"No, well he wouldn't even realise, would he?"

Staring down at his shoes for a few moments, Gordon-Cumming seemed to build up his courage again before puffing his chest out and blasting Holmes once more, "This is foolishness. You are the cheat, Sir, not me."

"Ah, well that may be what you believe Sir, but I have not only my observations but many other witnesses. Dr. Watson here, Mr. Wilson as well, plus I'm sure any number of other members at the playing tables either tonight or last night would be willing to confess that there were irregularities in your betting. I must admit it took me a while to work out how you did it."

"Did what?"

"Oh, come on Sir, don't play the innocent fool," said Wilson, obviously losing his patience, "I saw on numerous occasions, your stack of counters change in size once the play had passed you by. Mostly when the Prince was banker. A most distasteful display."

"I never. You have no proof."

"Ah, but that's where you may be wrong," said Holmes, "As I said, it took me a while, but I have studied with some of the best illusionists in the business. They each have their methods, but I believe you have studied with some of those in the United States while you were there on a hunting trip perhaps."

"Why would I do that?"

Holmes stepped forward, reaching for both the Lieutenant Colonel's hands, he flipped them over and bent them down. Suddenly, a small mechanical arm slid out from beneath his left shirt sleeve, it held a small red counter in the tiny claw at the end. As it reached the end of its track, the counter popped out of the claw and dropped to the carpet.

My eyes grew wide at the startling evidence on show. Wilson gasped and took one step forward. Holmes held out a hand towards him and spoke, "Because the illusionists in America have developed the use of mechanical gimmicks, rather than using simple sleight of hand, to add a level of mystery and showmanship to their tricks. Something that you have brought back with you from there, it seems."

The accused man simply stared down at the exposed machinery. Relaxing his hand, the mechanical arm withdrew until it disappeared into his sleeve. Lifting his head once more, his face wore the expression of a beaten man. "You don't know what it's like you know. Edward has the world at his feet, but he simply takes it all for granted and lets his life pass by without a care. He may well be crowned King one day, but I don't believe he will ever actually be ready to rule. I may have inherited my title, but I served my country in numerous theatres of war. When I returned, several of my businesses collapsed, robbing me of my family's heritage."

"But you maintained your relationship with the Prince?" asked Wilson.

A slight hint of rage came to Gordon-Cumming's voice as he answered, "Well, yes, I am a Baronet. I have a station in society to maintain, and I have been Edward's friend for many years."

"Even though you have stolen from him."

"Pfft, as I said, he wouldn't miss it. He has the riches of Croesus at his command."

"Envy is a poor reason to act as you have," Holmes added.

"Especially from a member of the Scots Guards, one of the most honourable regiments in Her Majesty's army," I felt compelled to include.

Indeed, it was my comment that struck at the heart of the man. He deflated upon being reminded of his service to Her Majesty, even if he was not as honoured by his association with her son. Hanging his head in shame, he mumbled, "You are right Doctor. By cheating the Prince, I have cheated his mother, someone I served in earnest overseas." He drew breath in a long sigh, lifting his eyes to look at his host. "What would you have me do Sir?"

His voice wavering with its own controlled anger, Arthur Wilson replied, "Sir, you have brought dishonour not just upon yourself, but also upon this house." He strode around, waving his hands to the side as his rage built, but he withdrew it inside and calmed down. "I am seriously considering bringing the law into this. We aren't that far from Hull they could be here within the hour."

At which point, Holmes intervened. "May, I suggest something Arthur?"

"By all means Sherlock, but if I don't like it then I'll send Smithers to fetch the local sergeant."

"As is your choice, but would it be more expedient to allow Sir William to repay his debt to the Prince, and possibly sign an affidavit, witnessed by your good self, that states he shall remove himself from any future gaming. Would that meet with your approval?"

"I don't see how?"

"Well, that approach would limit any possible damage to the Prince's reputation and would allow Sir William to save face himself."

"Hmmm," replied Wilson, still mulling over Holmes's suggestion.

"I agree," said Gordon-Cumming, "And I do appeal to your good nature, Mr. Wilson. I can only apologise so many times but would be forever in your debt if you would allow what Mr. Holmes has suggested."

Staring at Gordon-Cumming for quite a long time, Wilson finally nodded before opening the door to reveal the stoic figure of Smithers. He spoke to the butler who quickly moved away, before striding across and sitting at his desk. Pulling out a sheet of parchment, he dipped a pen in his inkpot and scribbled several lines on the page, before glancing up and motioning for the accused man to approach him.

"If you wish to end this tonight, then sign this paper."

Gordon-Cumming read the note aloud. "In consideration of the promise made by the gentlemen whose names are subscribed to preserve my silence with reference to an accusation which has been made in regard to my conduct at baccarat on the nights of 8th and 9th of September at Tranby Croft, I will on my part solemnly undertake never to play cards again as long as I live." He paused for a moment as he reread the missive to himself before reaching for the pen and signing his name below.

It was at that point that Lieutenants Levett and Lycett Green appeared in the doorway. Wilson greeted them and appraised them of the situation before turning to face Gordon-Cumming. "Both Levett and Lycett Green expressed their own suspicions last night and earlier this evening. They have consented to add their own testament." As all three approached the desk, I noticed dark looks of distrust, upon the faces of the younger soldiers, directed at their older colleague.

Wilson bent over and added his own name below Gordon-Cumming's before handing the pen to Levett. Within seconds the two names were appended. Looking up at Holmes and myself, Wilson thought for a moment. "I think the leverage that our three names have should be enough to ensure this will pass muster in any court of the land."

Holmes nodded. "I agree. Something such as this should remain within the auspices of Sir William's peers."

With one final look at Gordon-Cumming, whose eyes dropped to the floor as they met Holmes's gaze, my good friend exited the room. I hurried after him, not wanting to intrude on Wilson's next words.

As we made our way back to our rooms, none other than the Prince stepped from his room and into our path. Upon seeing Holmes, a wide grin broke out across his face. "Mr. Holmes, my word, fancy bumping into you at this latening hour. Not tracking down any miscreants among us, I hope."

"No, your Highness, nothing as exciting as that. Watson and I were just confirming our transport back to the train station in the morning, we will be returning to London tomorrow."

"Well, that's a shame, I had hoped to find some time to pick your brains over some of those wonderful adventures you've had. Never mind, now that I have made your acquaintance, I think it may be prudent to invite you over to Marlborough when I'm back in London. It would be so stimulating to talk with someone of your intelligence. Some of my entourage can become serious bores after a while."

"I thank you, your Highness, and would be delighted to attend at any time."

"Of course, only when you aren't saving England from some nefarious cove from across the channel, that is." Glancing across at me, the Prince continued, "Of course, Doctor Watson would be more than welcome as well."

I bowed slightly and said, "Thank you, your Highness, I would be just as deeply honoured as my friend here."

"Very good, very good," the Prince said, "Now if you'll excuse me, I have some things to attend to myself before I turn in for the night. I think her name is Elsie or something. Goodnight gentlemen." He shuffled off down the hallway.

I think I could feel my face redden as I realised what he'd just said. All I could manage in response was to murmur a goodnight.

Holmes waited until the Prince was out of earshot before chuckling to himself. "I think we should keep that little titbit, amongst the same stash of secrets with everything else that has happened tonight."

I gaped a little, but added, "I think you are quite right, Holmes."

***

It was a week later as I sat at my breakfast table and opened the morning copy of the Times that I almost spat out my coffee. The headline on the front page read *The Royal Baccarat Scandal*. The article related almost every aspect of the events that had played out at Tranby-Croft the weekend before. Thankfully, Holmes and I had been left out of the details, as it seemed to have been drawn from a corrupted version of events as if told by someone protecting themselves. As I finished the article I realised it was from an interview with Gordon-Cumming himself.

I excused myself to Mary, dressed and hurried to 221B Baker Street, where I found Holmes sitting quietly in his parlour with the same newspaper in hand. A smile crossed his face as his eyes fell on my exasperated expression.

"Hullo Watson, why so flustered?"

I held up the paper and said, "I see you've read this article, surely you must understand my perturbation."

"I do, my friend, but I also think you have nothing to really concern yourself with."

"But this Gordon-Cumming cad has basically blamed everybody but himself."

"Yes, yes he has. He has even called upon the Prince to be questioned over the matter. I must admit I am a little aggrieved by his stance but can only see his own status crashing around him."

"Do you understand why he would do such a thing?"

"Well, the fellow admitted that he enjoyed the station that his Baronet and association with the Prince brought him. He has stated that his reputation has been tarnished because of the whole affair, and especially because of the paper that he was made to sign by Wilson. At one point he said that the details of which were disclosed to the public. I honestly think that point is a fake claim to overshadow his own guilt."

"He is taking Wilson to court to clear his name. That's where he said the Prince may be called to give evidence."

"Yes. Again, I can only see this as folly on his behalf. He has clouded his own judgement with a false sense of innocence."

"What if we are called to the stand?"

Again, that enigmatic smile came to his face. "I think we would be the last people his lawyers would wish to have speak. I would only tell the truth as I see it, and you would be there to back me up in every detail. As we know, the truth is damning in this case."

I nodded. It was all too confusing and smacked of senselessness.

As history would tell, everything Holmes stated came to pass. Gordon-Cumming filed a writ of slander against Wilson and the other players on that night. The Prince was called as a witness, the first such occasion since the fifteenth century that an heir to the throne had been requested to appear to give evidence in court.

After a rather short trial, the jury found against Gordon-Cumming. His downfall was quick. The next day he was dismissed from the army, and within a short period of time found himself ostracised from polite society. The very thing he had feared all along.

Holmes and I never again crossed paths with Gordon-Cumming, all indications are that he retired to his Scottish estate after marrying an American heiress.

We did however accept several invitations to Marlborough House at the pleasure of the Prince. On each occasion, he plied us with both coffee and stronger drink, and many questions about Holmes's exploits. He seemed highly knowledgeable about all that I had written, and I would not be surprised if a large stack of issues of *Strand Magazine* could be found in pride of place amongst his possessions.

The Adventure at Castle Metzengerstein

After so many years spent documenting the various escapades of my good friend and close associate, Sherlock Holmes, I was still surprised by the way that an unexpected visitor would be the catalyst for yet another adventure.

One such day occurred when I was visiting Holmes on the way to my surgery. I didn't have any patients due for the morning, so spent a quiet moment with my friend talking about recent events and enjoying a lovely tea prepared by Mrs. Hudson.

A ring on the doorbell was followed by Holmes's brother Mycroft entering the parlour. His appearance was extremely unusual as he generally sent for Holmes by way of telegram and had him meet at the Diogenes Club, one of Mycroft's favourite haunts.

He appeared very dour and a little down in the dumps. I attributed it to his need to cross town and visit Holmes rather than the news he carried.

Seeing that morning tea was on offer, he quickly sat and availed himself of a cup of coffee and a scone smothered in jam and cream. Holmes and I simply watched until he had satisfied his hunger and was finally prepared to talk.

After wiping his hands on a napkin, Mycroft reached into his jacket pocket and withdrew a telegram. He passed it over to Holmes who immediately read it.

"Hungary?" Holmes muttered as he read, "It's been many years since I visited there."

He looked up at Mycroft and continued.

"I assume you can't be drawn away from affairs of the state?" he asked.

"No. Sadly, I'm at a rather delicate juncture on some precarious business. I think it best if you travel and represent the family," he said.

By this time, I was beginning to become quite confused.

"Would someone wish to let me in on the news?" I asked.

Holmes smiled and passed the note across. I quickly read it.

The telegram was from a Mr. Istvan Herzog, representing the estate of the Baron Metzengerstein. The message was a short notification that the funeral of the Baron and his wife would be held a week from today in the grounds of the Keszthely cathedral in Hungary. I read it again but could gather no more information. I looked up at the brothers who immediately saw my confusion.

"The Baron was an old family friend. The relationship between the Holmeses and the Metzengersteins goes back many generations," said Mycroft, "Though my brother and I, being the last in the patriarchal line, have rarely visited or engaged with anyone from the family."

"But we do have a duty to uphold tradition. A member of the Metzengerstein family has attended all of the funerals of our forebears for many generations," said Holmes, "It's also a lovely time of year, so a little trip would be most welcome."

"So, you'll go then," asked Mycroft.

Holmes pulled up a similarly folded note from his jacket pocket and held it up. "Mr. Herzog has already contacted me directly. He also asked if I could review the facts of the Baron's death, to ensure that everything is above board from a legal perspective." Turning toward me, Holmes asked, "Would your Mary allow you the extravagance of a little trip to the continent?"

"To Hungary?" I blurted out.

"Don't worry Watson, the Metzengerstein estate is on the western side of the country, not far from the Austrian border. The residents generally speak a rudimentary form of German, much like your own," Holmes replied, a slight smile on his lips.

"If I can ask you one favour, John," said Mycroft nodding his head towards his brother, "Please keep this one's level of geniality to a maximum. Some of our family still carry out a lot of business with the Metzengerstein companies and I'm sure they would like to keep doing so for many years to come."

It was my turn to smile.

"I will do all I can," I answered.

***

We were away in the early morning two days later. Mary was outwardly supportive, but I could tell there was a slight tinge of either envy or anger behind her façade. I located a locum to cover for me at the surgery as well, but once all was prepared I was more than eager to be on our way.

The hansom dropped us off at Victoria station where we were to take the first train to Dover. We managed to make the lunchtime ferry to Calais and were well on our way to Paris by mid-afternoon in a four-passenger carriage.

It would have been marvellous to have had some time in the city of love, but as always our time was precious. We arrived at the Gare du Lyon, and barely had time to purchase tickets before the Orient Express let out a loud whistle to indicate its immediate departure.

Luckily, we were able to procure a first-class sleeper for the twenty-seven-hour journey to Vienna and managed to unpack before the porter announced that dinner was to be served in the dining car.

The night passed without incident and it was whilst sitting in the club car the next day that I finally asked Holmes about the Metzengerstein family.

"Well, to be honest Watson, I've not had a lot to do with the family. Mycroft, being somewhat older than I, has met them on several occasions. My last interaction with them was over twenty years ago," he said staring out the window at the rapidly passing countryside.

"I do know they are a very old family who has lived in the South-Western area of Hungary for generations. They have familial ties to the Hapsburg dynasty and are very central to the Austro-Hungarian empire. The Baron was a highly prized advisor to the Emperor and spent a lot of his time in Vienna over the past twenty years, possibly why I've not crossed paths with him. My last meeting with him was briefly at the wedding to his first wife. My family made this same journey, though it was a lot less refined in those days and took over a week as this wonderful train didn't exist then," he continued.

"You said his first wife," I said.

"Yes. Poor soul died a year later during childbirth. Both she and the babe succumbed. I understand the Baron was devastated, but a few years later married another and not long after that they gave birth to a fine young boy, Frederick. He is now the Baron, I assume."

"What a tragic history?" I said.

"That's not the half of it," Holmes said with a wry grin on his lips.

I waited but nothing came forth, so I decided to nudge him further.

"Not the half of it?"

"No. The Metzengerstein family owns a sprawling estate of thousands of acres on the western shores of Lake Balaton, just to the east of the market town of Keszthely. They are the power in the district but have always been at bitter odds with the other powerful family of that area, the Berlifitzings. Even Mycroft has no idea what started the conflict, and if you ask the families they probably have no recollection either, but the feud has existed for centuries. I can only hope that the new Baron would be of a mind to lay such animosities to rest, but he is only young so who can say what thoughts have been placed in his mind."

"How intriguing," I said.

We passed the rest of the journey in virtual silence. Holmes sat back and stared out the window, I peeked at him a few moments later and he had drifted off. I busied myself with some papers relating to past adventures that I wished to read through and edit, by the time I looked up from my work we were pulling into the outskirts of Vienna.

I nudged Holmes awake and we returned to our sleeper and packed away our belongings.

When planning the journey, we realised that it would be quicker to alight at Vienna and continue in a carriage than to proceed through to Budapest and return. Taking a room in a nearby hotel, we rested before strolling to a nearby stable in the morning after a light breakfast.

Luckily, our telegram had reached the local office, and our request for a carriage to take us to Keszthely was answered. The onward journey across rough and sometimes narrow trails took the best part of the rest of the day and we arrived in the early evening.

Our contact, Istvan Herzog, the Metzengerstein family's solicitor, was still waiting for us at the local inn on our arrival. He was very apologetic about the state of the roads from Vienna and hoped that our journey was satisfactory.

I found him an affable man. He was in his mid-forties, balding and turning slightly too fat. He spoke excellent English with a slight eastern European accent, which to my ears was a blessing.

Holmes regarded him with a wry smile and after our introductions remarked, "I find it interesting that a man whose name translates to Duke would find himself in the service to a Baron."

I was flummoxed. Herzog simply smiled and nodded.

"Yes, I think though you will find there are just as many Herzogs in Austria and Hungary as there are Dukes in Britain. I'm afraid our early lofty origins have been diluted over the centuries. There are only so many Duchy's to go around I suppose," he said.

Holmes chuckled, "Well said. Well said."

"We did have a Count. Count Berlifitzing to be exact. The Berlifitzings have a marvellous historical line stretching back as far as the Metzengersteins," Herzog said.

"Had?" I asked.

"Yes. Sadly, the last Count died in a fire in his stables only a month ago. It was the Count's death, and that of the Baron that has caused such consternation around the region."

"Why?" asked Holmes.

"Well, the Metzengersteins and the Berlifitzings have been arch enemies for centuries, but a level of stability has occurred across both of their lands for at least the last hundred years. With one line effectively ended, and the other with a new Baron, the people are unsure and nervous."

"Interesting," said Holmes, "I presume that's why you would like me to look into the Baron's death then?"

"Yes, a satisfactory resolution would be of great relief to myself and many others."

We checked into our modest, but tidy rooms in the inn and within a few moments met Herzog back in the main bar to take a meal and some of the local beer.

As all three of us tucked into the local goulash with glee, Herzog filled us in on the details for the next couple of days.

"The funeral service is not for another two days, I'm afraid. I hope that doesn't affect your travel plans," he said.

We both shook our heads and Holmes added, "No, we weren't sure what would greet us when he arrived, so have left our departure date open and will take the train that is most appropriate at the time."

Herzog nodded, "Good. We had a small problem with the local Sheriff. He was a little indecisive over the circumstances of the Baron's death and needed to wait for assistance from Vienna. The Emperor himself asked for an investigation and sent his own man."

"And? what were those circumstances? I have only the event of his death, not the details of how he died," Holmes asked.

Herzog took a long draw from his beer, wiped his lip, and continued.

"The Baron and his young wife, God bless their souls, were travelling back from Budapest along the shores of Lake Balaton. They were traversing a rather narrow part of the road that runs along a high cliff when the carriage left the road. The Baron, his wife and the driver all perished in the crash," he said.

His lip quivered, possibly from his sense of loss, and he took another sip of beer.

"How sad and unexpected," I said.

Holmes piped up.

"Would it be possible to visit the scene tomorrow?" he asked.

Herzog looked pleased. "Of course. I'm glad you are so keen to begin. The Emperor's man ruled it as an accident, but I still don't quite agree."

"I believe it may be prudent to concoct a little cover story. Such as, that in my family we have a custom of paying respects to our lost ones both at the scene of their demise and at their respective funerals. We believe that their spirits may be trapped at the site of their death and can pass on easier if they know they are loved and missed."

Herzog smiled and nodded.

"Of course, that would be a very generous and kind notion. We are an old people in this area and have many similar traditions ourselves. To help you out, I have arranged for a driver to be at your service for the next few days. The two of you are among only a few who come from other countries. Most others will have their own transportation," he said as he turned his attention back to his meal.

***

Late the next morning, Holmes and I decided to seize the opportunity to tour the area and take in the sights along the shores of Lake Balaton, Hungary's largest lake.

After a hearty breakfast, we met our assigned driver, who introduced himself as Zoltan. He spoke no English but had a good understanding of German. Holmes was able to converse quite readily with him, and before long we were soon on our way.

I had managed to convince the Inn-keeper's wife to prepare a suitable repast for the three of us and showed the contents to Zoltan, who nodded very favourably, before ensuring the basket was safely stowed away for the journey.

We set off at a languid pace. The object of the day was more for sightseeing, though there was a specific point of interest we were seeking.

The carriage trotted down towards the lakeshore and turned left to follow the rutted dirt pathway along the northern side of the lake.

Within half an hour we had passed through several villages with a few residents tending to gardens or making their way along the narrow roadway on foot. Long names with many consonants appeared on signboards and passed through my gaze. I knew that when I came to write up this adventure I would probably need access to a map of the area to provide them with their proper spellings.

After about an hour we exited a heavily overgrown forested area and found that to our left there were wide open fields of low-cut grasslands and well-maintained hedgerows. Sitting well away from the road was a four-storey mansion with a wide frontage and several spires that jutted above the main roofline.

Zoltan pointed and said, "Dort ist Schloss Metzengerstein."

Even I could understand that this was the Castle and grounds belonging to the unfortunate Baron whose funeral we would attend on the morrow.

“It is certainly impressive,” I remarked to Holmes.

“We are only seeing the rear. The front entrance is something rather stunning,” he said.

We continued for another few minutes before plunging back into an overgrown forested area that ran down to the lake’s shoreline.

I noticed that the ground itself was rising as we ploughed on through the dark forest. Looking to my right, I found the lakeshore had dropped away significantly, so much so that we were now only feet from a sheer cliff.

The wooded cover broke and we were once again in the open air. Off to our left were more open lands, pockmarked with patches of wooded areas and some low-lying buildings in the distance.

“Was ist das?” Holmes asked Zoltan.

He remarked, “Das ist das Herrenhaus des Berlifitzing.”

I understood so murmured, “The Berlifitzing estate.”

Holmes nodded then asked Zoltan, “Wo ist der Unfall des Barons passiert?” (Where did the Baron’s accident happen?)

Zoltan pointed forward.

“Eine Meile voraus,” he said.

I realised he meant about a mile ahead.

As we reached the area, Holmes asked Zoltan to stop. He dutifully pulled across to a small layby. Holmes and I jumped down. Zoltan stayed put, giving us a queer look, and probably trying to figure out what the strange Englanders were up to.

I added up the number of days, and given the time since the tragedy, was curious as to what Holmes hoped to find.

“Holmes, the accident happened over a week ago, there’d be very little evidence left of anything, don’t you think?”

He turned and gave me a wry smile.

"I would never think such a thing, Watson," he said.

We stepped around the area, careful to stay on the edge of the track. I kept an ear out for the noises of any approaching carriages, this was a public road after all, but it was quiet. Only the sounds of birds and the odd knicker of our horse filtered through.

Holmes glanced from one end of the track to the other. About a hundred yards ahead, the road came around a sharp right-hand bend, then carried on straight for about two hundred yards before disappearing around another right-hand bend.

"Do you think they took the bend too fast?" I asked.

Holmes simply walked across to the other side of the track and pointed out some broken tree branches. I noticed it was in the middle of the long straight stretch.

"They went off here," he said pointing at several deep ruts that carved through the grassed area on the verge of the trail. Several tree branches had snapped off and were hanging by thin threads of bark or were lying on the ground.

The ground stretched out from the road for another few yards before dropping down to the lakeshore. We carefully stepped through the break in the foliage and peered down.

"Good Lord, the carriage is still there," I exclaimed.

"Interesting," said Holmes, "I would assume that the authorities recovered the bodies, but any thoughts of retrieving the carriage or, indeed, the horse, were abandoned because of the precarious nature."

Holmes looked over his shoulder and strode back towards Zoltan. After a few moments of conversation and hand waving, he returned.

He pointed up the road and said, "Our driver says there is a small track that leads down to the shore just up around the corner."

I stared off in that direction, a faint notion of despair in my mind.

"What do you hope to find, Holmes?" I asked.

"Why answers Watson, answers," he said, striding off towards the corner.

***

The climb down was long and arduous and for the whole time, I felt that I was perched in a more precarious position than your average mountain goat. We finally alighted onto the rock-strewn shoreline of the lake and made our way along until we reached the broken carriage and the bloated remains of the horse.

It was a horrible and sorrowful sight. The poor nag had expired upon impact with the ground. Her head twisted around with her now vacant eye sockets staring at the sky.

Holmes stepped around the carriage, examining the wheels, and murmuring to himself. From my position, I could see that each one seemed intact, remarkable given the thirty yards they had fallen. The horse and front of the carriage had taken the brunt of the force.

Finished with his examination of the carriage, Holmes moved towards the horse. I noticed him take a kerchief from his pocket to block the offending smell of the decaying mare. I joined him, keeping a kerchief over my face as well.

From the cuts and abrasions that ran along the animal's neck, shoulder, and withers, she had dashed through the dense underbrush before her final descent. That accounted for the broken tree branches above. Holmes made his way to her flanks and finally her rump. It was there he stopped and peered closer.

"What do you make of this Watson?" he asked.

Annoyed at the prospect of putting my face closer to the poor putrefying animal, I nevertheless leaned in to find a strange wound sitting high on the animal's rear hindquarter without any evidence of other injuries in the surrounding area.

It was about one inch high and opened to about an eighth of an inch across in the middle. There was very little blood around it, unlike some of the other injuries and wounds.

"Strange. Not made by a branch or twig, I would say. Perhaps it was an existing wound that opened up again when the animal died?" I said.

"Perhaps," Holmes replied, "Perhaps."

He looked around the rest of the area. His eyes intently searching and squinting to focus solely on some object of his desire. After a few moments, he stood up straight, looked towards the top of the cliff and spoke.

"I don't think I'll find much more down here," he said, "It's a glorious day, let us enjoy the rest while we can."

***

And we did. The remainder of our day was rather enjoyable. We found a grassed area down by the lakeside to spread a blanket and feast on the contents of our basket. The landlady had even included a rather nice bottle of local white wine. Zoltan's face split into a wide grin when he saw it. He told us it was from the vineyards on the Northern shores of the lake.

We returned in the early evening after visiting several small towns and wonderful vantage points. The Landlady had dinner waiting for us and Istvan joined us as we sat down to eat.

He reminded us that the funeral service would be held at around eleven o'clock the next morning at the large church in the centre of town. He also mentioned that we had been invited to the memorial at Schloss Metzengerstein later that afternoon.

We all agreed that tomorrow would be a tiring day and shortly after our meal was finished we bid goodnight to Istvan and retired to our respective rooms.

***

After a light breakfast and several fortifying cups of coffee, Holmes and I met in the small forecourt of the inn. We both sported our most sombre regalia of dark suits, vests and tie matched with a crisp white shirt.

The service was to be held at the *Magyar Hölgyünk*, or as Istvan had translated for us, *The Church of Our Lady in Hungary*. I assumed that there were many churches by that name across the country, similarly as there are numerous Notre Dame churches and cathedrals throughout France.

It was not far away, so we strolled through the bustling little town towards the imposingly grand bell tower and found a formidable-looking fourteenth-century church.

A large number of sombre people attired in dark, drab mourning clothes, similar to us, were gathered around the entrance to the church. Their numbers were dotted with the occasional appearance of a more ornately dressed person. I assumed these to be members of the local gentry and soon found myself overhearing conversations involving several mentions of the title *Count*.

I took in the presence of an older gentleman refined in an ensemble of green and white, complete with feathers and medals and assumed this was the object of most discussions. It was at that moment that Istvan found us and provided an explanation. The gentleman was József Horvath, the chief advisor to Count Berlifitzing. He had chosen to wear the Count's own livery for the occasion.

“As would be expected, his appearance here is out of respect to the Baron, even though there still existed much animosity between the two families,” Istvan said.

“But I thought you said that the Count had died not long ago, effectively ending the line,” I said.

Herzog nodded. “Yes, Mr. Horvath has stayed on to sort out the final legal arrangements. We have been in constant contact as there are some intricacies we are working through between the two families.”

“Intriguing, what intricacies?” asked Holmes.

“I may leave that until later,” Herzog said, nodding towards the road leading to the church.

I looked in the direction he indicated and noticed a large carriage, drawn by four black horses, arrive and pull up to the entrance of the church.

A young man, dressed in an overtly ornate blue and gold uniform, complete with a feathered hat and gold sword, exited the carriage.

Even before Istvan said, “That is the young Baron Frederick,” I knew who it was. He was joined by three other young men who left the carriage behind him. They seemed a little older but had the confident swagger of young men whose life has never seen real servitude. As I watched them move into the church I swear I saw one of them stagger as if under the influence of alcohol.

The service itself was long and unremarkable. Most of the speeches were in Hungarian, so I found myself mostly lost and simply watching the crowd. I was impressed by the gorgeous colours cast on the audience by the sun beaming through the large stained-glass window in the church’s bell tower.

I never gained an impression of whether the Baron and his wife were loved by these people or merely someone that must be paid respect out a sense of duty. The latter was our reason for being there, so I wondered how many others were similar.

The young Baron’s three friends were especially part of that coterie, as I noticed the staggering youth nodded off several times and had to be shoved awake by the nearest boy.

After the service, we made our way from the church and stood amongst the other mourners outside. Istvan joined us and we observed Frederick as he left. He was somewhat agitated by the youths around him, but when he regained his composure, he slipped into the fugue that besets the recently bereaved. Grief strikes people in different ways and the Baron's actions were in some ways similar to others I had witnessed but in many ways very different. The three youths around him seemed more of an encumbrance than assistance. I sincerely hoped there was someone else that he could turn to in this hour of need.

I turned away as the Baron's coach arrived to look further amongst the crowd. When I gazed back, the coach began to pull away.

Istvan mentioned that Zoltan would be along to collect us in an hour or so. From there we would head out to the Schloss Metzengerstein. As he shuffled off, Holmes and I parted with the idea of observing as many of the mourners as possible.

I walked around the grounds, admiring the beautiful architecture of both the church and the memorial crypts in the graveyard. Holmes went the other way to partake in a cigarette. His was the more interesting stroll.

It seems that as he made his way through the small gardens to the side of the church, he heard voices, one old and gruff, the other youthful, speaking in German around the corner of the church. He stopped and listened, as he is often want to do. Thankfully, he translated the conversation for me.

"Has he said anything about it?" said the gruff voice.

"Not yet. I'm working on him. He succumbs more every day. His mind wanders even as we speak. It is working. He is enamoured with the horse, rides every morning. It won't be long," said the youthful voice.

"Sandor, it is very important that he signs soon, otherwise all will pass to the state," the older voice said.

"I know that. The dosage can't be increased, or he might die."

"True but keep an eye on him and report back soon. You stand to gain a lot out of this yourself, but that can easily be stopped."

"What? I'm doing all you asked. Don't threaten me."

"Then hurry up. I'm already old. I want to see this through before I'm gone."

"Fine. Just don't threaten me again."

Holmes was taken aback as the blonde-haired young man that accompanied the Baron stormed around the corner, looked at him for a moment with distaste and carried on. Holmes steadied himself and took on a casual air. He waited a few moments before continuing around the corner.

There he found Ur. Horvath, sitting alone on a small bench beneath an arbour filled with fragrant flowers. Holmes walked beneath it and glanced down at the old gentleman.

"I do beg your pardon, Ur. Horvath isn't it?" The man nodded. "I was simply walking and thinking whilst I passed the time before the memorial," Holmes said.

Horvath waved a hand at Holmes, "Do not worry yourself. I was sitting doing much the same." Holmes peered around at the surrounding buildings. "Your town is so beautiful and peaceful. It is very rare to find this near my home."

"Your accent. Englander? Yes?" said the other man.

"Why yes," Holmes said, "My family are business associates of the Baron."

At the mention of the Baron's name, Horvath's face screwed up in a grimace. Quickly composing himself, he rose from his seat and looked up into Holmes's eyes, sizing him up before stepping forwards and bowing.

"On behalf of my dear departed friend, Count Gustav Berlifitzing, I welcome you to my country and to my town," he said.

Holmes likewise bowed, "A pleasure to meet you, I am Sherlock Holmes of London, England. If I can ever be of service, I can be found through Ur. Istvan Herzog."

The other man looked slightly puzzled.

"I doubt that I would ever require your service as I haven't travelled to England in many a year but thank you all the same." He trotted off slowly through the gardens and passed out of view.

Holmes regarded him for a while then finished his cigarette and found me to compare notes.

***

Istvan joined us in the carriage as we made our way to the Schloss Metzengerstein. We bumped along the dirt track out to the castle, each one lost in his own thoughts. I was still curious about the welfare of the young Baron and couldn't get the picture out of my mind of the three callow youths that surrounded him.

"Istvan," I asked, "With his parents deceased, does the young Baron have any adult presence in his life to guide him through the next few years?"

Istvan's face went dark.

"No. Sadly, not," he said, "I was one of his father's closest advisors, but Frederick has shut me out altogether."

"The three youths that seem to be his friends, where do they fit in?" Holmes asked.

Istvan almost spat out his reply, the anger on his voice was almost palpable. "Those three useless …," he checked himself before continuing, "They came with Frederick when he returned from school in Vienna last summer. They took up residence in the old servants' quarters above the stables. Frederick was to return to school in the autumn but given recent events, he will stay on here. Those three layabouts moved into the castle the day after the accident."

"The scoundrels," I said.

"Oh, they are more than that. Sadly, you may see for yourself soon," he said as he turned around in his seat.

Looking out of the carriage window, I saw that we had entered the grounds of the Schloss Metzengerstein. The view we had of the rear did not do justice to the magnificence of the place.

The path we were on turned into a wide gravel driveway that ran between beautifully manicured lawns and gardens and ended up in the forecourt of the castle.

It contained three great wings, the main one we had seen from the rear and one on each side. A large number of carriages were arrayed within the forecourt and in areas to either side of the castle.

Zoltan brought us to the front entrance where a footman opened the carriage door and led us up the steps. A doorman took our names and showed us into the castle.

Stepping into an ornate foyer, I noticed two staircases that wound their way to the upper floors, their gilded balustrades glittering in the light filtering in from windows high in the West facing front wall. The foyer was immaculately decorated in expensive furnishings and fabrics. I truly believe that even her majesty would have been impressed by the level of finish.

I looked to one side and could see into the grand ballroom which had been set up as a reception area for the guests.

Istvan was about to lead us into the ballroom when a white-haired servant scurried over to him and began to talk in excited tones, all in German. I managed to follow most of the conversation and was perplexed by its indications.

Miklos, who I found out was the head-butler, was very concerned about the young Baron's welfare. He went on at length to Istvan about how the Baron's mind had become confused and misdirected. Istvan placed a hand on Miklos's shoulder to calm him and continued to assure him that the young Baron was fine, just in grief at the loss of his parents.

Miklos baulked at the idea and said it had all begun well before the accident. Ever since he returned from school, his attitude had changed, and his behaviour had become most peculiar. Some of the servants had seen him wandering the grounds, alone, late at night. When he was approached he seemed confused and lost. Most times he was led back to the castle and went quietly back to sleep. Other times he would run away only to return in the morning, covered in mud, leaves and twigs, as if he had slept in the forest. Miklos went slightly red for a moment when he said that a few times the Baron had been completely naked.

He went on to say that the Baron spent much of his time in the ballroom, staring at the tapestry. Miklos had seen him in there for hours on end.

"It can't be healthy. He needs help," the old man entreated Istvan to do something.

Istvan answered, "I understand your concern Miklos, but to be honest, I am unsure of my own position in the young Baron's life, now that he is an orphan. He has the power to remove me from his service on a whim."

He patted the old man on the shoulder again before finishing, "But I will do all I can to advise the young man. We have known each other for years; I can only hope he heeds my advice."

Miklos nodded, his eyes a little downcast. He bowed and disappeared into the bowels of the castle. As Istvan turned towards us, his face showing signs of concern, he saw our expressions and replaced his own with a happier visage. "Shall we see what is happening?" he said, pointing to the ballroom.

We took advantage of the fair on offer and I noticed many of the same people that had attended the service that morning. I searched the room several times, but the Baron and his entourage were nowhere to be seen.

Istvan introduced us to several guests and we managed to conduct small talk in a variety of languages depending on the level of English of the other party.

From time to time, I noticed Holmes's eyes drift to one end of the room. I succumbed to the same distraction, in fact, nobody could fail to notice the astonishing main feature of the room and be enamoured with it.

At one end, taking up the entire wall between two thin windows, was a large tapestry detailing a medieval battle on wide-open plains that had a remarkable similarity to the castle's estate.

Istvan noticed our attention travelling to the scene and led us across to have a closer inspection. "Wonderful isn't it," espoused Istvan, "This tapestry has been in the family for centuries."

I stared at the intricate detail of the wall-hanging and marvelled at the scene played out. It showed a battle. There were knights in armour on horseback. Two sets of standards accompanied each force. One was bright blue and gold, the other a drab shade of green and white. Immediately it became clear that this was a battle between the Metzengerstein and the Berlifitzing families.

Istvan noticed my expression. "Yes, you have realised Doctor."

Holmes was peering at a startling presence in the centre of the tapestry. An incredibly detailed and life-like horse stood in the centre near the bottom of the tapestry. Its rider, bearing green and white, was pictured losing his life at the hands of a tall, armoured knight trimmed in blue and gold. The horse remained proud and resolute in the midst of what must have been a terrifying ordeal.

"The tapestry shows, what many believe to be the beginning of the troubles between the families. The dying man is believed to be the very first Count Berlifitzing, his assassin the Baron Metzengerstein who then laid claim to all these lands, including a vast area that had once been under the Berlifitzing family's control," he said.

"Fascinating," I said as I stared at the piercing black eyes of the horse.

Istvan and Holmes moved away to mingle with the other guests. I followed for a moment, but my attention was drawn back to the tapestry.

I gasped in shock as I viewed it once more. The white horse's head was now straight on, both eyes staring at me. I could have sworn it was looking off to the side before. I shook my head and turned away.

I must be tired.

I met up with Holmes to find that Istvan had moved away to speak with someone he knew, Holmes took me lightly by the arm and led me across to the doors leading out to the rear area. I tried to gain his attention to look back at the tapestry but failed. Glancing back, I stopped in my tracks. The horse was again looking to the side. Rubbing at my eyes, I heard Holmes speak over my shoulder.

"Intriguing isn't it?" he said, "It's a trick of the light. The weaver has managed to make the horse stare ahead and to the side depending on the angle the tapestry is viewed from."

I looked up at him, an expression of relief came across my face. "I thought I was going mad."

"I would think that anyone who stared at that tapestry for too long may think the same thing." Smiling, Holmes proceeded towards the exit doors, with me following close behind.

Once outside, we found the Baron. He was sitting on a chaise longue beneath a large umbrella to shield him from the sun.

His entourage was scattered around him, either sitting or partaking in some archery practice. Several targets had been set up around fifty yards away. A number of bows and quivers stood nearby.

A dark-haired member of the Baron's party was lining up one of the targets. His shot hit the target but well wide of the red centre circle. Two young ladies clapped and cheered. He turned and bowed to them.

I quickly realised that this was not the sort of endeavour I would have presumed would accompany a memorial wake, but again reminded myself that I knew nothing of eastern European customs.

Looking across at the Baron's party, I noticed Sandor, the fair-haired companion that Holmes had described. He stepped across into the path of a waitress who brought a tray of champagne. Taking the tray from the young girl, Sandor leaned in and spoke to her. She tittered out loud before composing herself and withdrew back into the castle. Watching her leave for a moment before turning towards the Baron, Sandor strode over and instead of offering the tray, simply gave a glass of champagne directly to the Baron then the other members of the party.

I saw Holmes wait until Sandor had moved away before stepping across to the Baron. He bowed and introduced us.

"Please let me give you my deepest condolences, your Grace. I am Sherlock Holmes, and this is my associate Dr. John Watson. Your father was a long-time business partner of my family and I bring their sympathy and best wishes for your future. If there is anything that I or my family can do for you then we are at your service," he said.

The Baron regarded him for a moment before speaking. His face retained the vacant expression I had seen earlier, in fact, it looked even more vacuous.

"Thank you, Mr. Holmes. My father spoke well of your family, there was a very healthy mutual relationship between us. I think I may have even met your brother, 'erm Mycrow was it?"

"Mycroft, your grace," Holmes corrected gently.

"Ah, Mycroft. Fat man if I remember," he said.

I smiled to myself at the description of Holmes's brother.

Holmes nodded, "Yes, he has enjoyed life."

The Baron changed the subject completely. “Do you shoot, Mr. Holmes,” he said nodding towards the targets.

As Holmes turned and glanced at the targets; I noticed a smile touch his lips. “It has been a while, but I can handle a bow.”

Without turning, the Baron motioned towards the blonde-haired man. “Sandor is our best, should give you a run for your money.”

I was still flummoxed at such a display on such a sorrowful day, but we were guests. Holmes didn’t miss a beat. He took off his jacket, passed it to me and strode over to the nearest bow and quiver.

I noticed Sandor pick up a bow and quiver from behind one of the lounge chairs and walk across to join Holmes. In German, he said to Holmes, "I am the best in these parts Englander, you will not come close.”

Holmes smiled and replied, “Fifty yards I make it.”

Sandor nodded as he watched Holmes knock an arrow, aim, and let fly. The calm day was split by a high-pitched whistle and thud as the arrow struck home.

I looked over and saw it sticking out of the target just on the edge of the red centre circle.

“Too bad, too bad,” said Sandor.

He knocked and loosed the arrow, hitting the target dead in the centre of the red bullseye.

“Fine shooting, Sir,” remarked Holmes.

“I am just as good over a hundred yards,” Sandor boasted, "In fact, the French man, Baron de Coubertin, has invited me to this competition he wishes to host in a few years, in Greece I think it is.”

As he started to move towards the target, Holmes held up a hand. “You won this round, allow me.” He strode to the target and withdrew the arrows. His own left a simple round hole, while Sandor’s left a long thin cut in the target. Walking back, Holmes examined the arrows. His own sported a simple rounded bullet head, while Sandor’s had a flanged triangular head made of iron or steel.

As he handed the arrow back to Sandor, he remarked “Interesting arrow for target practice. Is it for hunting?”

“Yes, I hunt, so I like to use the same arrows. No need to adjust to the different weight,” he said.

Holmes nodded. “Another round?” he asked. As Sandor nodded, Holmes stepped back, allowing the younger man to go first. “Winner first.”

Sandor knocked the same arrow, aimed, and struck dead centre again. I was sure I could see the original notch in the target sitting just next to his second arrow. As he moved away, Holmes stepped up to the firing line. He knocked, aimed, and loosed.

A loud noise rang out as Holmes’s arrow struck the target in the middle of the notch hole made by Sandor’s first arrow. Sparks flew as the metal heads struck each other.

Holmes turned to Sandor, who stared in utter dismay. “Must have needed to get my eye in.” He put the bow back on the nearby rack, motioned to the target and said, “I’d call that one a draw. Shall I get them?”

Sandor simply turned and walked away, much to the cheers and derisive comments of his friends. I stepped up to Holmes and walked with him to the target.

“What was that all about?” I asked following him towards the target. He pulled the arrows out and showed me the tip of Sandor’s arrow.

“When I saw the type of arrowheads I needed to know how good he was,” he said, “Now, I know the Baron’s death wasn’t accidental. I just need more proof.”

***

The rest of the afternoon was a long-drawn-out affair, to which we were growing tired. By early evening we decided to return to the Inn and began to say our goodbyes to those guests we had become acquainted with.

I noticed that the Baron had taken up residence in the ballroom once the light began to fade outside. He lounged on a settee and with a glass in his hand and simply stared at the tapestry. His three flunkies were nowhere to be seen.

I moved over to say my goodbyes but was met by a simple swish of his hand to wave me away. I felt slightly offended but hid my emotion, reminding myself that this was the Baron’s home, and my feelings were not important in that context.

Holmes noticed and declined to give his own goodbyes. He mentioned that we would return prior to departing for London in a couple of days and make good our farewells then. Returning to the inn, we partook of a light supper and retired to our beds.

In the morning I was greeted by a slightly subdued Holmes, the red tinge to the flesh around his eyes reminded me of many a night spent poring over some arcane volume of forgotten lore.

As I started to quiz him over his obvious weariness, the landlady stepped into the breakfast room and delivered a platter of fresh bread, cheeses, and a selection of cured meats. Within moments of placing the fare down, she returned with a steaming pot of rich, black coffee.

"Eat up Watson, we have a long journey this morning, followed by a return to say our possible farewells to the Baron."

"Where are we travelling?"

"I arranged for Zoltan to take us to the Berlifitzing estate, I wish to investigate the supposed accidental death of the Count."

"Supposed?"

"There have been too many accidents for my liking. Something that our friend Ur. Herzog has questioned as well, hence why we are here."

Upon mention of his name, Herzog burst into the dining room, a wad of papers under his arm and an anxious look on his face. "Mr. Holmes, Doctor Watson, I'm so glad I found you. The most shocking event has happened this morning, I'm still very confused over it, and need to review the legal papers that I leant you last night and compare them to those I received this morning."

Holmes pointed to a vacant chair and told Herzog to sit. "Calm down dear fellow and explain what's happened."

"That young upstart, Sandor Csalas, appeared at my home this morning and woke me up with a loud thumping on my door. Instead of exchanging pleasantries upon entry to my house, he simply thrust these," Herzog placed the papers on the table, "at me and claimed that he was now the Count Berlifitzing, by the fact he was the illegitimate son of the deceased Count."

"Why did Sandor come to you?" I asked.

Istvan replied that as part of a deal struck many years before, between the Count and the Baron, a large proportion of the Metzengerstein estate was to be returned to the Berlifitzings on the death of the Baron.

"I knew about the deal and had informed the young Baron that the legal paperwork was all in order. I have struggled of late to gain the Baron's attention and had been waiting for a more favourable time to press him to sign the final documents," he said.

Holmes regarded Istvan for a moment before speaking.

"This Sandor, is there any evidence to prove that he is who he says he is?" he asked.

"I've only skimmed through the documents, but I would much rather discuss this with Ur. Horvath to ensure he knows about it and can advise. He's much more knowledgeable about the Berlifitzing legalities."

"I imagine that the Baron finding out that one of his good friends is now his supposed familial enemy may be a strange turn of events for him as well," I added.

Istvan nodded.

"It may lead to a more congenial status across the region instead," added Holmes.

Herzog and I both shrugged. To be honest, I hadn't considered that eventuality.

***

The trip to the estate was long and arduous. The roads were quite good, but at the high speeds that Istvan had urged Zoltan to achieve, it became extremely rough and dangerous. We were shaken about as if we were table salt during a banquet, but still, I estimated our journey took us well over an hour.

The Berlifitzing estate was a less sumptuous abode but would befit a minor British royal quite nicely. The stark presence of the burnt-out building in the foreground of the estate detracted from the chateau. The stables had been consumed almost completely by the fire, only the thick skeletal beams of the frame remained. Even the stonework had splintered and collapsed along with the roof.

Zoltan pulled the carriage to a halt near the burnt remains. We all alighted, even the sturdy driver, who after such a drive required a leg-stretching stroll as much as his passengers.

Istvan wandered away, evidently in search of Ur. Horvath, while Holmes and I performed a circuit of the ruins to undertake a cursory examination. Noticing a pile of burnt fabric that was in contrast to the surrounding straw and wood, I stepped carefully into the blackened edifice. Holmes took one look, then moved on.

The heap turned out to be horse blankets that were blackened and charred, but only on one side. When I pulled them away and found the straw beneath to be compressed, but relatively unburnt, I assumed this was where the unfortunate Count had collapsed. The blankets had been used to douse the flames or to protect the poor man from further harm. I dropped my head in reverence for a moment, before stepping out of the remains.

Outside I found Holmes standing by an exterior upright beam that had been severely burnt. The top was a blackened stump, the cross beams burnt through and laying in charred heaps on the ground.

Intrigued, I watched as Holmes leant into the wood and sniffed, before wrinkling his nose and pulling away. "Kerosene." He sniffed lower on the beam, shook his head, then stretched to full height and repeated the action. Stepping around the upright, he picked up a piece of the cross beam remains and held it to his nose. Nodding, he repeated the word, "Kerosene."

"Is that normal?" I asked, "Is it a woodlice treatment or something in these parts?"

"I wouldn't think so, Watson, plus if it were, there would be more on the lower part than the top. Look at this as well." He pointed out a narrow notch in the upright beam that was scorched all around. A small trace of melted metal could be seen on the lower part of the notch.

Holmes held up another small flat lump of cold metal. He handed it to me for examination. It was misshapen after being partially melted by the fire, but the shape reminded me of an arrowhead. I then realised it must have been embedded in the upright beam, the shaft had burnt away, and the head had melted slightly and fallen to the ground.

"What do you think Holmes?" I asked.

He looked grim.

"If I'm not mistaken, that is the remains of an arrowhead, similar to something we saw yesterday. If it were, then the rest was consumed by the flames. It may be nothing or it may be everything," he said, "I have a bad feeling that this fire was no accident." Looking around for Istvan, he saw the young lawyer emerge from the chateau and stride sullenly across the gravel drive, his wad of papers beneath his arm.

I followed Holmes as he paced towards Herzog, but as he started to speak, the young Hungarian cut him off. "Ur. Horvath is in Székesfehérvár visiting the local magistrate." Pulling the papers out and waving them around, he continued, "I believe he knew about this all along, may have even known about this Sandor for quite some time and may have lodged edicts himself in my ignorance. I need to speak to the Baron and advise him on the next course of action."

"That may be out of our hands," said Holmes, snatching Herzog's attention away from his own worries.

"What?"

"I believe this fire was no accident. Which leads me to surmise that our young Baron is in danger and may be the next victim if all plays out as I expect it to."

Istvan glanced around and yelled at Zoltan. "Zoltan, a várba, gyorsan." (Zoltan, quickly, the Castle)

***

The journey to Castle Metzengerstein seemed quick but was possibly due to the silence of all three of us. Each was wrapped in our own thoughts. Zoltan pulled up in the courtyard and we made our way into the foyer.

Immediately, Miklos scurried over, his face a mass of apprehension and fear. I tried to follow along, but Holmes translated for me later.

"Ur. Istvan," he said, "The Baron. I am so worried about the Baron."

"Why?" asked Istvan.

"He has disappeared. He took the new white charger and raced off into the forest," he said.

"What new white charger?" Holmes asked.

"Two of the grooms found a beautiful white horse in the grounds early one morning two weeks ago. I presumed it had escaped from the Berlifitzing stables, such a tragedy that is, but I sent word and they did not know anything about it. The grooms managed to coax the animal into a stall. The young Baron appeared from nowhere, saw the animal and muttered something about the Count returned from the dead." The Butler pleaded with Herzog. "I warned you. I told you his mind is going," he said.

"What happened this morning to worry you?" asked Holmes intent on the story.

Miklos turned and looked up at Holmes with his watery eyes.

"For several days he has walked the grounds in the early morning, but of late he has taken to riding the horse for hours each morning. Today, he strode out before even I had awakened. The grooms said that he saddled the horse and rode off. That was several hours ago. We haven't seen him since. He's not in his right mind. I just hope nothing has happened to him."

Istvan patted the old man on the shoulder, as was his custom and sent him on his way with assurances that we would investigate and find the Baron safe and sound.

"The stables?" answered Holmes when I asked what next.

As we stepped into the Ballroom on our way to the rear exit, our eyes were drawn to the tapestry. A beam of sunlight from a skylight in the ceiling struck the central figure of the white horse giving it an ethereal and almost angelic quality. The effect was incredible.

"Extraordinary," I said.

"You can understand why the Baron is so enamoured with this tapestry, and this newly found white horse," said Istvan.

Holmes wasn't as convinced as the Hungarian. "Or else." Letting his statement hang, he stepped over to the settee on which we had last seen the Baron reclining. An array of dirty dishes and glassware sat on the ground and on a small table to the side.

Holmes picked up a champagne glass and examined the remains in the bottom for a moment before reaching in with his middle finger. Once extracted he rubbed his middle finger and thumb together and stared at the result.

"Watson, what do you make of this?" he asked.

I moved across and looked down at the silver residue on his fingertips. I took the glass from his hand and examined the sediment as well. Repeating Holmes's actions, I extracted some of the remains myself. After a few moments of rubbing the greasy compound around between my fingers, I looked up. "If I was to ponder a guess, I'd say this is elemental mercury."

"My deduction as well," said Holmes.

Suddenly, I was aghast. "You don't think that the Baron ingested elemental mercury?"

"Not only this once but on quite a few occasions," Holmes said, "Possibly for as much as several months."

"Mercury?" asked Istvan joining us at the settee, "What would that do? Is it poison?"

"There have been rare cases of some factory workers in London, where poisoning from elemental mercury caused brain and liver damage. In low levels the victim shows signs of dementia or a continued delirium, higher levels can cause sight problems, muscular atrophy and even liver or kidney disease. Some poor people had died horribly from renal shutdown," I said.

"Horrible," he said, "Would that explain the Baron's mental instability?"

"Yes. I think it would," said Holmes.

"Would it come from the champagne?" asked Istvan, "We import it directly from France."

I shook my head. "No, there is no history of high levels of mercury in champagne, that I know of anyway."

Holmes bent down and picked up a discarded soup bowl, a similar dark silver ring could be seen near the top.

"I would say that the mercury has been introduced into the young Baron's food by a third party," he said. Without a word he disappeared into the bowels of the castle, leaving the lawyer and myself alone.

Carrying on outside, we found the Baron's other two flunkies lounging around near the rear entrance. The number of empty champagne bottles explained a lot about their state of mind. One was asleep, the other one sat on a chaise lounge staring out over the lake.

Istvan walked up to the conscious man and spoke.

"Laszlo, wo ist der Baron," he asked.

"Ich habe ihn seit dem Morgen nicht gesehen, jetzt weiß ich es nicht, ist mir egal," Laszlo answered. (I haven't seen him since this morning. Now, don't know, don't care)

"Was ist mit Sandor?" (What about Sandor?)

"Habe ihn seit letzter Nacht nicht gesehen. Auch das ist mir egal." (Haven't seen him since last night, again I don't care)

By this time Istvan had his hands on his hips and was looking quite irritated. He dropped his hands, let out a harrumph and joined me. I could hear him mumbling under his breath. It was Hungarian, that's for sure, and I don't think I needed it translated to understand its intent.

At that point Holmes joined us, he took one look at the recumbent young men and said, "Forget them, I think their time is about to come. Let us check the stables."

Istvan and I both looked across the open fields towards the two-storey stable complex behind the servants' quarters. Holmes strode off. Istvan and I hurried to catch up to him.

When we were still several hundred yards away, a white horse broke from the nearby forest and raced across the field and into the stables. A blue-clad figure rode high in the saddle.

"There's our young Baron now," I said.

"Quite so," said Holmes hurrying up his stride.

Suddenly, a bolt of flame burst from the forest and flew across the open ground striking one of the stable's upper storey beams. Even from that distance, we could tell it was an arrow. The flames licked at the wooden beam which burst into blue and orange flames. Another flaming arrow flew from the woods and landed inside the ground floor; a fireball exploded from within leaving a curling trail of smoke that rose slowly into the sky.

"Kerosene," Holmes said.

Within moments more smoke began to belch out of the upper storey window and through the gap in the stable doors. Bright orange flames began to lick along the wooden beams and the roofline. A loud whinny echoed across the open field and the now riderless white horse bolted from the ground floor and headed towards the forest.

"The Baron," Istvan shouted and began to run towards the stables. I followed in his wake. Turning, I saw Holmes head for the forest, no doubt to apprehend the assailant. It had to be Sandor, no one else we had met could have made those shots with a bow and arrow.

By the time Istvan and I came to the stable, it was fully ablaze. Horses shrieked in abject horror within the flaming building. We, however, could see a pair of legs with riding boots, lying amongst the smouldering straw in the middle of the main area. Covering our faces with kerchiefs we dashed into the smoke and dragged the poor unfortunate Baron out into the clear air.

Once outside, a fit of coughing took both of us a few moments to recover before I was able to examine the Baron. He had as I feared succumbed to the smoke and flames. I tried several methods to revive him, but each failed to draw any breath or heartbeat.

Istvan's face dropped in horror at the realisation. He fell to his knees next to the body and visibly wept for his young charge.

"I failed you, I failed your father," he cried.

I stood and walked away, still suffering from the smoke I had inhaled and found Holmes walking towards me holding a bow and quiver full of arrows.

"No luck," I gasped.

Holmes looked at the body and crying lawyer and said, "Nor you, it seems." I shook my head in remorse. Holmes's face became stern. "Whoever shot these arrows was long gone. I followed a trail of boot marks, but they led to a line of hoof prints. The culprit escaped."

"But we know where," I said.

Holmes nodded. “Indeed. We shall send for the Sheriff and have him meet us at the Berlifitzing estate. I shall prosecute the case as I see it and justice will prevail.”

***

“But where is your evidence, Mr. Holmes?” said the blonde-haired youth as he sat on a high-backed chair in the middle of the large room of the Berlifitzing manor house, turning it into a de-facto audience chamber.

“I have presented it as I have seen it,” said Holmes, “Everything points to you.”

“Even though I am very protective of my bow and arrows,” he shrugged, “I admit that I may not have taken as much care of them as I should have. Leaving them at the Castle whilst I delivered my documents to Ur. Herzog, and then moved my possessions to the estate, was possibly a large oversight it seems, but you have no evidence that I was there this afternoon.”

“I must ask for more,” said the Sheriff, “As of this afternoon, Ur. Csalas, is now legally the Baron and Count of this entire area. A position that holds a great level of honour and power.”

Holmes nodded to the Sheriff. “I agree Sir, I agree, and I understand the gravity of these accusations, but you must agree that the evidence presented demands investigation. We have three very high-profile deaths, that have elements pointing to something other than accidents.”

The Sheriff nodded. “Yes, I do agree with that point.”

“If this is all you have against the Count, then I would ask you to leave your accusations at the door, and withdraw from our presence,” piped up Ur. Horvath, standing to Sandor’s right.

Holding up a single finger, and wearing a familiar sly grin, Holmes continued. “There is the other matter of the young Baron’s mental decline.” Holding out a hand towards me, Holmes said, “My good friend Doctor Watson and I found evidence that Frederick had been subjected to a subtle form of poisoning from the effects of elemental mercury being introduced into his food and drink.”

Horvath’s face grew red as his anger grew. “And you are blaming the Count for this?”

“Yes, yes I am.”

“On what grounds? If something was being administered to the Baron, then it could only have been the kitchen staff or that overstuffed butler." Horvath placed a fatherly hand on the Count’s shoulder. “Young Sandor here had only been a kind and generous friend to the Baron. Supporting him through his school days and offering a comforting shoulder during the days following his parents’ unfortunate demise.”

The act was well played, but even I couldn’t see how someone who supposedly had only met the newly installed Count in the last day or two would have been able to offer such a character reference.

“Ah, I cannot argue against those points,” said Holmes, “As I haven’t born witness to the friendship between the deceased Baron and the Count.” He stopped for a moment, waiting to see if anyone was prepared to butt in. When all stayed quiet, Holmes began again. “But one could draw a different picture from several facts.” As always, Holmes was apt to make a drama of the finale to an adventure. He stalked around the audience chamber and counted his facts off on several fingers as he spoke. “The chances of two strangers meeting at boarding school and becoming strong friends, only to turn out to be the last heirs of two extremely powerful neighbouring families, is quite infinitesimal.” Turning towards Ur. Horvath, he said, “I put it to you, Sir, that you knew of the Count's illegitimate son, and managed affairs so that this could happen.”

The Count’s aide went red with rage once more and started to speak, only to be cut off again. “Remember, I saw you in the Church garden. I also overheard your conversation, which brings me to the second point. Young Sandor, on your instigation, convinced the young Baron to sign documents that would see part of his newly inherited lands handed over to the heir of the Berlifitzing estates. All without the knowledge of his lawyer and confidant, Ur. Herzog. I would also add that the Baron was not of sound mind at the time. If he were, he would have discussed the details with Ur. Herzog. That was the precise reason that Sandor began the mercury poisoning.”

“Nonsense,” said Horvath, “You have only circumstantial evidence and conjecture. Any documents that have been signed have been legally done so. I have confirmation from the local Magistrate. Ask your lawyer for yourself."

"Well, intriguingly enough, I do have a witness, in fact, several witnesses."

A shocked look came across Horvath's face, his mouth gaped open. Even the young Count sat up straighter at the mention of a witness.

"Who?" he asked, meekly.

"When we were first introduced, I noticed an interaction between yourself and a young housemaid in the Baron's service. It was easy to track down this girl, or Zsófia as she is known."

Sandor's face grew even more horrified. Horvath's returned to anger, with his eyes constantly darting towards his young cohort.

"Zsófia was very effusive about our Count here. She waxed very lyrical about their love and how she would soon hold court in this very building, if not back at the castle itself. Young love is a wonderful thing, not so when it is simply one way though, as I believe your tryst with young Zsófia was." Holmes waited a moment for a reply, but the Count simply sighed. "As I thought. One tiny nugget of information that Zsófia unearthed was the continued assistance that she provided to you to administer the Baron's medicine, as she called it."

Holmes brought a hand out from his pocket. Between finger and thumb, he held a small glass vial with a distinctly silver liquid inside. "This is the medicine in question, I'm sure we can simply test it to verify that it is indeed elemental mercury."

"This girl, she is simply an opportunist, throwing herself at Sandor and leaching off his fortunate circumstance," said Horvath, his face red from rage or embarrassment, of which I was still unsure.

"That may be Ur. Horvath, but would you expect a young girl, born and bred in a region such as this to understand the effects of imbibing elemental mercury, and to what ends would such as she hope to achieve?" Holmes turned towards the young Count. "But you Count, have an intimate knowledge given your studies at the Vienna Institute alongside the young Baron."

"This still seems to be circumstantial, Mr. Holmes," said the Sheriff.

"Ah, you would think, but I have talked to Miklos the butler, who stated he saw the Count and this serving girl on many occasions, plus upon showing him the vial, he stated he had seen it pass from the Count's hand to the girl's. So, we have motive, we have evidence, we have witnesses, to at least impose a deeper level of investigation."

To this, the Sheriff nodded, before expressing his own concerns, "But, under the laws of this region, the Count and the Baron are considered exempt from investigation by virtue of their position. Therefore, regardless of your words, I cannot, in good faith, arrest the Count or even implicate him."

A wry grin came to Holmes's face. I'd seen that grin many times before, always before fireworks. "Yes, I thought that would be the case, but the former Count had been wary of the consequences of such a situation." Turning towards Herzog, he asked, "Istvan, if you will, can you read Clause 44.3 in the edict established by the Count upon his demise."

Surprised, Herzog moved to a nearby side table and placed the wad of papers down. He rifled through them until he came across the required page.

Looking across at Horvath, Holmes said, "These are the papers that young Sandor lodged with Ur. Herzog this morning, so you should have a copy of them, in case you wished to verify." Horvath simply huffed in resentment.

Mumbling to himself for a moment while he read, I noticed Herzog's eyes grow wide in disbelief. "You are right it's all here."

"Well out with it man," yelled Horvath.

"Clause 44.3. To lay claim to the estate of Berlifitzing, the claimant must be of good character and clean reputation. Any action undertaken by the claimant prior to investiture as the Count, that could result in a legal conviction, must be resolved before any claim can be progressed."

"The pertinent word is *could*," said Holmes, "Now, my dear Sheriff, is anything I have said here today given you cause for thought that perhaps Ur. Csalas here could be found to have orchestrated, if not executed, either the descent of the Baron's mental health or, in fact, his unfortunate demise."

"These are very serious accusations," said the Sheriff, "I do not think that anything like this has been seen in the history of this region." Shaking his head slightly, the Sheriff walked across to the table where Herzog stood and read the edict himself, mumbling under his breath as he did so. When finished, he looked back, his lips pursed in contemplation, first at Holmes, then at the young Count, back to Holmes then finally back to the legal edict.

The rest of us held our collective breath as if waiting for some form of judgement to issue from the Sheriff. I spied Horvath's anger seething behind his red face. I truly believe he might have been in serious danger of a heart attack.

After an interminable time, the Sheriff slowly turned to face the collected audience. He shook his head slowly and dropped his eyes. "I have very serious concerns about all of this. It is unprecedented for a Count or Baron of this region to be stripped of a title." Looking up into Holmes's face, he continued, "But if, as you say, Mr. Holmes, any of this evidence you have unearthed does indicate foul play in the deaths of the Barons and the Count, then I am duty-bound to investigate." Looking at the young Count, he said, "I am truly sorry your Grace, but the legal documents that were used to prove your investiture, also state that until this matter is cleared you are prohibited from taking the title of Count. Under those circumstances, you may be found guilty of the crimes of which you are accused. So, I have no choice but to place you under arrest until this is all resolved."

It was the young Count's turn to shout in anger, but his rage was directed not at the Sheriff or Holmes, but at Ur. Horvath. "You said I would be Count. You told me I would be protected by my rightful title." He stood and grabbed the older man by the lapels, pushing him back against a wall. "I killed because of you. I killed my father. I killed my friend."

The Sheriff, Holmes and I rushed across to the two men, dragging the young Count away from the frightened Horvath. His face showed the sorrow of someone who had lost everything in a matter of seconds. The Sheriff motioned towards a nearby doorway and two constables appeared, taking hold of the young Count, and dragging him, shouting, and screaming obscenities, from the room.

All eyes fell on the sad figure of Horvath. "Is he correct? Did you orchestrate all of this?" asked Holmes. The diminished man simply nodded.

It was the stoic figure of the Sheriff who had the last word. "You have brought shame upon the name of this family, and upon our community as a whole. If I do not take you from this place for your own protection, I cannot guarantee your safety."

Herzog, Holmes, and I watched the Sheriff lead the broken man away from the audience chamber, bringing a close to a very strange and wretched affair.

***

During the train journey from Vienna, I questioned Holmes over the next steps in both the houses of Metzengerstein and Berlifitzing.

He pondered for a moment, staring at the scenery rushing by outside before turning to me. "Despite the heard confession from young Sandor, the Sheriff will need to prosecute the case for murder and accessory to murder on both Sandor and Horvath. That may take many months, as I understand it will need to be presented in Budapest or to a Judge from the capital. Once that is finished, then our friend Ur. Herzog will be tasked with executing the final Will and Testaments of both the Baron and Count. Herzog seemed to think that his first steps will be to find a suitable heir to both estates. The families were large so there should be a relative somewhere that is legally entitled to each. There will no doubt be a cavalcade of suitors applying to be the next Baron or Count. I dare say that our friend will be employed on that exercise for some time to come."

"Well good for him."

"Yes, even once all is finished, I imagine Herzog will be kept busy managing the legal affairs for both estates for many years."

I thought for a moment, establishing the train of events in my mind in preparation for documenting the adventure when something occurred to me. "What about the young housemaid?"

"Ah, yes, the young at heart, in love with a supposed Count. I discussed her with Herzog, but nothing in her demeanour indicated she knew what the intention was of Sandor's deception. For all intents and purposes, she was simply a pawn in his twisted game. Hopefully, she will not be disposed of her employment because of it."

I nodded and settled back for the long journey home.

The Case of the Borneo Tribesman

Even though it was heading towards nightfall on that August evening, the dying sun of the day still beat down with a ferocity that had been unseen in London for quite some time.

Holmes and I departed our hansom and stood before the modestly appointed three-storey Kensington abode of our host for the evening. From what I knew of our host, the appointment of the building was more in line with the tastes of his wife, rather than the flamboyant nature of the man of the house. The couple had bought all three connecting terraced houses and made them a single abode, with all décor and modifications left to the wife.

It was two days since the simple but elegant card had arrived, inviting me rather than Holmes to what was coined an "event" at this address.

Our host was adventurer and businessman Sir Tristan Leavins, the head of the London division of the North Borneo Chartered Company. From my reading, I knew that he spent the majority of his time in the East Indies, coordinating the trading of resources and goods between Borneo and England.

A small handwritten note had accompanied the card and told me more than I could have gleaned from the invitation itself.

It seemed that Sir Tristan was to present, to the British Trade Commission, a selection of goods from far-flung Borneo to engender a want within them and secure funds for establishing a series of trade routes between the two countries. The event, as the invitation called it, was a prelude for a small but distinct class of attendees.

How I had been chosen to attend was indicated by the signature at the bottom of the letter. The name was Willard Kesson, or as I had known him Lieutenant Willard Kesson of the Royal Engineers, who fought in the Battle of Maiwand where I was unfortunately injured.

As a postscript, Kesson had noted that he would be delighted to see me again. He also suggested bringing Holmes to add colour to what may be a rather dull affair.

Taking the lead, I approached the door, readying myself to lift the brass knocker to announce our arrival. As I reached towards it, the door was opened wide, and we were met by an incredible sight.

Standing in the entranceway was a half-naked, dark-skinned man. He was resplendent in a brightly coloured cloth that wrapped around his waist, with a long section hanging down the front. Upon his head, he wore a feathered headdress, with several beaded necklaces that draped down his chest. I was so stunned by the man's appearance that I simply stood with my mouth open.

A bright white smile split the man's dark face. "Good evening, gentlemen. Welcome home to Sir Tristan's." Holmes bowed slightly to the man and introduced us. "Ah, good, good. Holmes and Watson. Yes. I hear that name." He stepped back and bade us enter.

As we passed by, Holmes stopped and asked the man. "I can only assume you hail from Borneo. Your headdress and loincloth are reminiscent of the Northern area, or indeed from the island of Labuan."

"Yes, sir. We all from Labuan. Many more inside," he said.

"And what is your name?" Holmes asked.

"Jamal. Your service I am," the man said, bowing before us.

"*Selamat Berkenalan*," Holmes said.

"And I pleased meet you too, sir," Jamal said.

"Your English is quite good," I said. "Where did you learn?"

"The sisters at the Mission." His face went dour at some remembrance. "I was many, who no parents."

"Oh, I'm so sorry, my good man. An orphanage." He nodded. I started to speak again, but another couple arrived at the doorstep. As Jamal attended to the new arrivals, we took our leave and moved into the house.

Looking down the hallway leading away from the entry foyer, we found another similarly dressed tribesman. He smiled widely as we approached but shook his head when I asked him a question in English. Instead, he simply held out a hand towards the nearby open set of double doors. Holmes repeated his Malay welcome, to which the man's face broke into a wide smile.

As we stepped through, I was simply awestruck. This would be called a ballroom in a country manor house, but here in a simple terraced house, it was something else entirely. The room stretched from the entrance hallway all the way to the far end of the third house. On one side a series of bay windows looked out across the gardens and onto the street, while on the other a succession of small alcoves had been created, with curtains supposedly hanging in front of doorways exiting the room.

I wasn't an architect by any measure, but I could see that as part of the expansion, the supporting walls between each house had been removed – something that I presumed would be extremely dangerous to the structural integrity of the floors above. "Holmes?" I asked my friend, turning to find him likewise studying the grand room.

"Yes, Watson, amazing isn't it? An incredible feat of engineering. The man responsible must be congratulated."

"I think you are seeing the room differently to me."

Holmes glanced at me for a moment, and upon seeing my slight discomfort, patted me on the shoulder and began to point out certain aspects of the room. "Fear not. If you look along the lines of the original walls, you can see arches built at the extremities, they meet up to sunken iron beams that virtually replace the function of the old bricks and mortar walls." He pointed along the length of the room and I could finally see the series of beams that had been added to strengthen the floor. "It's quite a remarkable design."

"Thank you," came a reply from nearby, "Sir Tristan asked me to help the builder with a new style of design that would enable the virtual disappearance of the load-bearing walls."

We both turned and found my old friend Lieutenant Willard Kesson standing just slightly behind us, a wide grin on his face.

"Willy!" I almost shouted, delighted to meet my old friend.

He stepped forward and thrust a hand out, grabbing mine and shaking vigorously. "John, it's been far too long, so good to see you again." Before I could introduce him, Kesson turned to Holmes and shook his hand as well. "Mr. Holmes, I am so glad you could make it. Even more pleased that you appreciate all of my designs in this room."

"It is a rather remarkable feat, sir," Holmes replied.

"Lieutenant Willard Kesson, here, was with the Royal Engineers at the Battle of Maiwand."

"Willard is fine if you please. John and I met in the field hospital after I succumbed to injuries as well."

"And you've been in Borneo for the last few years?" asked Holmes.

"Yes. I was recruited by Admiral Mayne, one of the North Borneo Company's directors. They needed engineers, and the Admiral wanted servicemen due to their diligence and perseverance. Plus, the warm weather is kinder on my injured leg."

"What have you been doing over there, Willy?" I asked.

"Ah, John, some amazing things. The North Borneo Chartered Company, as it is rightly called, was set up in competition with the East India Company. The Directors have been given the rights to investigate and exploit the resources available in the country."

"I'm intrigued," said Holmes. "What resources exactly?"

"Well to begin with foodstuffs, animal and plant goods, but there are moves afoot to investigate any mineral finds that we can unearth." Kesson indicated the room before us. "That's what tonight is all about. A first introduction to some of the produce, animals, and cultural artifacts that are on offer in Borneo. Sir Tristan has brought some of the local tribesmen with him, and a range of foodstuffs and produce to tempt the British Trade Commission, in the hopes of garnering further financial support and setting up future trade routes."

"Doesn't really sound like any of that is within your area of expertise," I said. "What do you do with your time and intellect?"

"Ah, that's where it is interesting," Kesson said, "The Admiral sent me out to Borneo with the intention of assisting with a way of bringing fresh food all the way from the East Indies to England. My first stop was in Australia where I met with a man called James Harrison, who had invented an ice-making machine. I brought his design and manufacturing techniques back to Borneo and using his initial design, I've improved it to a point where we can install the machine onto a ship and create ice at will, ensuring that any food shipped across the globe will be kept frozen or chilled for the entire journey."

"Marvellous," I said.

Kesson indicated the various displays and offerings around the room with a sweep of his hand. "What is on show tonight are some of the tastiest delicacies and intriguing objects of interest that we've discovered so far in Borneo." We stepped into the room, following Kesson as he led us around the various exhibits.

Following his movements, my eyes fell on several distinct areas around the room. In one small alcove, one of the tribesmen stood with an orange-haired orangutan on a stand. "This is of course an orangutan. We brought in another female as a donation to London Zoo to assist with their breeding program." Nearby was a table with an aquarium sitting on top. Inside, a long blue snake, with black stripes and a tiny swatch of yellow around its mouth, swam around. Its wide black eyes seemed to be fixed on my own as it moved. "This is the yellow-lipped sea krait," said Kesson, leaning in close to the aquarium. The snake jerked back before striking forward and smacking into the glass. "Quite deadly – and aggressive, as you can see. We did bring a breeding pair, but sadly one of them died on the voyage."

Not far from the aquarium was a six-foot-tall cage, with a wide-eyed animal, reminiscent of a small lemur, clinging desperately to a cut-down tree branch. "Ah, this cute little creature is locally called a cuscus. Again, we wanted to bring a breeding pair, but thought best to settle this little one in first and bring another on the next journey."

As we stepped away from the cuscus, we were approached by a tribesman carrying a large silver platter, covered in chips of ice, and topped with orange-and-white striped morsels of prawn meat. "Now this is special," said Kesson, picking one of the prawns from the tray with his fingers and biting into it with pleasure. "These are a large type of prawn caught off the coast of Borneo. We cooked and then froze them for transportation, ready to be thawed and consumed. You really should try some." He waved a hand at some of the other men holding serving platters. "We also have crayfish meat, brought over the same way, and some wonderful fruits, like jackfruit and rambutans. The fruit itself wasn't frozen but stored in a chilled room to ensure that it was kept fresh."

I did as Kesson said and using a small plate and fork offered to me by the tribesman, plucked one of the prawns from the tray and experimentally bit into the fleshier end. The meat was exquisite, the consistency of succulent chicken, but with a saltier, light fish taste to it. The morsel also had a slight smell to it, which remained on the plate afterwards, making me glad I had used the fork. "My word," I exclaimed, "That is indeed delicious."

"So, it isn't just the food that your company is promoting," said Holmes, "but also the freezing technology?"

"Indeed, it is, sir. The modifications I've made to Harrison's design could revolutionise food transport and open up the world."

Just as I was about to ask another question, a tall, immaculately dressed man entered with a much more demure lady by his side. Holmes leaned in and said, "Our host, I think."

Indeed, Sir Tristan Leavins, with his wife Blanche close by his side, made such a grand couple as they worked their way around the room that I almost forgot about the wonderful fare on offer and the fabulous beasts and items on display.

As they finally approached, Kesson introduced us to Sir Tristan and his wife. Usually, upon the mention of Holmes's name, people's faces light up with recognition and begin to deluge my good friend with questions aplenty. Sir Tristan's face was placid and engaging, but it was almost as if he'd never heard of Holmes. Lady Blanche was another matter. She gushed with enthusiasm and asked him all manner of trivial questions about some of his adventures. Sir Tristan moved off, leaving his wife to interrogate Holmes for a few moments before finally signalling her to join him and make the acquaintance of a couple across the room.

Turning to Holmes, I asked, "Do you think Sir Tristan was purposely rude, or actually didn't know who you were?"

"Well, given that the man has spent several years in Asia, building up the presence of his company, he may not have had a chance to peruse *The Strand*, unlike his London-based wife."

Nodding, I retorted, "Well, that would be fair. For a moment, I thought my writing had lost its touch." I searched for Kesson and found him munching on another prawn, smacking his fingers afterwards. I started to ask a question when a young man in his early thirties, with the tanned skin of someone that spends much of his time outside, stepped up beside Holmes and spoke quietly into his ear. Kesson quickly stated that he was needed to see to the ice machine and would return once the problem was resolved.

We amused ourselves by trying the crayfish meat and fruits on offer. Each was a delight and pleasure to the senses. Sating our appetite, we moved around the room and examined the special items that were displayed. Most were collections of weaponry, supposedly from the Bornean tribes during their pre-colonial state. One display contained several long wooden spears, and another a collection of short wooden, stone, and even iron knives. One of the most fascinating was a set of blowpipes, ranging in size and intricacy. There were five in all, starting at six inches in length, and growing to almost a yard.

In a small dish below the rack of blowpipes were a selection of actual darts used in the pipes. They were about three inches long, consisting of a slender needle for the most part and a thicker cone-shaped section at the end. I assumed that the thicker part pressed against the sides of the pipe, with the needle penetrating the skin of the animal or man. A small card explained that the darts were generally dipped in poison to incapacitate or kill the intended target.

I turned to ask Holmes's thoughts but found that he'd wandered away and was engaged in conversation with a couple across the room. Glancing back, I began to examine the longest blowpipe again. I was fascinated by both the simplicity and complexity of such a weapon. As I leaned in to look closer at the mouthpiece, a male voice spoke over my shoulder.

"Pick it up if you like," he said.

Standing nearby was an elderly gentleman. Although succumbing to a slight arch in his back, he stood as ramrod straight as he was able. "There's no mistaking a fellow military man," I said, holding out my hand, “I am Dr. John Watson, formerly of the Fifth Northumberland Fusiliers, and then with the Berkshires at Maiwand.”

The older gent took my hand and shook it firmly. A small smile crept to his face. “Rear-Admiral Richard Mayne, formerly of Her Majesty’s Royal Navy. Now I simply sit on the board of this damn company.”

“Very pleased to meet you, sir. I am a good friend of one of your employees, Lieutenant Willard Kesson.”

“Ah, Kesson. Good man, brilliant mind. I recruited him myself, you know. Was in the Royal Engineers. His superiors were very impressed. Sad that he was injured at Maiwand, though. Has been doing some great things in Borneo the past few years. That ice-making machine is a stroke of genius. His ingenuity will bring millions into the company. He’ll be well rewarded for his efforts, but,” the Admiral’s face turned slightly dour, “I’m afraid that he wants more than just money.”

“I don’t follow, sir.”

“Power, my boy! Power. Too many people want power for power’s sake. Kesson will go far, but it will take time. This company has been built on reputation more than genius.” Turning he pointed towards Sir Tristan. “Kesson needs to build up his own status, like Leavins over there. For the North Borneo Chartered Company to grow, we need people who can present to Parliament and Governments around the world. That requires status. We only put Knights of the Realm or highly-ranked military men in such positions." He stood for a moment and stared at the blowpipes, gathering both his thoughts and breath. “Kesson has time. His brilliance will shine through. He just needs time.”

The Admiral reached for the longest blowpipe and passed it to me. “Though genius can sometimes come undone. Even something as elegant and deadly as this weapon is no match for a good soldier with a gun.”

Examining the blowpipe, I was still impressed with the design. Looking down its length, I was unsure whether the tribesmen had hollowed out a straight length of wood or used something of a natural occurrence. It was light, and I could only assume that the length gave the projectile a much truer flight. When I turned back to remark to the Admiral, he was gone, almost as if he had never been there in the first place.

Replacing the blowpipe, I moved past the animals again, smiling at the huge eyes of the cuscus, and the ancient-looking face of the orangutan before joining Holmes and being introduced to the couple with whom he conversed.

After a few moments of answering questions, I chanced a glance across the room and noticed Sir Tristan and his wife speaking with another couple. They stood in a small alcove on the other side of the room not far from the racks of weapons. As I turned back, my eyes darted to the sharp movement of Sir Tristan's hand as it slapped at the back of his neck. I could have sworn he mouthed the word mosquito. At the time I thought nothing of it, amused by the idea that there would be any mosquitoes inside a Kensington residence, but I supposed at the height of summer, with Hyde Park not that far away, it was a possibility.

Re-joining the conversation around me, I found myself, once again, plied with questions about Holmes's adventures. I was, however, delighted when Kesson stepped up next to me. He leant in and whispered. "John, can you come with me? Sir Tristan has taken ill." I glanced over at the alcove where I had last seen our host and found it empty.

"Do you know what's wrong?"

"He fell faint, and it was only fortunate that another man caught him before he collapsed to the ground. He's been taken into a nearby room and laid on a settee. When I left, he was unconscious."

Holmes noticed our conversation and made his excuses as Kesson and I stepped away, joining us as we exited the large room and came upon the small crowd surrounding Sir Tristan.

I hurried up to the reclining man and ushered the others away. "Please, I'm a doctor. Give this man some space and air to breath." Kneeling down, I felt Sir Tristan's brow. His temperature was elevated, leading to my first thought that he had simply been overcome by the heat of the occasion. Glancing around, I noticed a maidservant standing nearby. I implored her to retrieve a cloth and some cold water.

"Would ice be better?" Kesson asked.

"Much."

"See to it, Gwendolyn." The young girl disappeared.

"What's wrong with him?" my friend asked.

"I think he has simply been overcome. I do wish I had my bag. I would like to check his heart." Dismissing any propriety, I reached down and undid the neck of Sir Tristan's shirt and tie. Touching my fingers to his neck I counted the rate of his pulse. It seemed to be slowing. I hoped that meant that he was relaxing after a mild case of anxiety.

I was so wrong.

Suddenly, Sir Tristan's body arched from the settee. His arms and legs twitched, his eyes snapped open, with the whites showing. Frothy drool gathered at his lips and streamed from his mouth.

Frantically, I glanced around at the nearby audience. "He's having a seizure. I need something small and hard. A spoon, fork, or knife. Quickly now." It was Holmes that found a letter opener with a thick wooden handle on a nearby desk. Snatching it from him, I tried to prize the man's mouth open, so I could slide it above his tongue, but as quickly as the seizure started it stopped.

It was then I realised the man in my arms was dead.

Checking his pulse again and finding nothing, I dropped my head in dejection. I hadn't realised who was still in the room but regretted my actions when Sir Tristan's wife cried out in despair. "No. No. Tristan. No."

Kesson went straight to the stricken woman and organised someone to take her from the room. My last sight was of the look of hopelessness on her face as her eyes stared at the corpse of her husband. Others were ushered out until it was only Holmes, me, and the corpse.

"If I'd had my bag," I spat, "I could have saved him." A hand patted me on the shoulder. Turning I gazed up into Holmes's stoic expression.

"You did everything you could, given the circumstances. More than anybody else could do." I realised his eyes lay on the corpse, rather than on my face. As always, Holmes was searching for clews. "I have my opinions, but from what do you believe he died?"

Staring back at the poor dead man before me, I answered, "Until a police surgeon investigates we won't have a solid answer. It could have been anything. Heart attack. A stroke. An epileptic fit. Perhaps a reaction to something."

"You may be onto something with the allergy angle." Moving closer to Sir Tristan, Holmes bent over and began examining the corpse.

I must have been weary, as I snapped at him, "Come, Holmes. A man has just died. In all likelihood it was natural. Not everything need be suspicious."

"That may be so, but until everything is eliminated, I will never drop my scepticism." He proceeded to kneel, examining him before gently lifting the man's head to reveal a small, dried bloodspot on the back of Sir Tristan's neck. "Now that is interesting."

Looking with weary eyes, I realised the spot was where I had seen Sir Tristan slap, only minutes ago. "That was where the mosquito bit him." But I was also recalling something else that I'd seen not long before – at the beginning of my conversation with Admiral Mayne.

Holmes glanced around at me, a look of surprise on his face. "Mosquito?" Nodding, I explained what I had seen earlier. His eyes drifted away as some inner thoughts began to run. Reaching into his pocket he withdrew his glass. Smiling at my look of shock, he said, "Always come prepared, Watson. Always come prepared."

I thought his comment a little rough, given my wish to have my doctor's bag at my side, but left it at that.

"Help me roll him on his side." I did as asked and watched Holmes study the small blood spot with great interest. "What do you make of this?" he said. He pulled away, leaving his glass hovering over the spot. Leaning in for a closer look, I noticed the blood spot was a lot larger than a simple mosquito bite. There was also a dried crust around the area. It was difficult to tell colour in the dull light of the room, but it looked cream or light yellow in tone. Definitely not a normal bodily fluid from such a wound.

"I have no idea, but whatever that dried substance is, I don't think it came from Sir Tristan."

"My thoughts precisely. Now, where was he when you saw the mosquito bite him?"

I described the alcove again – and the fact that there were blowpipes on display. Holmes was away within seconds. I was in two minds whether to follow or stay with the corpse until Kesson returned with help. There was nothing more that I could do for the dead man. Since he was beyond help and wasn't going anywhere in a hurry, I rolled him again onto his back and placed his hands on his chest. To anyone else he would look as if he was simply reposing.

Moving into the ballroom, I was surprised to find it empty of people and animals. I assumed that Kesson had sent word throughout the room that their host and hostess were indisposed and informed all to vacate the premises. I noticed that the racks of weapons remained, presumably to be removed at a later date.

I found Holmes on his hands and knees, studying the floor near where I had seen Sir Tristan supposedly bitten by an insect. "What the devil are you looking for?"

"Clews."

Remaining on his knees, Holmes looked at me and held up a small object. "I don't wish to suppose yet, but I'm beginning to paint a picture in my mind."

"Is that what I think it is?"

Holding the object between thumb and forefinger, he looked at it through his glass. "It appears to be small and cone-shaped, possibly made of wood or bamboo. There is a tiny indentation in the centre of the pointed end."

I noted that it very much resembled one of the darts that had been lying near the blowpipes.

"This is where it lay," he said, pointing to a small, discoloured area on the dark wooden floor. From where I stood it was either off-white or a light yellow in colour.

"Is that – ?"

"The same substance as we found on Sir Tristan's neck? It may well be." Holmes leaned in closer with his glass to study the substance again. "We shall need to examine it further, and possibly run a chemical test, but given the colour, consistency, and location, I am fairly certain they're one and the same."

"Any conjecture on what it could be?"

"No, but let us look amongst the weapons. In just a moment, I confirmed that the largest blowpipe was missing.

"The one I picked up and examined," I added.

Holmes gave the vacant spot a cursory glance, before picking up one of the darts and holding both it and his prize next to each other at eye level. The small conical object that Holmes had found was identical, although the needle was missing from the base of the dart.

I commented on that fact. "Do you think that it fell out?"

"I didn't find a needle anywhere." He wrapped the dart in one of the small envelopes that he habitually carried. "I think this is our mosquito."

"Perhaps the needle must be caught in Sir Tristan's clothing or something."

That sly grin grew on Holmes's face. "Perhaps. That would be one answer, but there's another I'd like to investigate."

"These darts are generally tipped with poison. It seems likely that this is what happened to Sir Tristan."

"I'm not prepared to say anything at this stage, but I want to eliminate as much uncertainty as I can." Turning to face me, Holmes asked, "Think back on Sir Tristan's symptoms before his unfortunate demise."

"He fell faint and reportedly passed out."

"Yes, and when you were attending him?"

"He was unresponsive. His heartbeat was slow but erratic, then finally he had a seizure before expiring. Everything happened so quickly."

"Yes. Not the sort of thing I would have thought could be attributed to a simple heart attack or apoplexy."

"True, but poison? Cyanide or even arsenic wouldn't affect someone in that way. Plus, they are much slower."

“What about some poison that attacks the central nervous system?”

“Well, I suppose, but where would someone obtain something so toxic?”

Holmes pointed behind me. As I turned, my eyes fell on the slowly moving solitary sea krait in its aquarium. “Good Lord? But how? I’m not even sure how to extract the venom from such a dangerous animal.”

“Ah, but if you recall, there were originally two.”

“Of course. If you removed the poison glands, you could extract the venom, and even concentrate it. That would make it deadly.”

“Something, I think, that the Bornean tribesmen have been doing for centuries.”

“What have the Bornean tribesmen been doing?” asked a voice from behind us. We both turned to find Kesson standing nearby.

“Watson and I were just ruminating on the use of blowpipes by primitive tribesman in Borneo.”

“That’s a strange thing to be talking about moments after a man died.” Kesson’s face was stern, almost brimming with anger at our indifference until his eyes grew wide. "You don't think Sir Tristan was killed by poison?”

I chipped in to try and guide Kesson’s thought patterns in a different direction. “We were simply passing the time until the authorities arrive.”

It was then that my old friend noticed the objects in Holmes’s hands. “Those are blowpipe darts.” His eyes rose to Holmes’s face, and then to mine. “You *do* think Sir Tristan was poisoned, don’t you?” Turning his head, he glanced at the empty spot in the rack nearby. “One is missing. Those cursed tribesmen! I knew they were a foolish idea.” Without waiting, Kesson stormed from the room. I started after him, but Holmes placed a hand on my shoulder to stop me.

“Stay, Watson. With the Lieutenant out of the way, we can investigate further in peace.”

Understanding my associate’s desire, a niggle of doubt surfaced in my mind regarding Kesson’s possible future actions. Turning those thoughts more towards things at hand, I glanced around to see what Holmes was up to.

He stood, hands-on-hips, near the alcove where the blowpipe dart had been found. As I stepped up next to him, he remarked, "I need you to do something for me."

"Yes?"

"Can you stand as close to the spot that you saw Sir Tristan when he was bitten?"

"Certainly." I stepped back a few strides and studied the area for a moment, whilst replaying as many of my memories of the event as I could. I then strode forward and stood as close to the spot and in the posture of our host as I could remember.

"Excellent," said Holmes, now stay still for me. He was silent for a while as he continued to stare, first at me, then at the small stain on the floor, before I heard him step away across the room. I chanced a glance over my shoulder, to see him searching behind the curtains at the other end of the room. Finally, he expressed an "A-ha!" Checking my position and location, I broke away and hurried to see what had piqued his interest.

There, behind one of the heavy drapes, and propped up against the wall, was the missing blowpipe. I glanced across to where I had previously stood and judged the distance to be some fifteen yards. "That would be a remarkable shot."

"Yes. I can only presume that whoever made it was quite conversant with the use of these blowpipes and had many years of practice."

"Oh, surely not one of the tribesmen?"

Standing, Holmes replied, "I will wait to answer that question." Pushing aside the curtain, he stepped through the doorway behind. Following, we found ourselves in a small, dark anteroom that led further into the bowels of the house. I pushed on and found an exit door that opened into a passageway leading through to the rear of the building.

Returning, I found Holmes holding a small silver dish. "What have you there?"

Pulling the draw-cord for the drapes, parting them to let light from the main room enter, I saw that the dish held two of the cone-shaped darts. They floated in a small puddle of coloured liquid, along with several chunks of ice.

"These are the ammunition for that blowpipe," Holmes said.

"But aren't those simply the larger cones? There are no needles – they simply wouldn't fly."

"Ah, there are needles – or at least there *were* needles, I believe."

"I don't follow."

"The day has been hot, has it not?" I nodded. "There are small bits of ice floating in this dish of water. I would conjecture that originally the dish was full of small chunks of ice, used to keep something cold – the needles of several blowdarts – perhaps formed of ice themselves."

"Incredible."

"Quite so. And quite ingenious. If one could create needles from ice, they would remain intact for the immediate purpose then melt away to nothing more than liquid in a matter of minutes or even seconds. The only remains would be the conical end used to stabilise the dart during flight. Something so small and trivial that most people would dismiss one as merely a piece of detritus and not give it another thought."

"Devilish. If the needles were formed from pure venom, then they would be deadly. The tip would penetrate far enough to break off inside the skin and deliver a dose of poison directly into the bloodstream. Death would almost be a certainty."

"Exactly."

A voice floated to use from across the room. "John? Are you still here?"

I stepped out through the curtains and found Kesson standing in the alcove leading through to where the unfortunate Sir Tristan lay. "Willard, over here."

"Good, good." He approached, his eyes darting to where the curtains were gently moving after Holmes had dropped them back in place. "The police and the surgeon are here. As you were the doctor that pronounced Sir Tristan dead, they would like to talk with you."

"Of course, of course." I glanced around before following Kesson, but there was no sign of Holmes.

Behind the curtains, we found a sorrowful looking man in his late fifties and a pair of young bobbies. All were staring down at the reposing form of Sir Tristan. The older man, whom I guessed to be the police surgeon, glanced across at us as we entered. Kesson quickly introduced us, and the man plied me with questions that I duly answered.

"Hmm," he said. "Based on so little, I can only conclude that it was natural, but I will have to investigate further back at the morgue. Thank you for being so diligent and thoughtful, Doctor Watson. Sir Tristan might have been saved if you'd had your medical bag, but given the rapidity with which he passed, I sincerely doubt it. Death appears to have been sudden, and probable."

"One thing you may wish to undertake is an analysis of the blood."

"What am I looking for?"

"A poison."

"What?"

"Possibly from snake venom."

"Surely you're joking! How would this man have been bitten by a snake in this environment?"

"Well, there was a live sea krait in an aquarium, but we do not believe that is how the venom entered his system."

"We?"

"My associate and I. Mr. Sherlock Holmes."

The old surgeon's eyes went wide. "You're *that* Doctor Watson?" I nodded in answer. "Do strange deaths just follow you around?"

"It does seem that way. Regardless, we have no solid proof as yet, but there are indications that this man has been the victim of foul play. The small mark on his neck. The dry crust around it. The seizure he had just before expiring. Holmes is working on other evidence as we speak, but it would add to our store of knowledge if you could undertake further investigation of this poor man."

He nodded. "I thought this would be a simple case, but you're right. I'll do as you say before writing up the certificate."

"Thank you. I'm sure we will be in touch if we have anything more, either directly or through Scotland Yard."

Kesson seemed to have lost all interest in overseeing his former boss's corpse and had taken on an air of agitation. Standing in the doorway, he indicated that I should follow. As I joined him in the adjoining corridor, he turned and said, "I think I have our man."

Slightly stunned, I simply trailed behind him as he wound his way through the house and down into a dimly lit area of the large basement.

There, one of the Borneo tribesmen sat on a straight-backed chair. Another man, apparently some sort of assistant to Kesson, stood behind him, an indifferent look on his face, but bearing a posture said he was ready to pounce if the man in the chair even moved.

The tribesman's face bore all the hallmarks of someone frightened out of his wits. His eyes were wide and darted between Kesson and myself upon our entry.

Taking a long look at the frightened Bornean, I asked, "Why?"

"What do you mean?"

"Why would this man have killed Sir Tristan? Motive is generally the first thing that Holmes establishes when faced with a puzzle such as this."

Kesson stared at me for a moment and then approached the tribesman. Leaning in he asked a question in Malay, which was followed by a fearful response. Standing, Kesson crossed his arms and glared at the man in anger. "I asked why he murdered Sir Tristan. His response was that we British must be killed because we invaded Borneo."

Leaning in close to the man's face, Kesson spoke another long string of Malay, which was followed by an equally long response, the man's mouth turned down in a grimace of absolute fear. "He is part of a Labuan resistance group who have sworn to destroy our company." Turning towards the man standing nearby, Kesson added, "Anderson, make sure he doesn't move. I'll bring the constables to take him away." Without another word, Kesson stormed from the room.

Standing for a moment, I stared at the poor tribesman for a while. Even though he didn't seem to speak English, his face spoke volumes. To me, this man wasn't someone fighting for a cause. He was simply a lone man, a long way from home, in a truly alien world. Glancing at Anderson, I asked, "Do you believe any of what Willard just said?"

Anderson looked my way, shrugged, and said, "I'm not paid to think, sir. Simply to do. If Mr. Kesson believes this man is responsible for Sir Tristan's murder, then I believe what Mr. Kesson believes."

A very convenient way of thinking.

"I personally don't believe a single word of what your friend said," came a voice from the shadows. The tall form of Sherlock Holmes appeared from the gloom. He still held the long blowpipe, and I noticed the shorter form of Jamal, the man who had greeted us at the front door upon our arrival, appear behind and follow him into the light. The Borneo tribesman still wore his ceremonial dress, but his smile had disappeared to be replaced by a dour look on his face. Indicating the seated man, Holmes said, "This man is innocent."

"How so? What further evidence have you found?"

"I'll get to that, but from what I overheard in the conversation between him and Kesson, I'm afraid that your friend is lying."

"How did you understand what they were saying? I didn't think you spoke Malay."

"Well, I don't very well, but I have studied."

"When?"

"The other night, after you received your invitation. Why? Didn't you?"

I gave Holmes a withering look before noticing movement as Jamal stepped over to the man and said, "Lian?" He followed up with a few words in Malay. Lian, the other tribesman, responded with his own string of sentences.

Finally, Jamal turned towards Holmes. "Lian, my friend here, he says that Mr. Kesson asked him to – how you say? – play a trick on Sir Tristan." Lian spoke further, with Jamal simply listening for a moment. "Yes, it was to show how the blowpipes work. The darts were only ice. Harmless. Mr. Kesson made them."

Holmes addressed Jamal, “I assume that Lian here was asked to hide behind the curtains and shoot one of Mr. Kesson’s supposedly harmless darts into Sir Tristan’s neck?” Jamal spoke to Lian who simply nodded. “The problem being that Kesson’s darts were poisonous.”

“What do you mean ‘Kesson’s darts were poisonous’?”

We all turned to the source of the voice. The man who until that point I had thought of as a friend stood in the entranceway, the two police constables standing behind him.

“Ah, just the person, I think,” said Holmes.

“Why?” Stepping into the room, Kesson’s eyes fell on Jamal. “And what is he doing here?”

“Jamal here has been helping us speak with Lian, your chosen perpetrator.”

“What? He can’t speak English. None of them can.”

“Ah, that isn’t quite true, sir,” said Anderson, his face a slight shade of red from embarrassment at contradicting his superior. “Jamal’s English is quite limited but effective. That’s why I placed him on door duty.”

“But he’s obviously lying, just like this one,” Kesson retorted, pointing at the seated man. “They’re all in it together. We’ve been defending ourselves from their type for years.”

“What do you mean by ‘their type’, Willard?” I asked.

“The insurgents. The resistance. They’ve obviously infiltrated the locals that we employ in the company, to get what they’ve always wanted. To kill Sir Tristan – or any of us, for that matter.”

Turning towards Anderson, I asked, “Is this true? Have you been struggling against these terrorists?”

Anderson’s eyes grew wide. They darted towards Kesson, who scowled at his underling, then to the policemen, then to Holmes, and finally back to me. His head began to shake slowly from side to side. A growl rose from Kesson. “Anderson, remember for whom you work.” The younger man’s gaze rushed back to Kesson’s.

“I’m sorry, sir. I cannot lie. Not about this. Not with Sir Tristan dead. Especially if you are involved.”

"Anderson . . . ." Kesson's voice rose in pitch and volume. His face flushed red with anger.

"No. I can't. There is no resistance. We've been at peace with the local tribes for years. They've never had it so good. Our company has furnished them with clothes, food, housing, and employment. Brought them out of their primitive ways and into the Nineteenth Century. They love us." His face turned towards Jamal. "Isn't that right, Jamal?"

"Yes, sir. It is. We would never wish harm on the white men."

All eyes turned back to Kesson. His own grew wide. "What? What am I supposed to have done? I have done nothing. If I have where is your proof?"

"Ah, proof," said Holmes. "Let me replay the facts for our constables here. One: Sir Tristan Leavins died earlier tonight, from a suspected heart attack, but more likely from the poison of the yellow-lipped sea krait. Two: This tribesman was coerced to unknowingly deliver the fatal dose of poison, using a primitive blowpipe, armed with darts made from frozen krait poison."

"Ridiculous!" cried Kesson. "That would be impossible."

"Except for the fact that you are a genius at ice-making and refrigeration," answered Holmes, bringing a small metallic object from his pocket and holding it before him. He broke the object apart, showing it to be a solid metal mould. "I visited your ingenious ice-making machine, and the little workspace you created nearby. This was simply sitting on the bench. It is a mould that can be used to create extremely delicate needles of ice." Pointing to a set of small conical cavities at one end, he said, "You can place a cone-shaped dart stabiliser in here, then pour liquid here, ready for freezing. And, *voilà*, ice darts ready for use in a blowpipe. Though you must be quick, or else they melt, as Watson and I discovered, when we found a dish with the remains of two darts and the ice that kept them chilled."

"That could have been used to make ice for drinks," Kesson countered.

"Perhaps, but the other mould I found inside a refrigeration unit upstairs would contradict that. It contained three cone-shaped moulds that still had traces upon them of a light-yellow liquid, seemingly formed into highly lethal poison darts."

"What liquid?"

"This liquid," said Holmes, holding up a small glass vial half-filled with a light-yellow liquid, "It was in a drawer attached to the workbench. I'm sure if we have it analysed, it will prove to be sea krait venom."

"Where would that come from?" Kesson demanded.

"From the poison sac of a certain yellow lipped sea krait that expired on the journey from Borneo most likely."

"But what possible reason could I have to orchestrate all of this? I was recruited personally to this company. I've worked diligently for years. I'm in charge of the entire engineering team in North Borneo."

"I think I can answer that," I said. All eyes turned my way. "I met Admiral Mayne. He was very complimentary of you but was a little concerned about your ambitions – ambitions that he believed might never be realised."

"What? What do you mean? I was virtually second-in-charge to Sir Tristan."

"From the Admiral's words, it seems that the company only promotes self-made men of station or with high military ranks into the top echelon of the company. He suggested that you could gain a higher level if you established yourself outside of the company or gained a title or honour."

"That old fool! When I was hired, he promised me a long and industrious career. I could take them far. My inventions will open new trade routes, bring millions into the company's coffers. But I can't do that as just as an underling, I need the power to direct the operations of the company. Sir Tristan was a blind fool, with no foresight. The company is better off this way."

"Does that mean you eliminated him for just that purpose?"

"What? No. I had nothing to do with this. Everything you have said is just circumstantial. You have no solid proof."

"Oh, I wouldn't say that," said a familiar voice from the doorway. Glancing across, I saw the short frame of a man whom we knew, filling the doorway. "In fact, from what I've just heard, I think the Yard could build quite a case against you, Mr. Kesson."

"Who are you?" said Kesson, his voice rising close to a yell.

"Inspector Lestrade, Scotland Yard, at your service," our colleague said, with a wry smile on his lips. Turning towards the two constables, he said, "You two, take Mr. Kesson here up to the wagon parked outside. Hold him for murder, and I'll interview him when I return."

The constables, each took hold of one of Kesson's arms.

"Anderson," said Kesson, "I need the company's solicitor. They'll have me out in a moment."

"Yes, sir, but I don't think the board will be very happy. They have very strict rules about the consequences of any improprieties of senior staff members – even where the person has only been charged, but the charges are overturned later. They simply do not tolerate any sullying of a person's reputation."

Kesson's face dropped as Anderson's words sunk in. "No. I've done nothing." The two policemen led him struggling and yelling from the room. I could hear his proclamations of innocence all the way down the corridor and up the stairs to the ground floor.

When all was quiet once again, Lestrade turned to face Holmes and said, "I received your message. I'd already heard about the poor unfortunate Sir Tristan, so now you'd better fill me in on the rest of this case."

***

It was several days later whilst I was finishing my breakfast coffee and reading the morning paper, that Mrs. Hudson brought Lestrade into the sitting room.

"Good morning, Doctor. I just wanted to drop by and give you and Mr. Holmes an update on this Sir Tristan Leavins business."

"Excellent," said Holmes stepping into the room. "I'd been wondering how you'd got on." He walked across to the table, sat down, and poured himself a cup of coffee. I offered Lestrade a cup, but he declined.

"It didn't take long, but this Kesson fellow broke down after a few poignant facts came to light. The police surgeon was quick. He found traces of poison in Sir Tristan's blood and labelled the cause of death as such. He also identified the liquid in the yellow bottle as krait venom. That linked to the frozen darts, and a full version of events from Lian, the Borneo tribesman, confirms everything."

"How did you get more information out of Lian?" Holmes asked. "We only had Jamal to translate, and while his English is good, it probably isn't good enough for that purpose."

"There was a Professor of Asiatic dialects at London University who is fluent in Malay. He was good enough to sit in with us and interpret."

"Has Willard been charged with murder then?" I asked, my heart heavy at the thought of Kesson's imminent fate.

"Yes. I know he was an army friend of yours, Doctor, but murder is murder, and it is especially heinous when the reason is for personal gain."

"He'll hang then, won't he?"

"Oh, yes. I can't see any other eventuality than that. Again, I'm sorry."

When the inspector had gone, Holmes glanced my way and spoke. "I, too, am sorry. We make far too few good friends in our lives. To find one that has transgressed the law in such a calculated way and used the ignorance of someone so innocent as a primitive tribesman is especially galling. You have my sympathies."

"Thank you, but I find that with all that we have found out about this man. I can neither condone his actions nor indeed regard him as a friend after such. My only hope is that the poor tribesmen that were caught up in this are treated properly and taken home quickly and with a minimum of fuss."

"That would be a proper conclusion to this adventure," Holmes said, sipping his coffee.

www.ingramcontent.com/pod-product-compliance
Lightning Source LLC
Chambersburg PA
CBHW030808310726
48980CB00006B/417/J

9781787057647